Just

Brandelene swallowed the gasp that threatened to escape her lips when Armand Kordell Bouclair walked out of the bathhouse. She stared, her eyes wide with disbelief. Surely he could not be the wretch she had purchased. This man was aristocratic. Very tall and powerfully built, he carried himself as though a prince. Moreover, he was incredibly handsome—breathtakingly so. The setting sun glinted golden highlights off his mane of tawny hair and a ruggedly chiseled face bespoke the power and ageless strength inherent in a man used to having his own way. Mesmerized by his carved, yet sensitive lips, she found herself wondering what it would be like to be smothered with ardent kisses by them. His was the overpowering, sun-bronzed face of a god, and Brandelene

Also by Brenna Braxton-Barshon

Through All Eternity

Coming Soon from HarperPaperbacks

BRENNA BRAXTON-BARSHON

Southern Oaks

HarperPaperbacks
A Division of HarperCollins*Publishers*

This is a work of fiction. The characters, incidents, and dialogues are products of the author's imagination and are not to be construed as real. Any resemblance to actual events or persons, living or dead, is entirely coincidental.

HarperPaperbacks *A Division of* HarperCollins*Publishers*
10 East 53rd Street, New York, N.Y. 10022

Cover illustration by Jim Griffin

First printing: May 1991

Printed in the United States of America

10 9 8 7 6 5 4 3 2

This book is dedicated to the people
who have surrounded my world with love.

In Loving Memory
of
Freda, my mother, and James, my father

and to

Sheri
the beloved child of my heart

To my cherished sister, Juanita Jane
To my adored mother-in-law, Luella Ruth

and

To my friend, my love, my beloved,
Marty

Acknowledgment and Gratitude

to

Meredith Bernstein

Of the Meredith Bernstein Literary Agency, who believed in this book, and proved herself to be everything an agent should be.

And to Kathryn Falk, publisher of *Romantic Times* and *Rave Reviews*, for the time, consideration, and sage advice she gave an aspiring novelist.

All thoughts, all passions, all delights,
Whatever stirs this mortal frame,
All are ministers of Love,
And feed his sacred flame.

SAMUEL TAYLOR COLERIDGE

Chapter 1

VIRGINIA
SPRING, 1803

"YOU COULD HAVE YOUR CHOICE OF ANY FINE GENTLEman, child. You just can't buy yourself a husband. You know they got nothing in there but thieves, murderers, and poor riffraff."

Sighing, Brandelene ignored the fussing woman, for she'd heard it so many times before. Besides, there was no turning back now. She swept gracefully toward the auction house, disregarding the gazes that followed her as much for her extraordinary beauty as for the impropriety, and rarity, of a lady of the gentry visiting the slave auction quarters—and without a male escort. Only the fact that she was far from home and unrecognized saved her from complete disgrace.

"A lady like you coming to a place like this," Ruby grumbled as she attempted to fan away her rising apprehension. "Your daddy'd turn over in his grave if he knew what you're gonna do, child." When those words received no response, Ruby's tone softened to one that never failed to sway her mistress. "There's just got to be another way."

"Ruby darlin', you know I don't have a choice," Brandelene said, a gust of wind whipping the delicate white silk of her gown. She stopped momentarily, handing her parasol to Ruby, and oblivious to the men's stares, she bent to smooth the skirts of her gown.

"Thank the good Lord your mama, God rest her soul, isn't here to see what's going on." Ruby glared at a well-dressed gentleman who was boldly appraising Brandelene.

Brandelene reclaimed the lace-edged parasol and stared at the building she'd been visiting occasionally for the last three months. Her porcelain complexion darkened and she shuddered, her distaste for the auction house rising like bile in her throat.

The exterior of the large, windowless wood structure belied the misery of humanity inside, for most of the building housed slaves. But another group also occupied a small portion of the warehouse—bond servants. People whose contracts of indenture were for sale; the unfortunates from debtors' prisons; the undesirables from the gaols of England; and the poor whites willing to indenture themselves for the cost of their passage to the colonies of the United States.

From this last group, Brandelene hoped to purchase a husband. A man she could control until she accomplished her objective; a bond servant who, in exchange for his freedom, would marry her for a short time. A husband in name only, whom she would discard, by annulment, after he had served his purpose.

More than three months earlier, when Brandelene had first devised her elaborate ploy, she'd learned that indentured servants no longer immigrated in large numbers to the United States, and there were no more shiploads of immigrants that landed in the South. Nevertheless, there were still some men willing to accept any accommodations, including living in the hold of merchant ships, in order to come to the American colonies.

This kept Brandelene hopefully searching the small indentured servant sections of Richmond's human auction houses, where the local agents who'd purchased the bondsmen kept them overnight until their contracts were sold. A continuous flow of merchant ships arrived in Richmond, but even so, the selection had been a pitiful lot. Not one man was even reasonably suitable to pass her uncle Cyrus's scrutiny.

Filled with emotion, Brandelene glanced up at the puffy white clouds drifting lazily in the sky. Then her gaze moved to the bright sun casting its warming rays over Richmond, but even this peaceful gift of nature could not ease her distress at the task she faced.

With characteristic determination, she started toward the auction house to view the men about to be sold into bondage.

"You wait for me, Miss Brandelene," Ruby insisted. "Don't you dare go into that awful place without me." She hurried to catch up with her strong-willed mistress. "I swear you're the most stubborn child I ever did see. They sure didn't teach you nothing at that fancy school up north. Nothing at all."

As Brandelene approached the entrance to the building she said, "I promise you, Ruby, this is the last time I will enter this wretched place. I can't afford to lose any more time. We'll go north and I'll continue my search there." Despite an overwhelming desire to flee, she resolutely set her fears aside, and with cool deliberation closed her parasol, opened the door, and swept into the auction house.

The immense guard appraised Brandelene with the same lecherous eagerness he had each time she'd been there, and the odor of stale ale and sweat assailed her nostrils.

"Good mornin', ma'am," the man wheezed, signaling another guard to escort her and Ruby to the small indentured-servant area of the large warehouse that had been haphazardly converted into slave quarters and an inside auction arena. "Mighty fine pleasure to see you agin."

Brandelene pressed one gloved hand to her nose to ease the stomach-wrenching stench of the auction house, while the other reached for a handkerchief. Wretchedness surrounded her. She watched a large rat scurry into the filthy straw that served as beds for the bond servants and slaves temporarily housed here until the auction. Then she followed the brawny guard.

A low murmuring grew as Brandelene passed among the chained slaves to the indentured-servant section and she solemnly averted her eyes.

The beautiful, luxuriantly gowned Brandelene was as out of place as a rose amid the tobacco—something to be seen but not believed, to be admired but not touched.

Once again the guard displayed the bondsmen whose contracts would be sold today. Brandelene looked carefully at each one, then regretfully shook her head as she dismissed the last man, the heaviness of disappointment settling in her chest. Time was running out.

Guards carrying clubs and whips herded manacled slaves into the rear of the building, distracting her. A pistol-wielding foreman supervised the line of black men and women, chained together by leg irons, as they filed into the auction house.

Unable to endure the sight, Brandelene had started to turn away when she saw him. A tall, tanned white man, shackled between two black men. He walked proud and straight in spite of his chains, his bearing strangely impressive.

"Aren't those people from the slave ship that just docked?" Brandelene asked.

The guard turned to look at the people being marched inside. "Yes, ma'am."

"What is a white man doing on a slave ship? Could he be a convict?" When he didn't answer, Brandelene asked, "Could you find out for me?"

Hesitating, the guard glanced nervously from Brandelene to the slow-moving line of chained humanity, then back to her. "Yes, ma'am," he replied reluctantly. "But you gotta come with me. I can't leave you here unguarded."

"Yes. Of course. I'll follow you."

Brandelene lifted her skirts and rushed to keep up with the guard's swift strides, her petticoats rustling as she hurried.

The guard stopped the procession of slaves and signaled the man in charge. As the two men talked quietly, Brandelene examined the object of her interest at closer range. The man looked as though he'd been spawned by the devil.

She turned to tell the guard she'd changed her mind, then hesitated to calculate the time she would lose traveling to New York, and in searching for and boarding each docking ship to examine the immigrants. Even more disheartening would be the explanations she'd have to make, and the additional days of the return trip.

Turning back, Brandelene once again studied the shackled white man. He was the only person with iron cuffs on his wrists as well as his ankles. Even so, he had an air of arrogance that belied his circumstances. He wore nothing but filthy, tattered breeches, and bruises covered his broad shoulders, powerful chest, and muscular arms. Even his thinly fleshed ribs, still muscled despite his obvious deprivation, were bruised. His spread-eagled stance emphasized the force of his thighs and the slimness of his hips under the shabby buff breeches, and his grimy, wildly tossed hair and scraggly beard could not hide the strength of his features.

Unaware of Brandelene's presence, for she stood well to the side and rear of him, the captive spoke in French to one of the black men to whom he was chained. "Dagert, I'll get us out of this predicament. Do not fear. Somehow I'll see that we get back home. I promise you." Then the white man scratched at his ratty beard, his chains clanking. "At least we're still alive." Probably guessing none of the guards spoke French, he'd made no attempt to speak softly, and his voice was deep and rich.

The black man turned to respond and abruptly noticed Brandelene studying them. His dark eyes widened in astonishment. Not quite as tall as his comrade, he was broad and muscular, and looked extremely strong, almost herculean.

The foreman left and the guard turned to Brandelene. "Sorry, ma'am, I couldn't learn much more than they got him with the other slaves in West Africa. Seems like he ain't no convict, but who knows? He don't speak no English."

"I would like to speak with him for a few moments," Brandelene said.

The guard hesitated until she turned her enormous, thick-lashed, violet eyes on him and smiled, revealing perfect white teeth. "I guess it'll be all right, but we gotta wait 'til all the slaves are inside. I can't hold up the line no longer."

Soon the last of the line had trudged inside and the large double doors were closed and bolted from the outside. The guard led Brandelene up to the only white man among the many blacks and Ruby, protesting all the way, followed the procession.

Aware she would not be permitted to detain the processing of the slaves for long, Brandelene wasted no words. "Are you married?" she asked the man in perfect French.

Startled by the flawless beauty who stood before him in a slave auction house, the man replied automatically, *"Non!"*

"Show me your teeth," Brandelene ordered.

Catlike golden eyes glared at her. "I am not a horse, madame.

"Shall I ask the guard to grant my request, or do you alread have enough bruises on your body?" she queried sweetly. Th prisoner grudgingly bared perfect teeth, white against his scruff beard. "Why," she continued, aware that their conversation i French was privileged from the guard hovering next to her, "ar you here in chains at a slave auction?"

"Madame, I assure you this is a dreadful mistake. I own a larg coffee and cacao plantation on the Ivory Coast. My chief oversee and I were on our way from a village in West Africa, where we' acquired additional labor, when we were all captured by slavers. The man stared at her with eyes that implored her to believe him his large hands clenching and unclenching in frustration. "Th fiends could not listen to reason, for they were Spanish and w didn't speak each other's language."

"Yes, of course." Brandelene's disbelief at this ludicrous explanation was not reflected in her response, and she wondered wha kind of fool the man took her to be. Obviously, she would no learn the truth from him.

"Then you'll help me?" he asked hopefully. "I'll see to it tha you're handsomely rewarded."

Brandelene's intuition warned her against the wretch who mus have committed some unthinkable crime to find himself in such circumstances. But time was so short and she was in such desperate need, and whatever else he might be, his refined speech indicated an educated man. She made her decision.

"I have need of a man such as yourself." She smiled charmingly. "I'll consider purchasing you and then we can discuss it. Perhaps we could perform a service for each other."

The man's eyes narrowed in contempt. "I've heard of wealthy women who practice strange pleasures. I am not a stud who performs on request, madame."

Gasping at the insult, Brandelene's hand flashed out, slapping him full across the face.

Before either of them realized what had happened, the huge

guard at Brandelene's side had shoved his cudgel into the chained man's stomach, putting every ounce of his massive bulk behind the blow. The manacled prisoner doubled over in pain.

"Stop!" Brandelene commanded. "Stop this instant! He was merely insolent," she said, not sure why she'd come to the rogue's defense.

The guard gave the injured prisoner a look of smug satisfaction, all the while slapping the palm of his hand with his club to emphasize his advantage. His stare dared the captive to err again. "Ya scurvy crud! You're talkin' to a lady—a lady o' quality. So you watch your mouth, you hear? One more word outta line an' you'll git plenty more o' what you just got. You understand?"

The prisoner nodded, his muscular arms clasped across his stomach.

Startled, Brandelene stared in wide-eyed amazement at the chained man. Clearly, he'd understood what the guard had said. If he understood English, he probably spoke English. She had to know. Cyrus did not speak French, but if this man spoke English, and if she could convince or even bribe him to assist her, she felt sure he could be groomed passably well to satisfy Cyrus's scrutiny.

Brandelene turned to the wary guard at her side. "I would like to question this man a little further, but I fear a strong, brave man such as yourself might make him too afraid to answer me," she drawled with all the southern charm she possessed. "If you would stand by that post"—she nodded toward a distant pillar—"he might be more at ease."

The guard looked doubtful.

"Surely, since you've already demonstrated how masterful you can be, he'll mind his manners. You've warned him and he is chained."

The guard once again smacked his heavy cudgel into his hand. "You tell him if he says or does one thing you don't like, I'll make him wish he'd died on that ship comin' over here."

Brandelene turned back to the shackled man who once again stood proudly straight, although it obviously pained him to do so. Again she spoke in French. "You heard the guard. Can you be trusted?"

She was answered with a piercing glare of hatred. The man gave no reply.

"You may be assured, I have no prurient interest in you, sir," Brandelene snapped, humiliated that the filthy wretch could possibly think otherwise. She silently cursed Cyrus Varner that she was in this unbearable situation. When she spoke again, she smiled deceptively, so the guard could not detect the intent of her conversation. "In fact, if I do purchase you, I fear I will have concerns of that nature from you. Can you be trusted?"

"Oui."

Brandelene assured the guard at her elbow, "It will be fine for you to watch from the pillar."

The guard grunted and moved to the requested post.

Facing the man whose only redeeming feature was his compelling, golden eyes, she queried in English, low enough so the guard did not hear, "What is your name?"

"Armand Kordell Bouclair."

"I don't have time to explain my predicament to you, Monsieur Bouclair, but I will tell you that if I do purchase you, you'll be well treated. In fact, you'll live the life of a gentleman, and if you cooperate, in six months' to one year's time you'll be given your freedom."

"I assume you live in the city?" His brief question in English carried only a slight indication of an accent.

The low, husky query sent an unwanted shiver of fear down Brandelene's spine. "No," she answered softly, feeling the tension course through his body at her answer. "I own a tobacco plantation quite a distance from here."

"I could be persuaded to 'cooperate.'"

"Yes, I felt sure the prospect of one year's servitude instead of the usual five would capture your interest." Then a troubling consideration flashed through her mind. "Ordinarily, I don't attend slave auctions. There's a possibility, since you were on a slave ship, that you'll be sold as such. I'm not aware if white men are sold as slaves. Regardless, I'm temporarily short of funds, and had anticipated only the purchase price of an indentured servant. Slaves bring a much higher price, for they're purchased for life instead of five years. I don't have the funds to buy a slave."

The prisoner leisurely appraised Brandelene from head to toe. "You might," he said, "try selling your jewels."

Affronted, Brandelene lifted a slender hand to the onyx brooch, surrounded by diamonds, pinned to the lace jabot at her neck. The captive's scrutiny flicked from the large matching dinner ring on her right hand to her matching earrings.

"I have need of my jewelry," she retorted indignantly. "Besides, there isn't time." The nerve of the man's suggestion grated at her, and it rankled that she'd permitted herself to be forced into an explanation. Perhaps she should give up the whole ridiculous scheme that had brought her into this building that surely was the depths of hell.

"Madame, I can see to it that my price is not too high, on the condition that you buy my overseer too." He nodded toward the large black man chained in front of him.

"That's absurd," Brandelene said. "I have just informed you, I may not have enough money to consider buying you."

The man's vexation was evident, but he fought to control it. "I can assure you that you'll get two people for the price of one, and my full cooperation."

"I don't need your overseer. I can hardly afford the amount he will cost to use him as a field hand for such a short period. You're not aware of my problems."

"Dagert is a talented overseer. I guarantee he'll increase your yield and your profits."

"Exactly how, pray tell me, do you expect a man who knows nothing about growing tobacco to accomplish that?" Brandelene retorted, irked by his cool, aloof manner.

"Madame, your naïveté is exceeded only by your beauty."

"For your information, monsieur, this naive woman knows as much about growing tobacco as any man in these United States," she said frostily, then was silent, irritated that again the wretch had goaded her into defending herself.

"Perfect. That's all the better." The prisoner smiled. "What Dagert doesn't know you can teach him—and he speaks English as well as I do. But what you won't have to teach him is how to supervise labor. He can get more productivity out of your plantation than any man alive, and without abusing the workers. Remember, madame, the two of us for the price of one. Is it agreed?"

Why was she holding such an absurd conversation, inside a slave auction house, with this insufferable creature? Then, as though to add to her misery, she heard Ruby's mumbled prayers.

"Two for the price of one?" Brandelene repeated. "Exactly how do you propose to accomplish such a feat?"

The prisoner grinned. "Leave that to me, madame. The man is my friend as well as my overseer. Do we have an agreement?"

Chapter 2

Again, Brandelene was impressed with the man's confidence in spite of his deplorable situation. His faint accent was quite pleasant, and his manner was certain to deceive Cyrus. Certainly, acquiring his friend would guarantee his cooperation, would it not? Hoping she'd not taken leave of her senses, she answered, "Yes, Monsieur Bouclair. We have an agreement."

"Then you may call me Kordell."

She turned to leave, anxious to be out of this house of misery. "Guard, please see to it the white man and the black man in front of him are auctioned today," she instructed. "I won't be able to attend the next sale."

"I can't do that, ma'am," the guard said apologetically. "These here are raw slaves straight from West Africa. They ain't been seasoned in the West Indies, like most slaves, so we gotta season 'em here a week or two before they're put up for sale."

Panicked by possibly having to wait another two weeks, Brandelene lifted her wide violet eyes. "I'm sure you can see to it that these two men are in today's auction," she said, as though the guard were in charge. Taking a few coins from her reticule, she pressed them into his hand.

Confusion crossed the guard's heavily jowled face as he pondered her request. Then his flat eyes glimmered as he figured a way to give her what she asked. "Your comin' here so regular like has been kinda disruptin' to the other guards, the slaves, and the gentlemen buyers. What with you bein' so purty an' all. If I was to tell the boss you wouldn't be needin' to come for a while if you could buy these two slaves today . . ."

"That's an excellent suggestion. I knew you could handle it."

Beaming at her praise, the guard boomed, "Follow me, ma'am." The trio started in the direction from which they'd come.

"Do not betray me, madame," the prisoner called warningly after Brandelene, in French, "or you will live to regret it!"

Momentarily Brandelene stiffened, then turned back to stare into the man's eyes, her ripe mouth curving into a smile. "Judging from the fresh bruises on your body, you've learned nothing at all on your journey here. Perhaps I should remind you, you are the one in chains and for sale. Not I." She tossed her curling raven tresses in haughty defiance. "You're hardly in a position to make threats."

"Touché!" he returned grudgingly, his gaze hardening.

Brandelene raised her hand and gave him a mock salute of triumph before she turned away. "Damnation! The contemptible, ungrateful miscreant," she muttered to herself, following the retreating guard. "And curse you, Cyrus Varner, for forcing me into this position."

The next two hours were the most trying of Brandelene's nineteen years. After arrangements had been made to put the two men on the auction block, she'd asked her gentle coachman, Joshua, to drive around Richmond. The time for a decision neared. She'd made an agreement with the prisoner, but should she go ahead with it? Should she risk all by purchasing him, especially when she was bound by her word to buy his friend also? Yet if she didn't marry soon there would no longer be a need to marry, for she would lose everything that mattered to her—Southern Oaks and the people she loved.

As the carriage jogged over the rutted streets of Richmond, Brandelene's recollections drifted back to Madame Duval's school in Boston. Sent there by her stepuncle, Cyrus, after her father's untimely death, she'd been relentlessly pursued by suitors. Often by men who'd only valued her for her exceptional beauty, and then later, as the fact became known, by men who desired her even more for her wealth as the heiress of the large tobacco plantation Southern Oaks. Of the acceptable suitors, not one had touched her heart. Now she wondered if she should simply relent and wed her old friend and neighbor Dean Paul Mason? There was no doubt he loved her, and although she loved him, it was only as a brother. Also, she had doubts that Dean Paul would permit her to run Southern Oaks as she chose.

That left Armand Kordell Bouclair. He spoke as an educated man, and could probably be made to look reasonably presentable with the right clothes. Moreover, if Bouclair cooperated—and he had every reason to, with the possibility of freedom, for both him and his friend, in only one year—he should deceive Cyrus. Perhaps she could buy the two men, then see how Monsieur Bouclair appeared after a bath, shave, haircut, and decent clothes. After all, she could talk to him at length, and if he were unsuitable she would resell the two men at the next auction.

Calm now, she knew what must be done and ordered Joshua to return to the auction.

It was to be held on the outside stage. Using all her feminine wiles, knowing a woman had to make the most of what she had in this man's world, Brandelene asked the auctioneer to place the selected two men on the dais last in their groups, with the white man auctioned before the black.

"Be happy to oblige, ma'am, but the white man isn't a slave." Lowering his voice so as not to be overheard by the men gathering for the start of the auction, the auctioneer said, "He's an indentured servant. However, I feel bound to warn you, he's a real trouble-maker. I'd hate to see a sweet little lady like you burdened with the likes of him. Perhaps you should consider another."

"I'll take your advice under consideration," Brandelene replied, acutely aware of the stares and comments from the growing crowd of men. "If I wish to bid I'll indicate so with my parasol. I'll be in the carriage under the large oak."

She gathered up her skirts and headed in that direction, aloofly ignoring the men who tipped their hats and stumbled over each other for a better look. "Men make such fools of themselves over a pretty face," she said to Ruby as the crowd parted to permit her to pass.

"Those gentlemen aren't talking about your beautiful face, lamb. They're talking about the lady making a fool of herself by attending a slave auction without a proper escort."

"If I listened to you, Ruby, Cyrus Varner would gamble Southern Oaks away, and we'd all be sitting out in the road," Brandelene retorted as Joshua helped her into the barouche. After arranging her skirts, she adjusted her parasol to protect her fair skin from the overhead sun. "Or, I suppose I could wed some wealthy plantation owner's son. Then, as my husband, he'd own Southern Oaks and he could keep the people in slavery. As his wife I'd be helpless to stop him. Perhaps that's what I should consider doing instead of this ridiculous scheme I'm attempting."

A one-time slave, Ruby smoothed her flower-sprigged, muslin gown in shock.

At Ruby's stricken look, Brandelene regretted her harsh words. "Don't start fretting, Ruby darlin'," she comforted. For this was the woman who'd nursed her when her mother could not; whose heart was filled to overflowing with love; whose plump hands automatically caressed, soothed, and comforted; whose voice, though sometimes harsh, could croon in the softest of dulcet tones, and Brandelene loved her more than any other living person. Now she studied Ruby's adored face, still smooth and wrinkle free, her caramel complexion, perfect and glistening, her large, dark eyes, warm and sparkling, and she smiled at her reassuringly. "I'll never let that happen, Ruby. I'll do whatever I have to do, which, I fear, includes buying this convict's, or whatever he is, contract of indenture. This whole nasty affair will be behind us in six months to a year and Southern Oaks will be as it was before Daddy died." Sighing, Brandelene leaned back in her seat while the few bond servants were led from the auction house to the block.

Normally in the South, agents, or even slave brokers, purchased an immigrant's contract from the ship's captain, and then bargained with a prospective buyer either in the auction house, from a horse-drawn cart, or on the courthouse lawn. When a bond servant had not sold within a reasonable time he was considered inferior goods, and then, and only then, the agent had the contract auctioned off. Yet Kordell Bouclair had walked off the ship and, within hours, would be on the auction block. That thought, just occurring to Brandelene, was not encouraging.

The contracts of indenture of those bond servants considered inferior were auctioned first, most going for the sum the agent had paid the ship's captain, with the agent losing his usual hefty profit.

True to his word, the auctioneer had Bouclair brought to the small stage last. When the manacled bondsman was prodded with a cudgel onto the dais, Brandelene's body stiffened, and she took a quick, sharp breath. Had she been blind when she selected this man? Certainly so, for not even her desperation could have so greatly clouded her judgment. Now she stared at him in horror. No attempt had been made to improve his appearance. Additionally, he was the only person brought from the auction house in shackles, confirming his unmanageability. The bruises covering his body were alarmingly conspicuous in the bright sunlight, adding credence to her suspicions.

The man was cruelly prodded forward by two guards. Walking straight and tall, the bondsman held his head arrogantly high, defying anyone who might try to break his spirit.

Probably the man could not be trusted. Brandelene wondered if she could control him long enough to achieve her end? Most likely not, she concluded. It was a risk too dangerous to take. With that decision, she leaned forward and instructed Joshua to return to the Richmond Inn.

The reins snapped, the horse trappings clattered, and the carriage moved forward.

"No man should be a slave!" Bouclair thundered over the crowd. "We can join together, rise up, and I will lead you to freedom."

"Joshua, stop!" Brandelene cried out, turning to stare in stunned disbelief at the bondsman. Then she gasped as the guard smashed his rifle butt into the mutinous bond slave's ribs, causing him to double over in pain. Before the manacled Bouclair could straighten up, the brutal guard raised his musket and delivered another crashing blow, driving the prisoner to his knees. Both times, she heard the crack of his rib cage, the sound reverberating to her carriage.

Unsubmissive, still proud despite his debasement, Bouclair lifted his head and his pain-filled gaze captured Brandelene's. Grinning briefly, although yet on his knees, he defiantly returned the salute of triumph she'd thrown him when she left the auction house, letting her know he'd kept his side of the agreement.

"Damnation," Brandelene muttered, realizing he had to have known the penalty he would pay for such an outburst—indeed had already begun to pay. Twice she'd considered breaking their agreement, but now she found she could not. She'd given him her word and he'd trusted her to keep it. Besides, could a man who'd risked what this man had, to help himself and his friend, be all bad?

Leaning back in her seat, she watched him struggle to his feet. "I made an agreement with him—I gave him my word," Brandelene uttered aloud, half in explanation to Ruby. "Daddy always said a person was only as honorable as his word."

"Lordy, Lordy," Ruby cried, fanning herself furiously. "We're all done for."

A normally timid Joshua turned from his high seat to stare down at Brandelene with frightened eyes. "I know it ain't none of my bizness, Miss Brandelene, but . . ."

"I won't hear another word from either of you. I'm only doing what I have to."

Abruptly, Brandelene was interrupted by the auctioneer's booming voice, "Who'll bid five hundred for this magnificent specimen of youth and strength? Five years of servitude from a choice man who looks strong enough to do the work of two men. He'll just need to rest up a few days after learnin' his lesson from the guard."

A murmur went through the crowd of well-dressed men.

"Gentlemen, gentlemen! Certainly, you aren't going to let a little show of spirit dampen your opportunity to get a bargain," the auctioneer encouraged. "Look at the shoulders on this man, think of the work those muscular arms and that strong back can perform. He's top prime! Where else can you get a choice man like this for a hundred dollars a year?"

"Yes, and he'll run the minute he's well enough," a voice barked from the large group pressing forward for a better look.

"Or," another voice loudly warned, "lead an uprising."

Then, to Brandelene's surprise, the auctioneer invited, "Someone make an opening offer." He had not asked for an opening bid with any other indentured servant, and to her it reflected his anxiety to be rid of the troublesome agitator.

"I'll take a chance on him for one hundred," a man called out hesitantly from the throng.

Trembling a little, Brandelene stared in fascination at the bondsman who now, with the aid of the wooden railing, stood straight, his naked trunk revealing the breadth of his shoulders and furred chest. The glinting sun brightly displayed the rippling muscles beneath the skin, and she could feel the animal power of his body. Shuddering at the thought of his strength, she forced herself back to the auctioneer's calling.

"I've got a hundred. Who'll give me two? Only two hundred for five years from a strong back. Who'll give me two?"

Without hesitation, Brandelene raised her parasol with one gloved hand while snatching Ruby's fluttering fan with the other.

"I've got two hundred. Who'll give me three? Only sixty dollars a year for a strong young man. This man is choice! Choice! Don't tell me a delicate lady has more gumption than any of you gentlemen?"

At that, an undertone swept through the crowd that turned as one to stare at Brandelene, for it was unheard of for any woman to buy a male bond servant, but for a young lady of the gentry to bid on a young, virile bond slave . . .

Brandelene was little concerned with what others might think.

Her only care was that neither anyone from Petersburg nor any of the gentry surrounding Southern Oaks was here to discover her purchasing a bondsman. For if Cyrus learned of it, then he would also uncover the truth that she'd also married the bondsman, and would have the marriage set aside. From her elevated position in the carriage, she examined each face. Finding none she recognized, she breathed a sigh of relief.

"Who'll give me three hundred?" the anxious auctioneer asked. "Two hundred going once. Two hundred going twice. Sold to the beautiful young lady for the ridiculous sum of two hundred dollars. Lucky fella."

The auctioneer's last words invoked a round of raucous laughter from the men in the crowd, and Brandelene felt her face flushing hot as all eyes once again turned toward her.

"And," Ruby prayed, "may the good Lord have mercy on us all the days of our lives."

Amen, Brandelene murmured under her breath. "Joshua, please accompany me to the cashier to pay for Monsieur Bouclair."

"Yes, Miss Brandelene," Joshua said, shaking his gray head while he climbed down to assist Brandelene. "This sure is a bad day."

"Now don't you start too, Joshua," Brandelene admonished softly, her affection for the man who'd been her father's valet apparent in the tone of her voice. "I don't want to hear it. Not even from you."

"Yes, Miss Brandelene."

The shackled bondsman stumbled down the stairs from the auction block, watching in fascination as Brandelene descended from her carriage and glided toward the cashier. Fashionably attired in a white-silk charmeuse gown, banded beneath full breasts in the high-waisted Empire style, she moved regally toward him. Wide bell sleeves, encircled with three rows of burgundy trim, exposed, with every movement of her arms, a burgundy lace undersleeve, ruffled at the wrist. A burgundy lace jabot spilled from her slender neck in a cascade of showy ruffles, and the softly flowing skirts of her gown swayed seductively as she gracefully moved through the throng of men parting before her. A white hat, perched at a saucy angle on her head, was adorned at the right front and side with large burgundy silk flowers and plumes and she carried a white parasol stitched with the same three rows of burgundy trim that echoed her belled sleeves. An oversize burgundy lace reticule swung from her wrist.

Bouclair stared at the approaching vision in unabashed awe. He'd known many women, but none compared with her flawless beauty. His gaze hungrily followed her to the cashier's podium.

"I've purchased the last bondsman's contract. Please have your guards escort him to my carriage, along with the auction doctor," Brandelene instructed the cashier, handing him two hundred dollars in silver and picking up Armand Kordell Bouclair's contract of indenture. After she'd examined the document, she slipped it into her reticule. "Have his shackles removed before he's brought, and I insist the doctor accompany him."

"Yes, ma'am," the clerk answered, signaling a nearby guard to do her bidding. "Right away, ma'am."

Anxious to be away from the prying eyes, Brandelene quickly returned to her carriage, becoming more uncomfortable by the minute as her dismay grew, building into fear and uncertainty that she'd done the right thing. Panic such as she'd never known before welled up in her throat. She took several deep breaths to regain her composure, vowing once again to do whatever it took to redeem Southern Oaks, and eventually marry a man she loved. A man of honor like her father.

Wordlessly Joshua helped her into the carriage, then climbed to his high seat.

Ruby felt sure Brandelene had made a terrible mistake; nevertheless, the deed was done. Now the young woman she loved like a daughter needed her support and comfort. "Everything's gonna be fine, lamb. You'll see, everything's gonna be just fine."

"Oh, Ruby, I hope you're right."

Two brutal-looking guards approached, the bondsman manacled between them.

"My instructions," Brandelene said, her eyes flashing fire, "were that this man be unshackled."

"This here's a dangerous man, ma'am," the guard warned. "Where's the gentleman what bought him?"

"There is no gentleman. I purchased this man's papers and I'm ordering you to unshackle him—now !"

The guard's mouth flew open in disbelief, and then he chuckled obscenely before his lascivious gaze raked her. "That ain't a good idea, lady." His formerly respectful tone had turned to one of contempt. "He might make a run for it, or attack you."

Seemingly from nowhere, Brandelene drew a pistol, then smiled sweetly. "I'm well armed and am an expert in the use of firearms. You need have no fear for my safety. Now, please unshackle this man."

Grumbling, the guard bent to unlock the leg irons from the bondsman's chafed ankles before removing the iron cuffs from his wrists.

To her fury, her newly acquired indentured servant grinned, and once again gave her a half salute. Brandelene turned to a man in rumpled clothes, carrying a black satchel. His ruddy face, wrinkled by life rather than time, made it impossible to guess at his age. Thin red veins spattered his nose and cheeks, and he reeked of whiskey. "I assume," Brandelene said, "you're the auction doctor?"

"Yes, ma'am." The doctor's tones were slurred and he weaved slightly.

"I believe your sadistic guards have broken some of this bondsman's ribs. Please bind him to relieve his pain. We have a three-day journey to my plantation."

"I'll not tend this man," the swaying doctor muttered, "without the presence of the guards."

"I'm sure the guards won't object to protecting you from an injured and abused man."

She watched as the doctor roughly pushed and pulled at his patient while binding his broken ribs. Though Bouclair grimaced in pain, he refused to permit a sound to escape his lips.

"Sweet mercy! Be gentle," Brandelene flared, standing up in her carriage, arms akimbo. "You're treating a human being, not an animal—or are you a horse doctor?"

The physician grudgingly finished his ministrations and closed his satchel to leave.

"I would like a bottle of laudanum to help relieve the man's pain."

"We don't waste laudanum on slaves, or riffraff!"

"Joshua, hand me the whip, please,"Brandelene requested softly, but firmly. Then, shifting the pistol to her left hand, she reached for the coiled carriage whip with her right. "Now, Doctor, I wish you to know I handle a lash almost as well as I handle a pistol. I'll be happy to pay you for the laudanum, but if I don't get it you'll not leave here without feeling the sting of my whip. Have I made that clear?" She thrust the butt of her whip against the physician's chest, watching the two guards, too shocked to move, out of the corner of her eye.

The doctor glared at Brandelene with open hatred in his bloodshot eyes. "You high and mighty rich women think you can do anything you want and get away with it. Someone should give you the thrashing you deserve and teach you your place. That'll get rid of your haughty airs."

With a calm that belied her flashing eyes, Brandelene raised the whip over her head and the tapering leather uncoiled with a flick of her wrist. "I warn you, Doctor, I will create a scene here that will stop this very profitable auction and have every gentleman running to my defense, for you have insulted a lady. How do you think your employer will like that? Now, do I get the laudanum?"

The sight of the exquisite, elegantly gowned woman, standing in her carriage with a pistol in one hand and a whip, threateningly raised, in the other, drew the attention of every man within sight. Not a man there did not admire her rebellious spirit, if only momentarily.

The doctor dove into his satchel and shoved the requested bottle into Ruby's hands.

"I felt sure you'd see it my way," Brandelene said with satisfaction to the doctor's retreating back. Victorious, she turned to her coachman. "Joshua, please help me down."

"Yes, Miss Brandelene," the coachman replied, grinning broadly while Brandelene laid her pistol on the seat, coiled and returned his whip.

She alighted from the carriage, took the laudanum from Ruby, and walked up to her new bond slave.

The man towered over her, disbelief flickering in his eyes. He stared down at a delicately molded face of unequaled beauty, a face stirringly framed by a wealth of lustrous blue-black hair the color of a raven's wing. High, exotic cheekbones were flushed with the soft rose of youth, and her complexion, perfection in porcelain, gave her an appearance of fragility. A visage that was a deceiving facade, for he knew this rare beauty was as fragile as a black widow spider. Then his gaze fastened on her large, violet eyes, fringed with long, sweeping black lashes. Unfathomable eyes; compelling, mesmerizing eyes that a man could lose his very soul in if he did not tread carefully. She had a full, sensuous mouth, a mouth that invited a man to taste fully of the passion waiting there. A woman not unlike, he imagined, the one whose siren song lured sailors to shipwreck on the rocks. A woman with whom it would be heaven to make love, a woman with whom it would be hell to fall in love. At that moment he vowed he would never be one of the many who loved her.

Chapter 3

"MONSIEUR BOUCLAIR," BRANDELENE DRAWLED, "IF you are finished staring at me as though you've never seen a woman before, I'll have Joshua help you to that tree where you may sit down. Then I'll give you a little medicine that will relieve your pain. I fear it'll be a long auction and your friend will be the last of the slaves to be sold."

Turning, he managed the few steps to the moss-hung oak and lowered his large frame to sit on the grassy knoll, leaning back with a grimace against the tree trunk.

Brandelene followed, then knelt beside him, carefully spreading her skirts before offering him the bottle of laudanum. "A small sip is all you'll need. It is opiate-based and you'll feel much better shortly."

At her softly drawled words, Bouclair did as suggested, then returned the bottle. "Thank you, madame. I appreciate what you did with the doctor. You will not be sorry."

Only Brandelene was already sorry as she stared at the bondsman at close range, in the bright light of day. Was there any way this stringy-haired, ratty-bearded wretch could ever be made presentable enough to pass Cyrus's scrutiny, as her beloved? Disturbed, Brandelene arose and returned to her carriage, unaware of the man's catlike gaze following her swaying hips.

"Miss Brandelene, you're taking your life in your hands," Ruby protested. "Where's your sense, child, getting that close to that riffraff, and you not even having your pistol handy?"

Seating herself in the carriage, Brandelene glanced at her bondsman. Bouclair's side was to her where he sat against the tree with one long leg stretched out in front of him while the other leg was bent at the knee, his muscular arm resting easily there. Studying his strong profile, she wondered what this man had done to find himself in such deplorable circumstances?

The afternoon dragged on interminably. Glancing at the bondsman, Brandelene saw that he slept. "Thank heaven someone can sleep through this nightmare," she murmured as she again scanned the crowd of southern gentlemen which had now thinned to a quarter of its original number. Most had made their acquisitions and left early enough to return to their plantations tonight or, if they had a longer distance to travel, to have their taste of the pleasures of Richmond and start for home early tomorrow. This would give her the opportunity she sought, to buy Bouclair's friend at a more reasonable price than if he'd been among the first auctioned off, when the bidding was vigorous. That much she'd learned from her father when she attended her first auction with him, at the age of twelve, shortly after her mother died. Now she smiled in fond recollection of Ruby forbidding her father to take her.

"Mister Barnett," Ruby had argued, "it's just not proper taking a young lady to a place like that."

Yet Brandelene had wanted to go, and her father would deny her nothing after her mother died. After that once, however, she'd refused to go again, until three months ago when her search began.

Standing up in the carriage, she took a deep breath. "Please assist me down, Joshua." After alighting, she walked over to her dozing bond servant and tapped his arm with the tip of her parasol.

Bouclair was instantly awake, his eyes alert as he glanced warily around him.

Carefully, remembering Ruby's warning, Brandelene handed him a canteen of water and he nodded his appreciation.

"Monsieur Bouclair, I read in the *Virginia Gazette* that field hands are bringing absurdly high prices at the auctions, and that it's due to the mills up north having installed the cotton gins." She traversed back and forth in front of the bondsman where he sat by the tree, then spoke absently as though to herself, "It takes one person a full day to handpick the seeds from a single pound of cotton fiber and I understand that marvelous cotton gin can do it in no time at all. Well, apparently the northern factories can't get enough cotton to keep up with their capability of production and the demand for cotton can't be met. So new cotton plantations are springing up all over the South and old ones are expanding to meet the need, which is why the price of slaves is so high." She stopped and searched her bondsman's face before she proceeded. "I, ah, I've never bought a slave before, and I admit I had no idea they brought such high prices as I've seen here today. And with Richmond being a major slave market. . . ."

At Brandelene's rambling words, Bouclair's eyes narrowed suspiciously as he wondered why she was telling him this now. Certainly, she hadn't awakened him to chat inanely about the wonders of the cotton gin and the high price of slaves. "What, madame, are you trying to tell me?"

"Earlier today, I saw a couple of young black men, in excellent condition, each go for the outrageous price of thirteen hundred dollars." With that, Brandelene anxiously fanned herself, then stepped back, away from his accusing glare. "Your friend should be coming up on the block shortly, and I didn't pay much attention to him in the auction house, so I don't know his age, or condition. I, ah, I only have a thousand dollars, and I want you to be aware that if I can't afford him. . . ."

Instantly Bouclair jumped to his feet, wincing in pain, his face a mask of rage. "That, madame, was not the agreement, and you sure as hell had better think of something quick, for you will regret it unto your dying day if you don't buy Dagert!"

"How dare you threaten me!" Brandelene's hand flashed out to slap his face.

Strong fingers clasped her wrist in midair, holding it in a viselike grip. "You got away with that once, madame. I don't advise you to try it a second time," the bondsman warned, glowering.

The deep timbre of his voice sent a chill of fear down her spine. "Let me go this second or I'll have you whipped!"

He released her immediately, his own anger turning to desperation as he realized his position. "You must buy Dagert." The tone of his voice reflected his anguish, his unusual golden eyes imploring. "You must. I give you my word, I will repay you."

A stab of guilt rushed through her. After all, she had agreed to buy his friend.

"If Dagert's sold to someone else, I might not be able to locate him by the time I can buy him back."

Brandelene glanced up at the murmur in the crowd. A slave was being prodded up the stairs to the auction block, and his dark gaze scanned the crowd, coming to rest on her. The man's unmarked torso, gleaming a rich ebony in the sun, was herculean and her eyes widened at the size of his immense chest and powerful biceps. If he looked like a blacksmith now, after weeks of deprivation, what must he have looked like before? All the while the slave's gaze remained locked on her, and she gasped, "Is that Dagert?"

"Yes."

"He'll bring a tremendously high price," Brandelene said, her promise weighing heavily upon her. "I'll never be able to get him for a thousand dollars. . . ."

"And I trusted you!"

Brandelene's conscience refused to be stilled. What if it were she and Ruby in such a situation? What would she do? With that painful image, her guilt melted into compassion and touched her heart. "I have money at the Richmond Inn, for safekeeping. I could pay the thousand and leave my brooch for collateral until I return with the rest of the money. Then I'll simply have to sell Mother's jewels to replace the money I'll need to get us home." She straightened to the full of her height. "You needn't worry, Monsieur Bouclair. I will buy Dagert." Her father's words about honor came rushing back. "A Barnett keeps her word, regardless of the cost." Glancing up at him, Brandelene caught the respect mirrored on his face. Relief and strength flowed through her and a dazzling smile lit her perfect features.

Bouclair returned her smile.

The auctioneer rapped for silence. "Who'll give me seven hundred for this prime buck with the strength of a bull?"

Before the auctioneer could acknowledge the bidding, the black man on the block bellowed in perfect English, "I am a free man." Defiant, he raised his massive arms over his head, his hands clenched into fists. "No one will make a slave of me!"

Bouclair grinned knowingly down at Brandelene.

Realizing the two men had planned this, based entirely on her word that she would keep her agreement, she whirled to see the guard's rifle butt crashing toward Dagert's ribs, but it was stopped short of its mark by the iron-hard palm of the black man's hand.

Brandelene knew that the threat Dagert hurled had raised the fear every slave owner harbored—that a slave would be commanding enough, intelligent enough, or strong enough to lead an uprising of the many slaves a plantation master owned.

"Stand back, guard, let's get this auction over," the auctioneer ordered, hoping to stop any incident that might further devalue an outstanding slave, and lower his commission.

* * *

A short time later Brandelene had bought Dagert for the reasonable sum of nine hundred dollars. Had she outwitted herself in her desperation?

"I know I can trust you to wait for me while I pay for Dagert," she told Bouclair. "If you became lost I'd be forced to have him resold at the next auction. Joshua," she called out, "please escort me to the cashier."

"Yes, Miss Brandelene," Joshua answered. After they were out of hearing range of Ruby and the bondsman, the aging coachman turned to her. "Miss Brandelene, how're you going to get those men home? They're bad-lookin' men. How're you ever going to get them home without us all gettin' killed?"

Pausing, Brandelene glanced up at the tall, lanky coachman. His hair was completely gray now, and his rich mahogany skin was wrinkled with age, but all she could see were his gentle and endearing ways, his tender heart. "I've been wondering about that too, Joshua. You know I'll never allow you or Ruby to be harmed, so don't you worry. I'll think of something."

Minutes later, when the trio returned to the barouche, accompanied by a guard, Kordell Bouclair grinned at Dagert, giving him a sly wink that did not go unnoticed by Brandelene.

Boys in men's bodies, she thought, smiling to herself, and then sobered. If but they were—if only for the next three days. She turned to her companion. "Ruby, please get the tape measure you've been carrying for three months. These men will need clothes. You read me their measurements, darlin', and I'll write them down." Brandelene pulled a scented handkerchief from her reticule and handed it to a shaking Ruby.

"Thank you, child," Ruby said gratefully, and after scrambling from the carriage began her task.

With that chore done, Brandelene addressed her newly acquired slave. "Dagert, please help Monsieur Bouclair up to the coachman's seat. The two of you may ride there with Joshua. One of the overzealous guards has broken several of his ribs, so be gentle."

After the two men were seated next to Joshua the guard left, shaking his head at the ignorance of the woman sitting in the carriage behind two potentially dangerous men. Brandelene found reason to agree with him and with trembling hands she pulled the pistol from her reticule.

"Oh, Lordy!" Ruby cried out.

"Monsieur Bouclair and Dagert, before we leave I wish to warn you that I am well armed."

The two men turned to stare into the muzzle of her pistol.

"Do not make the mistake of thinking that because I am a woman I don't know how to use a pistol, for I'll wager my aim against any man's. I won't hesitate to use this pistol to protect my property, my servants, or my person, so consider well before deciding to do anything I might consider a risk."

Wordlessly, the two men turned, facing forward, their backs to her once more.

"In addition, I have two sets of manacles, which I consider inhumane to use, but as I've already told you, I will do whatever I have to. I'm asking you, please, do not force me to do something I don't want to do." Brandelene inhaled deeply. "Have I made myself clear?" Her calm, cool voice belied the terror wrenching through her insides; she knew that to show either of these powerful men, who were every bit as desperate as she, one sign of fear or weakness could be disastrous.

The two men glanced at each other, then nodded.

"Good. As long as you conduct yourselves reasonably, you'll be well treated," Brandelene said, speaking to their rigid backs. Her voice was soft, the terror, the icy fear rioting within her slowly disappearing, and her confidence returned as she took control of the situation. "I am not a slave master. I'll discuss my predicament with Monsieur Bouclair later today. He, of course, will be free to inform you, Dagert. But first we'll get you both bathed and dressed so you are accorded the respect you deserve, and then we'll get you some decent food."

She leaned back in her seat, relaxing for the first time today. She quietly, and slowly, eased the hammer forward on her pistol, so the men did not hear, then said, "Joshua, please drive to the bathhouse."

Once there, Brandelene instructed the armed proprietor to bathe the two men in clean water, shave them, and to cut the white man's hair in a style a gentleman of quality would wear. After that a doctor was to attend them both.

Some hours later, Brandelene returned to the bathhouse, which catered to seamen and the owners of slaves and bond servants, with the new clothes she'd purchased. Joshua took the clothes inside and quickly returned.

Ruby, across from Brandelene, clucked her disagreement. "You can dress that white man up all fancy like a gentleman, but that isn't gonna change what he is, and you know it. We're all dead as possum meat with those two men loose and thick as wolves."

At those disturbing words, Brandelene glanced at the sinking sun, knowing she dare not risk being out after dark with the two men, pistol or no pistol in her hand.

"Joshua, please see what's keeping those two." The words had merely passed Brandelene's lips when Dagert, accompanied by an armed guard, appeared. He walked with a dignity he'd not shown before, then clambered onto the seat beside Joshua.

"Were you both well treated, Dagert?"

"Yes, madame," Dagert answered, turning to give her a smile that lit up his appealing face. "Thank you."

"Did a doctor come to bind Monsieur Bouclair's ribs?"

"Yes, madame."

Moments later Brandelene swallowed the gasp that threatened to escape her lips when Armand Kordell Bouclair walked out of the bathhouse. She stared, her eyes wide with disbelief. Surely, he could not be the stringy-haired, ratty-bearded wretch she'd purchased? This man was aristocratic. Very tall and powerfully built, he carried himself as though a prince. Moreover, he was incredibly handsome—breathtakingly so, looking more a confident gentleman of wealth in the store-bought clothes than any gentleman in tailored garments she'd ever met. The setting sun glinted golden highlights off his shining mane of tawny hair, a luxuriously thick mass of soft waves that framed a ruggedly chiseled face that bespoke the power and ageless strength inherent in a man used to having his own way. Brandelene, mesmerized by his carved lips, found herself wondering what it would be like to be smothered with ardent kisses by them. Shocked, she quickly lowered her survey to his clean-shaven strong, square jaw, now set in determination. He had a strong nose with slightly flaring nostrils, high, angular cheekbones, and magnetic, thickly fringed, golden eyes grandly accented by dark, curving brows. His was the overpowering, sun-bronzed face of Adonis, and Brandelene was flustered as never before.

Kordell stopped beside the carriage and grinned, his perfect teeth strikingly white in his sallow face and his cateyes, a molten gold in the sun, locked with hers. "If you are finished staring at me as though you've never seen a man before," he taunted, mockingly tossing her earlier remark back at her, his rakish grin widening into a dazzling smile, "I'll get into the carriage."

Chapter 4

"ARROGANT RAKE," BRANDELENE SNAPPED, HER FACE flushing hot.

With amusement still flickering in his eyes, Kordell started to climb to the coachman's seat.

"Monsieur Bouclair," Brandelene said, tightening her hold on the pistol covertly held beneath her reticule, "as much as it irritates me to do so, I must invite you to sit in the carriage with me. It would hardly be appropriate for a gentleman so dressed to be riding with the coachman."

"My pleasure, madame." Kordell grimaced in pain as he climbed into the carriage, his hard thigh pressing against hers when he eased himself down beside her.

"To the Richmond Inn, Joshua," Brandelene ordered, glancing at the setting sun. Once again the icy fingers of fear worked their way to her heaving breast. "Please hurry. It's been a rather trying day and I'm sure we could all do with a hot dinner." She made a weak attempt at a smile, for Ruby who sat in rigid terror opposite her. "Ruby darlin', please hand Monsieur Bouclair the laudanum. He seems to be in quite a bit of pain."

When Kordell leaned forward to take the bottle of medicine from Ruby's trembling hand, the reflection of the sun shining off the tip of the pistol concealed under Brandelene's large reticule caught his eye. It was pointed directly at his stomach. "Your concern is touching, madame," he said, knowing Brandelene was unaware of his discovery. "Heartwarming."

Not wanting to discuss the necessary room arrangements for Kordell and herself within hearing range of Dagert, Ruby, or Joshua, Brandelene instructed Joshua to drive directly to the area that housed the help. The Richmond Inn did not offer accommodations for servants within the guest's room.

"You will stay with me, Monsieur Bouclair," Brandelene directed when the inn's groom arrived to drive the carriage to the front. "Dagert, you'll please go with Ruby and Joshua." After a concerned Ruby had reluctantly alighted from the carriage, Brandelene smiled reassuringly. "I'll be fine, darlin'. Please see that Dagert has all he wants to eat."

Ruby nodded. "This sure is a bad day," she mumbled. "I'd rather be a slave again than dead."

Brandelene leaned over the side of the carriage, so her words would not be overheard by the groom. "Dagert, consider well before you decide you might wish to leave. It would not go well for Monsieur Bouclair if you did. And if any harm should come to my loved ones"—she nodded toward Ruby and Joshua—"your friend will regret the day he was born."

When Kordell heard Brandelene's words he knew her pistol was still pointed at his stomach. "Such a fragile, helpless woman," he said. "How do you manage by yourself?"

"You needn't worry about me, Monsieur Bouclair. I can take care of myself quite well."

"Of that I have no doubt. Not even the slightest."

Biting her tongue, Brandelene ordered the young groom to drive them to the entrance of the inn. "I wish to freshen up and change before we dine, so we'll need to reserve your room now. The room must adjoin mine," she told Kordell.

"Of course, I wouldn't have expected otherwise."

"Monsieur Bouclair, let me make one thing clear." Brandelene thrust her parasol at him, so she could reach in her reticule for her money with one hand without releasing her grip on her pistol with the other. "I have no designs on you romantically. Not today, not tomorrow, not ever! I have enough idiotic fools lusting after me without having to buy another. I've been pursued by enough gentlemen of quality that I certainly wouldn't buy a—a—whatever it is that you are in order to have a love affair. So, my overbearing, pompous friend, you may relax. I won't be making demands on you that you might not be able to fulfill."

Although infuriated at her insult, Kordell spoke with deceptive calm. "This may come as a surprise to a woman of your vanity, but usually women pursue me. I don't have to seek them—or *buy* them."

"How interesting," Brandelene replied, fury singeing the edges of her cool control. "Tell me, Monsieur Bouclair, do you think you were pursued so fervently for your immense wealth, or for your attractive shackles?" Never had a man aggravated her to such a degree that she happily would have thrashed him until he begged for mercy.

Kordell's icy glare could have frozen her to her seat. "You didn't believe a word I told you about my capture, did you?" Brandelene's lace-edged, opened parasol, which he'd been holding over her, he now, unknowingly in his irritation, held over himself.

At that point Brandelene glanced up at the delicate parasol shading him from the last rays of the sun and laughed throatily. "One would never suspect, Monsieur Bouclair, that you protected your complexion so zealously."

Looking up at the object of her ridicule, Kordell's cold resentment vanished. His laughter was rich, marvelous, and infectious, and Brandelene laughed with him. In their mirth they declared a silent truce.

* * *

A short time later Kordell was locked into his adjoining room while Brandelene bathed and dressed for dinner. She fashioned her hair into a chignon, with thick curls clustering over one ear to trail down her breast to her waist. Then she coaxed the wispy fringes to frame her face, and wove a multitude of tiny lavender silk flowers into a crown across the top of her head. With the latest turn of events, nothing would do but that she look her best this evening. Never in her wildest imaginings had she considered that the wretch she purchased would be the most handsome man she'd ever seen. A man with enormous self-confidence, fierce pride, a sense of humor, and, she imagined, more charm than necessary. What if Kordell Bouclair refused to marry her? It was a possibility.

Rising from the dressing table, Brandelene crossed the room to the wardrobe, selected her iridescent lavender silk gown, and carefully slipped it over her head. The beautiful fabric shimmered from lavender to purple in the lamplight.

She slipped her pistol into her matching reticule, stepped into slippers, pulled on long gloves, and took a deep breath, strengthening her confidence, for much depended on this night. Then she went to the connecting door and tapped lightly. "Monsieur Bouclair," she called softly as she slid back the bolt. "I am ready to dine."

After a minute Kordell opened the door, and a swift intake of breath escaped his carved lips as his gaze dropped from Brandelene's face to her décolletage. His bold, raking stare lingered briefly on the full mounds of temptingly revealed porcelain flesh. A woman of her flawless beauty would put any man to a test, but to one who'd suffered many weeks of forced celibacy on the high seas, the sight of her was an unbearable agony. Recovering his self-control, his gaze lifted to meet hers, to behold unfathomable violet eyes, more dazzling than the amethyst jewels she wore, fringed by an incredible length of sweeping black lashes. Her hand, inside her reticule, presumably gripped her pistol. "Madame Barnett," he acknowledged, his husky voice breaking, betraying his desire.

At length, during dinner at a table securely tucked into a corner that allowed little room for an easy escape, Brandelene inquired into Kordell's background. Too anxious to eat, she listened attentively to his story. Again, he repeated the same preposterous tale he'd told her in the auction house—that he owned a large coffee and cacao plantation on the Ivory Coast, situated on the Gulf of Guinea around the western bulge of Africa. Dagert, his chief overseer, and he had gone to a distant village in Mali to acquire additional labor, and while returning home with thirty black men they were set upon by slave traders.

Brandelene asked him numerous questions, and he answered in great detail, proving a personal knowledge of which he spoke. She was convinced he'd definitely been to the place he described so vividly, but she did not believe for one minute that he owned the plantation. More than likely, judging from his physique, he was an overseer, or even a common laborer.

Relaxing in the comfortable dining room over wine, Brandelene smiled and lowered her thick lashes demurely, then slowly lifted them to stare into the burning gold of his eyes.

"Monsieur Bouclair," she started softly, "I will be happy to help you right the wrong done you, if you'll help me in return. I'll explain briefly. Daddy owned a large tobacco plantation that I inherited at his . . . his death, over two years ago. However, Daddy's will stipulated that his only other living relative, his stepbrother, Cyrus, be named my guardian and controller of the plantation until such time as I marry . . ."

"You're not married?" Kordell interrupted, his heavy brows shooting up in surprise.

"No. I haven't yet met the man I will consider marrying. Wealth, or a pretty face, is but a curse to a woman. I've become the pawn of greedy or lustful men. They all want me for my inheritance or for . . ." Awkwardly hesitating, flustered, she felt her cheeks flush brightly.

With a knowing look, Kordell threw back his tawny head and laughed.

Humiliated, she felt all eyes in the room on them. "Sir, you are no gentleman! Do you wish to hear what I have to say, or do you prefer to play the fool?"

"Pardon me, mademoiselle. My apologies."

His voice, deep and resonant, seemed sincere until she glanced up to catch a devilish look in his eyes. "I can see this is a waste of time." Brandelene had started to rise when Kordell's hand shot out and caught her wrist, staying her.

"Please. I didn't mean to make light of your situation," he said a boyishly charming smile lighting up his face. "You were so . . so adorably flustered, so unlike the composed woman I've seen all day. You now have my undivided attention."

After consideration, Brandelene lowered herself back into her chair and Kordell's fingers released her wrist to trail lightly over her hand. I will have to take care with this charming rogue, she warned herself, ignoring her racing heart. "Following Daddy's death, my stepuncle sent me north, to Boston, to a school for genteel women. After two years of embroidering, watercolor painting, harpsichord playing, attending boring balls and soirees, and playing endless charades with milksops, fortune seekers, lusting gentlemen, and idiotic buffoons, I couldn't bear any more. So I went home. I found my plantation and finances in utter chaos. Cyrus had replaced Daddy's overseer with a cruel man, the indentured servitude of the workers had been rescinded, and the people were once again enslaved. In the slavery state of Virginia, which is where we are, they had no one to turn to for help, and have no personal rights."

Her voice broke, and she paused to compose herself. "Cyrus has total control of the plantation and all monies. I discovered he'd gambled away the considerable cash of my inheritance, and in addition, he borrowed money, mortgaging my estate, and gambled away that as well. The plantation has been disgracefully neglected. If Cyrus controls Southern Oaks much longer it will be beyond saving—if it isn't already." Stopping, she watched Kordell for a reaction, but his face was unreadable.

"I couldn't stand idly by and permit the people Daddy had freed to be subjugated, or watch my heritage, the estate that's been in my family for three generations, be gambled away. I'll do anything to save the indentured servants and freed people from the future to which my stepuncle is condemning them. I'll do anything to save my beloved Southern Oaks, my plantation, my inheritance, the only home I've ever known. I'll do anything except spend the rest of my life married to a man I do not love—that I will not do."

Kordell quirked his eyebrow questioningly, but said nothing.

Heaving a sigh, Brandelene explained, "My daddy and mother had the good fortune of marrying out of a deep and abiding love for each other. It remained so until death separated them. I want a marriage such as they had. Daddy promised me I could marry a man of my own choosing. I will marry no other. First, I would wish to become a chambermaid and wear rags. Yet I cannot even do that, for it would be condemning nearly six hundred people to a life of slavery under my stepuncle's control."

Anxious, Brandelene scanned the dining room, making certain no one was here who knew her, even though, so far from home, the possibility was remote. Then she girded herself to do the thing she found so detestable, feeling the knot in her stomach, the lump in her throat threatening to choke her if her pride did not do it first.

"I have carefully considered every alternative, and have even discussed it with Daddy's lawyer. My only alternative is to gain control of Southern Oaks by fulfilling the terms of Daddy's will. I shall marry. Since I haven't yet met the man I would consider marrying, my only choice has been to purchase an indentured servant who, in exchange for his freedom, will wed me without betraying the circumstances. After a reasonable length of time I will have the marriage annulled." Searching his face for some sign of his willingness to assist her, she found nothing.

Then Kordell's eyes widened in disbelief as he realized the meaning of her words. "Am I to understand that you wish me to marry you?"

At his question Brandelene glanced around mortification, fearing someone had overheard the astonished question. Satisfied no one had, she turned back to him, swallowing the pride that threatened to stop her plans. "Unfortunately, yes, Monsieur Bouclair. In exchange for your freedom, and only until I can have the marriage annulled."

"And if I refuse?"

Brandelene seethed that this insufferable bondsman would turn up his nose at her suggestion. Kordell was certain to deceive Cyrus; she would never find another nearly so fitting. Besides, there was no time. She knew her desperate situation required desperate measures and replied, "I'd have no choice but to return you and Dagert to the auction house to be resold. In addition, it would be very unlikely Dagert would be bought by the same gentleman as yourself, and as you've already mentioned, you might be unable to locate him in five years. Unlike yourself, he'd be a slave for his entire life."

"This is extortion!" Kordell snapped, glaring at her until she turned away. "What other options do I have?"

"None!" Brandelene was humiliated beyond endurance. How dare he treat her as though she'd offered him the black plague. She had beguiled many, and now she felt an unwavering determination. She would entice this rogue, she vowed. But she would not beg him, she resolved while she attempted to control her temper. Then, visualizing Ruby's soulful eyes, Joshua's trusting face, and the couples and children who might be separated if they were sold, she reconsidered. Yes, she would even beg him—but only if she had to. She rested her hand on his. "Monsieur Bouclair," she said softly. "I have no alternative. I don't have enough money to buy another bondsman without selling your servitude, and Dagert. I don't have the time to wait until you can reimburse me the price I paid for the two of you, for there would be nothing left of Southern Oaks to save. Please try to understand, monsieur. I'm a victim of circumstances, much the same as yourself." With that, she lowered her lashes and withdrew her hand to wipe away the lone tear trickling down her cheek.

All anger now gone, Kordell stared at her. All of a sudden, she seemed so defenseless, so vulnerable. "What is required in the United States to obtain an annulment?" His deep voice was filled with compassion, with concern for her.

All signs of tears now gone, Brandelene's lower lip trembled slightly before a small, enchanting smile touched her inviting lips. "There's nothing to it. It's a mere formality. You sign a document, I sign a document, and a doctor signs a document. The annulment s automatic after the documents are filed."

"A doctor signs a document? What kind of document does a doctor have to sign?"

Disconcerted, Brandelene turned away, a soft flush rising to her cheeks. "Certifying that the marriage has not been consummated." Her answer was barely audible.

"Are you telling me you're still a . . . ?" Kordell paused. "Do you mean what I think you mean?"

Brandelene colored fiercely. "Yes, I do, Monsieur Bouclair," she flared. "Since I'm unmarried why do you find that so astounding? Exactly what kind of women do you consort with in your country that you'd expect otherwise?"

Ignoring her question, Kordell said, "So we are to marry and not, ahh, not be married? Is that correct?"

"Yes, that is correct. How many times, or how many ways, must I tell you?" Then she leaned forward, placing her elbow on the table and her chin in the palm of her hand. "In fact," she assured him frostily, "I want this marriage to you as little as you want to marry me."

"If I agree to this ridiculous scheme, which I haven't, there are certain conditions you must agree to."

Staring at him with disbelief, Brandelene simmered. He was bargaining with her when she held his contract of indenture! Slowly good sense overcame anger. "What are your conditions?"

"One. That you assist me in straightening these unbearable circumstances in which I find myself."

"I have told you that I don't have the finances to help you."

"I will accept your word for that." Kordell hesitated, searching her eyes for the truth. "I'll need to send and receive correspondence freely."

"Agreed."

"Two. At the end of your 'reasonable length of time,' which is to be no more than the six months you mentioned, you will give Dagert a document of manumission and return my contract of indenture, which is forged, for I did not sign it."

"I told you at the auction house it would be six months to a year."

"Six months, and no longer!"

For a moment Brandelene's gaze challenged his. Finally she acquiesced. "Agreed."

"And the documents of manumission for Dagert and my contract of indenture?"

"Agreed."

Now Kordell leaned back, casually swinging one arm behind his chair with a confidence that rankled her. "Three. Dagert is to be your overseer."

"No! I refuse! I know what needs to be done to save Southern Oaks. I won't take the shambles and turn it over to a foreigner who knows nothing about tobacco. Do not take me for a fool because I am a woman and in unfortunate circumstances, Monsieur Bouclair."

She sat momentarily silent, struggling to contain her temper. Losing the battle, she ranted, "Who do you think you are to make such demands of me? My position is intolerable enough without adding to my problems with the likes of you, Monsieur Bouclair. This conversation has ended. You and Dagert will be returned to the auction house in the morning." With that she jumped up from her chair, almost knocking it over in her haste.

Whirling out of his seat to step in front of her, Kordell gasped aloud from the pain his quick movement had caused. "Please hear me out. My predicament is every bit as desperate as yours. I know we can come to some agreement." Now his tone was apologetic and he paused, glancing away, then back. "It's only that I can't bear to think of Dagert as a common field hand."

Kordell's last words touched her heart. Could he be all that bad to have such fierce loyalty and concern for his friend? Brandelene stared into his eyes, seeing the pain glowing there. She nodded, and once again, he assisted her into her chair.

"Since we are considering marriage—of a sort—why don't we pretend we are friends and you call me Kordell?" he invited. "I don't even know your given name, Mademoiselle Barnett."

Resting her chin on her hand, the beginning of a smile widened into approval as she scrutinized him. Beware of this charming knave, her senses warned her as she found herself unwillingly drawn to him. "Brandelene Lauree. My name is Brandelene Lauree."

"Brandelene Lauree," Kordell repeated, his voice as intimate as a caress.

A shiver tingled her spine. No man had ever affected her the way this one did, and she cursed her attraction to him, her temporary loss of self-control.

"Your name is almost as lovely as you are."

"Please . . . Kordell," Brandelene said, using his given name for the first time, commanding herself to put a barrier of ice between them. "You may save your charm for someone who'd appreciate it more than I. Shall we get back to the matter at hand?"

Fascinated, Kordell stared at her, rubbing his chin thoughtfully as he contemplated this unfeeling spider who held Dagert's and his future in the silk of her web. "Brandelene, my concern at this point in our discussion is for Dagert. He is . . ."

"And my concern is for my plantation!" she interrupted, her battered pride making her feel more degraded by the minute as she bartered with a bondsman—and her own bondsman at that. "Kordell, I cannot place a man who knows nothing about tobacco in the position of overseer." Then she added maliciously, "That should be clear even to a man of your obvious limitations." She watched him struggle with his anger at her insult. The rogue deserved her cutting remark, and she smiled with no small amount of satisfaction.

"My 'obvious limitations' are not at issue here. The talent of a natural leader and his knowledge of the land are. You told me you know tobacco as well as any man. Is that true?"

"Of course it's true."

"You've indicated your present overseer will have to be replaced. Why can't you teach Dagert everything you know, or at least everything he needs to know?"

"Why don't I be the overseer myself?"

"Brandelene Lauree Barnett, your beauty is only exceeded by your ignorance!"

"I must take care not to let you turn my head with such flattery," she said sweetly. "You've said words to that effect before—in the auction house, I believe. Do you not tire of repeating yourself? Or is your vocabulary so limited? I might add, Monsieur Bouclair, that, as for yourself, your audacity is only exceeded by your highly inflated and considerably undeserved ego."

At that remark, Kordell threw back his head and howled with laughter. "God help the man who really marries you. He'll surely need it."

"Strange you should mention that. I was thinking the same about the woman who marries you." Then, unable to help herself, she laughed with him.

The moment dissolved slowly and Kordell's countenance sobered. "Will you consider Dagert?"

"Consider? Yes, Kordell. If I can't find a competent overseer who'll work for me, or one I can afford, I'll consider him. In fact, I might even consider you." A teasing light shone in her eyes. "Before you give me your decision I need to inform you of what I will expect from you. If either you or Dagert attempt to escape, any agreements of this evening are forfeit. If you inform anyone of our arrangement, or if you or Dagert do or say anything to make our arrangement suspect by Cyrus, any agreements of this evening are forfeit. If you make any advances, in private, toward me, any agreements of this evening are forfeit. In addition, you'll be expected to play the loving husband in public, in front of Cyrus, and in front of the servants, for all eyes to see, until our annulment is filed in six months. Have I made myself absolutely clear?"

"Quite," Kordell returned. Uncertainty nagged at him. How on God's earth could he play the loving husband for six months to the most exquisite, the most desirable woman he'd ever met, and leave her untouched? How, knowing legally Brandelene Barnett was his wife, could he turn away from all that lawfully would be his? Did she think he had ice water in his veins?

"What is your decision, Kord?"

"I will give you my decision in the morning, *Brandy*." His voice was soft, soothing, almost sensual.

Fury almost choked her, and she fought to maintain her cool demeanor. Did he think he could best her? "Perfect. I will give you my decision at the same time," she said sweetly pleased with the look of surprise that crossed Kordell's face.

They left the dining room and Brandelene stopped to request that two baths be sent to their rooms early in the morning, to be followed by a visit from the doctor. As they went upstairs, she smiled cordially, all the while one hand firmly clasped the pistol in her reticule. "If one of us decides against this foolhardy venture, at least you'll be returned to the auction house in considerably better condition than you left it." Her voice was soft, with no indication of the tumultuous emotions rushing through her. Her dire predicament had not been resolved this night. Convinced, after their discussion, that she could not have found a man better equipped to deceive Cyrus than Kordell Bouclair, Brandelene vowed not to let the self-confident scoundrel know how desperately she wanted his assistance.

Chapter 5

IT SEEMED BRANDELENE HAD JUST FALLEN ASLEEP, BUT the sun shone brightly through her window when she was awakened by a knock.

"Water," a voice said, "for your baths."

"One moment please," she said, slipping on her dressing gown. She picked up the key to Kordell's room and her pistol, and hurried to the connecting barrier. Knocking softly, she slid the bolt, unlocked the door, and opened it. Kordell sat naked on the side of his bed, bent over in pain. "Oh," she gasped and partially closed the door.

Kordell chuckled. "If you're willing to enter a man's room

without announcing yourself first, you should be prepared for what greets you."

When they requested Kordell's adjoining room, they'd represented themselves as husband and wife, using the assumed name of Brown that Brandelene had used earlier. With that in mind, she whispered through the crack, so only Kordell could hear. "Your bathwater is here. You can imagine the gossip if the servants saw me unlock the door to my *husband's* bedroom. If you will kindly cover yourself I'll let the servants in while the water's still hot. Then I'll bring you some laudanum."

"Consider it done . . . Mrs. Brown."

"Insolent rake," Brandelene muttered, moving to unlock her own door to admit the servants, hiding the pistol beneath her wrapper. "Take the water into my husband's room first. He's not feeling well. Also, please summon a valet to assist him with his bath."

"Yes, ma'am," the pretty maid replied and scampered from the room after two young boys, bearing buckets of steaming water, entered.

Retrieving the laudanum, Brandelene returned to Kordell's room, unaware of the tempting picture she presented in her satin and lace dressing gown, her raven hair tossed in wild disarray. "If you were in so much pain, why didn't you wake me?" she scolded gently and handed her sheet-wrapped bondsman the medicine. Averting her gaze from the disturbing presence of a half-naked Kordell, she watched the young boys pour buckets of steaming water into the copper tub. Kordell took a sip of the pain-relieving laudanum, and suddenly she thought of a way, if he accepted her offer, to get him to Southern Oaks without fear of either her safety, or his escaping.

"Thank you, Brandy."

Kordell's voice was husky, oddly disturbing, and it rankled her that he again used the name by which only her father had called her. She took the medicine, her fingers brushing his, her gaze meeting his. Her heart lurched and her pulse pounded in her ears. In a hurry suddenly, she fled to her room, alarmed at her unwanted attraction to him.

Sometime later, after she'd bathed and dressed, she sat at the dressing table while the maid brushed her waist-length hair to a lustrous sheen. At the sound of the doctor entering from Kordell's room, she turned and smiled warmly.

"All I could do for your husband, ma'am, was rebind his ribs," the physician said. "That must've been some fight. Never saw so many bruises on a man."

"Doctor, it's imperative we return to my . . . to our plantation as soon as possible." Her voice was low enough that Kordell could not hear through his opened door. "I will need two bottles of laudanum since it is several days' ride by carriage, and many of the roads are quite bumpy."

"Your husband really should stay here for a week or two. The man's in no condition to travel, but I understand. It is planting season." The doctor opened his satchel and handed her the requested medicine.

"Thank you, Doctor," Brandelene said, and paid the physician. After he left, she took the bottles of medicine and hurriedly wrapped them in a petticoat, so they would not break, with an eye on Kordell's portal, making certain she was not observed. She hurriedly shoved the laudanum into her baggage, picked up her reticule with the pistol inside, and returned to her chair for the maid to finish brushing her hair. Anxious to be on her way, for she was determined to leave for Southern Oaks today, or north to find another bondsman, she decided to leave her naturally curling tresses loose.

"Wear your hair like that." Kordell stood in the connecting doorway, watching her. "It's lovely."

Defiantly, she began piling her locks on top of her head. "Have you reached a decision, Kordell?" she asked, sticking one pin after another into the weighty mass before topping it with her small blue hat, adorned with three white plumes.

"Of course I agree. Considering my alternatives, you've left me little choice." His words were said in an odd, yet gentle tone.

"I have reached the same decision, for further delay could cost the people I love their freedom, and me my heritage." With that, she rose from her chair and picked up the white parasol that coordinated with her white-edged, blue gown. "Shall we have breakfast and be on our way?"

Thoughtful, Kordell scanned her face, then her attractively gowned, curvaceous figure, fighting the wave of desire that ached in his loins, feeling much like the "idiotic fools" she had said lusted after her. "One would never suspect from your wardrobe that you're in such dire circumstances. You seem to manage very well on a pittance." Catlike golden eyes narrowed as he contemplated her, one dark brow arching uncertainly. "God help you, Brandelene, if you've lied to me."

Brandelene bit back a retort and started for the door. Once out of hearing range of the maid, she turned to Kordell as they walked down the wide staircase to the lobby. "And God help you, Armand Kordell Bouclair, if you do anything to upset my plans." Her hand tightly gripped the pistol in her reticule. "I may be small, but you'd better be warned that if you do, I will be a force to be reckoned with that you have never seen the likes of this side of hell."

Kordell's amused eyes gleamed down at her. "That I can believe from a feisty hellcat like you. That I can well believe."

"You're certainly not in any position to judge another's character. You're pompous, you're arrogant, you're crass, you're . . . I could go on and on."

Chuckling, Kordell said, "Regardless of what the next six months will be, Brandy, of one thing I am certain—they will not be boring."

"You may add insufferable to that list," Brandelene snapped before she swept into the Richmond Inn's dining room.

With the appetite of a man who'd spent several weeks in the hold of a slave ship, Kordell ate a large breakfast, while Brandelene drank juice and tea. Their meal had been taken mostly in silence, with Brandelene finding Kordell's gaze on her every time she glanced at him.

Becoming more uneasy by the minute, she knocked her parasol from where it leaned against her chair, deliberately kicking it under the table. "Oh, how clumsy of me."

"No problem," Kordell said, smiling. "I'll get it." He pushed back his chair and bent painfully under the table to retrieve the parasol Brandelene's foot rested on.

With Kordell fully occupied, she quickly poured a few drops of laudanum into his coffee, then removed her foot from the parasol.

"No harm done." Kordell brushed her footprint from the white fabric and leaned it beside her chair.

"Thank you," Brandelene said, studying his face, boyishly appealing when he smiled, wondering why he was in such good humor when he'd had to reach a decision so distasteful to him. What was he up to? She stared into his penetrating eyes hoping to discover some answer there, but found only her own disturbing thoughts. How could she spend six months with a man she found increasingly attractive, and remain detached? Could Kordell be a fortune hunter? That was the only sensible explanation for his cheerful attitude. True, he was more charming, more polished, smoother, and less obvious than the others had been, but possibly a fortune hunter no less. So thinking, she intentionally hardened her heart toward him.

"Shall we leave?" Brandelene inquired coolly after he finished his coffee, anxious to have her distasteful scheme over and done with, so she could claim her rightful inheritance and this rogue would be gone. Then she would have the time to find the husband she loved, who truly loved her.

A baffled look crossed Kordell's face at her sudden icy tone, but he said nothing and rose to assist her from her chair.

A short time later, with the boot of the barouche loaded with trunks, Brandelene and Kordell waited outside the servants' quarters for Ruby, Joshua, and Dagert. Not a word had been exchanged between them since they'd left the dining room. Brandelene felt restless and irritable, wondering why she was disappointed at her discovery of Kordell's probable intentions. Why should she care if he sought her inheritance? What else should she expect from a man who'd probably been running away from some dastardly crime he'd committed? Or, at best, he was a destitute man who could be presumed to seize the opportunity to improve his station in life. With this knowledge aforehand, why had it shaken her to realize he was no different from so many others?

Refusing to consider the matter further, Brandelene dove into her reticule and shoved a handful of bank notes at Kordell. "This should cover our expenses until we reach Southern Oaks. I selected a few things suitable for a man of means at the time I purchased the clothes you're wearing. I was fortunate that most of them had been ordered for a gentleman near your size, and for a healthy bonus the proprietor let me have them. We can have the cuffs let down and have them tailored to fit by the Southern Oaks's seamstresses."

At the humiliating necessity, Kordell stiffened. "I will consider this a loan and intend to repay you when I'm able to make the arrangements."

"That'll be fine." Brandelene sighed, unconcerned if Kordell Bouclair wished to continue with his deception. "The shopkeeper is holding my selections until noon today, so we'll need to stop there to pay for them and pick them up. If there's something I haven't thought of . . ."

"I'm sure you've thought of everything," Kordell replied, taking the money she offered and shoving it into his pocket. He scowled, a quivering muscle in his jaw betraying his injured pride. "I know it's useless to tell you that you don't need the pistol you have hidden beneath your skirts."

"Have no fear that I will accidentally shoot you, Kordell. I am experienced in handling firearms and only shoot what I intend to. Having my pistol ready gives me a more comfortable feeling since I'm traveling unescorted."

"I would sooner accost a black panther than you, mademoiselle. Much sooner."

"Good! You keep thinking that way and we'll get along fine."

"It had never occurred to me we wouldn't get along fine—for you will see to it." He glared down at her. "Tell me, Brandelene, do you wear breeches too?"

"If I do, would it threaten your masculinity, Kordell?"

To her dismay, he laughed. "The woman hasn't been born who threatens my masculinity. And she never will be."

"Your modesty is overwhelming."

"Yes. That is something we have in common, isn't it?" He gave her an impish grin.

Unable to help herself, Brandelene laughed and she found herself wondering what there was about this man that moved her from anger to laughter and back again.

At that moment Ruby, Joshua, and Dagert came out of the inn to see Brandelene and Kordell sitting in the carriage, laughing together.

"Look at that riffraff sitting up there with Miss Brandelene, acting like he was a fine gentleman," Ruby mumbled.

Overhearing her words, Dagert, with a disturbed expression on his face, helped Ruby into the conveyance, before turning to Brandelene. "Good morning, madame. I can't remember how long it's been since I had such good food. I ate enough for three men. Thank you for your consideration."

"My pleasure, Dagert."

Moments later Joshua and Dagert climbed onto their high seat and Brandelene made her announcement, "Monsieur Bouclair and I are going to be married."

Ruby gasped.

Dagert stiffened in shock, staring straight ahead, his disapproval obvious.

"This sure is a bad day," Joshua grumbled.

"Ruby, I expect you to treat Kordell with the respect that should be accorded my husband. Otherwise Cyrus will never be deceived."

"Hmmph!" Ruby's hands trembled as they anxiously smoothed the skirt of her brightly flowered gown, betraying her fear.

Kordell leaned forward and gently informed Ruby, "No harm will come to your mistress because of me."

His assurance was no comfort to the distraught woman.

At Kordell's considerate words, Brandelene glanced up at him. He was an ever-changing mystery, an enigma she had not quite figured out. "To the shop where I purchased Monsieur Bouclair's clothes and then home by the route we discussed earlier, Joshua," she directed.

They would not go directly from Richmond to Petersburg, for many eyes in Petersburg would see the carriage disembark from the Richmond river barge, and Cyrus would be certain to find out. So, Brandelene and Joshua had decided that instead of going south, they would go east as far as the Claremont plantation in the Tidewater area, ferry across the James River there, and enter Petersburg by road from the east. It would add one day's travel time, but she felt it would be worth it. If Cyrus investigated, he would most probably assume they'd come from Norfolk, and not think to inquire at Richmond.

Joshua, with his head lowered, his shoulders slumped, snapped the reins of the matching bays.

"I have several letters I'd like to post as soon as possible," Kordell said, pulling the letters he'd written the previous night from his coat pocket.

"Of course. Joshua, please stop and inquire where Monsieur Bouclair may post his letters," Brandelene instructed. Noticing both Kordell and Dagert relax at her words, she realized they were as skeptical of her as she of them.

Shortly thereafter, Kordell had posted his letters and was in the shop to claim the clothes Brandelene had selected for him.

Ruby leaned forward in the carriage, concerned she might be overheard by Dagert, who sat behind her on the driver's seat next to Joshua. "Miss Brandelene," she whispered, "how're we ever gonna get home without them murdering us all?"

"Don't fret, darlin'. I have my pistol ready and Kordell will be asleep most of the way home." Her hushed reply was followed with a delicate finger to her lips.

"How you know that?"

"I have enough laudanum with me to put a horse to sleep," Brandelene whispered. "Kordell has already had two doses this morning. I shall give him another when he returns to the carriage. Shortly he should be sleeping like a baby."

Moments later Kordell walked out of the shop, followed by a young boy laden with a trunk full of the purchases Brandelene had selected. She turned away, irritated by her heart trip-hammering at the sight of the remarkably handsome man. With the trunk loaded onto the carriage, Kordell swung himself up beside her, grimacing in pain.

"Home, Joshua," Brandelene called out and the carriage lurched ahead.

After removing the laudanum from her reticule, Brandelene turned toward the man who would be her husband in three days. Smiling sweetly, she handed him the medicine. "The ride home will be rough. You had best take a little of this to ease the pain." Noticing the slight flush of his face, she filled her voice with concern.

As though dazed, Kordell shook his head to refuse her offer. "I'm not in pain now and I'm a little light-headed. Perhaps I shouldn't have any more yet."

"Nonsense! You're weak as a newborn colt. I've gone to considerable trouble to assure you don't suffer any more discomfort than necessary." Brandelene handed Kordell the small bottle of milky liquid. "I have enough on my mind without having to care for an injured man, or having to postpone our wedding because you're too ill to stand up."

Reluctantly, he took the proffered bottle, swallowed a sip of the bitter liquid, and handed it back to her. "Your consideration for my welfare is comforting, to say the least," he said, knowing her other hand, discreetly placed under the folds of her skirt, held her pistol. "We have an agreement, Mademoiselle Barnett. You may be assured, you have bought yourself a husband for six months. Have no concern for that. If every rib I had were broken I would crawl before the magistrate for the joyous privilege of marrying a cold hellion like you."

"Have no fear, Monsieur Bouclair, for I'll see to it that you're not deprived of that 'joyous privilege.'"

"I never doubted it for a minute."

"Monsieur Bouclair, my circumstances force me to wed the likes of you. Heaven knows it certainly isn't your charm or considerable wealth. However, those same circumstances do not require me to suffer your offensive behavior, or your insolence. May I remind you of the entire agreement? You are to play the loving husband for all the world to see."

Although her mistress's voice was gentle, Ruby could see Brandelene's knuckles turning white as she gripped her parasol with, she imagined, the same ferocity Brandelene would have liked to use on Kordell's throat.

"I suggest," Brandelene continued, "if you value your freedom, and Dagert's, you start practicing that behavior now, as my betrothed. You apparently are unfamiliar with the conduct of a gentleman, and could use a little practice. Or shall I have Joshua return to the auction house?" She smiled smugly and her gaze bore into his, unaware of the captivating picture she made in her blue and white dress, with the breeze whipping stray strands of raven hair around her face.

The even whiteness of Kordell's teeth contrasted with the sallow tan of his face and his smile brought a softening to the chiseled features. "Do you," he asked, amused, his voice calm, his stare steady, "rein in a horse with the same expertise?"

"Most assuredly."

"I was certain you did. Well, my *beloved* fiancée, when am I to be given the honor of marrying you?"

"In four days in Petersburg. There it will be easy for Cyrus to verify the legitimacy of the marriage, so near to home."

"Ahh, yes. That would be most important, wouldn't it? And being farther from the auction where you purchased your husband would be of additional importance, would it not?"

Once again Brandelene silently cursed Cyrus Varner. She hated Cyrus, hated having to marry an insensitive rogue in an ill-advised scheme to regain her inheritance, hated her whole life. Most of all, she hated Kordell Bouclair. How would she ever get through six months with the man—if she lived that long?

"Do not make light of my situation, Kordell. If only for the reason that your own tenuous position is dependent upon the success of my plans."

At those words, Kordell's hand flashed out grasping Brandelene's wrist, his fingers digging into her soft flesh. "That was not the agreement."

"Remove your hand this instant." Brandelene pulled the pistol from beneath her skirts and pointed it directly at his stomach.

When Kordell glanced down at the cocked pistol he loosened his grip on her wrist. "So that's the way it's to be?" His eyes narrowed in contempt. "I knew I shouldn't trust a conniving viper like you."

Exhaling in relief, Brandelene slipped the hand holding the

pistol beneath her skirts. "Monsieur Bouclair, I made an agreement with you. I intend to honor it, if I'm able to." Now she shifted anxiously in her seat, lowering her eyes from his accusing glare. "Certainly you've realized that if Cyrus discovers my husband is an indentured servant, whose servitude I purchased three days prior to my wedding, he could have the marriage annulled with great ease and remain in control of Southern Oaks. Which also means he'd control your servitude and the ownership of Dagert. It didn't occur to me it was necessary to point that out to you."

"Mademoiselle, there is nothing in this absurd scheme of yours that has not occurred to you. What else haven't you told me . . . that didn't occur to you?"

Ignoring his question, Brandelene looked up at him with imploring eyes, then handed her parasol to Ruby, turning her body toward Kordell's. "If we work together we'll be successful, Kord. I know we will," she said softly, her fingers lightly brushing his hand where it rested on his knee, and her gaze dropped to the manacles lying on the floor of the rocking carriage, then lifted to his. "For the next six months we are shackled together as surely as if we wore those manacles, each dependent on the other for salvation."

Kordell studied Brandelene's upturned face, so exquisitely vulnerable; her supple lips, so invitingly close; her violet eyes, glistening like jewels in the sun, so mesmerizing. Since she'd turned toward him, he'd felt her breast singeing his arm, felt her hand burning into his. So light-headed was he that he could not think, he could only feel. Feel the yearning, deep in his loins, to possess her. She was a haughty temptress, a devastating whirlwind who would devour her mate as easily as a black widow spider does, and he cursed her beauty, cursed his foggy mind that refused to concentrate. Why couldn't he think? Why was he so light-headed? His vision blurred slightly, then cleared. All he could see was Brandelene's sensuous mouth, her slightly parted lips, and he lowered his tawny head to taste fully of the inviting pleasure.

Brandelene found Kordell's warm, moist kiss a tender caress, surprisingly gentle, yet hinting at the passion he controlled. Helpless to stop herself, her fingers clasped the back of his head. Her soft lips parted beneath his, sending the pit of her stomach into a whirlpool of emotion, and she found herself wishing his intoxicating kiss would go on forever. That it was his desire for her, not her inheritance. All of a sudden, he relaxed and his head slipped to her shoulder to nestle in the softness of her neck.

Stunned at his audacity, at the tumultuous feelings racing through her body, she jerked away from him and he slumped back against the seat. The laudanum had finally taken effect. Kordell slept soundly and her outward calm belied her wildly pounding heart, her racing pulse. Never before had she reacted to a man this way, and that fact sent her equilibrium spinning, pounding to the rhythm of her heartbeat. What was wrong with her? What foolishness possessed her? It was madness! Her senses reeled and it perplexed her, distressed her, then infuriated her, and she chastised herself for permitting this . . . this . . . bondsman to so affect her.

Bewildered and torn by conflicting emotions, she stared at Kordell's face, bronzed by wind and sun, marveling at the strength, the confidence, the vitality reflected there. Although reluctantly, she silently admitted she'd never met a more masterful man. Strangely, at the same time, as he slept a slight vulnerability manifested itself in his spellbindingly handsome features. Resisting the overwhelming urge to take him into her arms and comfort him, to promise him she would do everything in her power to help him in his plight, she forced her gaze away from his compelling good looks.

And then she knew. This was not a man she need fear would physically assault her, but a man who could win her heart with his charm, his wit, his hypnotic golden eyes. He would not murder her in her bed, but rather would tear her heart from her, leaving her an empty shell of a woman, and nonetheless dead. Disturbed, she realized that this Kordell was a man far more dangerous, far more to fear, than the men she'd formerly been so wary of. For this man could wield the power to destroy all her plans—if she permitted him. She must harden herself against him, enfold her heart in ice, for she could not let her attraction to him jeopardize Southern Oaks.

Ignoring Ruby's condemning glare for her impropriety, she glanced up at Ruby and gave her a wink. Still, she wondered who was really triumphant, she or Kordell?

The barouche doggedly traveled east on the dusty planters' roads of the isolated Tidewater countryside of Virginia. Tense, ever alert for trouble, Brandelene tightly gripped the pistol as the carriage rolled through miles of dense forest, where two desperate men could disappear in the blink of an eye, and rocked past thousands of acres of planted fields filled with workers, their backs bent to their labor. Seldom did they pass an approaching carriage, for it was spring, planting season, and only ladies of the gentry had the leisure time to travel anywhere. Fully aware of this, Brandelene realized there was no one to come to her aid should she need assistance. She, and she alone, was the sentinel of her two newly acquired servants, and her heart beat with fear at the thought of her risk. Her one advantage was that she felt sure one man would not flee without the other. Thus, as long as Kordell remained drugged she felt reasonably safe.

Kordell still slept that night when Dagert half carried, half dragged him into his room at a secluded wayside inn, while Brandelene watched with satisfaction. Consequently she was unprepared for what greeted her the following morning when she unlocked Kordell's door.

Chapter 6

"YOU ARE NOT DRUGGING ME ALL THE WAY TO SOUTHern Oaks! I should have known better than to trust you. If you were a man I'd thrash you!" Angrily, Kordell paced his small room, the muscle in his square jaw tensing visibly as he fought to control his rage. "That auction doctor was considerably wiser than I gave him credit for being. He said someone should give you the thrashing you deserve, and that's exactly what should be done with a hellcat like you!"

Brandelene stood with the key clutched in one hand, her pistol in the other.

Kordell glared at her. "What? No denial, Brandelene? No dramatic pleading for forgiveness so I'll still marry you?"

"I did what I felt I had to do."

"And I had damn well better do what I have to do." Kordell started toward her and she raised her pistol and pointed it directly at him. He froze in his tracks.

"We have an agreement," Brandelene quietly reminded him. "I have not lied to you. I need you, just as you need me."

"You had better use that damn pistol, or get out of my way." Yet, as angry as he was, he could not help but admire her spirit.

"What would you have done in my place, Kord?" Brandelene asked softly. "Think about it." Her voice was low, throaty. Her eyes were imploring as she sighted down the barrel of the pistol.

He was furious, but he realized, under her icy exterior, how terrified she must have been, traveling with two strong strangers through isolated country. Now she looked so small with her pistol pointed at his heart, and more than anything, he wanted to kiss her until she begged for mercy—or more. "I go to Southern Oaks of my own free will, or I don't go at all."

At his words, Brandelene lowered her pistol and released the hammer. He wanted to snatch the pistol from her, but thought better of it. At the moment he was but a bond slave in a foreign country. So instead, he brushed her aside and stormed downstairs to the waiting carriage.

Thereafter, Kordell lapsed into an angry silence, stubbornly refusing any of the pain-relieving laudanum, and the next two days dragged on endlessly. Brandelene's right hand felt as though her pistol were permanently embedded into it. Added to her dismay, Kordell developed a fever, but he obstinately refused to see a doctor. Each night she locked him in his room at the inns where they continued to give the assumed name of Brown.

At last, with dusk approaching, they entered Petersburg by the eastern road. They were only a few hours from the plantation.

Now, so near to Southern Oaks, where many people would recognize her or her name, they dared not continue to pose as husband and wife. The gentry of Virginia might have ostracized her because her father had operated his plantation with indentured servants and free black people instead of slaves, but she would not have her reputation further slandered by being called a wanton woman. Heaven knew her disgrace would be near complete by traveling with her fiancé without a proper chaperon, compounded by a hasty, unannounced marriage performed in a judge's chambers. Since they could not request adjoining rooms the only solution was to reserve one room in her name, on one floor, and a second room in Kordell's name, on another floor. It was the very least propriety dictated.

Some hours later, Brandelene, with Ruby, paced the hallway outside Kordell's room. Playing the nervous fiancée, she waited for the doctor to leave Kordell's room, but her concern was not feigned, for his weakness and rising fever had caused her to send Joshua for the best physician in Petersburg. It seemed an unusually long time before the doctor joined her.

"You're going to have to postpone your wedding, my dear," Dr. Malloy announced. "Your young man is quite ill. He never should have traveled after being beaten so badly by those thugs. I can understand his anxiety to be with you, but he's also suffering the effects of malnutrition, from his seasickness for so many weeks. What with his undernourished condition, then to be so brutally assaulted, and to immediately travel for so many days before healing, I'm afraid, due to his weakened state, he's gotten lung fever."

Brandelene paled. Her guilt at feeling responsible for Kordell's illness consumed her. "He'll be all right, won't he? You must help him, Doctor. Please!"

The doctor, believing her anguish to be concern for her beloved fiancé, pulled her into his thin arms to comfort her. "I've left some cough medicine to break up the congestion in Kordell's lungs, and some pills. The instructions are written on the medication. In addition, he's to remain in bed and drink all the liquids he can. He'll require twenty-four-hour care, my dear. He needs to be sponged constantly with cool water to help keep his fever down, for he will die from a raging temperature before the lung fever can. . . ."

Kordell couldn't die, Brandelene vowed. She had saved Toby and Belle from succumbing to the ravages of lung fever, certainly she could save Kordell too.

"I have no one to send to tend him right now," the doctor admitted. "The only woman I know who would be capable is assisting at a difficult delivery." The doctor looked down at her anxious face, then patted her with reassurance. "I'll stop by in the morning. Now don't you worry, Brandelene. Your young man is a fighter. He's going to fight all the way with a woman such as you waiting to marry him."

Brandelene groaned aloud at the doctor's words, for she knew the last thing in the world to give Kordell Bouclair the will to live was the thought of marrying her. "I'll get a suite of adjoining rooms, and have him moved there so we can care for him. I can't worry about my reputation now."

"You can't do that, my dear," the physician scolded. "Every gossip in Petersburg will know by tomorrow morning that you're staying in a suite with your fiancé. They wouldn't care about the reason, or that the man is too ill to care for himself, let alone be a party to improper conduct. You've got to think of yourself, Brandelene. What if your young man were to die? Every blackguard within a hundred miles would swarm down on you, thinking you a woman of easy virtue. You would live the rest of your life in disgrace, and no self-respecting man would ever marry you. You've already compromised yourself by having been in his room without a proper chaperon. Surely you know how inn servants gossip."

"I can't . . . I won't stand by and not help when he's so sick. No one will care for him as I will."

The doctor rubbed his chin, deep in thought. "Everyone in the Wolf's Lair knows me. I'll arrange for a suite of rooms in your young man's name and explain to the proprietor that he'll need attending. I'll tell them I'm sending someone over to see to his care. You keep your room and remain there until I come for you.

After we've moved Kordell, you and Ruby can sneak up the back stairs to his suite. Take caution you're not seen. Not even by the inn servants. I think that's the most you dare attempt."

"Thank you, Doctor. Ruby and I'll wait in my room."

The doctor nodded and hurried toward the front stairs.

Brandelene paced her room while she waited for his summons. "Oh, Ruby, what a mess I've gotten myself into. Mother didn't raise me to be devious. I'm glad she's not here to see what I've done. The inn doctor in Richmond told me Kordell shouldn't travel. And I never should have given him so much laudanum. Perhaps, if he hadn't been drugged, I would've noticed sooner how ill he was."

"Child," Ruby soothed, "you got to quit that fretting. Everything's gonna be just fine."

"If Kordell dies it will be my fault. We should have stayed at the Richmond Inn for a few days so he could recuperate."

Ruby pulled Brandelene into her comforting arms and as she'd done so often when the young woman was a child. "Nothing's gonna happen to that rascal. Me and you are gonna take care of him just fine. That handsome devil is too charming to die, little lamb. Now you know I'm right."

"Oh, Ruby, I hope so." Brandelene pulled free of the loving embrace. "I'll never complain about him again if only he'll live, I swear I won't," she said, then added, "Why, I wouldn't be surprised if he's deliberately doing this to get even with me just because I put laudanum in his drinks."

At the knock Brandelene ran to open the door to Dr. Malloy.

"Kordell's moved," the doctor said. "I'll escort you up the back stairs to his rooms and then I have to leave to check on Mrs. Cain. I'm sure the woman's carrying twins, and her last birth was extremely difficult." He placed an arm around her and gave her a supporting hug. "Don't worry, Brandelene. Kordell's resting well and there's nothing I can do for him now that you can't do. I'll be here as soon as I can in the morning."

The three of them hurried down the corridor to the rear stairs. At the door to Kordell's suite the doctor said, "I've dismissed the inn servants. Don't let anyone see you in this room. If you need assistance have Ruby send for Joshua. If you need me, send Joshua. My wife will know where I am."

The physician left, and Brandelene and Ruby slipped into the suite. Anxious, Brandelene crossed the sitting room to look in on him.

"I was sure you wouldn't be too far behind the doctor," he said. "I should've guessed you guarded my door. Where are your pistol and your laudanum?"

Aggravated, Brandelene lifted her reticule containing the pistol defiantly high. She sighed and averted her gaze from his bared, thickly furred chest. "How am I ever to get through the next six months with you?"

He struggled to sit up, grimaced in pain, and sank back into the bed pillows. "Perhaps you'll be spared such agony."

"You needn't worry, Kordell. I won't let you die."

"I wasn't aware anyone had appointed you God. I feel considerably relieved now that I know."

She crossed the room and bent to touch his brow, to check his fever. "Your temperature hasn't risen any. That's a good sign."

"And I thought you were getting affectionate," Kordell mocked and his glance paused on the fullness of her high, firm breasts, his eyes glowing with an inner fire.

"You can't feel too bad if you can act the rake and maintain your sense of humor."

"It's going to take more than your precious laudanum and a little fever to do me in."

"Kordell, I'm sorry about the laudanum. Really I am. I felt it was better than putting manacles on you, and besides, you were in such pain," she rationalized, unused to explaining anything to anyone. "It seemed the best thing to do, for both of us. You know I never would have insisted we leave Richmond right away if I had known you were in poor health. You looked so healthy . . . after your bath." Then Brandelene pulled a chair to his bedside.

Kordell looked into her violet eyes and their gazes locked before she turned away. "I believe you, Brandelene. If only for the reason that you wouldn't deliberately let anything unfortunate happen to me . . . before we're married."

Brandelene squirmed in her chair, vowing she would not let him provoke her while he was so ill. "Can I get you anything?" At his silent scrutiny she reached for the pitcher and poured a glass of water. "Dr. Malloy said you need to drink often. It will help keep your fever from rising." She bent and slipped an arm beneath his shoulder to assist him to a sitting position. The feel of his naked, muscled shoulder under her hand, the fresh aroma of soap mingled with his masculine scent, the heady touch of his curling locks that brushed her cheek, and his hand over hers on the glass sent a whirlwind of tumultuous feelings coursing through her body. Disturbed, she pulled her hand from beneath his and plumped the pillows on his bed.

"Why do I have the feeling I wouldn't receive such loving care and concern if we were already married? In fact, it would be quite convenient for you if I were to die once we were wed, wouldn't it, Brandelene?"

"How can you say such a cruel thing, Kordell Bouclair? I have treated you with naught but consideration . . . except for the times you've provoked me."

Tired and aching, Kordell sank back onto the pillows, his breathing labored. "Are you to be my caretaker, or is the doctor to send someone?"

His voice was weak, and Brandelene's brow furrowed in concern. "I will take care of you. The doctor didn't feel you were ill enough to require special care."

Smiling at her lie, he closed his eyes. "Good. Then I need have no fear, for you will ordain that I get well quickly."

During the next few hours Kordell's fever steadily climbed and Brandelene, now assisted by Ruby, cared for him. She gave him the medications as Dr. Malloy prescribed, forced him to drink the water, juices, and broths he tried to refuse, and finally pulled the bedcovers down to his waist to sponge his burning body with cool water. It was near dawn when, fatigued, she once again pressed her fingers against his brow, then sank down onto the edge of his bed in relief. The worst was over.

"Kordell, your fever dropped. Do you hear me? Your fever has dropped."

Dazed, he nodded and his eyes opened for a few seconds before he smiled and drifted back into a foggy, dream-filled sleep.

Shortly thereafter, the doctor arrived and examined Kordell. Afterward he spoke to Brandelene in the small sitting room. "My dear, I must be frank with you, as I was with your young man. Kordell's extremely ill. I realize he must seem considerably improved, since you and Ruby worked so painstakingly with him last night. It was that effort that lowered his fever. However, his lungs are more congested than before. There are so many things we don't know in medicine, and this kind of illness is one of them. We are so limited in our knowledge of how to treat it—sometimes I think the mother's remedies work as well, if not better than what I have been educated to do."

The doctor's words penetrated her groggy mind. "What are you telling me, Doctor?"

Dr. Malloy sighed and placed an arm around her shoulders. "I can't assure you that Kordell will live. He has a fifty–fifty chance—at best."

"Oh, dear God! What have I done? What can I do?" Brandelene implored, her guilt engulfing her. "I'll do anything. Anything!"

"Continue with the medication, liquids, and sponging as you've been doing," the doctor instructed. "Do your best to keep his fever down. As I said, that will be his undoing before the lung fever. Kordell must stay in bed. He's probably much too weak to get up anyway. He'll need constant care if he's to have any chance at all."

"I refuse to let him die!"

The physician ignored her outburst, knowing that it came from an independent, strong-willed young woman used to having her own way. "Brandelene, he also needs the assistance of a man to take care of his personal needs. Kordell mentioned someone named Dagert."

"Yes."

"I'll bring him here as soon as possible. He can share in Kordell's care. Besides, it's too much for only you and Ruby."

Brandelene stared at the doctor. Dare she permit him to bring Dagert to this suite where she would be defenseless? Yet dare she further risk Kordell's life by refusing additional help? "Yes, please bring Dagert."

"I'll see to it as I leave, and I'll be back this evening to check on Kordell. He'll probably reach his crisis point during the night." Dr. Malloy tilted her chin up. "You have a strength I've seen in few women. If anyone can pull him through this, you can. The rest is up to God."

"Then I shall get on bended knee. Kordell is not going to die."

While Brandelene talked with the doctor, Kordell lay brooding. After the physician had discussed his condition, his first concern had been for Dagert. How could he protect his friend from slavery if he died? Finally he arrived at a viable solution to which he felt Brandelene would be amenable. Now, with his mind free of burdens, his thoughts turned to the high-spirited temptress who'd purchased his contract of indenture. Last night, when she'd nursed him with a gentleness he would have sworn she did not possess, she'd shown a side of herself he'd not seen before. It might have been interesting to see all the sides of the complex Brandelene Lauree Barnett. Even now, as ill as he was, he could not still the ache of desire that burned in him. He sighed, for he knew the doctor had tried to spare him the full truth of his chances for recovery. Too many times Kordell had seen the devastating results of lung fever in England, France, and on the Ivory Coast, and was aware of the exceedingly high mortality rate. Few survived.

He was deep in thought when Brandelene swept into his room. Their gazes met, and Kordell felt himself being helplessly drawn into the violet depth of her eyes, and he had neither the strength nor the will to fight it.

She glanced away, but not before she noticed the light flush that still lingered on his disturbingly handsome face. "You're looking much better this morning, Kordell," she said and smiled cheerfully.

"You can drop the pretense, Brandelene. I know how grave my condition is. Will you sit down? I'd like to talk to you . . . please."

There was a huskiness to his voice now and Brandelene shivered at the ominous tingle splintering down her spine. She sat as requested, then glanced up in questioning silence.

"I ask you to hear me out without interruption," Kordell insisted and Brandelene nodded her assent. "I must accept the probability that I will not live through this night, or, at best, my condition will worsen considerably. It's with that possibility in mind that"—he paused, laboring to breathe—"that I make this request. In our discussions, my demise was never considered, and I realize that in such an event all agreements are rescinded. Now my first concern is for Dagert. I'm aware that if I don't survive you won't have the money to proceed with your plans, and you'd be forced to sell Dagert in order to start anew." He raised his hand to still her interruption. The beginning of a smile tipped the corner of his mouth. "We can both have what we want, and what I must have if I'm to die with peace of mind, or live with honor." Breath short, he coughed. "I will marry you today if you'll agree to give Dagert his document of manumission, to be effective in six months, or at the time of my death, whichever comes first."

Brandelene gasped at his suggestion. How could he bargain so calmly over his own death? "Kordell, you're not going to die, unless you insist on a wedding now. You need bed rest. I'll care for you, and I won't let you die."

"I still haven't been informed of the proclamation that appointed you God, so you're not going to have any say in this matter."

"Damnation! Must you make a joke out of everything? I am doing all I can to show you consideration and help you get well, and you do naught but make light of a serious situation."

The slight tremble of her lip was the only indication of her inner turmoil and Kordell sobered. "You're right. I apologize for my lack of consideration. However, my proposal is in all earnestness." He gave in to a racking coughing spasm, pausing to rest before he was able to continue raggedly, "Will you marry me today in exchange for Dagert's freedom, in the event of my death?"

Chapter 7

"I WILL NOT MARRY A MAN ON HIS SICK BED. BESIDES, it would be for naught. Cyrus would know the marriage wasn't consummated and would have it set aside."

"Then I will marry you wherever you select."

"What kind of monster do you take me for? If you attempt to ready yourself for a wedding, and leave this inn for the ceremony, you'll be signing your own death certificate. I won't consider it."

"Brandelene, it is my life! It is my right to risk my life for whatever purpose I choose. I've seen the devastation of lung fever. Not many survive. What difference if I die tonight, or tomorrow night, if one day can buy Dagert's freedom, and give you Southern Oaks too?" He sank back into the plump pillows. Exhausted by his labored breathing, he rested for a moment. "I ask you to give a dying man his last wish." His golden eyes, dulled by fever, searched her face for the answer he sought.

Her gaze captured his and pleaded for understanding before she whispered, "I cannot . . . I cannot." Kordell turned away from her, but not before she saw the despair nakedly reflected in his eyes. "I'll draw up the document of manumission now for Dagert," Brandelene said, and hoped this concession might give him ease. "Dagert's on his way here to help care for you. I'll give the paper to him as soon as he arrives, so you may rest peacefully. You're never going to get better if you continue fretting." Although forced, she laughed softly. "Sweet mercy, Kordell Bouclair, you fret more than Ruby. How am I ever to survive the next six months with the two of you to contend with?"

Surprised, Kordell turned back to stare at Brandelene, seeing another side of the woman she tried so hard to conceal, then he closed his eyes and prayed to a merciful God to let him live.

Brandelene rose quietly and walked into the sitting room to write out the papers to free Dagert. Refusing to think about the consequences of her actions, for she had to right the wrong she'd done, she returned shortly to Kordell's room with the document of manumission in hand. She went to his bedside and glanced down at his flushed face. She poured a glass of water, then helped him sit up to drink. "I'm sorry to wake you, but the doctor said we can't let your temperature rise." She held the cool glass to his fevered lips. After he drank the water she handed him the document. "I thought you might prefer to give this to Dagert yourself."

Gratefully, Kordell took the paper from her outstretched hand. "You make the arrangements and Dagert will help me prepare for our wedding. But it must be today, Brandelene. I may not have the strength to walk tomorrow."

Straightening, Brandelene knocked the chair over in her turmoil. "No. I told you. I won't let you take such a chance for a charade of a marriage that's been a ridiculous endeavor from the first I thought of it. You will not get out of your bed."

Kordell chuckled. "I can see you need a little practice to become the obedient wife."

Speechless, Brandelene spun to storm out the door, then paused. "You are a fool, Kordell Bouclair! An utter fool!"

"I've been called worse. And by you."

Minutes later Dagert rushed to Kordell's bedside and Brandelene left them alone while she paced the sitting room. When Dagert walked out of the room, his face was grim.

"Is Kordell worse?"

"No. He's fallen asleep. May I speak with you, Miss Brandelene?"

"Yes, of course. Please be seated." Brandelene sat opposite the immense man.

Dagert wrung his huge hands, then crossed his large feet, his discomfort obvious. "Miss Brandelene, you must marry Kordell," he blurted. "You must marry him today. As soon as possible."

Brandelene's quick intake of breath betrayed her astonishment, and she stared at him, at a loss of for words.

When she did not reply, Dagert spoke quietly, "Kordell told me of your predicament, and your agreement—all of it."

"I don't wish to be rude, Dagert, but this is none of your affair."

"Yes it is, Miss Brandelene," Dagert replied gently. "Kordell's father found me orphaned in the bush country, and took me into his home when I was just a tot. Kordell and I grew up together, were educated together, were never separated until he left for Oxford. I love him like a brother and that makes it my affair. What Kordell wants is to marry you today." Pulling the document of manumission from his hip pocket, he said, "He gave me this."

Brandelene rose from her chair, walked to the window, and pulled back the curtains to stare blankly into the uncobbled street below. "We shall marry when Kordell's well enough. I won't let him get up and go through a ceremony today. He's burning with fever, and he's weak as a newborn kitten." She turned back toward Dagert. "I don't understand the urgency. The cost to Kordell is too high."

"Miss Brandelene, Kordell is dying. He has . . ."

"He is not dying! I don't want to hear those words again, Dagert."

"Miss Brandelene, I've seen this illness many times on the Ivory Coast, and few live through it."

"Then Kordell will be one of the few," Brandelene shot back, pacing. "I've nursed two through this same thing and they both survived . . . and Kordell will too."

"Miss Brandelene, I want him to live more than you ever could, for I love him, but Kordell believes he is dying. You've been exceedingly generous to write my document of manumission. I begged Kordell to return it to you, for I didn't want him to risk his life either. But all my pleading couldn't persuade him to give this paper back to you. I can't refuse a dying man's gift, given out of love." Dagert's voice broke and he blinked back tears before he continued, "Kordell needs to know, in the event he doesn't survive, that he's fulfilled his part of your agreement. He's an honorable man, Miss Brandelene, and with your refusal to let him keep his commitment to you, you're robbing a dying man of his honor, his pride, and his dignity. That's all Kordell has left right now."

"Are honor, pride, and dignity worth dying for?"

"You tell me. Kordell says you have an abundance of all three. What would you do in his position?"

"What if I agree and he dies? I'll carry the guilt of his death, to serve my own purpose, to the grave. You ask too much. I cannot."

"If you let him die, robbed of all his values, what guilt will you carry to your grave?"

Brandelene began to pace again. Could she steal a helpless man's pride to assuage her own feelings of guilt? She thought not.

"Kordell needs your attention," she said. "Tell him I'll leave now to have my lawyer make the necessary arrangements." She straightened with a firm resolve. "I will not let that stubborn Galahad die, even if I have to breathe my own breath into his lungs."

Much later that day, feeling old beyond her years, Brandelene made herself relax in warm, scented bathwater. Her ivory, silk-brocade wedding gown, freshly pressed, hung by the door. She knew Cyrus would expect her to wed the man she loved in a sumptuous wedding gown and she could ill afford to draw suspicion by not doing so. Even so, she'd cringed as Ruby packed the elegant gown, when they left Southern Oaks to go to the auction houses in Richmond. She balked at wearing a veil during the farce of a marriage ceremony, for she'd always envisioned herself with a beautiful trailing veil when she married the man she loved. So instead, she'd designed a crown of silk rosebuds to wear on her head, and Ruby had made the wreath, clucking her disapproval all the while. Brandelene wondered if she would be able to get through this nightmare of a day without Ruby by her side. Ruby, unfailingly, had always been there for her at her lowest times—when her mother passed away, when her father died, when she came home to find Southern Oaks once again immersed in slavery and her inheritance seriously jeopardized, and now on this her wedding day.

Earlier this morning, Charles Thompson, her father's shrewd

lawyer, had once again warned her against going through with her risk-filled scheme. With reluctance, he'd drawn up the undated petition for annulment, to be signed by Kordell and her before their marriage. "A precautionary measure in case the young man changes his mind later," he had explained. "Nevertheless, Brandelene," the lawyer had added, "it's an unethical precaution for me to take, and I insist on a doctor's certification that the marriage hasn't been consummated at the time I fill in the date. So be warned, my dear, if you can't obtain that certification I will not file this annulment without a newly signed document." In addition, another document, to be signed by Kordell as her husband, disclaimed any right to her estate. Although this last document would probably not hold up in court, the lawyer had said, at least it would give her husband pause to consider before he contested the validity. Then the bespectacled lawyer had insisted on taking the papers to Kordell himself, stating that he needed to witness his signature. He was with Kordell now.

After she'd returned from the lawyer's office, Brandelene had rushed to Kordell's bedside to explain about the documents. She also informed him that her father's lawyer was arranging for a special license and they would be married in the judge's chambers at seven o'clock.

"Wear your hair down . . . please," Kordell had requested, his face flushed with fever, and she'd assented, rushing from his room, another stab of guilt piercing her breast.

"Child, you stay in that water any longer and you're gonna look like a prune in that beautiful gown."

"Oh, Ruby, Kordell was so flushed when I was in his room. How can I go through with this?"

"Don't you start fretting again," Ruby admonished. "That handsome devil isn't gonna die."

Brandelene slipped into her dressing gown and sat in a chair while Ruby towel-dried her long, thick hair. "I hope Dagert bathed Kordell in cold water as I instructed. His fever is climbing, and Dr. Malloy said the high fever would . . . would harm him before the lung fever. It was the cool water that helped get Toby's and Belle's fever down."

Ruby fluffed Brandelene's damp hair before she reached for the brush. "I remember when Belle was so sick. I thought your daddy'd die when that horse doctor told him he was gonna have to shoot his favorite mare. And when your daddy refused I told my Matthew that you and your daddy'd never get that horse back up on her legs. I couldn't believe my eyes the next morning when that mare was standing there eating like she'd never been sick. That sure was something."

After that, the two lapsed into a dismal silence as they prepared for Brandelene's marriage.

And then it was time.

Brandelene and Ruby entered the sitting room as Kordell, followed closely by Dagert, walked out of his bedroom. Clothed in formal attire, his powerful, well muscled body moved with an easy grace, belying the seriousness of his illness, and Brandelene tried to control the dizzying current of excitement that raced through her at the mere sight of him.

She had paid a dear price for his outfit, specially ordered from England for another customer of the Richmond tailor, but she did not regret a penny of the cost. Approvingly, she appraised the mocha satin-brocade dress coat, cut away at the waist, with long tails. His frilled shirt, neck cloth, and cravat were of ivory lawn, and ivory trousers, lightly striped with mocha, closely fit his muscular legs.

So elegantly dressed, Kordell's magnetism was strong, drawing Brandelene against her will, and his golden cateyes riveted her to the spot. With pounding heart, she finally realized where she'd seen such compelling eyes before. His were the eyes of a lion she'd once seen. A proud, arrogantly confident lion. Lord of the jungle. "I'm happy to see you're strong enough to walk unassisted," Brandelene stammered.

"I thought it impossible for you to look more beautiful," Kordell said, his gaze capturing hers. "I was wrong."

Dagert and Ruby looked from Brandelene to Kordell, for the air between the two was charged.

Kordell stopped to rest and leaned against the overstuffed chair for support while he admired his bride-to-be.

Her luxurious raven hair, crowned with a garland of ivory satin rosebuds, cascaded in natural curling waves over her full breasts to her small waist. Tendrils of curls, woven with trailing lily of the valley, framed her perfect face. The low décolletage of her ivory, silk-brocade gown revealed high, rounded breasts. A man could die happily, lost in such pleasure as she displayed, he thought. Perhaps she would grant a dying man his last wish? Her soft shoulders rose above the tight-fitting, long sleeves. The skirt of the Empire gown, banded beneath her breasts with narrow ivory satin, was fitted to her slender body and flared gracefully to the floor. A matching train flowed in a waterfall of pleats attached at the back of her shoulders. A large cameo, surrounded by a three-strand pearl choker, was the only jewelry she wore. If he lived, by law he would have every right to possess her, but by their agreement he would be forbidden to do so.

The brief carriage ride to the retired judge's town house proceeded in complete silence. The solemnity of the occasion seemed more fitting for a funeral than a wedding, Brandelene thought, then paled as she glanced worriedly at the flush on Kordell's face.

When the carriage stopped in front of the two-story house, Dagert scrambled from the high seat to assist a weakening Kordell. The black coffee and cognac, which Brandelene had suggested he drink to give him strength, was fast wearing off, and Dagert wondered if his friend would be able to make it through the ceremony without support.

Kordell took several short breaths before he straightened and walked around the carriage to proffer his arm to Brandelene. She gathered her voluminous train in one hand and placed the other in his to alight from the carriage.

Bending low, Kordell spoke so only she could hear. "No pistol, Brandy?"

Enjoying his sense of humor, she gave him a dazzling smile. "I didn't think it necessary, since this is your doing, not mine."

His mood suddenly buoyant, Kordell returned her smile and slipped his arm around her tiny waist. "Now the charade begins, Brandy, for all the world to see," he murmured, recalling her words as his part of the agreement. His gaze boldly raked the rapid rise and fall of her softly rounded breasts, so enticingly revealed above her gown. Silently he cursed the enormity of his lust for her and wondered if it were from his forced celibacy, the shadow of his imminent death, or the enigma of Brandelene herself?

Brandelene shivered with pleasure at Kordell's touch, then glanced up at him. Her heart turned over and she cursed her powerless attraction to him. When his gaze locked with hers and he lowered his tawny head to touch his lips to hers, flashes of fire splintered through her body.

"For all the world to see," Kordell repeated huskily, then guided her toward the judge's house.

Waiting outside the private entrance to the judge's chambers, Charles Thompson was a silent witness to the brief public display of affection. When the lawyer had gone to the Wolf's Lair Inn to obtain Kordell Bouclair's signature on the documents, he'd been astonished by the bondsman's striking appearance. As well, he'd been further surprised, during their short conversation, to find Kordell to be not only intelligent, but well educated. Nevertheless, a penniless bond servant was still a penniless bond servant, regardless of his attributes, and now Thompson found himself concerned that Brandelene might fall prey to the charm of a man who apparently intended to take full advantage of his good fortune—if he did not succumb to lung fever first. The lawyer decided he would make it his business once again to caution Brandelene strongly about the bondsman. It was the least he could do for her father.

The lawyer followed the stiff-backed butler to the private chambers of the retired Judge Jenkins, trailed by Brandelene, Kordell, Ruby, Joshua, and Dagert. Thompson had made no explanations to the aging judge for the urgency of the hasty marriage and left his good friend to draw his own conclusions.

Anxious and apprehensive, Brandelene glanced around the large, dark, wood-paneled room. The book-lined walls reminded her of her father's library, a warm, beautiful room, but not one in which she would have chosen to be married. Inhaling deeply, she recalled the witticism she'd heard that when a groom married, his life flashed before his eyes, feeling the same experience herself as she fought the irresistible desire to turn and flee.

Sensing Brandelene's distress, Kordell's muscular arm tightened around her waist.

In a fog, Brandelene heard Judge Jenkins introduce himself and exchange social amenities with Kordell. She felt as though she were suffocating.

Aware of her trembling, Kordell glanced down at her face, now drained of all color. "Your honor, my fiancée and I would prefer to have the ceremony in your gardens."

Chapter 8

THE WHITE-HAIRED JUDGE LED THE WAY THROUGH THE French doors.

Once outside, Kordell leaned down to whisper to Brandelene, "Take three deep breaths and you'll feel better."

Brandelene did as instructed, then smiled gratefully up at him. Remembering the ring, she thrust it into his hand. An enormous ruby, surrounded by sparkling diamonds, glowed bloodred in the light of the setting sun. Kordell glanced at her in perplexity. "It was my mother's wedding ring," she explained softly. "Cyrus has never seen it, and will expect me to wear something extravagant—from my wealthy husband."

Judge Jenkins placed them in position for the ceremony and an overwhelming surge of hysteria once again rushed through Brandelene. She glanced up at the devastatingly handsome stranger who stood next to her. A stranger who would soon be her husband. "I can't go through with this," she whispered, searching Kordell's eyes for some hidden reassurance. He hugged her, conveying a warmth of understanding she had not suspected he possessed.

"Do you really have any choice now?" Kordell asked so only she could hear, then grinned rakishly before he added, "Also, consider what it would do to my reputation if you changed your mind now."

There was something warm and calming in his humor and Brandelene smiled at his gentle wit. Kordell bent and plucked a vivid red rose from the flowering bush next to him and handed it to her. She hesitated, then took the flower from his hand. For the first time, she glanced around, her ears deaf to the words the judge intoned, and she noticed the beauty of the gardens where she stood. The last rays of the sinking sun transformed the grounds into a mystical, orange-red wonderland. And that beauty let her escape intolerable reality by fantasizing that the vows she now repeated were for the one man she loved with all her heart and soul. The man who would love her for herself. It was a vision that allowed her to participate in the farce of this marriage as she pledged to love, honor, and obey Armand Kordell Bouclair, until death, even though she'd already signed the petition for annulment. It was a lie, and a sacrilege.

Kordell slipped the beautiful ring on her finger, the ring that had symbolized true love between her mother and father, but now only represented deception. The thorns of the rose she squeezed in her right hand tore into the soft flesh of her palm.

"I pronounce you man and wife," Judge Jenkins announced. "You may kiss the bride."

Kordell's gaze locked with Brandelene's with a tenderness that completely shattered her composure, and as the descending sun showered its glorious rays of enchantment over the flower garden, he pulled her tightly into his embrace. His nearness overwhelmed her and her heart fluttered wildly in her breast. She closed her eyes when he lowered his tawny head to claim her lips. Disturbed by the emotions tearing through her, she turned her face away, and Kordell's warm lips brushed her cheek, then trailed to her ear, making her senses spin. His hot cheek pressed to hers and he placed light, feathery kisses on her ear, his touch oddly gentle, caressing.

"Would you deny your dying husband a kiss to seal our vows?"

His husky voice was sensuous and his breath warm against her ear. He affected her as no other man ever had.

"I ask only this of you, Brandy. For this one time, kiss me as though I were the man you loved with all your heart."

Unknowingly, Kordell had said the only words that would allow Brandelene's pride to share with him what he asked. Leaning back in his encircling arms, she gazed longingly into the golden depths of his eyes, which now burned with unmistakable desire. Her gaze dropped to the fullness of his carved lips and lingered there. She slipped her hand, still clutching the rose, behind his neck while her other hand cupped the back of his head, drawing him down to her inviting, slightly parted lips and her world whirled crazily around her. She could feel his heart pounding erratically. Groaning, Kordell crushed her to him, igniting a flame that refused to be smothered. Brandelene melted in his arms as waves of pleasure surged through her body and his warm mouth captured hers in a sensitive, tender kiss. A spellbinding kiss that hungrily deepened into much more and sent the fire of the flame splintering through her, leaving her weak, breathless. She succumbed completely, responded ardently, and returned his seductive kiss with a reckless abandon that seared her soul. Then his moist lips moved over hers, devouring her passionately, totally, as she longed for him to, consuming her with his intensity, his magnetism.

Judge Jenkins coughed loudly. "Mr. Bouclair, you have the rest of your life to kiss your lovely wife. There are documents to be signed and I'm already late for a meeting."

A heady moment later the bride and groom separated in confusion, their gazes locked questioningly, searching for an answer to what had happened between them.

"God help me when you're well," Brandelene jested softly, with a lightheartedness she did not feel.

Kordell stared down at her, stunned by a depth of emotions he'd never experienced with another woman. "God help us both. I'm afraid, Madame Bouclair, it is going to be an extremely long six months." He did not add that he had no hope of being alive three days from now.

Fear rose up within Brandelene. Fear not of Kordell, but of her own tumultuous emotions. Disturbed and confused, she returned Kordell's gaze. None of the suitable men who'd paid her court had aroused the range of feelings in her that this bondsman did. Feelings she dared not examine for what they really were, for she could ill afford to have personal sentiments for Kordell Bouclair. He was a man forbidden to her in every way. She would never, never give her heart to a fortune hunter. Abruptly she turned away. Curse you, Cyrus Varner! Damn you to hell and back! she swore as she nervously toyed with her mother's wedding ring on her left hand. She glanced up to find Kordell still watching her, and their gazes met with an intensity that left her weak.

Judge Jenkins coughed again and with practiced ease Kordell guided his wife behind Judge Jenkins and into the judge's chambers. His hand on her waist was gentle and he drew her possessively closer to his side.

First Kordell, then Brandelene, signed the documents. When that was done, she stood up, threw back her shoulders, and lifted her chin haughtily as though to say, I have done what I needed to do to save Southern Oaks. Silently observing her, Kordell briefly touched his lips to hers. Brandelene quivered at the sweet tenderness of his silken kiss.

"For the judge to see, Madame Bouclair," he whispered, then took her hand to lead her back into the flower garden where they'd wed. The judge wrote in the registry and completed the documents of marriage, followed by Charles Thompson's signature as witness. Once there, Kordell lapsed into a spasm of coughing before he sank weakly to a stone bench and pulled Brandelene down beside him. His gaze was drawn to the red rose she still carried in her hand. His arm encircled her. "Brandy," he gasped, "I do not feel well. I didn't want to alert the judge to my condition. I may need Dagert to assist me to the carriage."

Alarmed, Brandelene noticed the high flush of his face, the glaze of his eyes. She pressed her lips to his burning brow, upset that she'd been so absorbed in her own emotional trauma that she had not noticed Kordell's rapidly deteriorating condition before this. She jumped to her feet, but his hand stayed her.

"Brandy, compose yourself. We have come too far to ruin things now. Please inform Mr. Thompson and Dagert that I would like to speak with them. A few minutes more will be of no consequence." Then he gasped for breath and slumped slightly from the exhaustion of his worsening illness. "I will also need some cognac if I'm to walk out of here. Judge Jenkins must have no suspicions aroused, for Cyrus is certain to question him at length."

Agreeing, Brandelene nodded, and with a deliberate calm that belied her anxiety, she strolled into the judge's chambers where the last of the documents were being witnessed. Smiling radiantly, she exemplified the picture of the happy bride. She crossed to the side of her lawyer, then Dagert, and informed the two men Kordell wished to have a word with them in the garden. Moving to Ruby, whose face looked as though she were in mourning, Brandelene spoke softly.

"Please ask Joshua to come to Kordell's suite as soon as he stables the horses. I'm going to need all the help I can get this night. Kordell's extremely ill. He's much worse. Oh, Ruby, I fear for his life."

"Child, I told you. That good-looking scoundrel isn't gonna die. What you really need to be fretting about is how you're gonna keep yourself from falling for that charmer. I saw the way you kissed him," she scolded. "Mmmm-um! That handsome devil could charm the hounds from a hunt."

A short time later, in their suite at the Wolf's Lair, Kordell was in a cool bath in his room, closeted with the lawyer.

In the other bedroom, Ruby assisted Brandelene out of her wedding gown. Surprisingly happy, Ruby placed the gown on a hanger and lovingly brushed the skirt. "You sure were a beautiful bride, Miss Brandelene. I don't reckon there could be a more beautiful bride than you."

"I'll be a lovely widow if Mr. Thompson stays with Kordell much longer. Doesn't he know how sick the man is? Quick, Ruby, fasten me, so I can go take care of Kordell."

Moments later Brandelene crossed the sitting room when a knock sounded at the hall door. She glanced at Dagert's forlorn face, then moved to open the door to Dr. Malloy.

"Oh, thank heaven you're here, Doctor." Brandelene smiled with relief.

"Kordell's worse?"

"Yes. His temperature is extremely high. But he's soaking in a cool bath now."

"You have him in a cool bath when he has lung fever? Have you lost your senses?" Dr. Malloy started toward Kordell's room. "No wonder he's worse!"

Flustered, Brandelene felt Dagert's accusing glare burn into her. Surely he didn't think she deliberately tried to insure Kordell's death—did he?

"Dr. Malloy, you told me Kordell would die from a high temperature before lung fever," Brandelene explained, running after the angry doctor. "I knew no other way to get his fever down fast."

The physician stopped and turned to face her. "I'm sorry, Brandelene. I'm frustrated because I don't have an answer either. Certainly the cool bath will lower his temperature, temporarily, but it could congest his lungs even more. If the medicine I left you, plus bed rest, and his own strength don't improve his condition, then . . ."

"Dagert, get Kordell out of the bath," Brandelene cried. "Hurry! Hurry!"

Distressed, Dagert, followed by the physician, raced to Kordell's side, relieved to find the high flush of his friend's face gone. Could the doctor be wrong? Brandelene had saved two other people from the devastation of lung fever. Surely she'd used this same technique?

He helped Kordell from his bath, concerned by his weakness. Unquestionably, Kordell's exertion earlier today, his congestion, and the fever were rapidly taking their toll. Hastily he assisted him to his bed.

Kordell sank back into the soft pillows and closed his eyes in exhaustion.

"Kordell, if you'll sign your name to your will, I'll have Dr. Malloy witness it," the lawyer said and handed the document, with quill and ink pot, to the sick man.

Kordell signed, then the doctor.

Unwilling to wait any longer, Brandelene knocked on Kordell's door, and slowly opened it.

"Come in, Madame Bouclair, I'm just leaving," Charles Thompson said. "Your husband seems to be in good hands now."

Dr. Malloy glanced from the lawyer to Brandelene. "You have married?"

Brandelene nodded, anxiously lacing her fingers.

"I'm surprised you would further risk your reputation, Brandelene," the physician admonished, "by marrying in a room at the Wolf's Lair Inn."

"Brandelene would never compromise herself in such a manner, Doctor," Thompson protested. "We've just returned from a ceremony in Judge Jenkins's gardens."

The doctor's face darkened with rage. "Am I to understand you took this man from his sickbed in order to marry in a garden? Have you no sense? Do you want this man's death on your conscience?"

Brandelene met the doctor's contempt-filled glare, feeling the same disgust for herself that his look betrayed.

"You don't speak to my wife in such a manner," Kordell gasped, rising up on one elbow to face the doctor. "It was at my insistence that we married today." With that he paused to catch his breath, then continued, "I gave Brandelene no choice, although she did her best to discourage me. There are circumstances of which you are not aware, Doctor, that forced us to marry now." Kordell collapsed back onto the bed, his face red as he gasped for air.

Dr. Malloy glanced at Brandelene's slender waist, then turned back to Kordell and mumbled, "My apologies to you both. You now have twice the incentive to get well, young man."

Humiliated by the doctor's assumption, Brandelene felt the heat rise to her face. Clearly, Kordell had done his best to defend her, and she could not fault him because his words had been misconstrued by the physician. Besides, Kordell had acted in a manner many gentlemen would not have, assuming the full responsibility himself, and now Brandelene looked at him with an admiration she could not disguise. There was more to this man than his handsome face and charm, for, unquestionably, he had risked his life to marry her. Other than her father, she had never known a man of such honor.

"I wish you well, Kordell," Thompson said and left.

At the doctor's bidding, Kordell sat up and the physician pressed his ear to his back.

"What are you doing, Doctor?" Brandelene queried.

"Listening to his lungs. He has worsened considerably."

"May I?" she asked and moved to Kordell's bedside with no intention of accepting the doctor's refusal.

"It's best you don't," Dr. Malloy said, removing the thermometer from Kordell's mouth.

"I insist . . . please." Brandelene sat on Kordell's bedside before he could lie down. Then she bent and placed her ear to his back as she'd seen the doctor do. Her heart stopped at the wheezing rattle of Kordell's labored breathing. The room whirled and she fought the darkness that threatened to engulf her.

Dr. Malloy said, "His temperature is climbing too."

Brandelene picked up the thermometer from the bedside table. "Please leave this with me, Doctor. It might help me in Kordell's care."

That action alerted Kordell to Brandelene's concern, so carefully hidden beneath her calm demeanor.

Once outside Kordell's bedroom, Dr. Malloy placed a thin arm around Brandelene. Dagert followed them and stood to one side. "My dear, I need to be straightforward with you now that you're married and there's much at risk. I have little hope for your husband to survive—"

"I refuse to listen!" Brandelene ranted.

"He's in God's hands now," the physician added gently. "There's nothing more I can do, and whatever you do now most likely will be futile."

"Will it hurt to try?"

"No. I've seen home remedies do some unexplainable things, but don't get your hopes up, my dear. And don't overtire yourself.

I don't want to have to make an emergency call on you." The doctor's face was grim as he started to leave, then he turned back. "I'll stop by in the morning. There's nothing more I can do here now and I must get back to my other patient, Mrs. Cain. She's in labor and most likely won't make it either."

After the doctor left, Brandelene turned to Ruby. "I stopped at the apothecary this morning after I left the lawyer's office. There's a package in my bedroom. Will you please bring it into Kordell's room?" Then with iron resolve, she turned to the man standing beside her. "Dagert, I'll need all the help I can get for the next twenty-four hours. We have much to do." She hurried into his bedroom and a grim Dagert followed.

Concentrating on the task ahead of her, Brandelene bent over her sleeping husband and touched his heated brow, his labored breathing rasping in her ears. "The way I helped Toby and Belle was to work on what seemed the most important at the time. Kordell's fever isn't any higher, so I'm going to try to ease his breathing."

Ruby bustled into the room with the package.

"Ruby, bring me every bed pillow and a sheet, then order extra sheets, blankets, four pillows, a carafe of hot coffee, a carafe of hot water, more candles, and a bottle of brandy," Brandelene instructed. "Can you remember all that?"

"Yes, child," Ruby said and cast a worried glance at Kordell before she hurried from the room.

"Dagert, we need to make a tent over Kordell's head," Brandelene directed. "Please set the commode table tightly against the bed."

Ruby bustled into the bedroom with the requested sheet and pillows. "I rang for the inn servant, but those people are slower than molasses in January."

"Thank you, darlin'." Now that she controlled the situation, rather than helplessly watching Kordell get worse, she felt confidence flow through her body. "Dagert, please sit Kordell up and I'll put these pillows behind him. I discovered with Toby that it eased his breathing if he wasn't lying flat."

"Yes, madame." Dagert rushed to do her bidding.

In his illness, Kordell groaned as he was wrested to a sitting position and Brandelene plumped the multitude of pillows behind him. His eyes opened.

"We're going to get you well, Kordell, and we'll be doing all manner of strange things. I'll need your help, so please don't fight me."

Kordell managed a weak grin. "You're going to fight the devil for me, are you? It should be interesting to see who wins." He paused to rest. "I'd much rather fight the devil than you, Brandy. So I suppose that means my money is on you, Madame Bouclair."

"I'm sure, during the next six months, you'll give me considerable cause to regret saving your hide, Kord, but I'm committed now, so it's too late to change my mind," she said softly.

Kordell's chuckle turned into a helpless spasm of coughing. He closed his eyes, the pain from his unbound broken ribs tearing through him, his face red from the exertion.

Brandelene dipped a cloth into the basin of cool water and bent to sponge his face, then moved down to his neck and chest. That done, she grabbed the sheet Ruby brought her.

"Dagert, let's get this tent set up," she urged. "As soon as the carafe of hot water arrives I'll put oil of eucalyptus in it and the hot eucalyptus steam should ease Kordell's breathing. We've used it at Southern Oaks as long as I can remember, and it does wonders. I can't imagine why Dr. Malloy didn't suggest it."

Hours later, long after Brandelene had sent Ruby and Joshua to bed, she and Dagert continued to work tirelessly over her critically ill husband. They constantly sponged his hot body in an attempt to reduce his rising fever while the eucalyptus oil steamed into the makeshift tent they'd erected over his face and shoulders. Tiredly, she sank onto Kordell's bedside while she lifted the sheet from his face and slipped the thermometer between his lips. Cloudy eyes opened and he smiled at her. With his lips so close to her own, she fought the desire to cover them with hers, to assure him she would not let him die. Yet she could do neither. Filled with emotion, Brandelene bent her ear to Kordell's chest. Endlessly, he wheezed and rasped with every breath, confirming his ever-worsening condition. She removed the thermometer and frowned. His temperature had not dropped, even with their constant sponging.

Kordell kicked fretfully at the sheet covering him, deliriously muttering about Nicolle and Bobby. Brandelene glanced at Dagert questioningly.

"Nicolle is . . . is the woman Kordell is going to marry and Bobby is her son."

Chapter 9

ASTONISHED THAT KORDELL HAD NOT MENTIONED HE was to be married, Brandelene merely nodded. "We must get his fever down, Dagert. Dr. Malloy said his fever will . . . we must get his fever down. The doctor said he shouldn't be put in a cool bath, but the cool water is what broke Toby's and Belle's fever. However, I'm going to try something else first. I've never tried it before, but I've heard about it. Strip Kordell, and cover his loins," she instructed, turning her back to reach for the two bottles of alcohol from the apothecary.

Dagert did as requested.

When Brandelene turned back to Kordell, she inhaled deeply at the sight of the superb specimen of masculinity stretched out, near naked, on the bed before her. Handing Dagert a bottle of alcohol, she moved to the other side of the bed. "We are going to gently rub the alcohol over Kordell's body. I'll do his neck, arms, and chest, and you do his legs. I've been told the quick evaporation has a cooling affect." She shrugged. "If this doesn't reduce his fever it's into the tub of cool water. We cannot dally with Dr. Malloy's medicines any longer."

They bent to their task and there was no protest from Kordell who, out of his mind from the fever that raged through his body, kept up his delirious ramblings about Nicolle and Bobby. His chest heaved as he gasped for air and his breathing was a rasping labor that left him exhausted and ever weaker.

An endless time later Brandelene checked his temperature and smiled at Dagert. "His fever has dropped."

Kordell's eyes opened and he stared blindly at her. "Nicolle? Nicolle," he mumbled hoarsely, then closed his eyes and fell into a delirium-free sleep.

Sighing, Brandelene lowered the sheet over Kordell's face and shoulders and glanced up as a tired Ruby, returning from a brief sleep, walked into the room.

"Ruby, will you pull the bell cord and order four bottles of whiskey? I'm out of alcohol and we'll never be able to get more this time of night. Also, another pot of black coffee and more water."

Ruby had just left the room when Brandelene once again pressed her ear to Kordell's chest. "His lungs are worsening, Dagert," she said, her face bleak. "I'm going to fix a mustard plaster for his chest. You sponge him with cool water again. It should help control his fever somewhat until the whiskey gets here. If we don't have to try to battle two things at once, we have a better chance of saving him—I hope."

Exhausted, Brandelene sighed and wiped the perspiration from her brow with her sleeve. Crossing the room, she retrieved the package from the apothecary, opened the bag of pungent yellow powder, and moved to the basin where she mixed the potent herb into a plaster. In a fog, she heard Ruby answer the light knock on the door and her instructions to the inn servant, but she could only concentrate on the grating sound of every rattling breath Kordell took. She wet a towel with steaming hot water from the carafe and covered it with the thick paste, then gently laid it on Kordell's heaving chest.

For the next two hours the threesome worked continuously over Kordell. They bathed his nearly nude body with whiskey and forced cool water down his protesting throat, kept the hot, pungent-smelling mustard plaster on his chest and added another to his back. All the while, the oil of eucalyptus steamed into his nose and mouth. Finally his congestion loosened and they needed to force him to cough.

"How we gonna do that?" Ruby asked.

"It won't be easy," Brandelene answered, rousing herself from the numb weariness weighing her down. "Toby was young and easy to threaten. His mother and I half dragged him, and he half walked, and that exertion forced him to cough. But with a big man like Kordell . . . I don't know." Suddenly her face lit up with the solution. "We knew if Belle was down for too long she would die. We couldn't get her to her feet. I poured black coffee and brandy down her throat to give her energy, then I whipped her until, with two grooms pulling, she got up on her feet. We blanketed her and walked her around. She—"

"You whipped an ill woman to force her out of her sickbed?" Dagert asked.

"You didn't know Belle is a mare?"

"Belle is a horse?" Dagert gasped. "What is Toby?"

"Toby is a young boy, Dagert," Brandelene said softly, understanding his alarm. "Do not fear I am trying to kill your friend. You heard what Dr. Malloy said—I can do him no harm, and I've no doubt that Kordell might be dead right now, but for our ministrations." Tiredly, she moved to the herculean man's side and placed a comforting hand on his powerful arm. "You see, Dagert, the illnesses of animals are often treated in the same manner as those of a human. Lung fever is lung fever, be it man or animal."

"What do we do next?" he asked.

"You love Kordell, so I leave the decision to you. Do you want me to continue with the only way I know?"

After long consideration, Dagert nodded.

Hours later the first rays of light were shining in the window. They had brought Kordell safely through the night.

Brandelene sank tiredly into the chair beside Kordell's bed. She leaned her head back, closed her eyes, and hoped the worst was over. "Dagert, is Nicolle beautiful?"

"Yes. Very."

"What does she look like?" When she received no response, she glanced up at him questioningly. "If it makes you uncomfortable, you needn't answer."

"No, it's all right. Kordell would tell you if you asked. Nicolle is as beautiful as an angel. She's tall and slender, has hair the color of corn silk and eyes as blue as the sky."

Disturbed by Dagert's answer and not sure why, Brandelene was compelled to know more and she asked with feigned indifference, "How old is Nicolle?"

"She's a couple of years younger than Kordell. Twenty-eight or so." Dagert fussed anxiously with the sheet tent over Kordell's face and shoulders. "The three of us grew up together."

"Then you must care considerably for her," Brandelene said, wondering if the woman could be the coffee plantation owner's daughter—or widow?

At her comment, Dagert's face grew reflective, and he paused in his ministrations to Kordell. "She's the kindest, the gentlest, the most considerate person I have ever met, and I could not love a sister more."

"You said earlier that Kordell is going to marry Nicolle. Has he asked for her hand?"

"Well kind of, I guess. Maybe not. But everyone knows there's an understanding between them."

"And Nicolle accepted?"

Without answering, Dagert lowered his large frame to the side of the bed.

Suspicious, Brandelene blurted, "Nicolle refused him?"

"Oh, no! Nicolle said they'd talk about it after we returned from Mali, but then slavers captured us." At Brandelene's silence, Dagert added, "Kordell said he was going to make a formal proposal when we got back from the bush country. It's obvious she loves him. However, we both know what her answer will be when he asks her. Nicolle, or any woman he wants, cannot say no to Kordell."

Brandelene asked her next question with all the casualness she could muster, the blood pounding in her brain all the while, "Does Kordell love Nicolle?"

"You'll have to ask Kordell that," he said, then added, "Everyone loves Nicolle. Kordell should have married her years ago, before she married his friend Robert."

An unwanted pang of jealousy shot through Brandelene. Never had she felt the distressing emotion before, and now she shifted uncomfortably in her chair. "Is Nicolle wealthy?"

"Very wealthy."

Brandelene reeled with shock, but soon her surprise yielded to anger. Whether he realized it or not, Dagert had confirmed what she already suspected. Kordell Bouclair was a fortune hunter! Brandelene swallowed hard, vowing to harden her heart against him, promising herself never to let him pierce the barrier of indifference she would put between them. Suddenly she needed to be alone.

"Dagert, I'm going to freshen up. I'll be back shortly." She all but ran to her room. Tormented, her gaze fell upon the rose, now withered, Kordell had given her at their wedding.

That rose represented a man's honor.

Unable to throw the flower away, she stared at it where it drooped in the glass of water on her bedside commode. "Curse you, Kordell Bouclair!" she cried out in the dimness of her candlelit room.

The battle for Kordell's life continued for long, exhausting, back-breaking hours. He moved from burning fever, where he writhed and groaned in anguish accompanied by ranting delirium, to periods of teeth-chattering, quaking chills no amount of blankets could stop. Still he did not improve.

At dawn, on the morning of the third day after their wedding, a dazed Brandelene worked over Kordell. She was oblivious to everything else, having had no sleep since before their marriage. She shook continuously from the black coffee she drank to keep herself awake, her heart raced nonstop from lack of rest, and her entire body was engulfed in tides of numbing exhaustion and despair. Afraid to leave Kordell's side, she took only hurried, refreshing spongings at the basin in her bedroom, and her hair was permeated with the odor of mustard and eucalyptus. Her usually sparkling eyes were dulled with a consuming weariness she'd never before experienced. With blurred vision and a mind that no longer concentrated, she resolutely dragged on and automatically performed her ministrations.

She lifted the mustard plaster to replace it with another steaming one, and glanced up at Dagert who swabbed her husband's warm body with alcohol. One more time, she bent and placed her ear to Kordell's chest, no longer caring that the odorous mustard clung to her hair. Listening intently, she stiffened, then jumped to her feet and cried, "Dagert! Dagert! Kordell will live! Thank God, he'll live!" Whispering a prayer of thanks, she collapsed to the floor.

Ten days later, sensing their nearness to home, the matched bays lifted their hooves handsomely high as they trotted toward Southern Oaks. The lush countryside abounded with white-flowering dogwoods and orchards of pink-blossomed apple trees, with a yellow-blooming beech scattered here and there among the varied assortment of leafy bowers. They now traveled the fertile Piedmont Valley of Virginia.

Tobacco country.

A gentle breeze wafted, fragrant with the scent of dense vines of honeysuckle, wild grape, and creeper, and a riot of colors from wildly blooming flowers forced themselves through the tangle of green beside the lane. Brilliant red cardinals flitted everywhere, and the robin's sweet chirp competed with the call of the meadowlarks and whippoorwills. Now and then roadside quails whirred up as the well-sprung carriage moved down the country planters' road, and once a doe, closely followed by a buck, bounded across the road and into the thicket on the other side.

As the barouche rolled on there were glimpses of oak-studded lawns and stately plantation mansions, interspersed by a sea of green fields.

Tobacco.

Virginia boasted the finest tobacco in the world and only the Tidewater area of Virginia was as rich as the Piedmont Valley.

Kordell sat beside Brandelene in the carriage, facing Dagert and Ruby. Brandelene had been aloof, even icy during his recuperation. Indeed, from the moment he was well enough to talk, and he did not know why. "I am indebted to you for my life," he'd said after Dagert told him what she had done. "I offer my thanks and sincere gratitude—until you are better paid."

"Think nothing of it, Kordell," she'd replied coldly. "I would have done the same for any of my bondsmen."

What had caused her frigid response after she worked so selflessly over him, for three days and nights? What could have happened after their wedding, when she'd kissed him with passionate abandon and shown genuine concern for his welfare, that had turned her back into the black widow spider he'd originally thought her to be?

Who was the real Brandelene, the one at their marriage and his death bed, or the one she'd showed him the last ten days—a cold, heartless woman whose only concerns were for herself?

With deliberate slowness, Kordell raked the angel of his dreams, the witch of his nightmares. For a while she had been heaven. Now she was hell, and he craved her with an intensity he knew his ravaged body could not quench.

Brandelene broke the awkward silence. "Dagert, these last two weeks I've come to know you, to admire you, to respect you. Kordell at one time suggested that you be my overseer. At the time I wouldn't consider it. However, after working so closely with you throughout Kordell's illness, I realize he was right. Would you consider being my overseer for the next six months?"

Taken unaware, Dagert stared wordlessly at Brandelene.

"I couldn't pay you until after the harvest, and if I'm not able to save Southern Oaks, or if my scheme with Kordell doesn't work, Cyrus will still control Southern Oaks and I might never be able to pay you. Of course, I'll understand if you decline."

"Decline! How could I decline? You've already done more for Kordell and me than we ever dared hope for when we were in the hold of that hell ship. Of course I'll work for you."

"Dagert, I'm not asking you out of any sense of obligation I feel you owe me. You're a free man now, and from the beginning I had no intention of having you work for me without wages. Kordell paid for your cost by making himself unsalable at the auction, and I might add he almost paid the highest price he could—his life. You've Kordell to thank for your freedom, not me. I could not have paid the price to acquire you otherwise."

"I appreciate your honesty, and I still accept your generous offer. However, I don't know anything about tobacco."

Brandelene could feel Kordell's gaze boring into her. "Kordell has assured me you're an expert at supervising labor, without resorting to mistreatment, and that is the kind of man I need. As for your lack of knowledge about tobacco, I know tobacco as well as any man, and better than most. Daddy taught me well, so I wouldn't permit Southern Oaks to dwindle away after he was gone. I'll work side by side with you, guide you, and teach you everything I know. You already know we work well together." Leaning forward, Brandelene folded her hands in a graceful pose that belied her inner strength. "It will be a gamble on your part, but if my plan works, and we have a good harvest, I will give you and Kordell a bonus in six months, so you can return to the Ivory Coast."

Brandelene saw Dagert's quick, puzzled glance at Kordell, but ignored it to continue. "Since you don't know our country, I'll tell you what you need to know in order to make a wise decision. A free, educated, English-speaking black man such as yourself will get no work in the South—you'd be feared too much. Feared that you would lead an uprising of the slaves. It was only three years ago that an educated black slave, named Gabriel Prosser, organized thousands of slaves in Richmond, the capital of Virginia, and planned a major slave revolt with the goal to make Virginia a state of free black people. The plot was reported to Governor James Monroe. The governor called out the state militia and captured Prosser and many of his followers. They were caught before they could carry out their plans. Since then fear has governed most whites in Virginia.

"Therefore, Dagert, I believe you would have to go north for employment, and according to the *Virginia Gazette,* work there isn't plentiful, and is mostly low-paying. Please consider my offer and advise me of your decision."

"I don't need to think it over. I'll do it," Dagert replied. "However, madame, a genteel woman can't work in the fields to teach me what I need to learn. Isn't there someone else?"

"There is no one else who knows tobacco as well as I, who'd help me, for Southern Oaks is ostracized—"

"Ostracized?" Kordell's deep voice interrupted.

"Yes. I'll explain later," Brandelene answered, unwilling to share, now, the truth of the shadow that hung over Southern Oaks. Turning back to Dagert, she said, "There are many experts on Southern Oaks, but no one person knows tobacco from the planting of the seedling through the priming of the leaf as I do. I spent five years at my daddy's side and learned everything he knew, and he was the best. Besides, no one has the interest I do, and there's too much at stake."

Disturbed, Dagert glanced at Kordell, his brow furrowed. "Kordell, are you going to permit your wife to work in the fields . . . ?"

"Kordell permit me!" Brandelene flared, her voice several octaves above her usual tones. "Kordell has no say over what I do! He is my husband in name only, and even if he weren't, no husband will ever forbid me to do anything. I am not some helpless, simpering female." She blushed at her unladylike outburst, then asked gently, "Do we understand each other?"

"Yes, madame," Dagert answered, glancing from Kordell's amused grin to Brandelene's furious face. "We do now."

Brandelene looked at Kordell and her heart lurched at his strong profile, at his mane of softly waving, tawny hair, sun-streaked with golden highlights. He exuded a masculinity, a power, an irresistibility she'd never found in any other man. He was a perfection of animal magnetism and undoubtedly women had pursued him his entire life. Unsettled at her vulnerability to the fortune hunter she'd married, she wondered how she was ever to get through six months unscathed. All thoughts of his honor were now gone. Again she vowed that this common bondsman, who sought to better his station in life by using her, would never best her, or play her for a fool.

"Kordell," she said impetuously, "we haven't discussed it, but there's a stipulation to which I absolutely insist you agree."

Her tone was testy and Kordell glanced at her, curious.

"I will not have you disgrace me with any of the wives or

daughters of the local plantation owners. If you must satisfy your, ahh, appetites, then you'll need to go into Petersburg. Even then I would ask that you exercise discretion, for I'm known there. After two weeks or so you will be free to travel to Petersburg. Of course, Dagert cannot go at the same—"

Kordell grabbed Brandelene by the shoulders and bellowed, "Joshua! Stop this damn carriage!"

Chapter 10

INSTANTLY BRANDELENE'S HAND SHOT INSIDE HER RETICULE to retrieve her pistol. She shoved the cocked weapon into Kordell's waistcoat. "Turn me loose this instant!" she stormed as the carriage came to a swift halt.

Coming to Brandelene's assistance, Ruby raised her clenched fists to flay Kordell when Dagert's burly arm surrounded her to easily pull her back into her seat.

"Calm yourself, woman," Dagert said, for Ruby's ears only. "Kordell will not harm her."

Ignoring the pistol jabbed into his midsection, Kordell kept his iron grip on Brandelene. His fingers bit into her soft flesh and his eyes glared into hers. "I have suffered your insults from the moment I met you in that godforsaken auction house, but this is the last."

"If you value your life, Bouclair, let me go," she warned with icy aloofness.

Ignoring her threat, Kordell's hands tightened on her shoulders, and she flinched.

"Go ahead and shoot. Then you can explain to the magistrate—

and Cyrus," Kordell snarled, and cursed her beauty, her proud willfulness, as he stared into her violet eyes, now darkened into a shimmering, jewellike black magenta.

Brandelene's finger trembled on the trigger. Torn by conflicting emotions, she hesitated. "I am warning you one last time. Turn me loose!"

Kordell grudgingly admired her spirit, her daring. Undaunted by the cocked pistol he warned, "Before our marriage you instructed Ruby to treat me with the respect due your husband. I will release you when you agree to do the same. I expect no more and I will accept no less."

Ruby's muttered prayers intruded into Brandelene's frantic thoughts. "Agreed."

Lowering his strong hands from her, Kordell glanced down at the cocked pistol still shoved into his stomach. Brandelene removed the pistol and carefully lowered the cocked hammer. With unexpected swiftness, he snatched the pistol from her and shoved it into the waistband of his breeches. "Madame, if I'm to play the loving husband, then I am to be a man."

He smiled with a smugness that sent her temper soaring.

"If I am a man, no woman, not even my wife, holds me at bay with a pistol. I might add, madame, I could have taken your pistol at almost any time from the moment I first set foot in your carriage. I am here because we have an agreement, and most certainly not due to your forcing me at gunpoint." With that, Kordell instructed Joshua, "Drive on."

Brandelene fumed as the carriage jerked to a start.

"With that matter resolved, my loving wife, as to your earlier remark, do not have concerns that I will humiliate you with other women. I will not. My only intention is to get through the next six months and return to the Ivory Coast. Now that I have satisfied your qualms about me, there's a matter about you that perplexes me." Ignoring Brandelene's hostility, he placed his arm on the seat behind her to rest his hand lightly on her shoulder.

Brandelene flinched at his touch.

Already regretting his bold move, Kordell could feel the softness of her shoulder burn through her gown into his hand, and an unwanted response fired through his loins. Compounding his plight, her fragrance drifted up to plague him further and he glanced down at the perfection of her beauty, in profile, as she stiffly stared straight ahead. He tried to remember what he'd been talking about. "Ahh, as I was saying, there is a matter I am mildly curious about," he confessed and managed a warm smile that betrayed none of the craving hunger for his wife that had obsessed him for the last ten days. "You mentioned something about being ostracized. Also you've hinted that your reputation is less than desirable. What have you not told me, Brandy?"

Before his appealing smile, her defenses melted away. Unquestionably, he needed to know everything. Brandelene swallowed hard and tried to manage a simple answer. "Do you remember, about ten or twelve years ago, when Toussaint L'Ouverture led hundreds of thousands of slaves in a bloody revolution and overthrew the French in Haiti?"

"Yes, quite well."

"Then you are aware that thousands of French whites were massacred in that revolution."

"Yes, I know."

"So you must know of the fear most slave-operated plantation owners have lived with since that time?" At Kordell's nod she continued: "It was two years after the start of that revolution that my grandfather died. I was ten years old. At that time, Daddy converted most of our slaves into indentured servants, and freed the rest. Then Daddy set up a system for all of our bonded servants to work their way to freedom. In the South it is unheard of for plantation black people to be indentured servants, or freed. The local plantation owners ostracized us, and I became the unwelcome daughter of the traitorous and hated James Barnett, whom the gentry felt had betrayed them."

"What else is there, Brandy?"

She began to tell him the story of a free Southern Oaks and how Shadrach, the plantation preacher, and the common house had come to be a Southern Oaks tradition.

Two Sundays following her grandfather's death, and James Barnett's conversion of his slaves to indentured servitude, James was in Petersburg and came upon a young man who preached the Gospel to a gathered few in a vacant field. James paused for a moment to listen to the young man's inspiring words and stayed to hear the entire sermon. Afterward, the educated mulatto preacher passed his hat and gratefully pocketed the few coins he received. Curious, James asked to speak with the man. In a short time, Barnett had learned the penniless Shadrach and his mother had just arrived in Petersburg. They had been freed at the death of his white father.

After their conversation James offered Shadrach a position at Southern Oaks teaching the newly indentured servants to read, write, and cipher tolerably, so that when their term of servitude was satisfied, if they chose to leave they would be better able to survive. He was to preach the Gospel on Sundays, perform marriages and baptisms, bless births, read Bible verse, lend comfort at deaths, and perform all things that both a schoolmaster and minister would. In exchange for this service, Shadrach would receive a reasonable wage, a private cabin for himself and his mother to share, and their food. It was an offer that he immediately accepted.

With the Haitian slave revolt so fresh in people's minds, James feared that if he legally freed his eight hundred slaves, he would suffer severe retaliation from the neighboring plantation owners. Consequently his conversion of the plantation from slavery had been an informal one rather than legal. So when Shadrach came to Southern Oaks, the bond servants, according to the Commonwealth of Virginia, were considered slaves. Therefore, they could not legally marry, for the state law did not recognize any civil or legal rights for slaves, which included entering into a contract such as marriage. However, Shadrach performed a ceremony for any couple who wished to marry, then recorded it in his journal along with the records of births and deaths that he kept, and the marriage was then accepted as being recognized in the eyes of God and the couple, if not by the state.

From the hiring of Shadrach, a man who proved to possess all the potential James Barnett had seen in him, came the building at Southern Oaks of what was to be called the common house.

The common house was a large building. The main room was furnished with tables and benches, later replaced by chairs as time permitted, which seated as many as nine hundred people. This room was used by the indentured servants, other than the house servants, to eat a morning and evening meal, prepared for them in the adjoining kitchens, six days a week. During the winter months, the room became a schoolroom for the young people in the morning, and the adults, for two hours, in the afternoon.

On Sundays the common room sufficed for morning and evening religious services, one midafternoon meal, prepared the day before, and a general congregation of people wandering in and out to socialize. If there were entertainments, disputes, special meetings, or celebrations such as weddings and births, they were held in the common room. Southern Oaks was a small community, shepherded by Shadrach.

From the first day the common house was put to use, James Barnett, feeling a person should have the pleasure of libation with his evening meal, allowed the adults either a cup of wine with their suppers or a brandy afterward.

The success of the common house vastly improved the quality of life of the bond servants on Southern Oaks and resulted in the increased efficiency of all. James Barnett and Shadrach had taken great pride in the success of the project.

"Not one bond servant attempted to run away from the time Daddy converted to indentured servitude until Cyrus took over," Brandelene said, then added softly, "It is against the law to teach slaves to read, write, or cipher in Virginia, and these people are still considered slaves by the state."

Kordell's hand tightened slightly on her shoulder and he found he wanted to shelter her from any further pain. He was beginning to understand what had shaped her into the fascinating enigma she was. He studied her in fascination, her delicate femininity a contradiction of her fierce independence and strong will; her ethereal beauty a contrast to the fiery, high-spirited wildcat he knew her to be; her petite stature and slender figure a deception of her true strength and stamina. For the first time, he realized the picture Brandelene Barnett Bouclair presented to the world of a pampered woman was a facade behind which the complex woman, the intelligent, shrewd, and cunning woman, hid.

"What aren't you telling me, Brandy?" Kordell probed.

She took a deep breath. "After Prosser, the slave who planned the revolt in Richmond, was captured, there were armed patrols on all the roads for several weeks. Most whites were terrified, and carried rifles and pistols at all times. From that time on, all slaves were required to have a written traveling pass anytime they were off the plantation of their owner." Inhaling sharply, she blurted out, "Three weeks after that near revolt . . .

"Daddy was murdered!"

"Murdered!" Kordell repeated in astonishment.

Brandelene nodded, stared straight ahead, and held her head high, allowing the tears to trickle down her cheeks.

Kordell pulled her into his arms and stroked her silken head while she sobbed into his chest.

"Some white demon shot Mister James when he was coming home from Petersburg," Ruby cried. "Everybody knew what a good shot Mister James was. The coward waited in the black of night, so Mister James couldn't see him."

Astounded by Ruby's revelation, Kordell could think of nothing to say to comfort his wife. He pulled a linen handkerchief from his pocket, lifted her chin with gentle fingertips, and wiped her tears.

"That little lamb never shed a tear over her daddy, 'til now," Ruby sputtered, tears running down her own cheeks. "She loved her daddy like no child I ever did see and she's held it in all this time, knowing the dirty coward that murdered him is still running around loose."

Kordell held Brandelene with her face buried in his neck while she yielded to her grief. Confused by the tenderness of the feelings he was experiencing for the first time in his life, he tightened his arms around her, unwilling to examine what he really felt. All the unbidden craving for his wife that had raged through his loins a short time ago disappeared. He wondered why his heart still beat so wildly and decided he did not want to know. Firmly, he set the matter from his mind, for his life right now was complicated enough without further entanglement. He bent and pressed warm lips to her brow, and his voice gentled as he whispered, "It's all right, Brandy. I'm here now."

After a while Brandelene pulled herself from his comforting embrace to sit straight, her head held high while she rode toward the plantation in somber silence.

When the carriage passed the borders of the vast estate, Ruby proudly pointed it out to Kordell and Dagert. Kordell ordered Joshua to stop the carriage and proceeded to instruct Dagert, Ruby, and Joshua about what they could and could not say, in regard to Brandelene's and his introduction, courtship, and marriage. He coached them until he felt sure there would be no major blunders. Brandelene listened quietly, surprised by Kordell's ability and patience, speaking up only now and then, for it was obvious he'd given his directions considerable thought.

"If you're afraid you'll give a wrong answer, or if you're asked a direct question that would require your answer to be an untruth, refer the person to Brandelene or me. I remind you again, do not at any time mention Richmond. We certainly don't want Cyrus Varner to snoop around there. All of us have considerable to lose, so we must be alert with every word we say, with every person we talk to, for only the five of us, and the lawyer Thompson, know the truth of everything." Satisfied that he'd done his best, he sighed. The burden of being able to successfully accomplish a deception of this magnitude weighed heavily upon him.

Sometime later the carriage turned into a wide, tree-lined lane. A majestic white plantation house emerged on the horizon.

Southern Oaks.

Fifteen towering oaks graced each side of the lengthy drive. Their thick foliage mushroomed over the driveway, permitting only rare shafts of sunlight to penetrate their crowns. Beyond the giant trunks lush green lawns gently sloped, broken at random intervals by the great trunks of several lofty oaks, their leafy bowers spreading shade over the manicured grounds.

A steep, widely overhung roof, bedecked with dormers, stretched endlessly over a row of twelve massive columns along the front and wings of the mansion. French doors surrounded the house and opened from all rooms onto the main veranda and second-story balcony. Two wide oak doors were bordered by cut glass and crowned by an arched, cut-glass transom. Twin pillars, a miniature of the twelve massive columns, guarded each side of the intricately carved oak doors. On the second story, a large, arched, cut-glass window, centered over the entrance doors, revealed an elegant, one-hundred-candle crystal chandelier hanging in the three-story foyer.

Kordell sat wordless as they approached the mansion. Since he learned of James Barnett's murder, he had been able to think of little else, and wondered if Cyrus Varner could have had anything to do with his stepbrother's death. The man had much to gain, if he had been aware of the terms of Barnett's will. Deciding it was a riddle that might never be solved, he turned his thoughts to the problem at hand—the protection of his wife. In the absence of a will, if Cyrus could find grounds to have their marriage annulled, and Brandelene died, Cyrus would undoubtedly inherit the entire estate. Under those circumstances, Mr. Varner had considerable reason to see the marriage set aside and, further, would benefit immensely if his stepniece suffered a premature death, as her father had.

Kordell tried to concentrate on how to prevent such an occurrence, if indeed there was any threat at all. The resolution came to him in a flash—he would trick, or force, Cyrus into acknowledging the marriage publicly.

The carriage stopped in front of the mansion of Southern Oaks. Matthew, the tall, lanky family butler and husband of Ruby, waited on the veranda with their beautiful daughter, Pearl.

Kordell alighted and proffered his hand to his wife.

Brandelene's face glowed and her violet eyes shone with happiness at being home, giving Kordell a glimpse of the child she'd once been.

Pearl, Brandelene's lifelong companion and friend, raced down the veranda stairs to embrace Brandelene, and Ruby looked on in happy approval.

"That's my baby," Ruby proudly announced to Kordell and Dagert. "I bounced Pearl on one knee and Miss Brandelene on the other when they were babies."

Then Kordell caught Dagert's awestruck look at Pearl. The stunning young woman was taller than Brandelene and slender as a young boy. Her large, thick-lashed, dark eyes were accentuated by a lovely toffee complexion and her cheeks flushed with the soft rose of youth. A full, soft mouth was set in a daintily pointed, oval face and Pearl's long hair was plaited into a coronet of braids on top of her head. Grinning in amusement at Dagert, Kordell's gaze moved back to Brandelene, who'd suddenly stiffened.

The object of her disapproval was a balding, heavy man, dressed all in white, who'd shuffled out onto the veranda, and now stood glaring through button black eyes at Brandelene, then Kordell. The man's mouth curled in an unpleasant twist. Although not tall, his immense bulk and sinister demeanor created an intimidating presence.

Kordell needed no introduction to know this was Cyrus Varner, and he instantly disliked the man. He moved to Brandelene's side and placed his hand firmly on her waist, then squeezed gently in a gesture of support.

At that, Brandelene, feeling her composure under attack, glanced up at her husband in gratitude. Her fear that he might betray her subsided.

Kordell smiled confidently down at her and increased the pressure of his hand to guide her up the stairs of the veranda to face their adversary. "Cyrus Varner, I presume," Kordell greeted the enormous man. Although he extended his hand, his eyes silently challenged Cyrus. "I am Kordell Bouclair."

"Mr. Bouclair," Cyrus wheezed. His hand, clasping Kordell's, was strong and sweaty. He bent his head back to scrutinize Kordell, then turned toward Brandelene. "You certainly show a blatant disregard for your father's good name by traveling in the company of Mr. Bouclair without a proper chaperon." Cyrus made no attempt to disguise his annoyance in front of the others. He rudely turned his back on Brandelene and Kordell to enter the mansion.

"Varner!" Kordell boomed angrily. "Do not make the mistake of addressing my wife in a disrespectful manner again!"

Cyrus whirled about surprisingly fast for a huge man. "Your

wife!" he said, his broad face twisting in rage. "I am this girl's guardian and I gave no permission for her to marry. Nor will I!"

"Brandelene feared that would be your attitude," Kordell said calmly, "which is why we married without your consent." Unconsciously, he moved into a spread-eagled stance and sized up the man he already considered his enemy. "We were wed two weeks ago by Judge Jenkins in Petersburg."

"Two weeks ago!" Cyrus bellowed and his pallid face whitened. "The marriage is not legal without my permission. I will have it annulled!" His heavy jowls shook in his anger and he gave Kordell an ominous glower. "Do not bother having your bags brought in, Mr. Bouclair. Joshua will drive you back to Petersburg."

Chapter 11

BRANDELENE FELT A SINKING DESPAIR OVERWHELM her. Why had Kordell confronted Cyrus in such a manner? He had forced Cyrus to challenge him—and their marriage. Frantically she searched for a method to salvage the disastrous beginning, but was interrupted by Kordell's retort.

"I will stay with my wife, Varner—*here*," Kordell declared firmly, emphasizing each word. "If anyone leaves Southern Oaks it will be you." Then he placed an arm around Brandelene, pulled her close, and hoped his next ploy would deceive Cyrus. In a most pompous voice he said, "As for annulling our marriage, I trust you are a rich man, for I am willing to do whatever is necessary, at whatever cost, to protect Brandelene and our marriage." A swift shadow of fury swept across Kordell's face and his eyes narrowed. "Heed my words well, Varner—*whatever is necessary*! Wealth such as mine will buy many things, including the destruction of any man who stands in the way of my marriage to Brandelene!" With an air of authority, he turned to an alarmed Joshua. "Joshua, Brandelene will instruct you where to have the footman put our trunks."

Stunned by this stranger who challenged him, Cyrus stiffened. "No man comes in here and threatens me!" he thundered. Then, as though rethinking his position, he added, "Why don't we go inside and discuss this over a drink? I was merely concerned for my niece, that she didn't fall into the hands of an unscrupulous fortune hunter."

Astonishment touched Brandelene's face, and she glanced up at Kordell with a respect she'd not felt before. There was much more to this self-assured man than she'd realized.

Pain flashed through Kordell's ribs and his chest ached fiercely. The weakness from his recent illness was fast overtaking him. He needed to rest. However, it was important that he smooth the havoc he'd wreaked before they left the veranda. "Mr. Varner, I understand your concern for your niece's welfare, and realize our marriage has come as a shock to you. Nevertheless, my first concern is for Brandelene's happiness, and surely she couldn't be completely happy if her only living relative were estranged from her, now could she?" After maneuvering Brandelene around the wide girth of Cyrus and through the entry into the foyer of the mansion, he turned to solicitously pat the rotund man on the back. "Our trip was tiring and I've been somewhat ill." Kordell smiled widely, exerting his considerable charm. "Why don't we, as you suggested, discuss this matter further, perhaps over dinner? I'm sure we'll have a meeting of the minds that will be acceptable—to all of us."

Cyrus cast a sly look at Kordell, grunted, and nodded.

At that, Kordell smiled and placed his arm around his wife's waist. "Will you lead the way to our room, my sweet?" He cast Brandelene a warning glance. "I could use a little rest."

"Of course, darling." Showing none of the alarm that gripped her, she pressed her head to Kordell's shoulder for only a moment, for Cyrus's benefit. Although it rankled to have to use the master bedroom that had been shared by her parents, she realized Cyrus would expect it and turned to call to the butler, "Matthew, please send a maid to the master suite."

Kordell and Brandelene crossed the marble floor of the large foyer to the wide, curving staircase encased by an intricately carved balustrade. The stairs swept gracefully upward to a wide landing, where a large mullioned window overlooked the rear gardens, before winding in two opposite, graceful curves to the second floor.

Midway up the staircase, Kordell paused in front of the many-paned window to catch his breath, his brow beaded with perspiration. He looked out over the oak-shaded gardens behind the mansion before Brandelene led him up the open stairs branching off to the west wing.

Sometime later Kordell rested in the master bedroom while Brandelene, in the large adjoining bedroom, relaxed in her bath. Pearl sat nearby.

Pearl had been two months old when Brandelene was born and Laura, Brandelene's mother, had nearly died in childbirth. With his wife near death, James Barnett had sought out Ruby to nurse his newborn daughter, and the two babies had grown up together, were educated by the same tutor, and were as close as sisters.

After James Barnett's father died, James freed Ruby, Matthew, Pearl, and Joshua and converted the remaining slaves into indentured servants; from that time Pearl had been Brandelene's only female friend. Yet in many ways, Pearl was more than a friend, for she was always Brandelene's staunchest supporter and never so much as lifted a brow in disapproval.

Brandelene sank lower in the warm, fragrant water and finished telling Pearl the whole of her agreement with Kordell. "Pearl, I cannot help it. That is Daddy's bedroom and it presses me sorely to have a man who is not, and never will be, my husband sleeping in Daddy's bed."

Pearl leaned back in the high-backed European chair and smiled mischievously. "Heaven above, Brandelene, how could you not consider that man for your husband? The way he set your uncle Cyrus down. How can you resist such a man? He's marvelous!"

"He's an arrogant rogue!" For some unexplained reason she hadn't told Pearl that her husband was naught but a charming fortune hunter, or of her unexpected attraction to him. She wondered why she was unable to reveal this last when, after swearing Pearl to secrecy, she'd told her everything else?

Brandelene stepped out of the tub, toweled herself dry, slipped into a wrapper, then crossed the room to sit down at the dressing table. "I noticed Dagert couldn't take his gaze from you," Brandelene teased, bringing a blush to Pearl's cheeks.

"I didn't pay much attention," Pearl replied shyly, towel-drying Brandelene's long hair. Then she picked up a hairbrush to begin the task of brushing the raven tresses to a luster.

Brandelene glanced at Pearl in the ornate gilded mirror. "What gown shall I wear for dinner tonight? You select a lucky one for me, Pearl darlin'."

"Your burgundy gown," Pearl said, her dark eyes sparkling. "Then you can wear Miss Laura's ruby and diamond jewels. Cyrus has never seen any of your mama's jewels and he'll think your wealthy husband gave them to you since they match your wedding ring." She piled the shining black hair in rolls of curls that partially covered a chignon, high on the back of Brandelene's head.

"You're clever, Pearl." Brandelene pulled loose tendrils of hair to curl softly around her face. "I wish I'd had you with me when I bought Kordell and Dagert. It was a nightmare."

"I can't imagine spending two weeks with a man such as Mister Kordell being anything but heavenly. Don't you have eyes, Brandelene?"

Flushing a soft pink as she caught Pearl's gaze in the mirror, Brandelene conceded, "He is attractive—somewhat."

"If you let that man get away you are a fool."

"I want Kordell considerably less than he wants me—which is not at all."

"You could always give him a little more of that laudanum he's so fond of. That might improve his disposition." Pearl giggled and then the two women laughed together, as they had when they'd been naughty children.

A short time later Brandelene donned her petticoats, gown, and jewels, then stepped before the tall cheval glass to examine her reflection. Her mother's ruby and diamond necklace, earrings, and bracelet glowed bloodred amid the sparkling diamonds, and combined with the rich velvet of her burgundy gown. Indeed, she looked every inch the wife of a man of wealth. "It's much too late in the season to be wearing velvet. I will smother, and this is more a ballgown than one for dinner."

"All that greedy Cyrus will see is the obvious cost," Pearl reminded Brandelene, pinning three burgundy velvet rosettes to the back of her hair. "You look especially beautiful, and sooo wealthy."

Moments later Brandelene tapped lightly on Kordell's connecting door, then unlocked it when he bid her enter. He rose from his chair. Attired in gray cutaway, charcoal breeches, and black Hessian boots he looked a dapper gentleman of means. Devastatingly handsome.

Irritated by her thoughts, Brandelene spoke quickly. "You're looking better, Kordell. I trust you're also feeling better."

"Considerably, thank you," he responded in the deep, resonant voice she was becoming accustomed to. Then his roaming gaze touched her elegant gown and extravagant jewels. "Your mother's?"

"Yes. Cyrus has never seen any of mother's jewels. He was seldom here before Daddy's death."

For a time, Kordell's slow regard rested on the rapid rise and fall of her full breasts, invitingly displayed above the décolletage of her Empire-waisted gown, then reluctantly moved to her soft bared shoulders, and dropped to her curving figure, temptingly revealed beneath the soft flowing folds. She was regal. Majestic. He groaned inwardly. "It was considerate of you to assign Joshua as my personal valet, but not necessary."

"Kordell, a man of means is never without his personal valet. It's a necessity rather than a luxury."

"Of course. You wouldn't overlook the smallest detail whether you can afford it or not."

"It appears to me," Brandelene retorted, "the question is not if I can afford to, but if I can afford not to!"

Silently, he cursed her clever mind and sharp tongue, watching the black widow spider he'd first met slowly emerge and the warm, passionate, and loving Brandelene disappear. Why? he wondered. Had he not done everything she could have expected of him, plus some? Why was she once again the frigid, aloof woman?

Despite their harsh words, the air between them was charged, and Pearl froze at the door, unwilling to intrude, observing Brandelene and Kordell look at each other across the empty room, their mutual attraction more obvious to her than either would willingly admit. Quietly she retreated into Brandelene's room.

"You look beautiful, Madame Bouclair," Kordell murmured and took a step forward, his hoarse whisper breaking the silence.

"Thank you," Brandelene breathed, frozen where she stood. "Kordell, since you brought it to my attention in the carriage, I've been wanting to apologize to you for my rude behavior toward you." She lowered her lashes, then raised her gaze to capture his. "I have no excuse for my behavior other than the burden of my tenuous situation. I hope you understand."

Kordell crossed the room in swift strides and placed his large hands on her bare upper arms. A slight tremor shot through his body at the touch of her soft skin. "I didn't ask for an apology, Brandy, nor did I expect one. However, I do appreciate your graciousness in extending one."

His golden eyes penetrated her very soul, and she felt her knees tremble at his touch. She reached up and gently removed his burning hands to hold them in her own. "I also wanted to thank you for the way you handled Cyrus. You were superb."

"Thank you, madame." Her hands seared his flesh, her delicate fragrance played havoc with his senses, her slightly parted lips tempted him beyond all reason. His head lowered slightly.

His lips were inches away and she wanted to rise up on tiptoe. Her heart raced, her mind whirled. It was craziness that she was so drawn to him, even though she knew he would press every advantage he had, for his wealthy Nicolle was so far away, and Southern Oaks was so near. If Cyrus were gone, there wouldn't be such a problem.

"Tonight, Kord, I want you to ask Cyrus to leave Southern Oaks within the next two days." When he made no reply, she sighed with relief at his silent agreement.

Already warm in her velvet, she said, "I forgot my fan. I'll be right back." Brandelene disappeared into her room.

The night before Kordell had agreed to marry Brandelene, he had deliberated her proposal at length, for he'd realized that if Cyrus Varner were to learn the facts of their marriage and have the marriage set aside, he, Kordell, would be an indentured servant for five years under Cyrus's control. Her stepuncle was not only the guardian of Brandelene, but also of her estate, of which Kordell's contract was an asset. In that event, Dagert's document of manumission, written by Brandelene, would in all probability be invalid. Worthless. Then Cyrus would also control the ownership of Dagert, who not only would be a slave for life, but also could be sold away. So, all things considered, he knew he had to play out this charade with Cyrus until the man was convinced. That, unquestionably, would not be within two days, and Kordell wasn't going to risk Dagert's and his own freedom. Brandelene might want Cyrus Varner to leave in two days but he certainly didn't.

Brandelene returned with her fan and smiled up at him.

Desperately craving her, he knew he had to get her out of his bedroom before all his self-restraint disappeared. "Shall we go to dinner?"

"Of course, my husband." She flashed a dazzling smile at him and he glanced away.

Didn't she realize how she affected him? Kordell guided her across the room, opened the door, and stepped aside for her to precede him. "Where is Cyrus's room?"

"He's in the east wing, so we only need be concerned about the servants." When he said nothing, she commented, "I've told Pearl everything."

"Is that wise?"

"She is my dearest friend. In fact, she's my only friend since none of the plantation owners' daughters are permitted to speak to me, let alone associate with me. I would trust her with my life. We need a friend to help us get through the next six months, although, granted, it won't be nearly as difficult if Cyrus will leave tomorrow, or the next day."

When they reached the top of the curving staircase, without

warning Kordell pulled her into his arms and kissed her soundly.

Astounded, Brandelene pushed at his chest with open palms.

Lifting his tawny head, he whispered softly, "Cyrus is watching."

Brandelene entwined one hand in Kordell's hair and pulled his head back down to hers. But then of its own accord her other hand moved under his muscular arm to the center of his back, drawing him closer. His mouth reclaimed hers as he crushed her to him, shattering her calm with the hunger of his searing kiss that sensuously explored the soft fullness of her lips and shot spirals of ecstasy through her. She'd been kissed before, by experienced men, by men of the world, by handsome, sophisticated men. But not like this. The others had been brief, chaste kisses and none had ever prepared her for the intoxicating ecstasy of Kordell's.

All intentions of charades for Cyrus's benefit fled and, helplessly, nothing mattered except the lips locked hungrily to hers. His mouth moved over hers and devoured her with a savage intensity that left her weak. She returned his fiery kiss with reckless abandon, submitting to the emotions that whirled through her body, out of control. His warm lips trailed across her cheek to nibble at her ear and her senses reeled. Vigorously, he kissed her again and his moist mouth overpowered her in a wondrously passionate kiss. The flame of that intoxicating kiss pounded in her head while her heart raced in cadence with the fire coursing through her body. When he lifted his head, their gazes met and she felt him tremble.

"Brandy, Brandy," he whispered, gazing into her eyes, "what are you doing to me?"

Unable to answer, she stepped back and her knees threatened to buckle beneath her. She slipped her shaking hand through his arm for support and caught a glimpse of Cyrus, downstairs, before his large bulk moved out of sight.

"We have only two more days to get through, and then this must stop," Brandelene whispered breathlessly. "As soon as Cyrus is gone . . . that is the end of it, Kordell!"

He stared down at her wonderingly, for she was a flaming passion that gave him no ease. Perhaps she was right. Let Cyrus be gone and that be the end of it. But he knew he dare not risk success by staying with Brandelene's scheme. All their futures were at stake. He had to proceed with his own plan.

He placed his hand over hers, where it rested on the crook of his arm, and started down the wide, curving staircase.

Matthew informed them that Cyrus awaited, and Kordell escorted his wife to James Barnett's impressive library, where Cyrus Varner stood with drink in hand.

Cyrus stared at her shimmering jewels, and raised the stubby hand that grasped his glass. "A drink, Mr. Bouclair?"

"No thank you, Cyrus." Kordell watched the immense man's eyes narrow at the uninvited use of his given name.

"Let's eat," Cyrus muttered and lumbered from the room, making no attempt to hide his irritation. "You're late and I'm hungry."

The wall of French doors that overlooked the flowering, tree-shaded gardens of Southern Oaks was opened wide to permit the gentle breezes to enter the spacious dining room. An abundance of candles flickered in the two crystal chandeliers that hung over the large table, set in glittering service for three. A white-gloved footman stood silently by, waiting to be of service.

Kordell glanced at the location of the place settings. The head of the table was bare, the opposite end contained a place setting, and the other two were at the center of the table, opposite each other. Kordell stopped shortly inside the room and removed Brandelene's hand from his arm. "Excuse me a moment, darling." He turned to Matthew who'd followed the trio into the room. "Matthew, have the place settings changed. I will sit at the head of the table, my wife—"

"No!" Brandelene protested, paling visibly. "That is Daddy's seat."

Swiftly, Kordell's arm circled her tiny waist and his hand tightened with warning. "Of course, my sweet," he responded gently. "I shall occupy it with accordant reverence, but I am the head of our household now." Then he turned back to Matthew. "As I was saying, my wife will be seated immediately to my right, and Mr. Varner may occupy his usual place."

Hesitating, Matthew glanced at Brandelene.

She stood rigid, her calm demeanor belying her inner rage.

"Yes, sir," Matthew acknowledged, then motioned for the waiting footman to do as Kordell bid.

For a moment, Cyrus stared in stunned disbelief at the strong-willed Brandelene, who had always zealously defended anything of her father's, before his look turned into a leering grin. Apparently, from the display at the top of the stairs, the fiery-tempered hellion had been tamed by her own hot blood.

Kordell seated Brandelene in her designated chair, and bent to briefly press warm lips to her bare shoulder. "My darling, I know how you loved your father," he said for all to hear. "I only intend to occupy your father's chair, not his place in your heart." Then he leaned against the table and lifted her chin with gentle fingertips to gaze into the depths of the black magenta eyes that blazed back at him. "Give me a bewitching smile, my beauty, so I know you understand."

Brandelene smiled, knowing she had no choice, but though her lips curved warmly her eyes narrowed. A betrayal now? she wondered as she watched Kordell slip into James Barnett's chair. Was this his first step in attempting to maneuver himself into the role of her husband and, as such, the ownership of Southern Oaks? Well, let him play all the games he wished, the sun would turn to ice before Kordell Bouclair became her husband in fact as well as in name.

During dinner, a belligerent Cyrus threw one question after another at Brandelene's husband. Kordell answered each query casually, and at times in vivid detail, with the air of detached self-confidence one would expect from a gentleman of considerable circumstance.

To her surprise and relief, Brandelene found herself marveling at Kordell's composure, and his mystique deepened as she wondered at the truth of this bond servant who knew exactly how to comport himself, to the smallest detail, as what he represented himself to be. Fate, she surmised, must have led her to the only indentured servant in the United States who could make her want to believe his ludicrous tale of a heritage and life of extravagant wealth, when she knew it to be untrue, for she'd purchased the penniless fraud herself.

Brandelene turned to observe Cyrus. Completely duped by Kordell, he was no doubt consumed with greed. She could sense him anticipating how, or if, he could benefit from this unexpected windfall. Relaxing slightly, she smiled to herself and Kordell's words interrupted her musings.

"I felt," Kordell's deep voice was saying, "since you've wisely befriended the local plantation owners, it would be most appropriate for you to announce our marriage at a reception at Southern Oaks, perhaps the week-end after this."

Chapter 12

BRANDELENE WAS BREATHLESS WITH RAGE, WHILE Kordell's booted foot pressed down on her slippered foot in warning. How dare Kordell suggest a reception?

Cyrus's wide face mirrored his indecision at the unexpected suggestion, and he wheezed heavily as he spooned a large helping of apple brown betty into his mouth.

Confident, Kordell placed a comforting hand over Brandelene's, which were tightly grasping the edge of the table. "I felt it a good idea to meet all the neighbors and get to know them before we leave for France and then the Ivory Coast."

At that, Cyrus's eyes widened in surprise. "You're returning to the Ivory Coast?"

Kordell smiled with satisfaction, for the avaricious Cyrus Varner had responded as he expected. "My apologies for not making that clear," he said in a patronizing tone. "I assumed, after describing

my own circumstance, you would realize I could never be satisfie
to live . . . here."

Although Brandelene seethed inwardly, she managed to contai
her acid tongue, fully realizing the import of Cyrus's public ac
knowledgment of their marriage. She could almost hear Cyrus'
thoughts as he considered his position if Kordell and she were t
live on the Ivory Coast, in France and England, an ocean an
many weeks away. Surely he had to realize it would be the nex
best thing to his owning the plantation—if he were left in control

Hesitant, Cyrus cleared his throat. "I can't imagine Brandelen
leaving Southern Oaks." His expression was skeptical.

"My wife," Kordell announced arrogantly, "will go where I go.

Brandelene simmered, yet she smiled sweetly at Cyrus.

"I sent that defiant, independent vixen north for over two years.
Cyrus spoke as though Brandelene were not present. "Sent her t
an expensive school for genteel ladies and they did nothin' to curl
her feisty, rebellious ways, and taught her more tricks to boot.
find it hard to believe Brandelene will listen to anyone."

"It was Brandelene's fiery spirit that first attracted me," Kordel
admitted truthfully. "Actually, you might say I have literally be
come her servant because she is so independent."

A swift kick to the shin, under the table, was Kordell's rewar
for his flash of humor.

"Considering the relatively short time you've known Brandelene
you seem to have tamed her quite a bit," Cyrus allowed grudgingly
"I wouldn't have believed it possible."

"Damnation!" Brandelene cursed and threw her napkin on th
table. "Enough is enough!" Bristling, she jumped to her feet, almos
knocking the chair over in her anger. "You, Cyrus Varner, wil
never live to see the day any man tames me, so don't bothe
holding your breath in hopes that you do!" With that, she sailec
from the room and then paused at the open French doors to turr
back and glare at Cyrus. "On second thought," she snapped
"please do hold your breath." With that parting remark, she disappeared into the gardens.

Stroking his chin thoughtfully, Kordell watched the man whc
was still eating. "Cyrus," he began with a low but firm tone, "

had felt I made it quite clear earlier that if my wife has been insulted, I have been insulted. I'm a patient man, Cyrus; however it is not advisable to provoke me."

Although the room was comfortably cool, sweat appeared on Cyrus's brow.

Casually, Kordell leaned back in his chair and stared at the man. "You didn't answer my earlier question, Cyrus. I assume your silence is your agreement to host a reception to announce our marriage."

Cyrus belched loudly. "Yes," he said reluctantly.

"Excellent!" Kordell pushed back his chair to rise. "Brandelene will go over the guest list with you tomorrow." Satisfied, he stood up, rising to the fullest measure of his considerable height, deciding to dangle one more false lure before the gluttonous Mr. Varner. "I can see where you might be a valuable man to me, Cyrus," he said slyly. "Someone here in the United States who understands my thinking, and could be trusted to look after my varied investments and interests could be worth a good sum to me. That is if you would be interested in traveling."

"I love to travel."

"Good," Kordell said, now satisfied that Cyrus had taken the bait. "Remind me to continue this discussion in the not-too-distant future. After we become better acquainted. Now, if you'll excuse me, I'll go find my bride and soothe her lovely ruffled feathers."

He sauntered through the open French doors onto the rear terrace that overlooked the flowering gardens of Southern Oaks. He glanced up at the full moon and watched as it slowly slipped behind a puffy gray cloud, casting haunting shadows of the giant oaks that dotted the gardens. The chirrup of crickets and the croak of tree frogs filled him with a sense of peace, and he searched for his wife in the diffused moonlight. Walking down the stairs, the fragrance of wisteria, jasmine, roses, and bougainvillea filled the air. His reflections trod gently backward to another garden, where he'd wed the ravishing Brandelene, the fascinating Brandelene, the mysterious Brandelene, who was slowly bewitching him and luring him into her silky web. The moon peeked out from a billowing cloud and bathed the gardens in a magical aura of moonlight. Then he saw her. She walked under the spreading boughs of a towering oak and he crossed with purposeful strides to her side.

Brandelene saw Kordell approaching. "How dare you suggest Cyrus hold a reception for us," she exploded when he reached her, and her accusing voice stabbed the air. "We agreed that evil man would be gone within two days and you are deliberately sabotaging our agreement." With a swish of her skirts, she turned her back to him. "I should've known you wouldn't keep your word. Well, be warned, Kordell Bouclair," she tossed over her shoulder, "if you're not bound by your word, then neither am I." To Brandelene's dismay, Kordell moved so close behind her she could feel the heat of his body.

"Are you finished?" he asked and received no response. "Brandy, if you will think back you will—"

"Don't call me Brandy!" she snapped. "My name is Brandelene—to you!"

"You are my wife, and as such I wish to call you Brandy, although *hellion* is more fitting at times. Which would you prefer?"

"I would prefer that you disappear." She whirled to face him. "I knew I would have cause to regret saving your worthless neck."

"As I was saying, Brandy, when I was rudely interrupted, if you will think back you will recall that you suggested Cyrus leave in two days." His husky voice was softly gentle and he clasped his hands into fists to prevent himself from taking her into his arms and kissing her breathless. "I did not agree to that suggestion and made no indication I did. Be assured, my lovely wife, I will keep my word on all our agreements."

"I'm not your wife," Brandelene replied frigidly. "And don't make the mistake of thinking by keeping Cyrus here that I shall succumb to your attentions. It's miraculous, monsieur, how quickly you forget your lovely Nicolle when there's another wealthy woman near!"

Kordell stiffened as though she'd struck him. "Brandy," he murmured, gently clasping her bare shoulders in his strong hands, "since Cyrus squandered away all the cash reserves of your inheritance, that wealth you guard so zealously is rather questionable right now, if not entirely nonexistent. Are you so insecure of your own worth that you think a man could only want you for your inheritance?"

Stunned into silence at his accusation, she squirmed uncomfortably at the possibility he had spoken the truth, then forced her mind from such an unsettling thought. "Kord, we need to talk. Civilly."

"Fine. If you're finished playing the high and mighty Brandelene I met at the auction."

"You have the temerity to speak to me in such a manner?"

"I'll admit to having one or two faults, madame. Can you admit to the same?"

Why was she either helplessly attracted to him, or furiously irritated by him, with nothing in-between? "To answer your question, Monsieur Bouclair, I would admit to them—if I could think of any. However, if it will ease your mind, I will ponder the question. Surely I'll find some tiny flaw. I promise to let you know if I do."

"Is this how we talk civilly?"

Moments passed before she said, "Truce?"

"Truce."

"Shall we sit?" She pointed toward the wrought-iron furniture a short distance away.

He nodded and they started walking in that direction.

"Kord, I . . . I've given some consideration to our agreement." Brandelene floundered before his sharp and assessing gaze. She inhaled deeply and blurted out, "I realize it was my insistence that you play the role of a loving husband in public. However, I've changed my mind. I still wish you to play that role, but with no physical contact between us."

Kordell stared at her as though she'd taken leave of her senses. "Ahh, Brandy, exactly how do you suggest I do that?" he asked and graced her with an irresistible grin, his perfect teeth a brilliant white. "Shall I bellow words of endearment across the room to you?"

Brandelene inwardly cursed him.

At her stony silence, Kordell shrugged matter-of-factly. "Fortunately, I've never had the misfortune of being in love, dear innocent, but I've seen many who were. The bewitched couples couldn't keep their hands from each other, barely remaining within the bounds of propriety. I have only comported myself in a manner to fulfill our agreement."

"Damnation! The agreement be hanged. I won't submit to your lusty attentions."

He laughed. "What is the lady afraid of? Herself?"

"You are conceited! You are arrogant! You are an audacious, pompous rake!" Brandelene exploded, and the lively twinkle in Kordell's eyes only incensed her more. "And, I might add, your opinion of yourself is highly inflated. This may come as quite a shock to you, Monsieur Bouclair, but I do *not* find you irresistible."

"Madame Bouclair, your tender words are most comforting," Kordell mocked. "However, the lady's protestations do not match her behavior. The kisses you shared with me at our wedding and at the top of the stairs were hardly ones you would bestow upon someone you found to be offensive."

To Brandelene's mortification, her cheeks burned in remembrance, her pulse pounded in her ears, and she stiffened in humiliation.

"Since it is impossible to hold a mature conversation with you, I am ordering you to keep your hands off me. Do not touch me again. Publicly nor privately."

"Sit down, Brandelene," Kordell said softly.

She started to walk away and his hand flashed out to grab her wrist.

"Madame, I said sit down, or would you prefer I sit you down like the child you're acting?"

"You wouldn't dare."

"Try me."

Wordlessly, she glared at him.

"I said *sit*, Brandelene."

"I take orders from no one. Least of all from you."

With his patience more than a little tried, Kordell sighed in frustration, the weakness of his illness overtaking him. "Brandelene, will you please be seated? What I have to say is of the utmost importance to us both, if you wish to save Southern Oaks."

"Are you threatening me?"

"No, Brandy, for my fate is now tied to the success of your ridiculous scheme. Please be seated."

After a moment's hesitation, she stiffly sat on the settee, then said, "My name is Brandelene."

He lowered himself beside her. "Brandelene, regardless of how we feel about each other, we're shackled together for the next six months, as surely as a team of horses." He smiled before continuing, and the warmth of his smile echoed in his voice. "Yours is a foolhardy venture, at best, and only has a chance of succeeding if we both play our parts to perfection. At any rate, there's no turning back now. I agree with your original plan. First, we must convince Cyrus I'm a wealthy plantation owner from the Ivory Coast, which I believe I have done. Secondly, I show uncompromising strength, so Cyrus will consider twice before he again challenges me. And thirdly, until Cyrus leaves, we must play the part of a bewitched couple who married hastily, without a betrothal period, out of a deep love and infatuation for each other."

"No."

Kordell raised his hand to silence her. "Please hear me out."

His deep voice was gentle, lulling her into relaxation, his hand on the settee behind her unusually warm against her bare back.

"Brandy, if Cyrus isn't convinced of the latter, he'll never accept the first two. Are either of us ready to pay the exceedingly high price of failure because we find it distasteful to play the charade of lovers?"

Brandelene sighed.

"Let me assure you, madame, it's considerably more difficult for me than it is for you, for you're an innocent child. Yet even that is far more palatable to me than the alternative that will accompany defeat, for I'm in a foreign country, without friends or money. I'm at the mercy of the situation in which I'm temporarily trapped."

Disturbed, Brandelene contemplated Kordell's words. She knew he was right. She nodded.

Kordell stood and offered her his hand.

When she rose she brushed against him. "But no reception, and see if you can encourage Cyrus to leave in two days. I could tolerate the devil himself for two days."

All his control and good resolve disappeared at her scathing remark and Kordell roughly pulled her into his arms, his mouth capturing hers as she struggled to free herself. His callous kiss was punishing and angry, a cruel ravishment of her mouth.

But then, just as quickly, his moist, firm mouth became tender, affectionate, moving gently over hers to devour its softness, drugging her with the intensity of his ravenous kiss. Brandelene stopped struggling and her arms slipped, of their own accord, around his nape. When his demanding lips caressed hers, all remaining sense flew from her mind and she eagerly returned his fiery kiss while a delicious warmth flooded her body, leaving her mindless. At that moment, Kordell's potent kiss deepened, his arms crushed her against his hard chest. Breathless, she hungrily kissed him back, reveling in the smoldering heat that splintered through her veins, momentarily stunned by her own ardent response to the intimacy of his endless kiss. When his lips left hers, her mouth burned with an unquenched fire. Slowly, he trailed lingering kisses across her soft cheek, nibbled at her earlobe, then seared down her neck to sensually kiss her wildly pulsing throat, and she moaned softly before she arched her neck to the delicious touch of his hungry lips.

"Kord," she whispered, then cupped his face between gentle hands and drew his carved mouth up, to recapture hers in a timeless kiss of flaming passion that left her weak from the aching desire that possessed her completely.

Their lips parted, and he smothered her face with tiny butterfly kisses, then buried his face in her soft, fragrant hair, trembling as he clasped her to him, and his racing heart pounded in her ear pressed to his granite chest.

All reason had flown and now Kordell's torrid desire for only her flamed. "Brandy. Brandy," he whispered, "I want you!" His words were a proclamation, for he knew the only way he could quench the fire that raged in his loins was to appease it and let it burn itself out.

"Never," Brandelene protested weakly, unable to move from his embrace for fear she would collapse, resting contentedly against the warm strength of his body. Silently, he held her like that until her senses slowly returned. But her face, that had so recently burned from his volatile kisses, now flamed with humiliation that Kordell had deliberately tried to prove her weakness for him, and she'd responded with an abandon that proved him correct. Mortified beyond words, she jerked free of his arms. "You are contemptible to take advantage of my distress. May I remind you, the agreement was that you do not touch me in private."

"Is that what you really want, Brandy?" Kordell asked, his voice low and seductive, his desire a physical pain. "Can you deny what is between us?"

"There is nothing between us," she retorted and turned from his penetrating gaze that shimmered golden, even in the moonlight. "What I want is for you to keep your hands off me, as we agreed. I will not be mauled. Not even for Southern Oaks."

"Madame," Kordell said patiently, "I simply sought to show you I haven't exactly forced myself on you. That the feelings between us are not only overpowering, but mutual." He lifted his hand and gently brushed back the curling tendrils that blew softly across her face, and she shivered at his intimate touch. "Feelings that are inexplicable to me, for I have never felt this way about a woman before. It is overwhelming."

"The only thing I find overwhelming is your arrogant conceit, your incredible ego, and your insufferable pomposity," Brandelene returned. "To me you're nothing more than a bond servant who is the means to the salvation of Southern Oaks. Don't make the mistake of assuming the feelings I publicly display toward you are anything more than make-believe. Have I made myself clear?"

"Explicitly," Kordell replied tonelessly, and Brandelene stormed off toward the mansion. "However, Madame Bouclair," he softly murmured after her retreating back, "I don't believe a word of it."

Brandelene went straight to bed, but found no relief from her tortured thoughts, or her tormented body.

She rose, slipped into the silk and lace peignoir that matched her blue night rail, and then walked through the open French doors of her bedroom onto the moonlit balcony that overlooked the sweeping front grounds of Southern Oaks.

A fragrant breeze whipped her tousled hair and she rested her hip on the balustrade and leaned back against the massive pillar. Her gaze wandered to the swaying shadows of the majestic oaks that stood like silent sentinels of the mansion, then lifted to the full moon, playing hide and seek behind the dark puffy clouds. Again, her reflections, as though they had a will of their own, returned to the memory of Kordell's crushing embrace, his passionate kisses, and her pounding heart refused to be stilled. Her body grew warm at the recollection and would not be cooled by the breeze.

"For I have never felt this way about a woman before." His words echoed in her mind, and she felt betrayed at every turn. Betrayed by her body, betrayed by her mind, and betrayed by Kordell. How many times had he murmured those same words to his perfect Nicolle, and all the Nicolles before her? "Curse you, Kordell Bouclair!" she cried aloud. "Curse your wretched soul!"

"Are you speaking to me?" Kordell inquired from behind her.

Chapter 13

STARTLED, BRANDELENE WHIRLED TO FACE THE LARGE shadow that leaned against Kordell's portal. "How long have you been standing there?"

"Far longer than you, madame."

"You should have let me know."

Kordell laughed softly as he walked from the shadows to stand before her. "And miss that beautiful tribute to me?" Bare-chested,

Kordell stood with his hands in the pockets of his breeches and looked down at her.

Brandelene was glad that he also had spent sleepless hours and hoped she caused his distress, as he did hers. Distraction melted into fascination as her gaze moved from his muscular, furred chest to the breadth of his shoulders that completely filled the boundaries of her vision, and she shivered from his nearness. Stepping back, she bumped into the balustrade and teetered precariously. Instantly Kordell's hand flashed out and grabbed her arm to steady her. Then he released her as quickly as he'd saved her from falling and she could still feel the touch of his hand burning her arm, but it was nothing to the fire that raged through her body.

"Thank you," she said over her loudly beating heart, afraid if she uttered another word her voice would reveal her tumultuous feelings.

"My pleasure," Kordell murmured, his voice deep and sensual, as though he had spoken the most intimate of words. "Are you unable to sleep for the same reason as I?"

"If you've been pondering our tenuous position with Cyrus, I am," Brandelene lied.

The moonlight shaded his chiseled features and the soft light gave him the appearance of a Greek god. Suddenly Brandelene felt small and vulnerable; it was a feeling she detested, a feeling she hadn't experienced in many years, since she'd first put up her invisible wall to shield herself from the pain, the anger, and the resentment of friends who abandoned her.

Forcing her thoughts to her present problem, she spoke softly, "Kordell, I cannot consider a reception to announce this farce of a marriage."

He threw up his hands in disgust, and Brandelene instinctively backed away from him.

"Why not?"

Her full lips parted, inviting him, yet forbidding him, to taste fully of their sweetness. He shuddered and lifted his gaze to her eyes, consciously refusing to allow himself to look at her tantalizing body, thinly covered in the blue silk and lace that had so sorely tempted him when first she walked onto the balcony. With her unaware of his presence, he'd watched her at his leisure. With one rounded hip balanced on the balustrade, her body leaned back against the pillar and the wind revealingly billowed her night clothes about her. The moon silhouetted her voluptuous body, a temptation no celibate man should have to endure. Now his gaze held hers and once again he fought the ache in his loins, for never in his life had he desired a woman as much as his wife.

Brandelene recognized the open lust that covered her husband's face, for she had seen that same look many times, from many men. Before Kordell, she'd found that look disgusting, but now it seemed strangely exciting and compelling, drawing her as a magnet to iron. She turned away and walked a few steps down the length of the balcony, bathed in a moonlight that transformed the area into a beauty she'd never before seen. Turning to face him from a safe distance, she replied, "I don't want a reception because I can't face all those censorious people who've treated me as beneath contempt these many years." She wondered why she'd revealed her innermost fears to this man she'd known less than three weeks. "Besides, there is no time. I need to see the fields are properly prepared to transplant the tobacco seedlings, and furthermore, I doubt if one person would come even if invited by Cyrus, who would never host such a function anyway."

"Cyrus has already agreed," Kordell said, slowly moving toward her. "With a little coercion."

"He has?"

"Yes. We had a discussion after you left the dining room this evening, and Cyrus saw how advantageous it would be for him." He described his conversation with Cyrus after she'd left.

Unable to help herself, Brandelene laughed at the vision of the greedy man being duped. "You're marvelous, Kord." She straightened to find he stood so close she could feel the heat from his body. Still smiling, she stepped back. "I wish I'd been there to see him. I can well imagine that snake's face."

"Cyrus's little beady eyes were actually spinning."

Stepping back again, Brandelene found herself against the wall of the mansion.

In the shadows, she was celestial, not of this earth, but Kordell's craving was definitely earthly, and his restraint had reached its limit. He had to have her. Besides, he justified to himself, he'd already signed the petition for annulment. Surely the laws of Virginia would not require the doctor's certification. That, most certainly, he further reasoned, had to be a precautionary action by the clever lawyer Thompson and not a requirement of the courts. If that were the case, the marriage could be annulled without the damnable doctor's certification that prevented his satiating his now obsessive yearning for Brandelene. Satisfied with his hasty deductions, Kordell stepped forward, and his hands shot out to brace himself against the wall where he pinned her between strong arms. He had to get her out of his system. All he could think of was Brandelene in his bed, Brandelene submitting to him with fiery passion. "I want you, Brandy," he murmured huskily, his breath warm against her face. His hard body pressed against her softness and his gaze captured hers.

"I don't want you," she replied weakly, her words barely audible. Her heart raced uncontrollably.

"You're lying." He dropped one hand to trace gentle fingertips across her cheek, her chin, and down her throat. "Kiss me and then tell me you don't want me as much as I want you."

"I don't want you for my husband, and I won't have you any other way!" She ducked under his pinning arm and ran into her bedroom, slamming the double French doors behind her.

She'd hardly fallen asleep before Ruby woke her the next morning. With her doors shut she'd tossed fitfully the entire night in her stifling room.

"Good morning, child."

"There's not much good about it," Brandelene grumbled, yawning. "I got very little sleep, thanks to Kordell."

"Mmmm-um. I can believe that, lamb. I saw you carrying on in the garden last night with that rascal. Miss Brandelene, you're asking for trouble. That fancy lawyer told you if you don't get a doctor's certificate, you don't get an annulment. Then you got yourself a husband, child."

"Don't fret, Ruby darlin'. Mules will fly before Kordell will be my husband."

After dressing, Brandelene knocked softly on Kordell's connecting door and entered when bid to do so.

Kordell walked in from the balcony where he'd waited for Brandelene to awaken. "Madame," he said, "I wish to apologize for my conduct last night." Stroking his chin thoughtfully, he waited for her reply. When he received none, he explained, "I was quite swept off my feet by your beauty, and the night."

"Shall we go down to breakfast? Cyrus must be pacing by now."

"Is this how you accept my apology?" Kordell challenged, silently admiring her high-necked, dusty rose gown with its froth of ecru lace at the collar and cuffs.

"I really had come to expect better from you."

"Is this how you accept my apology?" Kordell repeated with quiet emphasis, his tone oddly gentle.

"How often," Brandelene frigidly rebuked, "am I going to have to endure your unwanted attentions?"

"How often are you going to walk the balcony in your silk and lace night clothes?" He grinned.

"Your humor is not amusing. This is my home. Must I dress and carry my pistol when I wish to stroll my own balcony in the middle of the night? I refuse to, Kordell. Instead, you will learn to conduct yourself as a gentleman."

"Tell me if you will, my beloved wife, do you always handle uncomfortable situations with such a sharp tongue?"

"Would you prefer I punch you in the jaw?" Brandelene retorted, her hands on her hips curled into fists. "Now that I think on it, I much prefer that method."

"Please, mistress, have mercy on me," he teased. "Do not beat me, for I'm but a simple bondsman. Say you will accept my apology."

"Kordell, don't play the fool."

"Have you accepted my apology?"

"Yes! Now let's go."

As he moved toward her, a grimace of pain crossed his face.

"Your ribs." Brandelene vividly recalled his naked torso when he'd been on the balcony. "You didn't have your binding on last night."

"Joshua removed it when I bathed for dinner. Then after you flew into the house from the gardens, I felt it best not to disturb you to rewrap me."

"A wise decision." She laughed. "I probably would've bound your hands and mouth instead of your ribs."

Kordell grinned. "I assumed as much."

"Remove your shirt and I'll bind you now," she instructed and moved to his armoire to retrieve the bandages. "I'll not have you in pain even if you are a . . ."

Ignoring the latest scathing remark she'd been about to hurl at him, Kordell started to remove his cutaway coat. "Brandy, I'm asking you to reconsider the reception. I . . ."

"No. I refuse."

He unbuttoned his waistcoat. "Brandy," he began patiently. "I'll be with you every second. It . . ."

"No."

He doffed his blue cravat and started to unbutton his white lawn shirt. "It is so much more important than simply having Cyrus publicly acknowledge our marriage. We . . ."

"No!"

Finally, Kordell tore off his shirt and threw it on the bed in a rumpled heap and swiftly crossed the room to clasp her arm. "Dammit, Brandelene, will you at least hear me out?"

Surprised, she glared down at the hand that gripped her.

Without hesitation, he released her, his face boyishly appealing in his frustration. "I'm sorry, Brandy," he apologized, his voice husky with remorse. "I'm sorry."

Ignoring his apology and the incident that preceded it, Brandelene said, "Raise your arms and I'll bind you." Her heart thudded in her ears at his bared muscular chest, so close to her, at the light furring that tapered at his waist, at his masculine scent that played havoc with her senses. "You may tell me what you wished while I'm doing this."

As instructed, Kordell lifted his arms and his body trembled at her gentle touch. Groaning inwardly, he hoped she didn't look down and notice his obvious response to her, his canopied bed so temptingly near it was an agony to him.

"Brandy," he said, his voice softer, huskier than he intended, "it is extremely important for Cyrus to recognize our marriage publicly. The reception will accomplish that. With luck it will also delay any investigation he might decide to undertake. In addition, if Cyrus publicly acknowledges the marriage it should discourage him from inquiring too deeply into the facts, if we do nothing to alert him. However, I don't delude myself. Reception or not, if he somehow finds the truth of the matter, or even part of the truth, he will rush to have this marriage set aside. Of that I have no doubt."

Brandelene glanced up at him. "Your binding is finished," she declared. The air between them was vibrantly alive, and once again Brandelene cursed her intense attraction to him.

Slowly and seductively, Kordell's gaze slid downward. "Perhaps we should finish this conversation on the balcony," he suggested, his voice breaking. Abruptly he strode to his armoire for another shirt. "Madame, I realize you are my wife, and as such have every right to be here. However, unless you desire to become my wife in every way, I suggest you wait for me on the balcony."

At his words Brandelene's cheeks flamed and she fled through the open French doors. It was a beautiful Virginia spring morning; a gentle, fragrant breeze rustled the leafy bowers of the giant oaks. The birds chirped and twittered their welcome to a sunny new day while the butterflies flitted from one vivid flower to another. Even the puffy white clouds gaily chased through a vivid blue sky. Brandelene had never been more miserable in her life. She realized her situation with Cyrus was tenuous at best. What plagued her even more was her growing feeling for Kordell. All good sense regarding him seemed to have vanished.

The best way to deal with Kordell was to acknowledge that he was her adversary, as surely as Cyrus Varner, and outwit and outmaneuver him. Surely if she could best one unsuspecting man, she could best two. After all, it was simply a matter of clever juggling, plus overcoming her attraction to him. In this matter, she determined, she would turn her strong will to her benefit. With her resolve firmly set, Brandelene smiled, the day suddenly beautiful, and she felt herself rather clever to use one adversary, Kordell, to defeat the other, Cyrus.

"What are you smiling at?" Kordell asked as he strolled onto the tree-shaded balcony.

"It's such a lovely day, and I've decided neither Cyrus nor any of my adversaries is going to defeat me."

"Madame, I knew that when you stood in your carriage with a whip in one hand and a pistol in the other."

Kordell's laughter was rich and infectious, and Brandelene laughed with him. "I must have looked utterly ridiculous."

"Quite the contrary." His voice lowered. "I thought you were magnificent."

Ignoring the heartbeat that pounded in her ears, she questioned, "You wished to speak further with me?"

Kordell gave no indication that he noticed her sudden coolness. "Back to the matter pressing us. Cyrus Varner is many contemptible things, but in my opinion he didn't murder your father. If for no other reason than he wouldn't take that kind of risk."

At Kordell's unexpected statement, Brandelene whirled to face him. "I never suspected he had. He was in another state when it happened, and besides, he had no way of knowing about Daddy's will. In fact, Cyrus was quite surprised, and exceedingly irritated, at first, by the will."

"Good. I'm happy you agree. However, that means James Barnett's murderer is probably a neighboring plantation owner, or someone who works for him." Kordell leaned against the pillar. "If Cyrus had not sent you north it's quite possible you might have been murdered too. I want this reception to meet your neighbors, to attempt to assess each man for his ability to commit murder, or to order it done for him. I know this is rather farfetched, but it will give me a chance to size these people up. To see whom we're up against. There'll be no opportunity once you've fired your present overseer and restored the slaves to indentured servitude."

"You're suggesting I not appoint Dagert overseer before we have a reception—if we have a reception? That would mean I leave Cyrus in control of Southern Oaks for another ten days, when each day is so important in the planting season."

"How important will it be if you're dead?" Kordell asked, and his face reflected the power, confidence, and strength of an autocratic man. "The slave revolt planned by Prosser was only two and a half years ago, Brandy, and less than a hundred miles from here. When these plantation owners find out you've restored Southern Oaks to indentured servitude they are going to be filled with fear. And perhaps panic."

An ominous foreboding engulfed Brandelene.

Then Kordell reached out and ever so gently clasped her forearms. "Brandy, I can't protect you, or myself, if I have no idea what, or whom, I'm up against. When you fire your overseer and reinstate your indentured servants, every plantation owner in this valley will know it the day it happens. And I would venture to say the animosity will be worse than when your father did it the first time." With that, he let his hands slide down her soft arms to take her hands in his. "You informed me slaves and indentured servants are not permitted to bear weapons. That means, Madame Bouclair, it will be you and me against the world, for we'll get no help from Cyrus, and we'd better know against whom to guard our backs."

"Oh, dear God! What have I gotten you into?"

"Somehow I knew when we reached our agreement that regardless of how good or how bad it was with you, it would never be dull." Kordell grinned an irresistibly infectious smile that reached his magnetic leonine eyes.

With a hammering heart, Brandelene returned his smile, reminding herself he was her adversary as surely as an unknown assailant in the dark of night. No matter, she would accept Kordell's offer and guard her back—against him too. She squeezed the hands that still held hers. "Agreed!"

"The reception will be the week-end following this."

She stood on tiptoe and pressed her lips to his brow. "I suspected as much. You have a slight fever. It's straight to bed after breakfast."

"Madame, that is the best offer you've made me since first we met."

"You do not take no lightly, do you?"

"Do not take me lightly, Brandy. Before I return to the Ivory Coast, I will possess you. And you will come to me willingly."

Chapter 14

INVITATIONS TO THE RECEPTION WERE WRITTEN BY Pearl and delivered that morning by liveried grooms. Men and women, who could little be spared during planting season, hustled in from the fields for the next ten days, to paint, clean, polish, and shine the mansion, and meticulously manicure the grounds. The mirrored ballroom, which had been closed when Brandelene's mother died seven years earlier, was aired and cleaned. Each delicate prism of the fixtures was washed, and the crystal chandeliers sparkled, recalling memories from her childhood, reminding Brandelene of happy times when soirees abounded in the mansion. The European furnishings in the ballroom were uncovered and thoroughly cleansed and, to Brandelene's delight, looked elegantly new. Guest rooms that had not been used since Southern Oaks had been converted to indentured servitude nine years earlier were aired and cleaned, for most of the guests would stay over rather than drive the long distances to their own plantations in the middle of the night.

For two days, Southern Oaks would be the center of social life, as it was built to be, as it once had been.

Meanwhile, Kordell, under Dr. Malloy's care, still needed considerable rest, and since he could not work he took it upon himself to keep Cyrus fully occupied, hoping to prevent him from leaving the plantation to start an inquiry into the facts of the marriage. The two men talked for hours each day, and Kordell insisted on teaching Cyrus to play chess, displaying a patience at which Brandelene marveled. Her stepuncle's usually belligerent moods brightened with each passing day, and as the event approached he became actually pleasant at times.

To Brandelene's astonishment, they were inundated with acceptances to the invitations from Cyrus, and a trip to Petersburg was necessary to select the special supplies and foods for the reception.

Kordell insisted on accompanying Brandelene, despite her protestations, for he would not hear of her traveling without an armed guard. Suspicious of his motives, she felt sure she knew the real reason he wanted to go to town, and it most assuredly was not to protect her. She found herself growing disturbed at imagining Kordell with another woman, and at that realization became annoyed with herself. What was wrong with her? After all, she reasoned, if he shared a woman's company while in Petersburg, perhaps he would not continuously lust after her. Was that not what she wanted?

In Petersburg, they hired musicians, selected the fabrics for Kordell's clothes, and bought a few gourmet delicacies. Brandelene, making purchases on credit, worried as the cost of the reception went higher. Kordell assured her they would find a way to handle the expense; after all it was a small price to pay for the benefits they might reap—Cyrus's public acceptance, and possibly their lives.

Finished with her shopping, Brandelene turned to Kordell who had not suggested having any time to himself. "If there's anything you wish to do while we're here," she hinted, discomposed, as a light flush crept into her cheeks, "I'll meet you in two or three hours, for tea, before we leave for Southern Oaks."

Understanding her meaning, Kordell held back the laughter that threatened. "I've already posted my letters"—he pretended to misunderstand her suggestion —"and it didn't take two or three hours."

At that, Brandelene shifted uncomfortably as she stood by the carriage. "If there's anything else you'd like to do, tell me the time to meet you, and we'll pick you up here," she offered, her blush deepening to crimson.

With a most sober countenance, Kordell pondered, and Brandelene fanned herself in agitation while she waited. "You don't ɿeed to take me to a bathhouse," he mused aloud, "for I now see o those needs myself, and I hardly think that would take two or hree hours."

Frustrated, she fumed impatiently, not certain if he were serious ɔr teased. "There's nothing you personally wish to do?"

"Madame, have I overlooked something?"

"I had said you would be permitted to come into Petersburg ɪfter two weeks. I'm offering you the privacy to do whatever you :hoose. Perhaps then you can keep your roving gaze and lusty ɿands from me."

Enjoying himself immensely, Kordell's eyes widened in surprise. 'Do you mean what I suspect?" He grinned at Brandelene's help-.essness to halt her embarrassment. "Madame," he said, his mouth ʠuirking with humor, "that doesn't take two or three hours either."

"Insufferable . . ." Brandelene's words were interrupted by the ɔrief, delicious touch of Kordell's lips on hers.

"Brandy, have you so quickly forgotten? I am a married man." Kordell swept her up in strong arms to deposit her in the carriage. Then he climbed up beside her. "Home, Joshua!"

"Yes, sir!" Joshua answered smartly and snapped the reins.

Brandelene smiled to herself, unexpectedly happy.

For the next three days wonderful aromas of baking and cooking filled the plantation house while the boisterous cook grumbled and supervised her multitude of help, complaining of the many women constantly underfoot. All of the preparations could have been better handled in the large kitchens of the common house, but Brandelene felt it would be inconsiderate to have special foods prepared in front of the near six hundred slaves with whom she could not afford to share.

For as long as Brandelene could remember, Matthew had been the family butler. Yet the efficient, always busy man was more than a butler, assuming most of the duties of a majordomo. And so it was that Matthew helped oversee the multitude of chores for the reception. Bedding and curtains for the numerous guest rooms were unpacked, laundered, and left to hang a full day in the fragrant Virginia air. Draperies, bedcovers, and area rugs, removed years earlier when all invitations to Southern Oaks had been declined, were unpacked and aired in the warm sunshine before being placed in the rooms. Formal uniforms, for the numerous maids and footmen required to see to the guests' every comfort, were unpacked, laundered, starched, and ironed. The long-unused, costly crystal, china, and silver were removed from storage, unpacked, and washed and polished to their original sparkling beauty. In the cellars of Southern Oaks, the cases of port, the gallons of whiskey, the kegs of brandy, the hogsheads of Madeira, and the casks of rum, which, unbeknownst to Cyrus, had been in storage for the past nine years, were made ready for the reception on Saturday. The guests of Southern Oaks would be entertained with a prodigal lavishness.

Friday evening, Brandelene, exhausted but smiling, approved the completed work, admitting to herself Southern Oaks had never looked better. For the first time, she appreciated the organization, coordination, and enormous amount of work required for such an undertaking, a feat performed with seeming ease by her dainty mother throughout Brandelene's early childhood, for before their ostracism the Barnetts had entertained with the same regularity as the other Virginia gentry.

All too soon, Saturday arrived. Becoming more uncomfortable by the minute, Brandelene felt her apprehension grow as uncontrolled emotions overwhelmed her. In her chemise, she sat at her dressing table while Pearl wove delicate strands of silver through her elaborately coiffed tresses. Suddenly, Brandelene jumped to her feet, slipped into her velvet dressing gown, and raced across the room to throw open Kordell's door.

Humming to himself, Joshua was assisting Kordell into his waistcoat.

Brandelene ran to Kordell and he wrapped strong arms around her.

"What's wrong, Brandy?" he asked, feeling her shake in his arms. "Are you ill?"

Pearl ran into the room after Brandelene, shrugging at Kordell's questioning look.

"Kordell," Brandelene said against his chest, "I can't go through with it."

In the ten days since Brandelene had agreed to the reception, Kordell had had ample opportunity to question, at great length, Ruby, Matthew, Joshua, Pearl, and other servants. While he rested in his bedroom, where conversations were private and free from interruption, he'd talked to the people who were closest to her and knew her best. When he finished he felt he knew and understood her almost as well as the people who loved her. He wondered if he would have asked her to endure the agony of this reception if he'd known then what he knew now.

Kordell's face darkened with the memory of part of what he had learned—of the bloody slaughtered animals and chickens left on James Barnett's doorstep after he turned his slaves into indentured servants, placed in the middle of the night as a warning; of the night people had come in the dark with blazing torches; of the fear that pervaded the mansion when no white man would work for Barnett, and Brandelene slept in her parents' locked bedroom, surrounded by her father's loaded guns, in the event the local plantation owners decided to retaliate; of the insults hurled at her when she was in public with her parents; of the time a woman spat at her, or a child threw dirt in her face or the many times children called her names while the child's parent looked on; of the country general store that refused the Barnetts' patronage; and how, eventually, Brandelene answered each sneer, each insult, and each taunt with a proud toss of her head and a haughty smile. Finally, he was told how she'd thrown her body over that of her blood-soaked father, and defiantly refused to cry.

Kordell tightened his enveloping arms. "It's all right, Brandy. I'm with you now."

Pearl and Joshua turned to leave, but Kordell motioned them back.

"How," Brandelene murmured, her tone sardonic, "can I permit those people to enter Southern Oaks when I know one of them murdered Daddy? I will be examining the eyes, the face, of every man who walks through those doors, wondering if he is the villain."

"I understand, Brandy. You don't have to come downstairs.

Pearl will help you to bed to rest." Pulling her closer, he rocked her gently as he might a child. "I'll make my excuses for you."

At those words, Brandelene stiffened in his arms. "Excuses! No one makes excuses for me!" With that, she pulled free, her pride seriously bruised by her behavior. "I shall be ready shortly," she said with firm determination, her head held high. "I won't hide in my bedroom because of them—or anyone." She hurried to her room, but stopped at the door and turned back to give Kordell a bewitching smile. "I know this isn't your problem, Kord," she said softly. "Thank you for understanding."

"Your problems are my problems, Brandy. We're in this together—all of it."

Bewildered by his words, she turned away, quietly closing the door behind her.

Brandelene moved to her wardrobe and removed a sheet-wrapped article. "Pearl, please remove the silver strands from my hair. I've decided to wear another gown."

Pearl gasped. "Brandelene, surely you're not going to wear *that gown*?"

Meanwhile in Kordell's room, Brandelene's delicate fragrance lingered behind her, and Kordell cursed himself for allowing this woman to slowly enchant him when no other ever had. Sighing, he turned to Joshua. "Does Brandelene charm every man she meets?"

"Yes, sir!" Joshua chuckled, his wrinkled face beaming. "She sure does."

"I really didn't need to ask," he retorted in good humor, standing patiently while Joshua adjusted his cravat. "I had better beware, wouldn't you agree?"

Joshua laughed heartily. "Yes, sir, I sure do. But . . ."

Kordell glanced up as Joshua's words trailed off. "You were saying?"

"Well, sir." Joshua fidgeted. "I just don't think it's gonna do you no good, no ways."

At that, Kordell threw his head back and roared with laughter. "May heaven help me, for I will surely need it."

"Yes, sir, you sure will."

A short time later Kordell strolled the balcony, attired in formal evening dress. Brandelene swept through her open French doors to join him and he inhaled sharply at the sight of her, marveling at her innocent beauty. She was a raven-haired seductress, as regal as a queen, in a gown that shimmered with every movement, and his devouring appraisal roamed the breathtaking beauty of her flawless face and temptingly curvaceous form.

No woman before Brandelene had ever stirred Kordell's emotions, but now, regardless of how he tried to banish her from his thoughts, her eyes, her soft, inviting lips, invaded his mind to the point where all coherent thought gave way to his ever-present burning desire.

"Does my gown meet with your approval?"

"You are incredibly beautiful, Madame Bouclair." His voice was sensuously husky and his naked hunger shone in his eyes for her to see. "This is your night, Brandy, for you will be the envy of every woman here. And I will be envied by every man."

"Thank you, kind sir," she drawled and smiled her pleasure at his compliment. She swallowed her comment that there could not be another man in the entire world who looked as handsome as he did right now. Nor did she tell him that after she left his room, she had put on this special gown instead of the one she'd originally planned to wear. She didn't know what had possessed her to do so, for this was not simply an elegant gown, but the wedding dress Ruby had labored over for many months, the dress Brandelene had planned to wear when she married the man who loved her for herself. The only things missing were the veil—and the man who loved her for herself. She reached back, lifted the short train, and accepted Kordell's proffered arm to go and face her enemies.

Downstairs, the marble floor in the foyer shone and reflected the sparkling prisms of the crystal chandelier, alight with a hundred flickering candles. Tall trees and potted plants had been strategically placed around the three-story entry hall and lent a warmth as well as beauty. Cyrus stood in the foyer to receive the guests, and present Brandelene and Kordell to each new arrival. Although this was an obligation he performed disgruntledly as host of the reception, it was a role Brandelene had assumed he would refuse to play.

With considerable effort, Brandelene smiled and responded graciously to the cool congratulations from the steady stream of arriving guests. Seething inwardly, resentful of her situation, she wished she could spit the insults back at those who'd hurled them at her over the years. Adding a bitter bile to her already unbearable position was the possibility that one of the men she cordially conversed with, a guest in her home, her daddy's home, might be responsible for the murder of her beloved father. With determination, she carried on with her role-playing while the neighboring gentry continued to arrive. Clasped tightly around her since they first took their positions in the foyer, Kordell's arm held her protectively close to his side, for all the world to see, and rather than objecting she found it unusually comforting.

Shortly, after all the guests had arrived, Brandelene sighed with disappointment. Dean Paul Mason, the man she had considered marrying, had not come. She had hoped, even depended on, her only friend among the gentry being here to lend his support. In hopeful expectation, she glanced through the open portals and down the lengthy driveway of Southern Oaks, but no other carriage rolled into sight.

Most of the guests who'd had long drives retired to their rooms to freshen up.

Brandelene mingled for a while, then excused herself and made a final survey of the mansion. The entire main floor, except for James Barnett's library that she'd locked, was open for the guests' use. Floral arrangements, spilling their fragrance, abounded throughout the plantation house and filled the air with a heady perfume. Women servants, meticulously attired in stiffly starched black gowns with ruffled white aprons and mob caps, bustled through the rooms with silver trays containing crystal goblets and decanters of assorted spirits, or appetizers. Minstrels strolled throughout and filled the manor with lilting music.

Satisfied with the results of her hard work, Brandelene paused to wish that Ruby and Pearl were here, not only to share in her achievement, but to lend the moral support she needed from loved ones. However, Ruby, Pearl, Joshua, and Dagert had been instructed to absent themselves from the reception to avoid any questions that might be asked of them.

Joshua had retired to his room, but Dagert invited Pearl to walk with him. Indeed, at this moment the couple strolled the edge of the gardens. Ruby, who insisted on accompanying them to chaperon her daughter, followed at a short distance.

Inside the mansion, Brandelene accepted a goblet of sparkling wine from a passing servant and then moved to the dining room for a last inspection. It was customary on occasions such as this, since some guests had spent hours traveling the long distances between plantations, that the guests eat shortly after arriving.

Silver candelabra, gracing the beautifully laid table and sideboards, were alight with flaming candles that cast their flickering light over her mother's china, silver service, and crystal stemware.

The crystal sparkled and the silver gleamed in remembrance of days long past.

Brandelene's eyes shimmered with unshed tears at the memory of the last time the tableware and fine linen had been used, when her mother lived.

When Brandelene had prepared the menu for the reception she'd refused to consider using expensive, imported delicacies, for her meager financial reserves were dwindling fast. Instead she opted to use Cook's considerable expertise to prepare assorted hot and cold dishes using the plantation's fresh beef, pork, duck, and chicken for the entrees, plus the large assortment of foods stored in the enormous cellars. A wide variety of side dishes complemented the main course and the sideboards in the dining room abounded with desserts of every kind. White-gloved footmen, with snowy white, starched fronts, stood quietly waiting to serve the guests. Sighing, she instructed Matthew to announce the invitation to dine and moved to join her guests.

Due to the large number of people in attendance, dinner was an informal affair with the guests selecting their choices from the hot buffet. Following a footman who carried their plates of food and drinks, the guests repaired to the elegant, mirrored ballroom where tables had been set up for the occasion. The hundreds of candles in the chandeliers flickered reflectively in the ceiling-to-floor, gilt-framed mirrors surrounding the room and created the magical illusion that the room had no walls, with one mirror reflecting endlessly into another. A bouquet of flowers graced each table and hanging baskets of flowers, decorated with burgundy bows and streamers, surrounded the high-ceilinged room. The numerous mirrored French doors stood slightly ajar, permitting the soft Virginia breeze to float through the room, and the fragrance of the multitude of flowers wafted in the air. Musicians played on a raised dais at the northern end of the large ballroom and entertained the guests with the beautiful strains of music that filled the room. It was exactly as Brandelene had imagined her wedding reception would be. It was perfect—except her beautiful, gracious mother, her loving, honorable father, and the husband whom she loved to the depths of her heart and who loved her equally were missing. She quickly blinked back tears of self-pity. It was an indulgence she could not afford.

After dining, the guests wandered throughout the mansion and lantern-lit gardens while servants cleared the ballroom for dancing.

It was then that Kordell sought Brandelene among the guests; when he saw her, she took his breath away. Crossing to her side, he guided her to the ballroom, pausing at the door to take in the loveliness of the room. As instructed, half the candles in the chandeliers had been snuffed, leaving the room bathed in soft golden light. The tables were gone, replaced by tall, potted plants and small trees that Brandelene had selected individually from the Southern Oaks's forest. They merged with the hanging baskets of flowers and were reflected again and again in the surrounding walls of mirrors, giving one the feeling of being in an airy indoor garden. Rich burgundy and dusty rose velvet European settees and chairs were arranged around the perimeter of the floor, amid the potted plants and trees.

Amazed by her accomplishment, Kordell bent and whispered, "My compliments on the outstanding job you've done, Brandy."

Brandelene reveled in the warmth of his remark.

The musicians played and Kordell turned to Brandelene. "May

I have the pleasure, Madame Bouclair?" His voice was deep and sensual as he extended his arms.

Unusually happy and not sure why, she smiled, lifted the train of her gown in one hand, and slipped her other hand around his broad shoulders. Then Kordell pulled her soft body enticingly close to his, and aware of the many couples drifting into the room, she did not draw away. After all, the bride and groom were expected to start the dancing. She shivered in his tight embrace and wondered if it was the wine, or his intoxicating nearness, that caused her to feel light-headed as he whirled her around the floor with an expertise that surprised her. Now his masculine scent filled her nostrils and she could feel his muscular chest crushing her breasts, his firm flanks swaying against her. His body gently massaged hers and sent a searing flame through her abdomen. Rapidly, her heart beat against his granite chest and she tingled warmly all over. With gazes locked, oblivious to everything and everyone else, she floated in Kordell's arms. His leonine eyes burned with desire as they devoured hers and their intensity caused her knees to tremble, but she was powerless to turn away, drowning in their depths.

Then Kordell lowered his tawny head to press his warm cheek to hers and Brandelene closed her eyes, surrendering completely to the moment. Her senses swam from his suffocating sensuality. Their bodies, melded together, moved as one to the music and she was lost to everything but the delicious feelings that engulfed her.

Groaning inwardly, Kordell's lips moved to her ear where he pressed a light kiss before he whispered, "Tell me now, Brandy, that you don't want me as much as I want you."

She felt her heart flutter crazily and so weak was she that she feared her own legs would not support her if he should suddenly release his tight clasp. "I don't want you for my husband," she murmured, her throaty voice breaking with the tumultuous emotions that rushed through her unbidden.

"My husband will be a man I love with all my heart and soul. A man who loves me for myself, a man who will love me forever, and I will have no other!"

Possessively, Kordell pulled her tighter into his arms and she gasped. "You already have a husband, my beloved," he breathed into her ear. "Certainly you haven't forgotten already."

His breath was warm, his voice strong and velvet-edged. "You . . . my . . . beloved," Brandelene accented each word silkily, then continued, "are not my husband and never will be." She felt him nuzzle her neck as he spun her around the mirrored ballroom and she abandoned herself to the whirl of sensations that splintered through her body, telling herself she dare not pull free with so many guests to witness it. Barely able to speak, she murmured into his neck, "I'm not interested in a fortune hunter who lusts after me. The streets are lined with those kinds of men."

At that, Kordell twirled her through the open doors onto the shadowy, lantern-lit terrace. "Is that what you think, Brandelene?"

"Yes. That's exactly what I think." She leaned back in his strong arms, but hard thighs molded her even closer as his hand, at the small of her back, held her unyieldingly.

"I am not a fortune hunter, Brandy."

"I suppose you're going to tell me you're madly in love with me?"

Silence greeted Brandelene's question and Kordell's gaze once again held hers.

"At least you didn't lie to me, Kord. I respect you for that." Although she recognized the seductive look in his smoldering eyes, still her heart whirled giddily as his head lowered to capture her slightly parted lips. Why did he affect her so? Why did her resistance completely slip away in his arms? Dreamily, her consciousness seemed to ebb. Abruptly she turned her face away before his beguiling mouth claimed hers, partially regaining her senses while her heart beat a rapid tattoo. "We are in private now," she said, but her shaky voice betrayed her actual feelings.

Kordell lifted his head to gaze down at her face, exquisite in the dim shadows. The music filtered through the open doors to where he held her in his arms and he reluctantly released her. When Brandelene was near, as now, all principles, all thoughts of Nicolle, and all self-control vanished. Only his insatiable desire existed, his uncontrollable yearning for this one woman, and he was powerless to help himself. She had become a persistent, unrelenting obsession. He could not continue like this. She was driving him half-mad with longing, and he cursed his continuous craving for a woman who was forbidden to him by agreement. The agreement be damned! He would have her. Tonight! Brandelene would release him from their cursed agreement, he would see to that, and then he could spend the next five months satiating his obsessive craving, and then return to Nicolle and the Ivory Coast. In the depth of his savage hunger for Brandelene, reason fled, replaced once again by a solution that would give him what he desperately wanted, what he had to have—Brandelene—until he returned to the Ivory Coast.

Besides, did not her every kiss say she wanted him as much as he wanted her? And had he not already signed the petition for annulment? Therefore, since he would not contest the document, Brandelene could have what she wanted—the annulment; and so too he could have what he wanted. Brandelene. In his bed. Tonight.

Chapter 15

A COUPLE STROLLED ONTO THE TERRACE, CLOSELY followed by another.

"We are not in private now," Kordell murmured and crushed Brandelene to the rock-hard wall of his chest before she could object. His mouth possessed hers and stole her breath away.

Surrendering, she lifted her hands to twine in his hair while she pulled him ever closer. Eagerly she pressed her body to his and the feel of his virile physique drew her as a magnet. Her heart palpitated wildly, about to tear free of its moorings, as his demanding lips smothered hers with a hunger that sent shock waves through her entire body. Then his devouring kiss overwhelmed her, commanded her intimate response, and her mouth melted into his in a searing fusion that left her weak and confused.

Kordell clasped the feminine softness contoured against him as his other hand wandered over her bare back, and though he pressed her closer, still it was not enough. His body hungered for hers, and he could think of nothing but possessing her completely as his desire tore, unsated, through his loins. What was wrong with him? Never had he thrown caution or good sense to the winds over a woman. But Brandelene was a potent drug in his veins and he was helpless to deny the powerful hunger that only she could satiate. Nor did he want to. Finally he drew his mouth from hers. "I want you, Brandy! God help me, for I want you so much. You can still get an annulment without the doctor's certificate. I'm sure of it. Be mine . . . tonight."

"No. Never," Brandelene protested softly, her lips still moist from his intoxicating kisses. She could sense the barely controlled power coiled in his body. "Never!"

As she spoke, Pearl and Dagert were walking in the copse of trees at the edge of the gardens while Ruby trailed behind, and all three unwittingly became witnesses to the scene between Kordell and Brandelene.

"Oh, Lordy! I warned that child to watch out for that good-looking devil. I told her!" Ruby hustled to catch up with her daughter and grabbed Pearl's arm. "You get yourself into the house before that happens to you and we got double trouble." Ruby pulled a reluctant Pearl through the gardens and they started up the rear stairs. "You're not gonna see that charming giant again."

On the terrace, Brandelene pulled herself from Kordell's embrace. "We should return to our guests."

Kordell nodded and said, "Brandy, I need to spend as much time as I can talking with the plantation owners." Then his hands slipped down her arms to clasp hers. "If I don't dance with you as much as you think necessary to convince all the wagging tongues that we are happily married, I hope you understand."

"I rather imagine the way you already danced with me, and the couples strolling the gardens who witnessed us here on the terrace, will stop any gossip of that nature. Wouldn't you agree?"

"Perhaps I should be absolutely certain." With that, he pulled her back into his arms, lowered his head, and his mouth hungrily covered hers in a burning kiss she passionately returned. After a time he lifted his lips from hers. "Brandy, you will be . . ."

Reaching up, Brandelene placed her fingertips to his lips to still his words. "A faded memory, someday," she finished his sentence, then took his hand and led him back into the crowded ballroom. Once inside, she turned to glance up at him. "I'll mingle with our guests and see if I can detect more than the usual hostility or antagonism toward me." Standing on tiptoe, she brushed his mouth with a brief kiss. "For the benefit of the guests," she teased, and her eyes glinted mischievously before she moved off into the crowd, unaware of Kordell's gaze following her.

Sweeping through the ballroom full of ladies in pale, elegant ball gowns and gentlemen in evening dress, she ignored the women's scornful glances and the men's assessing gazes. Why had they come? But she already knew. There was not a woman here who'd not been forced, by a curious husband or father, to attend. Would the new master of Southern Oaks adhere to Cyrus's policy of slavery, or the hated James Barnett's operation with freed blacks and bond servants? The atmosphere was charged with unasked questions.

Brandelene determined she would learn nothing by dancing with any plantation owners. If any asked her to dance, he would have only one reason and she would have to contend with endless queries. Therefore, she deduced as she attended to her duties as hostess, more benefits would be reaped from talking with the wives and daughters, whose inquiries would be of a far different nature than the men's. She intended to reply to no queries about Southern Oaks. This decided, she spent most of the evening answering a multitude of questions about Kordell. Fearful of drawing suspicion, she answered openly and related almost verbatim the tale Kordell had told Cyrus. By the time the evening turned to early morning she'd repeated the story so many times she almost believed it herself.

She was disappointed, for she'd been able to find out little, other than that the wives and daughters still considered her a traitor. She could feel their contempt, their animosity, barely concealed below the surface of their polite, trite conversation. Now, her head held high, she was moving to find Kordell when, turning a corner, she almost ran into Dean Paul Mason.

"Ahh, beautiful lady. I thought I'd never find you alone," the tall, attractive man she'd known since early childhood said pleasantly. "How are you, Brandelene?"

"Dean Paul! How nice to see you." She remembered when the young man had courted her, before her father's death. Dean Paul had been the only neighbor, indeed the only white person other than Dr. Malloy and the lawyer Thompson, who had attended her father's funeral. The rites had been held in the family cemetery on Southern Oaks where her mother, grandmother, and grandfather rested. When she'd been unable to cry at her father's graveside, her grief beyond consolation, Dean Paul had tenderly held her in his arms. Pulling herself from her memory, she glanced up into the bright blue eyes of the attractive blond man and held her hands out to him.

Dean Paul pulled Brandelene to him and briefly they hugged each other.

At that moment Kordell stepped into the wide hall and observed his wife in the arms of another man. Stepping back, he watched from a distance. He was furious with Brandelene, but even more so with himself for the feelings that tore though him.

"Oh, Dean Paul, it's so wonderful to see you again," Brandelene said excitedly and leaned back against the silk-covered wall. "I do believe you're the only friend I have here."

"What of your husband?"

Flustered, Brandelene flushed uneasily. "Of course, he's my best friend," she said and glanced back up at the man who, five months earlier, had asked her to marry him. "I meant you're my only friend among all these guests. In fact, you're probably the only guest who isn't my enemy." With that admission, she quickly moved to another subject. "I watched for you all evening. How ever did I miss you?"

"I arrived only a short time ago," Dean Paul admitted, and reached out to touch Brandelene's arm, then dropped his hand helplessly to his side. "The last place in this whole world I wanted to be was at the reception for your marriage to another man. But I had to come."

"Don't talk like that," Brandelene scolded gently. "You'll find a woman who deserves you more than I do." She slipped her hand through his arm. "Why don't we go into the drawing room where we can sit and talk?"

"Your husband's quite handsome and personable," Dean Paul commented coolly, but the blue eyes that raked her face openly reflected his infatuation. Placing his hand over her own that rested on his arm, he slowly walked with her toward the drawing room.

It was a gesture and a look that did not go unobserved by Kordell before he moved away.

Brandelene and Dean Paul had been childhood playmates until her father had turned their slaves into indentured servants and the boy had been forbidden by his parents to play with her. However, when Brandelene turned sixteen, the then eighteen-year-old Dean Paul had started calling on her, unbeknownst to his family. Their friendship had bonded when he'd courted her that year before her father's death, and her feelings had developed into deep affection and respect. However, Dean Paul was in love. When he asked her to marry him she had never experienced being in love, so she could not say what it was like, only what it wasn't. True, she cared deeply for Dean Paul, but she didn't love him, and she yearned to marry a man she loved.

Even so, after she returned from school, over five months earlier, she'd considered marrying Dean Paul. To save Southern Oaks from ruin, and its people from slavery, she would willingly have given up her dreams. For Dean Paul agreed that, as her husband, he would reinstate Southern Oaks to the state of bonded servitude, as it had been before Cyrus assumed control. She had no doubt he loved her, and for herself alone. As the only son of the Masons, Dean Paul was heir to a large estate, second only to Southern

Oaks in the Piedmont Valley, so he did not seek her fortune. Still, if Dean Paul freed Southern Oaks's slaves it could result in the young man being disinherited and disowned, for his father was a zealous advocate of slavery. It could possibly result in a blood feud. And her conscience would not permit her to ask so much from him.

But the deciding factor in her refusing Dean Paul's offer of marriage was an unsettling fear at the back of her mind that once she and Dean Paul married, he would be so strongly influenced by the father he loved and admired that he would give in to his father's strong will and keep Southern Oaks immersed in slavery. As his wife, with the law siding with her husband, she would be powerless to do anything about it. It was a risk she was afraid to take. The thought of such a happening was intolerable, for, to the depths of her soul, she believed every person should have the right and privilege of living free.

Brandelene and Dean Paul entered the drawing room occupied by only three women who chatted at the far end. She sat down and turned to face Dean Paul who had lowered his tall frame into the chair next to her.

"Oh, Brandelene. Why did you marry another? You knew how much I loved you." Dean Paul had to pause to recapture his composure. "I know you cared for me."

"I do care for you. I care a great deal." Deciding it might be less painful for him if he did not know the whole truth, she added, "I loved you too much to come between you and your family."

Understanding, Dean Paul sighed. "Do you love your husband? I need to know."

"Kordell is very considerate of me, Dean Paul, and I need him. You must forget me, for you and I can never be more than friends."

He reached out and lightly fingered a loose tendril of raven hair on her cheek. "I will never forget you, Brandelene. Nor will I ever stop loving you." Suddenly aware of the impropriety of his action, he withdrew his hand. "The only reason I came was to warn you."

"Warn me of what?"

"That all these people are here for two reasons—to find out if you're going to reinstate Southern Oaks to indentured servitude, and to try to determine how strong your husband is, how powerful, how wealthy. I'm sure none of them are pleased with what they've seen, for it is obvious Monsieur Bouclair is not a man to be tampered with." He took a deep breath and asked her the question to which so many had tried to find the answer, but lacked the nerve to ask directly.

"Are you going to restore Southern Oaks to bonded servitude?"

Brandelene hesitated, her gaze moving from the watered-silk that veiled the walls to the Aubusson rugs that decorated the oak floors. Then she answered simply, "Yes."

"I was sure you would," Dean Paul confessed. "Oh, Brandelene, I fear you're in for trouble. If you ever need help of any kind, send for me. If your husband isn't good to you, send for me. If you merely need a friend, send for me."

"Thank you, Dean Paul. I appreciate your consideration. There is one thing I would ask of you."

"Anything, Brandelene. Anything."

"Please don't tell anyone what we're planning at Southern Oaks. We haven't informed Cyrus yet."

Dean Paul laughed softly. "You have my word on it. So Varner is hosting your reception unaware that you're going to go against his wishes."

Paling at his last words, Brandelene remained silent.

Dean Paul rose from his chair. "I'll take my leave, Brandelene. Remember, if you need me . . ."

She rose and placed her hand on his arm. "Dean Paul, forgive me if I've hurt you. I never intended to. It's simply the way things worked out." Brandelene slipped her arm through his and walked with him to the foyer, her swaying, crystal-beaded skirts flashing a rainbow of colors in the candle lights.

"You've sacrificed everything for Southern Oaks," Dean Paul said. "I know you well, Brandelene. If you don't love this man you've married, you'll never be happy." With that he bowed low over her hand, turned and left.

Matthew, his face an unreadable mask, wordlessly held the open door for young Mr. Mason to leave.

Turning back, Dean Paul called out, "Remember, if you ever need me . . ."

Brandelene watched Dean Paul out of sight, then straightened her shoulders and lifted her head high with determination. Turning back, she found Kordell lounging casually against the balustrade.

"How long," Brandelene demanded to know, "have you been standing there?"

"Long enough to know we had better dance if we are to stifle any gossip about my wife and her former lover."

"Dean Paul is not my former lover," she snapped, her eyes blazing.

With barely controlled rage, Kordell crossed the foyer in quick strides to glare down at her. "He damn well better not be." Roughly, he grabbed her elbow to escort her to the ballroom. "If you have played me false, madame, you will regret it, I assure you."

Brandelene jerked free of Kordell's grasp and the open palm of her gloved hand struck him full across the face. "Think twice before you insult or manhandle me again."

"Without doubt, you are a black widow spider."

"Rather appropriate, wouldn't you say? After all, I'm married to the devil incarnate."

Matthew, a silent observer of the scene openly played out before him, coughed loudly and Kordell turned to see two guests stroll into the foyer on their way to another part of the mansion.

Reaching out, Kordell dragged Brandelene back hard, close to his side. His arm encircled her and he led her, unprotesting, toward the ballroom. Once inside, he pulled her into his arms and whirled her around the floor.

Where Brandelene had melted into his arms earlier, she was now rigid, seething with anger; his captivating gaze that had thrilled her before, she now returned with fiery indignation; and his tight embrace that had sent wonderful intoxicating flames searing through her body now filled her with barely controlled fury.

"Smile, my lovely spider, unless you wish to undo all we've accomplished, if you haven't already."

Hastily Brandelene forced a smile to her lips and hated the involuntary thud of her heart when Kordell rewarded her with a larger smile of his own, a smile that never reached his eyes.

"Since you conveniently neglected to mention your Dean Paul to me," Kordell said in French, "what, or whom, else have you conveniently forgotten to mention?" The strong hand at the small of her back was firmly possessive as he deftly guided her among the other couples on the dance floor.

"Dean Paul is none of your affair."

Scarcely suppressing his anger, Kordell whirled Brandelene through the open doors onto the crowded terrace, and swiftly led her to a large oak in the gardens. None too gently, he placed her back against the towering tree, and his hands against the knurled trunk pinned her between his strong arms. Enraged, he glared down at her shadow in the starlit, moonless garden and she could feel the heat of his anger. "It damn well is my affair if another man has bedded my wife when our annulment is contingent upon her virtue being intact."

Now calm, Brandelene's voice came from out of the shadows, soft, controlled. "Our annulment's certainly been of no consideration to you lately, while you've pursued me like a rutting stag to get me into your bed. Where was your concern for the annulment then?"

Frustration the likes of which he'd never known overwhelmed Kordell and he fought the urge to shake the truth out of the black widow spider he'd had the misfortune to marry. "We're not leaving here until you tell me the truth, Brandelene."

"And, my *beloved* husband, will you believe the truth if I tell it to you?" With that, she reached up and placed gentle fingertips on Kordell's chiseled face, then let them slide sensuously down his square jaw to his strong chin. "And even then, how will you have the proof of it?"

"It would seem, if you've had a lover, you've played me the fool, madame. Therefore, if I'm trapped into being your husband, I am claiming my rights." All rational thought gone, he swept her up in strong arms to carry her toward the mansion.

Chapter 16

STRUGGLING FUTILELY, BRANDELENE POUNDED KORdell with clenched fists. "Put me down, Kordell!" she raged. "You lay one hand on me and I'll blast you to kingdom come!"

With his mind set, Kordell ignored her threats and tightened his grip on her struggling body, striding swiftly with her clasped firmly in his arms.

"I've never been with a man, I swear on everything holy," Brandelene pleaded as she kicked and squirmed to free herself from his iron grip. When he neared the west wing of the plantation house Brandelene went limp in his arms.

"Please, don't! I'm begging you. Don't." She sobbed helplessly into his neck, her tears trickling slowly down into his shirt. "Oh, please, Kord, don't do this."

Kordell stopped midstride. He glimpsed the white, wrought-iron settee, changed direction, and carried her there. Easing himself down with Brandelene still in his arms, he cursed the day he'd first looked into her mesmerizing violet eyes, then cursed the desire that now raged uncontrollably through him. All reasoning ability had fled and all he could think of was Brandelene beneath him, Brandelene passionately returning his kisses, Brandelene surrendering to him.

Instantly her sobs subsided and she sat up straight, and wiped the tears from her face with the back of her hand.

Kordell fumbled in his pocket and handed her his handkerchief. "Do you," he snapped testily, "never carry a kerchief of your own?"

"I would have," she retorted, sniffling, wiping her face with the rough linen cloth, "if you'd warned me you were going to attempt to ravish me."

"I would've been happy to give you advance notice, madame, if you'd informed me I'd find my wife in the arms of another man."

Brandelene stiffened. "You saw that?"

The warmth of her burned through the layers of fabric separating their bodies, and Kordell groaned inwardly. "I and God only knows who else saw that. I suppose your conniving little brain already has an explanation."

"If you saw, then you know there is naught to explain."

Instantly his hands flew up to clasp her arms. "You had damn well better try, Brandelene, or I will finish what I started."

"I knew I'd regret saving your hide."

Kordell sighed. "Brandy, considering our agreement, don't you think you owe me an explanation?"

"You won't believe me."

"Try me."

"Dean Paul was the only white person who would be my friend after Daddy changed Southern Oaks. He called on me, without his family's knowledge, for almost a year before Daddy . . ." She took a deep breath and continued, "Dean Paul asked me to marry him after I returned from Boston." She paused, gazing into Kordell's eyes, and tried to determine in the dim light if he believed her.

"And why didn't you?"

"I was afraid he'd maintain slavery at Southern Oaks. And . . ."

"And what, Brandy?" His deep voice trembled with his controlled anger, his bridled desire.

Now Brandelene turned away from him and inclined her head. "And although I love him, I'm not in love with him."

At those words, Kordell released her and moved his fingers to gently cup her chin, turning her face to his.

To her stunned surprise she heard him say, "I believe you, Brandy." His voice was tender and his breath, warm on her face, was strangely soothing.

Kordell slipped one arm under her legs to lift her as he stood up, and after setting her on her feet, he pulled her close to his side as he started toward the ballroom. "We'd better join our guests, while I'm still able."

Sometime later, after the guests had retired to their rooms, Brandelene tossed fitfully in her tester bed. She stared wide-eyed at the canopy overhead, and tried to find the answer to a question that plagued her. Why had Kordell so readily released her when she'd told him she was not in love with Dean Paul? Before that he'd been incensed. Even angrier than when he realized she'd slipped laudanum into his drinks. Yet, at her simple explanation, he'd instantly believed her when he would believe nothing else she said. Why? She had no answer but finally she fell into a troubled sleep.

The following morning Brandelene dressed and hurried downstairs before any guests were up and smiled with satisfaction at the immaculate rooms. Following her mother's example, she'd given instructions for a fresh team of servants to come in and clean after the guests retired. Even the ballroom and the kitchen sparkled, ready to begin anew. Quite successfully, she had planned, organized, coordinated, and overseen a soiree of the highest magnitude, and she knew her mother would have been proud of her.

Breakfast was casual, with guests ordering their choice of foods and most were served in bed. Later, Brandelene organized a game of croquet while Kordell started a game of cricket.

The lawns of Southern Oaks, in the warm afternoon, were filled with happy, laughing guests, as they'd been the first ten years of her life. Yet where she'd been happy and carefree then, today she was filled with barely concealed bitterness as she once again searched each guest's face for the slightest hint of guilt.

The aroma of spit-roasted beef filled the air. A barbecue, complete with the wines, brandies, whiskeys, and rums from her father's private reserve, was held in the late afternoon. It plagued her to suspect James Barnett's murderer might be not only roaming James's home, but also drinking from his private stock. Regretting she'd allowed Kordell to persuade her to have this mockery of a reception, she looked for him. He was strolling across the lawns, deep in conversation with two plantation owners, carrying himself like Caesar, and he looked more the aristocratic master of a plantation than any of the gentry in attendance. He was magnificent. Disturbed, she turned away, and the afternoon wore on interminably.

At long last the guests were gone and Brandelene fled to her room. She rested for a while and later went out on the balcony, still dressed. Although she'd rung for Pearl to assist her out of her gown, the young woman had not answered the call. Troubled by her thoughts, she breathed in the cool, fragrant night air, and waited for Joshua to leave Kordell's room before she asked her husband's assistance. Crickets chirruped, tree frogs croaked, leaves rustled in the indolent breeze, and she was filled with a yearning she'd never before known.

"Brandy." Kordell chuckled as he came out of his room. "You needn't fear to walk your own balcony without being fully dressed. I don't intend to replay my exhibition of last night."

"Actually, I came out here to have you undo the fastenings on my gown. I rang for Pearl, but she must be asleep. She didn't answer the bell." Noticing a movement out of the corner of her eye, she turned toward the oak-lined driveway where the unmistakable shadow of Dagert walked beside a considerably smaller, slender shadow.

Kordell's gaze followed Brandelene's, then he grinned down at her. "I think that explains why Pearl doesn't answer your ring."

Astounded, Brandelene looked back to the two hazy shadows. "Dagert and Pearl?"

"You didn't know?"

"No, but I've been so involved with all the arrangements for this sham of a reception . . ." Brandelene watched the two shadows melt into one and her eyes widened in alarm. "Kordell, Dagert's not married, is he?"

"His wife and son died in childbirth several years ago."

"I'm so sorry. Dagert never mentioned it. It must've been very painful for him. He's such a caring man."

Surprised by her reaction, Kordell glanced down at her, a perplexed expression on his face.

Smiling to herself, Brandelene watched the shadow separate and become two. Pearl slipped into the house and Dagert turned toward his quarters.

"Dean Paul warned me we might have trouble if we reinstate bonded servitude. He said if . . ."

"You told Dean Paul?"

"Yes. But only because he can be trusted."

Without a word, Kordell climbed over the balustrade and jumped silently to the ground, then ran off in the direction Dagert had taken.

Confounded, Brandelene lifted her skirts and raced back into the house and downstairs, meeting Pearl. "Come with me, Pearl. There's no time to explain."

The two women hurried onto the veranda and saw Kordell returning with Dagert.

"Kordell, what has possessed you?" Brandelene asked. "Dean Paul won't tell anyone."

"Brandy, if you wouldn't trust the man enough to marry him, why would you trust him with this information, especially after he believes you've spurned him for another?"

Alarmed, Brandelene asked, "What do you want me to do?"

"Rouse twenty men who can be trusted and have them meet me here," Kordell ordered. "Be as quiet as possible, so you don't wake Cyrus, or the overseer. Dagert, you escort Brandelene. Pearl, you stay here and watch for movement of any kind. If you see anything at all scream at the top of your voice. I'll be right back." With that, Kordell ran into the house.

Dagert hurried toward the slaves' quarters and Brandelene rushed to keep up with his long strides. When they arrived Brandelene pointed out the selected cabins, one by one, and cautioned Dagert to be as quiet as possible in order not to awaken Cyrus's chief overseer.

Heavily armed, Kordell waited on the veranda with Pearl when Brandelene and Dagert returned with the group of men.

Although Brandelene could not see them in the dim starlight, she could imagine Kordell's dancing eyes and a smug look on his face. Then she saw the guns. "Where," she snapped, knowing the answer before she asked, "did you get those weapons?"

"From your father's gun cabinet in his library, of course. My beloved wife would certainly expect me to protect her."

"That room," Brandelene sputtered, "was locked."

"As was the gun cabinet."

"Kordell . . ."

"Brandy," Kordell interrupted her, "I'd love to discuss this with you now, but unfortunately there are other matters more pressing at the moment." Drawing in his breath slowly, he glanced down at her, still dressed in her lovely gown, her hair still woven with tiny flowers. She looked so softly feminine, so vulnerable, and a fierce need to protect her filled him; a desire to place his strength between her and the world, so nothing, or no one, would ever harm her again.

Confused by his emotions, he turned to Pearl. "Will you accompany Brandelene to her bedroom. She must be exhausted."

"Not you, not anyone, tells me what to do." She stood her ground and glared at him where he stood, spread-eagled, on the veranda. His full-sleeved shirt, open to his waist, revealed his muscular chest, and his breeches fit his slender hips so snugly she felt the heat rise to her face. He wore cordovan knee-high boots, and tucked into his waist was a brace of pistols. In each hand, he held a rifle. She had never seen a more masculine man.

"Curse you," she muttered softly.

Kordell nodded toward the gathered slaves. "My darling, have a care. Now be a good girl and run along to your room where you'll be safe."

"I'll go . . . my darling," Brandelene answered with a syrupy sweetness, for the benefit of the gathered men, "but only to change my clothes." With a swish of her skirts, she whipped past him, then paused. "I shall be back directly."

With Brandelene gone, Kordell quickly issued his orders. All were to patrol, unarmed, on horseback. Four men were to patrol the grounds of the plantation house, four the slaves' cabins, two the stables and outbuildings, six the fields, and the other four were assigned to outposts. They were to sound an alarm to alert Kordell and Dagert of any intruders, or attempts to destroy any part of

Southern Oaks. Additionally, they were instructed not to fight, but to protect themselves if necessary. The men had been dispersed to their assigned areas when Brandelene and Pearl returned.

Kordell leaned one shoulder against the wall and watched Brandelene, a pastime, he scolded himself, he seemed to be indulging in quite a bit of late. She wore a figure-hugging riding habit and boots, and had not brushed out her elegantly coiffed hair, still woven with tiny flowers. "Madame Bouclair, is it true you have some knowledge of guns?"

"I'll stake my aim against yours anytime."

Kordell handed her a pistol. Taking the weapon, she checked it was loaded with powder and shot, and slipped it into the waistband of her riding habit.

"At least," he smilingly approved, "you were well instructed."

"Daddy did everything well."

"Including pampering his feisty, strong-willed daughter?"

"If we're going to examine each other's character," she flung back, "I have much to say on the subject of yours. Shall I start with last night when you . . ."

"Brandy, another time please."

"Yes, I would think so."

"Madame Bouclair."

"Must you call me that?"

"I was under the impression that was your name," Kordell said, determined he would not let her goad him into another verbal duel.

"Only for as long as absolutely necessary."

"That remains to be seen, madame." The words had no sooner left his lips before he wondered why he'd said them.

At Kordell's remark, Dagert and Pearl, who'd silently listened to the exchange, glanced at each other in astonishment. Dagert held out his hand and Pearl moved to his side to lace her slender fingers with his.

"Before you start counting your money," Brandelene said, "may I remind you that you've already signed the annulment documents?"

Groaning inwardly at his foolish remark, Kordell forced his

thoughts back to their current problem. "Did your father also teach you how to use a musket?"

"Of course."

"Brandelene," Pearl volunteered proudly, "can hit a pebble with a musket while riding horseback."

"Why am I not surprised at that?" Kordell said and handed a flintlock to Brandelene.

Automatically, she cocked the flint and checked the priming pan, then glanced up at him expectantly. Kordell informed her how he'd deployed the twenty men and she nodded her approval. "I understand your precaution, but it's unnecessary. Dean Paul would never betray me. He gave me his word he wouldn't tell anyone."

At that, Kordell chuckled. "My beauty, if there's an assault on Southern Oaks, I assure you it will be led by the men who work for the father of your wonderful Dean Paul."

"Why do you say that?"

"As you informed me, and I was fiercely reminded by our guests, a revolt by slaves is greatly feared, even by the most considerate of slave holders," Kordell answered and reached out to tenderly brush her cheek with his knuckles.

Abruptly, she drew away from his disturbing touch.

"The senior Mr. Mason was adamant, and quite vocal, in his disagreement with your father's position of turning slaves into indentured servants. He's strongly against it and extremely pro-slavery."

"You think he is responsible for Daddy's murder?"

"No, I would guess not," Kordell replied, thoughtful. "That person, I'd imagine, would keep a low profile and not attract attention to himself. After all, we are talking about the murder of an extremely prominent citizen of the Virginia gentry." Deep in thought now, he walked the long veranda, then returned to Brandelene's side. "Now that your Dean Paul knows your plans—I know you trust him, but how dependable is the word of a besotted man who believes he was scorned for another? We have no choice but to inform Cyrus at breakfast and make the changes tomorrow.

I had hoped to have a couple of days to prepare, but we'll have to make the best of it."

"All right."

Abruptly, Kordell straightened and took her arm. "You must be exhausted. You can see you're well protected if we get unexpected visitors, so why don't you get some sleep?" Placing his hand at her elbow, he led her toward the entry doors. "I'd feel better if you were out of harm's way."

"Out of harm's way!" Brandelene exploded, jerking free of his warm touch. "I don't need protection by you or anyone, Monsieur Bouclair. I'm surprised I need to remind you, I'm quite capable of taking care of myself."

"You can't resolve this matter with laudanum, Brandy."

She bit back a bitter retort. "There is a matter I wish to discuss with you. Perhaps I can take this opportunity."

At her words, Kordell turned to Dagert. "Dagert, take this rifle and pistol," he directed in a low voice. "I'll get myself another. As soon as I return, station yourself on the rear terrace and alert us of any trouble that arises. I strongly caution you about using those weapons. We don't know the laws in the United States governing free black men using guns."

"I know Dean Paul won't deceive me," Brandelene said hesitantly, "but it would be helpful if Pearl went with Dagert. Then if there's a problem she can run through the house to warn us." Turning, she smiled at her delighted friend. "Would you mind, Pearl?"

"I'll be happy to help in any way I can."

Kordell slipped into the mansion and quickly returned with another pistol and rifle, and then Dagert and Pearl entered the house to take their post on the rear terrace.

After they'd left, Kordell motioned to the furniture on the veranda. "We may as well be comfortable, Brandy. There's something I've been wanting to ask you."

At his gesture Brandelene lowered herself into a chair. She placed her rifle across her knees and waited until Kordell sat in the chair next to her before she asked, "What did you want to ask me?"

"Brandy"—Kordell's deep-timbred voice boomed, then dropped to a spine-tingling softness—"why did you labor so passionately to save my life when it was to your advantage to let me die?"

At his velvety question, she froze. After an interminable minute, she asked in a hushed tone, "What did you say?"

"Why did you save my life when it was to your benefit to let me die?"

"I'm sure you will give me cause to ask myself that same question, many times, during the next five months—exactly as I'm doing now."

"You didn't answer my question."

The intensity in his lowered voice touched a chord that compelled her to give him an answer. "I don't know why," she said softly. "You needed me, and I couldn't let you die without trying. I couldn't live with the guilt of knowing that if I hadn't insisted we leave for Southern Oaks right away, or if I hadn't slipped laudanum into your drinks, you might not have become so ill. And . . ."

"And what, Brandy?"

"Damnation!" she flared. "And nothing, that's all. There is nothing else."

The silence was long and tension-filled. Finally Kordell said, "You said you wanted to discuss something with me."

"I fear Dagert and Pearl are becoming quite involved with each other."

"You fear? I'm happy for both of them. You've nothing to fear. Dagert is everything good you know him to be, plus more."

"I was sure of that. However, that is not my concern. My apprehension is that five months from now Dagert will return to the Ivory Coast, which is understandable. That's his home and he can live there in complete freedom."

"If you want me to assure you Dagert will marry Pearl and take her home with him, I can't do that."

"That's exactly what I am worried about. That Dagert *will* marry Pearl and take her home with him."

Astonished, Kordell merely stared at her. "Do you have some

objection to two people who love each other being happy?"

"Of course I don't."

"Then what possible objection could you have? Dagert would be a wonderful husband and father."

"I'm sure he would be. But it would break Ruby's and Matthew's heart to have their only child leave, to know they'd never see her again, or their grandchildren."

Kordell leaned forward in his chair and said, "Brandy, from what I've seen the last few days, Dagert and Pearl are falling in love. Do you suggest I intervene? Would you deny Pearl her chance at love? You, who have gone to ridiculously absurd lengths in order to have the one you would love?"

Brandelene absently watched the men who patrolled the grounds, then raised her gaze to find Kordell looking at her.

"Why don't we leave them alone, and let fate make the decision?"

At his suggestion, Brandelene weakly nodded her assent. "But . . . Pearl is so sensitive and she has no experience with men. I'm also afraid she'll come to love Dagert more than he loves her, and then he'll leave her behind with a broken heart."

"Is that why you avoid me?" Kordell pressed softly. "You're afraid I'll leave you when the six months are up?"

Brandelene's eyes widened in astonishment. "You're the most conceited, the most egotistical person I've ever met. Why do you find it so impossible to believe I have no personal interest in you?"

One brow rose and Kordell's gaze captured hers in the dim starlight. "Even you cannot deny the passion we share." He paused. "Brandy, are you afraid you will come to love me?"

Chapter 17

"I WOULDN'T FALL IN LOVE WITH YOU, KORDELL BOUCLAIR," Brandelene blazed, "if you were the only man on this earth!"

"Why?"

"Because I abhor arrogant fortune seekers!"

The shadows of the dim night on Kordell's carved face were strangely unnerving as he leaned forward in his chair and pinned her with his stare.

"I suppose you deny you're a penniless fortune hunter," she said.

"I don't seek a cent of your damnable inheritance, which under the circumstances is nebulous at best." He picked up her hand and examined it where it rested in his. "Pretend, for the moment, Brandy"—his voice was soft, almost mesmerizing—"I could prove I don't want any of the questionable fortune you so zealously guard. What would be your objection to me then?"

Bewildered and at a loss how to reply, she was anxious to escape his disturbing presence, his probing questions, but dared not leave her post. Why did he press her so?

"Brandy, you didn't answer me. What would be your objection to me if I could prove I do not seek your inheritance?"

"I don't wish to play this game with you any longer, Kordell," Brandelene shot back and jerked her hand from his. "It no longer amuses me." Then she leaned against the cool hardness of the wrought-iron chair to listen to the soothing sounds of the night. Sighing, she wished it could have been otherwise with Kordell, but she was acutely aware it was not. Her misery forced its way to her soft lips. "It certainly didn't take you long to forget your precious Nicolle. Your beautiful, wealthy Nicolle, the fiancée you were so in love with," she scoffed, breaking the silence that was thick between them.

Now Kordell's brow shot up in surprise. "I never claimed to be in love with Nicolle. And she isn't my fiancée." He leaned back in his chair and casually studied her. "You mentioned Nicolle once before. How do you know about her?"

Flushing warmly, Brandelene flinched at his question. She could not betray that Dagert had reluctantly answered her probing queries. "You rambled about a lot when you were delirious," she divulged in a half truth. "You talked about Nicolle."

"I love Nicolle, but I'm not in love with her. That's why I could so readily accept it as the truth when you told me the same about Dean Paul. Only someone who has experienced such feelings could have uttered those words."

"And yet," Brandelene said critically, "you were going to marry her?"

"It's a long story, Madame Bouclair. I'll tell it to you sometime, if you're interested."

"What I am interested in, Monsieur Bouclair, is why you would abandon a woman you admittedly love to consummate a marriage to a woman you do not love? Please explain that to me, *my beloved husband,* if you can!"

For some time, Kordell's penetrating gaze held hers. "I can't," he admitted. "I only know there is something special between us. I cannot name what it is, for I don't know."

"Well, Kordell Bouclair, I can name it," Brandelene snapped and jumped to her feet, clasping her rifle firmly in her hand as she glared down at him. "It is your lust. Your lust for a woman, and your lust for gold. Go to Petersburg for the first, and home to Nicolle for the latter, for you are not going to satisfy your desires for either with me."

Irritated, Kordell stood up, towering over her. "Then you have named it, Brandy. But it is *our* lust. And since you've brought up the subject, I have accepted your word about Dean Paul, and that your virtue is intact. However, if I ever have cause to believe otherwise . . ."

She shivered as if he'd touched her physically. "Go to Petersburg, Kordell, or go to hell. I don't particularly care which, but leave me alone." Then she flew down the stairs of the veranda with her musket in hand. She marched to the nearest towering oak and sank down to the cool grass, then leaned her back against the rough tree trunk. Gazing up at the star-filled sky, she rested there and allowed her tormented thoughts to wander where they would until the charcoal sky melded into the first rays of dawn's light. Tired, and with every bone in her body aching, she came to her feet, brushed her skirt, then walked past Kordell, where he sat on the veranda. She stopped before entering the mansion and said smugly, "I knew Dean Paul wouldn't betray me."

"If you were so positive, why did you sit up half the night with a flintlock across your knees?"

"Damnation!" she said and sped to the rear terrace to get Pearl. Stopping short inside the French doors, she watched in fascination the couple who were unaware of her presence.

Pearl leaned against a massive pillar, her face radiant as she gazed up at Dagert who dwarfed her slender form. Dagert's arm was outstretched with his hand braced on the pillar as he stared down at Pearl, a look of awe on his face. Then the pair laughed at something they discussed and Pearl, in her mirth, leaned her head against Dagert's brawny arm. Dagert's countenance sobered and his arm slipped around the young woman. Tenderly, he pulled Pearl to his herculean body and rocked her in his arms, his head bent to rest on hers with a gentleness that brought tears to Brandelene's eyes.

Filled with a deep longing that ached to her core, Brandelene watched Dagert tenderly stroke Pearl's head, and she straightened with a renewed resolve. She would find that kind of love for herself, the kind of love that had so elusively escaped her, if she spent the rest of her life searching. Sighing, she turned away, not wishing to observe the lovers in secret, and collided with Kordell.

His hand went out to steady her.

"Must you spy on me?" With that, Brandelene jerked free of his disturbing touch and bustled from the room to seek a servant to bring her water for a bath before breakfast.

Turning back, Kordell glanced outside to the scene between Dagert and Pearl. A scene Brandelene had been so absorbed in that she'd not heard him approach, and a grin widened his carved lips. "Ahh," he said with understanding, "Madame Bouclair wishes to be courted. If that's what it takes to rid myself of this eternal craving—this ridiculous obsession—so be it!"

A short time later Brandelene, bathed and dressed, tapped lightly on Kordell's door.

He was waiting for her, so they could go downstairs together, as they'd done each morning since arriving. "Good morning, Brandelene."

His deep voice was soothing, yet oddly distracting.

He moved in swift strides to her side and she reached out her hand to take his arm, as she had each morning since they arrived. Only today Kordell took her hand in his, and bowed low to briefly press warm lips to the back of her hand, his gaze holding hers all the while. He straightened, handed her a freshly picked red rose, and murmured softly, "That color is quite becoming on you. But then you make every color more lovely, Brandy." Pleased, he smiled at her puzzled look, and slowly regarded her upturned face with a look as intimate as a caress. He slipped her hand through his arm and placed his hand over hers.

Charmed, Brandelene sniffed at the fragrant rose in her hand, recalling another time Kordell had given her a rose. When they had married. It had been that considerate gesture that had kept her from fleeing the gardens where they exchanged their vows.

In the dining room, even Cyrus was in exceptionally good spirits, and chatted all during breakfast about the success of the reception.

After breakfast, Kordell glanced briefly at Brandelene, then turned his attention back to the man. "Cyrus, shall we retire to the terrace? There's a matter I wish to discuss with you."

Cyrus lumbered out onto the terrace, trailed by Brandelene, then Kordell.

Brandelene watched Cyrus sink heavily onto the iron settee as she moved to the edge of the terrace with her heart in her throat. This was the moment she'd dreaded, from the time she'd first contrived her scheme to regain control of Southern Oaks.

Confidently, Kordell sauntered to her side. He placed an arm around her and gave her a comforting squeeze.

The look in Kordell's eyes told her he realized the importance of this moment as well as she.

Cyrus glanced up questioningly at them.

"When we agreed to marry," Kordell began, "I assured Brandelene I wanted no financial interest in Southern Oaks. I consider this her personal property to do with as she pleases. I have my own estates." Pausing, he pulled his wife closer to his side and smiled down at her. "And, as such, Brandelene wishes to reinstate Southern Oaks to its former status of operating with bonded servants as her father—"

"No!" Cyrus bellowed, outraged, pulling his immense bulk from the settee. "No! I won't have it!"

"You won't have it?" Kordell said coldly. "You have nothing to do with it, Cyrus. This is Brandelene's estate. We are merely apprising you of the change as a courtesy to you since you're . . . since you were the only family she had."

"As her guardian I forbid it!" Cyrus raged and his bloated face turned from red to purple.

"Cyrus, you ceased being Brandelene's guardian the day we wed."

"You married without my permission! I'll have this marriage set aside." Cyrus fumbled for a handkerchief, wiped the sweat from his face, and turned to leave. "I'll have it annulled."

"Cyrus!" Kordell thundered. "I've warned you about interference with my marriage."

Snorting, Cyrus turned back. "If you're so wealthy, why haven't we seen any of your money? Which banks do you keep it in, Bouclair?"

At those dreaded words, Brandelene half slumped in Kordell's arms.

Kordell swept her up. "Cyrus, see what you've done. You've upset her terribly. Dr. Malloy thinks she is with child."

Appalled, Cyrus's pudgy face paled. "You're lying! Brandelene wouldn't disgrace her father's name in such a manner."

"Ask Dr. Malloy, if you think I'm lying."

"I will!" Cyrus shrieked and tramped into the mansion, bellowing for Matthew to have the carriage brought around.

"Put me down," Brandelene demanded, casting Kordell a hostile glare. "How dare you tell Cyrus such a thing!"

"Dammit, Brandelene!" He set her gently on her feet. "I know this is your game, but if it fails, Dagert and I are going to hang with you. I'll tell Cyrus anything I can to keep him from annulling this marriage." A flash of humor crossed his face and he grinned at her. "And it happens to be the truth. You know Dr. Malloy mistakenly thinks you're with child."

"You've as good as told Cyrus we, ahh, that we, ahh," Brandelene stammered, flustered, "that we knew each other before we married."

Kordell's laughter was full-hearted. "I wonder what Cyrus would say if he knew we not only did not ahh before our marriage, but we haven't ahh'd since our marriage either."

"How can you make jokes at a time like this? You're the most insensitive . . ." Then as she considered what she'd said, she tried to suppress a giggle. "You're impossible." Unable to help herself, she laughed. "You were right about one thing, Kord. It's not been dull." So saying, she sank down into a chair. "Well, husband, since we're shackled together, do you have any suggestions?"

Kordell's face sobered. "Actually the situation is no worse than you'd originally anticipated, and with Cyrus's public approval, it's considerably better than we'd hoped. This is exactly what we'd expected from Cyrus when we first arrived at Southern Oaks, but we were lulled into a false security when we were able to persuade him to host our reception. Correct?"

"Yes."

"So let's continue with your plans. I'll summon the chief overseer and terminate him immediately. I don't want the man on the premises now that Cyrus knows our intentions. Then I must make haste and go to Petersburg, so I can return before dark."

"Why do you need to go to Petersburg?"

"Surely you haven't forgotten so soon," he teased and his eyes twinkled mischievously. "Only a few hours ago you told me, 'Go to Petersburg, or go to hell.' Personally, I prefer the former."

Astonished, Brandelene stared at him, then turned away, experiencing mixed emotions. Suddenly she was overwhelmingly tired, and leaned her head back in the chair and closed her eyes.

"I'll summon the overseer," Kordell announced, and Brandelene nodded, her eyes still closed.

A short time later Kordell, with Brandelene at his side, dismissed Varner's harsh overseer. He gave the man a month's pay along with the explanation that his services were no longer needed. Kordell instructed him to pack and leave immediately. Dagert escorted the man, who spewed profanities and threats, to his cabin to assist him in gathering his belongings.

With the two men out of sight, Kordell turned to a pale-faced Brandelene. "If there's anything you need from Petersburg, write it down. Keep it to necessities only, I won't have any spare time. I'm going upstairs to change before I leave."

Unable to help herself, Brandelene studied his tall, dapper figure. His massive shoulders filled the light blue cutaway coat he wore, his navy waistcoat stretched tautly across his powerful chest, and his snug-fitting navy breeches, above knee-high, black Hessians, emphasized the strength of his thighs and the slimness of his hips. Annoyed, her voice dripped with venom as she said, "You're not dressed well enough to call on a strumpet?"

Kordell's eyes flashed with amusement. "Ahhh, Madame Bouclair, there's hope for us after all," he chided gently. "I had not realized you cared. Is that a hint of jealousy I detect in your tone?"

"Only your insufferable conceit could permit you to twist a simple question to your own interpretation," she retorted and her face flamed at his accusation. "Personally, Kordell Bouclair, I don't care what you do."

"The lady's question would seem to indicate otherwise. Are you so positive you don't?"

Brandelene refused to dignify his question with an answer.

"In the event you do care, my proud beauty, let me assure you I have no desire to be with any woman other than my wife—"

"And," Brandelene interrupted icily, "it will be snowing in Hades before you'll ever be with this wife."

"As I started to say, you need not worry that I'll be with a woman while I'm in Petersburg."

To her dismay, she felt relieved at his words. His golden eyes smiled at her, touching her everywhere, and she had the sensation of being stripped naked. It was a heady, exhilarating experience. Without otherwise touching her, he lowered his head to briefly touch his lips to hers, then turned and hurried from the room.

She frowned at his back and closed her eyes in exasperation. She knew what Kordell was up to and yet she was helplessly drawn to him. "I won't play the simpering ninny for him," she vowed aloud. "I've been wooed by others as charming as he . . . well almost, and resisted. Damnation, why did I have to save the life of a rogue contemptible enough to reward my deed by using me?"

"I wonder who you're talking about?" Pearl grinned as she walked into the room. "Brandelene, you're in serious trouble when you start talking to yourself."

"Oh, Pearl," Brandelene wailed. "I detest him! He's a fortune hunter! He's pompous! He's . . ."

"Extremely charming and incredibly handsome," Pearl added, "not to mention so masculine."

"Thank you, Pearl, for your support. You've been very helpful," Brandelene said, her voice heavy with sarcasm as she walked toward the arched opening. "Now, with your comforting words in mind I'll go list a few things for Kordell to get while he's in Petersburg."

Pearl followed behind Brandelene. "Why do you fight that man so hard? I don't understand you."

"Pearl, he only wants me for my inheritance."

"Be happy you have the money to buy a man like that."

"Buy a man." Brandelene was appalled. "I'd die a spinster before I'd buy a husband."

"Seems to me, you already have."

"I'm in no mood for your humor." Brandelene turned to continue on her way to the library.

"I can sure see that," Pearl called out to Brandelene's retreating back.

Brandelene made a short list of necessities and gave it to Matthew for Kordell. Not wishing to see her husband again before he left, she'd started toward the rear of the mansion when she heard the rattle of wagon wheels. Returning to the library, she glanced out the French doors to see Kordell, astride her father's stallion. He wore a brace of pistols in his waistband and was slipping two long flintlock rifles into leather sheaths on the spirited horse. Behind him, two men sat on the driver's wooden bench of a plantation wagon, and the fired overseer, with his possessions, sat in the otherwise empty bed. There was no carriage in sight.

Tormented, she recalled the easy target her father had been in the relative safety of a carriage that traveled at a much faster speed than Kordell would ride accompanying a wagon. What did he need a wagon for? What if he was detained and did not return until after dark? He would be an open invitation to ambush.

"Oh, dear God!" she gasped and threw open the French doors to run out onto the veranda. "Kordell!" she screamed as he pressed his booted heels into the flanks of his mount and started down the driveway.

"Wait! Don't go!"

Chapter 18

At the sound of Brandelene's voice, Kordell reined in his horse and trotted back to her.

Picking up her skirts, she raced down the stairs to meet him. "You can't go on horseback," she insisted, her fear reflected on her face.

Kordell leaned down, encircled her waist with a strong arm, and scooped her up into the saddle in front of him. He felt her quivering in his arms.

"I'll be back before dark, Brandy. Please don't worry."

Unsteadily, she twisted in his arms and looked up at him with large eyes. "You shouldn't be riding horseback," she murmured, distressed, yet unable to voice the depth of her fears for his safety. "Your ribs aren't properly healed."

"I had Joshua bind me especially tight."

"You're too recently out of a sickbed. Why, you're still weak. You'll be of no use to me if you're sick in bed. Besides, I'll not have time to tend a sick man again." His strong arms were warm and comforting, and she chastised herself for loving the feel of his embrace. "There is so much to be done. Why must you go into Petersburg today? It's far too dangerous. Unless, of course, you're really going to visit some trollop."

Kordell contemplated her upturned face, inches from his. "Why would you care if I sought out another woman for the favors you deny me as your husband?"

"Damnation! I don't care with whom you consort. But must it be today?"

"Madame, I'm not going into Petersburg to dally with a woman. I have much to do, since you confided in your wonderful Dean Paul. I need to prepare a warning system for Southern Oaks. I'm sure you'll agree we can ill afford to have twenty bondsmen patrol the grounds during planting season."

"Of course I do. But why can't you send a servant? No one would try to harm him."

"I realize that. But a servant might be detained by the plantation owners. Unquestionably, no one will detain me. What if one of the merchants refused to sell to a servant? We don't know what's going to happen, Brandy." Smiling, Kordell brushed a strand of wispy hair from her face. "Besides, if I can't find one item, I'll have to use another. This is too important to allow someone else to do it. I won't rest easy until I know we have an alarm procedure set up."

Kordell grinned and gave her a heart-stopping squeeze. Her heart raced, pounding in her ears, and her gaze fastened on his irresistible carved lips, so temptingly close. If only . . .

"Kiss me good-bye," Kordell demanded huskily and his mouth curved into a captivating smile. "For the servants."

Helpless to deny him, Brandelene closed her eyes and bent her head back to receive the burning lips that sweetly pressed against hers. Gently he covered her mouth in an endless kiss, a tender, drugging kiss that set her aflame. Her hand slipped to clasp the back of his head and she kissed him with the wild hunger that raced through her veins.

Lifting his mouth from hers, Kordell looked into her eyes, searching for the reason for her response, but he found no answer there. "I had better leave."

"Kordell, take care. Daddy . . ."

"I have no intention of making you a widow, my beauty, after all the trouble you went to keeping me alive," he assured, and slowly lowered her to the ground. Then he bent from the back of his stallion to brush her lips one last time. "*Au revoir,* Brandy."

She watched him trot down the oak-lined driveway, seated ramrod-straight in the saddle, as impressive as a prince. Simply dressed in a white linen shirt, snug-fitting breeches, and knee-high boots polished to a high sheen, his tawny hair glinted with golden streaks in the early morning sun, and she could but admire his virile masculinity. The feel of his ardent kiss still lingered on her lips. She turned back toward the mansion, to see Dagert's puzzled look and the knowing grin on Pearl's face.

Suddenly elated, Brandelene cried out, "Dagert, I can't wait to tell everyone the good news. Please have the people gather on the common grounds, and you and Shadrach join me there on horseback. It will be a day of celebration."

"Yes, madame," Dagert replied.

Southern Oaks, like most large plantations, was like a small village with its lanes of cabins that housed the slaves. Also on the plantation were a gristmill, sawmill, tobacco warehouses, tobacco curing barns, and open sorting sheds, as well as a granary, livestock barns, stables and coach house with quarters for grooms, and several outbuildings and sheds, as well as small structures such as a blacksmith, cobbler, leather worker's, or buildings where wool was carded, hides were tanned, mattresses, quilts, and pillows were made, and where clothes were cut and sewed. There was a midwifing house and a five-bed building for the sick. Additionally, there were several food-storage buildings, a laundryhouse, slaughterhouse, meathouse, smokehouse, icehouse, and tool sheds.

But at Southern Oaks, unlike other plantations, there was the common house and the large surrounding recreational area referred to as the common grounds.

James Barnett had made Southern Oaks's transition from slavery to indentured servitude informal to attract minimal attention to the conversion. He had not furnished each slave with a document of manumission, granting freedom, and then, in turn, acquired a signed contract of indenture. He had simply explained what he was doing and how he intended to do it. Records were kept as though each person were an employee with an hourly wage. Food and clothing expenses were then deducted from that wage and the surplus was credited toward the original purchase price of that slave. He issued documents of manumission when earned, as any gentleman of honor would have done.

While James Barnett lived nothing else had been necessary.

After James's death, Cyrus Varner arrived and realized that the informal conversion was not legal, nor recognized by the Commonwealth of Virginia. By law the bond servants were still slaves, and slaves they would always be while Cyrus was in control.

Cyrus had refused to pay wages. Consequently, nearly two hundred former slaves, who had earned their freedom under James, left, except for Ruby, Matthew, Pearl, Joshua, Shadrach, and his mother.

Although Cyrus had not been a cruel master, he permitted his newly acquired white overseer, a hard taskmaster, to have free reign over the slaves and life became drudgery for the former indentured servants.

Now the slaves of Southern Oaks gathered on the grassy land of the tree-shaded common grounds. There had been little reason for happiness since Cyrus Varner assumed control.

The hundreds of dark faces turned toward Brandelene as she, Dagert, and Shadrach rode among them. She nudged her stallion to a small knoll and reined the horse around to examine the crowd of expectant people. What she saw was the shame and disgrace of slavery; those who'd labored for too many years and were old before their time; those who'd seen too much pain, too much suffering, and lived without hope; the mothers who now desperately, fearfully, clung to their babies and children; the couples who cleaved to each other in fear.

Fear of being sold.

Brandelene loved these people and was responsible for their well-being. Now her fervent wishes, and those of her beloved father, were about to be fulfilled. Pausing, she glanced around at the familiar faces. She'd known many of these people all of her life. Blinking back unbidden tears, she knew, without reservation, this moment was worth all the sacrifices she'd made.

Exhilarated, she smiled with an elation she'd not known since her father died. She had envisioned this from the day she returned to the South and discovered Southern Oaks immersed in slavery.

"Friends," Brandelene started, but her voice broke with emotion. Composing herself, she started again, "I waited to tell you of my marriage so I could tell you two wonderful things at the same time. My husband wanted to be here with me when I told you, but he had to take care of a matter of importance to us all. However, his friend, Dagert, is here in his place." With that, she smiled up at Dagert who sat astride his horse, next to hers.

"My daddy wrote a paper called a will that said if he should die his stepbrother, Cyrus Varner, would be in charge of Southern Oaks until I married. He hardly knew Cyrus, but he believed the man was honorable and would carry out his wishes. We've all seen that Cyrus was not the man Daddy thought him to be." She swallowed the lump in her throat, took a deep breath, and pushed to the back of her mind the events that must have transpired in her two-year absence. That was the past and she could not change the past, but she could change the future. "In that same paper Daddy wrote that when I married, my husband and I would control Southern Oaks."

Inhaling deeply, she shouted, "You are no longer slaves! This is once again James Barnett's Southern Oaks!"

Deafening cheers rang through the air. Then everyone laughed, or danced, or cried, or all three at once. Ecstatic, Brandelene smiled as tears of joy streamed down her cheeks. She wished Kordell could share in the rejoicing for what could not have been accomplished without him. She glanced at Shadrach, who openly wept.

Now she turned to Dagert. "I have something more to say," she shouted over the boisterous revelry of celebration.

"Quiet!" Dagert's voice boomed over the din. "Quiet!"

An anxious hush fell over the crowd and all eyes apprehensively turned toward them.

Brandelene smiled dazzlingly. "Daddy's lawyer will prepare documents of manumission, your papers of freedom, in writing, and contracts of indenture with all the conditions, for each one of you. After you have those papers, you can *never* be enslaved again. Shadrach will explain these papers to you and answer any questions you may have." At the jovial shouts she held up her hand for silence and her spirited stallion nervously pawed the ground. Patting the animal's withers, she continued, "While the papers are being written, Pearl will talk with each of you so we can adjust and update the records for the time Cyrus Varner was in charge when no records were kept. You'll be given credit for that time toward your servitude. All children born during that period will immediately be issued documents of manumission, so you need never fear for them."

Murmurs of disbelief echoed through the throng and Brandelene once again held up her hand for silence. When the cheers subsided, she said, "Starting tomorrow, Dagert will be the chief overseer. But today will be a day of celebration." Standing up in her stirrups, she waved her riding hat in the air as the crush of people closed in on her. Her tears flowed freely as she shouted, "Welcome back to James Barnett's Southern Oaks!"

Over the din, Brandelene yelled to Matthew, "It's to be a day of little labor. There will be no butchering for fresh meat today. Open the meathouse and the wine cellar."

That evening, Brandelene stood with Dagert and Pearl on the veranda. The festive sounds of fiddles, banjos, and handmade flutes, accompanied by singing and laughter, floated up to them. Anxiously Brandelene watched the slowly setting sun, her apprehension obvious. "The guards are all at their posts?" she queried, already aware they were, but hesitant to voice aloud her fears for Kordell.

"Yes," Dagert answered.

Curious, she glanced at his emotionless countenance. "You've been distant this entire day, Dagert," Brandelene said. "What is the problem?"

"There is no problem," Dagert said quickly and stared straight ahead.

At his swift denial, Brandelene glanced up. "I know better."

"It's something that's none of my affair, and not my place to say."

"That may be, but I still insist you tell me."

"It's Kordell . . . and you."

Brandelene asked, "What about Kordell and me?"

"I've seen what's happening between you two. I figured it was part of your ploy to deceive Cyrus—until this morning."

"Does that bother you, Dagert?"

"Yes."

"Dagert!" Pearl exploded in alarm, pulling on his arm.

"Why?" Brandelene pressed.

"Because Kordell's almost betrothed to Nicolle. Because Kordell has a trail of broken hearts behind him. Because I care for you and respect you, and I'm afraid you, or Nicolle, are going to be terribly hurt."

"And," Brandelene added gently, "you love Nicolle dearly, like a sister, and want Kordell to marry her?"

Dagert's gentle, dark gaze met hers, pleading for understanding. "Yes."

"I understand, Dagert," she assured and the warmth of her smile echoed in her voice.

"Brandelene," Dagert said, "Kordell will wed Nicolle. Not because it's what I want, but because it's what he wants. Don't let him hurt you."

"This morning shouldn't have happened, Dagert. I won't be tempted again. If Kordell doesn't return to Nicolle, it will not be because of me." She realized that if she did not halt her overpowering attraction to Kordell, she soon would not have the strength to deny him. She resolved to put an end to her growing feelings, regardless of the difficulty. With Cyrus no longer present, the principal reason for their charade was gone. There would be little required to keep up pretenses for the bond servants. So, she reasoned, by eliminating all physical contact with Kordell, time would cool her unexplainable ardor. Besides, she would now be in the fields most of the time.

Kordell rode his stallion toward Southern Oaks and the pain from his unhealed ribs shot through his chest with every hoofbeat. The wagon, filled with supplies and hounds, their barking and baying now quiet, slowly followed. It had taken much longer than he anticipated to find and purchase the twenty-six hounds that rode nervously in the wagon.

Frowning, Kordell glanced at the setting sun, aware he would not arrive at Southern Oaks until long after dark, and he wondered if Brandelene would worry about him. Smiling, he realized how often of late his mind had led him to Brandelene. She taunted and tortured his thoughts at every turn, twisting him into an emotional tightrope. Yet, just when he decided she was an ice maiden and determined to dismiss her from his mind, she gazed at him with jewellike eyes and melted into his arms, setting him ablaze with a fire no other woman could ever extinguish. The fiery memory of her yielding softness against his body this morning overshadowed all else and filled his chest with a pounding heart. She was in his blood as no other woman ever had been. Silently he agonized over what to do about it and gently nudged his mount into a faster pace.

Once again violet eyes invaded his unwilling mind and Kordell surrendered and allowed his reflections to drift where they would. They turned to sweet, gentle, lovely Nicolle, with hair of gold and eyes as blue as the sky. Had Nicolle ever pressed him to the point of uncontrollable rage? Never! Had Nicolle even caused him one moment of aggravation? He could not remember one. The fantasy of Nicolle standing with a pistol in one hand and a whip in the other was so ludicrous he could not conjure up the image in his mind. Try as he would, he could not envision Nicolle, a widow who'd shared a man's bed, ever responding to his kisses with passionate wild abandon as Brandelene had, and that disturbed him. As a memory of Brandelene came to mind he asked himself if Nicolle, or any woman, had ever started a fire raging in him that threatened to totally consume him with its heat.

The answer quickly came of its own accord. Although countless women had fired his loins, only one woman had ever torched his soul.

Abruptly, his thoughts snapped back to the present and Kordell glanced at the disappearing sun, conscious that he had many miles to travel on the dusty planters' road, and all of it passing by the lands of hostile neighboring plantation owners. He confirmed that his pistols were primed and loaded with powder and shot. Then he hefted one long flintlock from its holder and thoroughly checked the priming pan before he placed it back in the scabbard. Examining the other musket, he held it in the crook of his arm. Leaning down, he reached in his saddlebag to feel the box of premeasured charges in silk tubes. Brandelene had not saved his life to have him murdered on the same roadway as her father had been.

Alert now, he scrutinized each shadowy tree that lined the road for any sign of movement. When he once more was surrounded by open fields of tobacco, he relaxed and Brandelene, once again, lingered around the edges of his mind. He wondered if her emotional farewell this morning could be an indication her feelings for him were ripening. Had she decided to give in to the overwhelming, unexplainable magnetism they shared, and waited, even now, to welcome him to her bed? Eagerly he urged his stallion on.

When Kordell arrived at Southern Oaks, he leaped from his mount, threw the reins to a waiting groom, and hurried into the mansion, envisioning the passionate welcome from his wife.

Chapter 19

"YOU CERTAINLY TOOK YOUR TIME TO RUN A FEW errands," Brandelene said when Kordell strode into the library. Relieved to see him, she fought her overwhelming urge to run and throw her arms around him, to tell him how worried she'd been. Instead, her voice held only aggravation. "I was about to send Dagert to search for you and I can ill afford to take him from the plantation."

Kordell glared at her, then stomped from the room.

It was several hours before he returned. Exhausted, he dropped into a chair in James Barnett's library, his brow beaded with perspiration. The pain of his partially healed ribs tore through his chest and the weakness from his recent bout with lung fever left him exhausted. He had finished overseeing the task of preparing Southern Oaks with a warning system against intruders, and had reduced the necessary patrol guards from twenty to five. This released the other fifteen men to work in the all-important job of transplanting the tobacco seedlings. Southern Oaks's tenuous salvation was dependent on a good crop this year.

Kordell felt almost as bad as he had at the beginning of his illness. He realized he'd pushed himself near the limit of his physical endurance, and considering that it was only a month earlier that Brandelene had labored so exhaustively to save his life, he hoped his overexertion would not spiral him into a relapse. Briefly he glanced around the library, dimly lit by one oil lamp with the wick turned low, then leaned his head against the high-backed leather chair while his hand rested on his flintlock. Only ne other time in his life could he remember when he'd been so ired—during his recent illness. He closed his eyes for a moment.

The twenty-six hounds Kordell had purchased were tethered t strategic locations around the plantation and their barking would lert the five guards of the presence of any intruders. Tomorrow, e planned to have one of the plantation carpenters start making he animals small shelters, but for tonight they would sleep on he ground. Experience had taught him that dogs, after being tied nd fed at their assigned location for a month, would consider his their home and would no longer need to be restrained. They hen could roam the area, which would make them even more aluable.

In addition, places where anyone on horseback would be exected to ride were ensnared with braided twine. Cowbells were ied to the twine so that anyone riding on the paths or driveway fter dark would clamor a warning that could be heard a great listance. With these two alarm systems, plus the five mounted nen who patrolled, he felt sure that no one could sneak up to the lantation manor house, the bond servants' quarters, or the fields eing prepared for planting. That done, he took comfort in being easonably secure that he could protect Brandelene and Southern Daks.

While Kordell rested in the library, Brandelene, unable to sleep, lipped on her flowing ivory silk and lace dressing gown, picked p her pistol and musket, and descended the stairs.

The white-haired house servant assigned the task of alerting he household in the event of trouble sat in the dark of the foyer vith the twin entrance doors to the veranda wide open. "Can I get you somethin', Miss Brandelene?" Isaac meekly inquired out f the darkness.

"No thank you, Isaac. I'm restless and can't sleep." Aimlessly, he walked across the foyer toward the veranda. Seeing a light in he library, she changed direction and moved to the open door. At first glance she saw Kordell, asleep in her father's favorite chair. Her instantaneous reaction of irritation rapidly melted into concern vhen she saw the drawn look of exhaustion on his handsome face. On closer examination, she noticed the beads of perspiration on his brow and the slight flush of his cheeks. Quietly she stole across the wood-paneled room to a large, carved armoire and, setting her candle, pistol, and musket on a nearby table, removed a lap robe. She crossed the room and placed the warm blanket over her sleeping husband. Then she curled up into the companion chair next to him.

He had risked his fragile health today to protect Southern Oaks and only one reason could she find: noblesse oblige. His honor.

Sometime later, Kordell awakened to the loud barking of dogs and the frantic cry of a mounted bondsman.

"Trouble's a-comin'! Trouble's a-comin'!" The guard raced his horse across the manicured lawns of Southern Oaks to bellow his warning.

Kordell jumped from his chair and threw aside the blanket that covered him. Puzzled, he glanced from the warm covering to Brandelene, where she'd fallen asleep in the chair next to his.

Isaac pounded heavily on the library door. "Trouble! Trouble!"

"Ready!" Kordell shouted back, hearing Isaac's heavy footsteps disappear as the servant ran to awaken the rest of the household. The clock chimed twice and Kordell picked up the oversize pistols from the commode table by his chair, shoved them into his waistband, then hurriedly checked the loading in the flintlocks. With a musket in each hand, he ran to the French doors. Through the many paned doors he could see, in the black of night, the numerous flaming torches that swiftly approached the mansion. Turning back, he watched Brandelene pick up her musket.

"Brandy! Douse the lamp, then go immediately to the rear terrace. Dagert has been instructed to meet you there and see to your safety." At the look of defiance on her face, Kordell commanded, "I don't want you involved in this. That's an order!" With that, he threw open the French door, bounded across the dark veranda and down the stairs. Fearlessly he stood in the driveway, waiting for the torch-bearing men on horseback who galloped up the long entrance to Southern Oaks.

Barefooted, Brandelene silently raced across the drive, behind Kordell, and stopped by the trunk of a giant oak to catch her breath. The dogs barked frantically, and the approaching horses' hooves thundered ominously.

"Don't come any closer!" Kordell boomed, his voice threatening. He stood, his flintlock to his shoulder, and faced the men with blazing torches. He drew a bead on the broad chest of the lead man. "Unless you want your head blown off!"

At Kordell's threat, the seven men reined to a rumbling halt, then glanced hesitantly from one to another, unprepared to find someone waiting for them this time of night.

With the intruders' attentions on Kordell, Brandelene crept across the lawn from tree to tree. Stark terror swept through her body when she noticed that each of the seven men on horseback carried flintlocks, and wore a kerchief to cover the lower half of his face. She was standing close enough to the nearest masked man to see, by the flickering light of the fiery torch he carried, the cold gleam of hatred in his eyes.

The glow from the flaming torches cast eerie orange shadows over everything it touched, and she felt a vivid, icy fear, the likes of which she'd known once before, twisting around her heart. It was déjà vu—the same sounds of horses' hooves thundering over the driveway, the same horrifying, yellow-orange glow from the torches that blazed in the black of night, the same terrifying fear that knotted in her stomach, and the bile that threatened to rise in her throat. Only that other time she'd been ten years old and trembled in her mother's shaking arms, while her father stood on the veranda to face the torch-bearing, masked riders. She shuddered.

But this dark night she would cower to no man. Never again would she live in fear, she resolved. With trembling but determined hands she raised her flintlock and carefully aimed it at the large figure of Harold Lee Mason, Dean Paul's father, whom she would recognize anywhere. Burning pitch from the flaming torches assailed her nostrils, and the acrid smoke that stung her throat hung heavy in the air.

"Harold Lee Mason!" Brandelene's voice shot out of the darkness beside the mounted men. "If anyone harms my husband, or puts a torch to Southern Oaks, you will be the first to die!"

Speechless, the masked riders turned toward the voice of the petite woman, in silk and lace nightclothes, with her flintlock pointed directly at Mason's head.

The torchlights glimmered on the long, threatening barrel.

"Do not make the mistake of thinking because I'm a woman that my aim is not accurate, for I am James Barnett's daughter." Brandelene laughed coldly. "Of course, at this range anyone could blast Mason to kingdom come."

"And whoever she doesn't shoot, I will!" Dagert's voice bellowed threateningly from out of the darkness near the mansion.

"Wait!" Harold Lee Mason cried, frantic. "Wait! We didn't come here to hurt anyone!"

"You're not here at this time of night, bearing arms and torches, to pay us a social call," Kordell snarled savagely and peered down the sight of the musket he held steadily. "Throw down your weapons!"

"We didn't come here to jest," sneered one of the riders.

"He's deadly serious, Billy George," Brandelene asserted firmly. "You may remove those ridiculous masks, for I recognize each and every one of you . . . you . . . *gentlemen,* as well as your horses." Although she remained in the shadows, no one missed the glint of her musket barrel. "Which one of you so-called gentlemen murdered Daddy? Was it you, Harold Lee, or you, Billy George?"

"I didn't kill your father." Both men answered at once.

"How about you, Richard? Or you, Robert?" she accused, but her gun never wavered from Harold Lee Mason. "You hated Daddy, John. Were you the coward who gunned him down in the dark?"

"No! No! We never killed him," Richard, Robert and John swore in unison.

"I wouldn't kill anyone!" Harold Lee Mason insisted.

"None of us would," Robert swore.

"What do you think would have happened if you set fire to a house full of sleeping people?" Kordell accused. "It would have been murder, regardless of how you try to dress it up."

"We weren't going to fire the house!" Richard's voice shot out of the group.

"I'm giving you one minute to throw your weapons down," ‹ordell barked, "or I promise you there will be blood shed here ɔnight!"

"That leaves you, Kenneth Frank, or you, Andrew," Brandelene pat vindictively. "Which one of you *aristocratic pillars of the ʾiedmont Valley* fired the shot that killed my Daddy?"

"None of us!" they chorused and nodded to one another in greement.

"We weren't going to fire the house either," Richard assured gain. "I swear."

"Dagert," Kordell shouted, "at the count of three shoot Mason's orse out from beneath him if all of these . . . gentlemen haven't hrown down their weapons. One . . ."

"Don't shoot!" the stout Mason pleaded and threw his pistol nto the drive, then hurriedly unsheathed his musket to do the ame. "Dammit, men, throw down your weapons!"

Slowly they all followed suit.

"I would exercise caution, John, if you value your friend's life," ʾrandelene warned as the man slowly inched his horse forward. If my trigger finger gets nervous, Harold Lee Mason is dead. ınd not a judge would fault me."

"You bastard, John!" Mason cursed. "Do as she says!"

John tamely complied.

"Very good, *gentlemen,*" Kordell said. "Now, one at a time, ismount and step slowly forward to be searched. I wouldn't want ɔ be shot in the back by one of you . . . *honorable gentlemen.*"

No murmur of protest came from any of the seven who meekly id as instructed.

"Dagert, shoot the first man who makes a suspicious move. Ve'll ask questions later," Kordell ordered, then drew the pistol ːom his waistband and cocked it before laying his flintlock at his ɜet beside the other one.

"Will do!" Dagert's voice barked out of the darkness.

"And I'll shoot the second," Brandelene said. "I hope someone ives me an excuse. Any excuse will do. Consider yourselves ʼarned. It's more than Daddy got."

"Place your hands behind your heads and turn around and back up slowly to me. One at a time," Kordell boomed, and before he searched them he took each man's torch and threw it on the grounc where it continued to blaze brightly.

After searching the last man, Kordell stood before them anc pulled himself up to the full of his considerable height. "Tomor- row, *gentlemen,* when cooler heads prevail, you may come for your guns—individually. Come in the light of day, so I can see wel the face of a coward who sneaks under the cover of darkness tc do his disgusting deeds against a woman and her home." With that, he picked up his flintlock and called out to Dagert, "Escor these men on foot to the roadway. They can mount up there." Then he picked up one of the burning torches and handed it to the nearest man. "You may lead the way. If you value your peers you'll hold that torch high, so my friend doesn't lose any of you and shoots someone."

Andrew took the torch and turned to leave.

"You'd be a helluva lot better off," Kenneth Frank blurted out "without that haughty witch you married, friend!"

Kordell's fist smashed into Kenneth Frank's face with such force the man was unconscious before he hit the ground. "Any othe of you brave men have anything to say about my wife?"

At their silence, Kordell glanced coldly down at Kenneth Frank's crumpled body, then ordered, "Throw my 'friend' over his saddle and all of you get the hell out of here before I regret being so lenient!"

Several of the men struggled to sling Kenneth Frank's heavy body over his horse, then started to walk humbly down the drive they had boldly ridden up, leading their horses behind them.

"Consider well before any of you decide to trespass on Southern Oaks again," Kordell shouted after them, "unless you are preparec to shed your own blood and have me and our six hundred bonc servants lead an uprising of your slaves!" The stacked torches, a small bonfire, blazed brightly and Kordell's towering, muscula body, with feet wide apart, was ominously silhouetted against the firelight. "I was exceedingly generous tonight," he called out to the retreating men in a calm but sinister voice. "But I give no man a second shot! You bother us again and I guarantee you the ground will run red with your blood!"

For an endless time, Brandelene stood mesmerized by Kordell's fiercely awesome figure, overwhelmed by the incredible persona he created, the fearsome tower of strength and power, the intimidating self-confidence, the treacherous intensity, and the tremendous fierceness akin to an erupting volcano. And the heat of that magnificently volatile volcano seared her soul, leaving its brand upon her heart.

The six men shuffled away with slumped shoulders and hanging heads, leading their mounts and the limp body of Kenneth Frank, while a musket-bearing Dagert followed at a distance.

Kordell instructed the bondsmen to place the surrendered weapons in the foyer and douse the torches. Then he turned to Brandelene, who still leaned against the giant oak with her flintlock in hand, watching him. Never before had a woman come to his defense, and it felt good.

Strangely wonderful. Great!

Momentarily, he watched her, then extended his hand and smiled gently, his eyes filled with an understanding of what had forged the mettle, the unfailing strength, and the overwhelming perseverance into the woman he admired more with each passing day. Each adversity Brandelene met head-on, lifting her proud head higher, and surviving ever stronger. An unfamiliar emotion, an indefinable feeling for her, swept through him. Engulfed him.

Brandelene walked to Kordell's side, took his proffered hand, and wordlessly returned his smile. Then, as the flames of the torches died they were cast into the black of a moonless, starless night.

They stood in the driveway together and waited for their eyes to adjust to the darkness.

After a time Kordell spoke. "I'm certainly glad you were on my side and not theirs."

There was something warm and inviting in his humor, and Brandelene laughed softly. "I was thinking the same about you."

Slowly they made their way across the dark drive and up the stairs to the veranda where they awaited Dagert's return. His recent illness taking its toll, Kordell suddenly dropped into a chair. Brandelene sat beside him and listened to the peaceful sounds of the plantation at night. Comforting sounds that belied the near tragedy that had occurred only minutes earlier.

"Kord, I don't know how to thank you for what you did tonight."

"It was my pleasure, Madame Bouclair." Kordell's deep-timbred voice was seductively low. "It was the least I could do for the woman who saved my life."

"Any indebtedness you may have felt you owed me has been repaid by what you did tonight. Many times over."

Kordell laughed tauntingly. "Think nothing of it—I would've done the same for any of my wives."

She recalled snidely uttering almost those same words to Kordell when he'd thanked her for saving his life. She smiled. "I deserved that."

Now they could see, by the light of the torch in Andrew's hand, the six men mount their horses. The large form of Dagert, with firearm ready, was silhouetted in the torchlight before the seven rode off leaving only darkness.

"Kordell . . ."

He inhaled deeply. He loved the way she said his name, so softly, almost in a whisper, caressingly, almost reverently. No one had ever said his name the way Brandelene did, and it sent an unwanted shiver down his spine.

"Kordell," she began again, "I never intended to put you or Dagert in jeopardy when we made our agreement." Pausing, she breathed deeply of the fragrant wisteria and honeysuckle that filled the air and wished she could see his face, his reaction. At his silence, she went on, "You've done far more than we agreed upon and I won't put you at further risk. I think we've accomplished what I wanted. Tomorrow morning I'll return your contract of indenture." She paused.

"You and Dagert are free to go."

"That's quite generous of you, Brandy. Exceedingly so, since I know it's a generosity you can ill afford. However, I cannot accept. We have an agreement, and I intend to honor it. Dagert and I will be here for another five months. For better or worse, exactly as in the vows we made."

A pain stabbed through her heart at his last words, and a spontaneous shiver trickled down her spine at the velvet warmth of his voice. She cursed him for he knew the words that could twist a woman's heart. He had to be the devil incarnate to deliberately tug at her heartstrings so.

At her silence Kordell changed the subject. "I didn't have the opportunity to mention it earlier, but I brought you a small present from Petersburg."

"A present?" Brandelene exclaimed, childlike, all thoughts of his being the devil now forgotten.

Kordell chuckled. "Yes."

"Why would you buy me a present?"

"It reminded me so much of you I had to buy it." A huskiness lingered in his voice. "For the time being we'll have to add it to the moneys I owe you. I intend to pay for it."

"Tell me what it is. I've never had a gift that wasn't for a special occasion." Though Brandelene could see only a dark shadow in the pitch-black of night, Kordell's presence was powerful. Visions of him standing in the drive, feet wide apart, flitted before her.

"It would spoil the surprise to tell you."

"Kord! May I have the present tonight—I'll get no sleep at all if I don't."

Now he laughed. "How could I refuse the woman who came to my defense, even if it was against my orders."

"You know I don't take orders from you."

"Yes, I know. I will have to work on your wifely obedience," he teased. "It's sorely lacking."

"Kord."

"Hmmm."

"If it makes you feel better, I don't take orders from anyone else either."

"I've noticed that, Brandy. But it soothes my bruised ego to have you tell me so. Thank you."

Instantly her heart warmed at the bond that grew between them and she felt an icy fear follow in the wake of that knowledge.

"I know you must be tired," Kordell said. "If you want, go to bed. I'll be up as soon as I speak with Dagert." Hesitating the moment the words were out of his mouth, he quickly realized the position of temptation he'd placed himself in. Still, even though his craving for her was a constant, never-ceasing agony, he was loathe to withdraw his suggestion, aware it would require an explanation he did not wish to give, so he continued with what he'd been about to say, "Then I'll give you your present."

A short time later Kordell tapped on Brandelene's connecting bedroom door. When she called for him to enter, he did so to see her seated at her dressing table while Pearl brushed her long raven hair. Behind him, servants were filling his tub with buckets of steaming water.

Their gazes met in Brandelene's mirror, with knowing smiles, for each knew the other had taken the necessary precautions to make certain they were not alone.

"I'll go see if I can help Joshua," Pearl said and hurried into Kordell's bedroom when she received no protest.

Brandelene rose and motioned for Kordell to be seated in one of the two velvet chairs in the sitting area of her large room. She moved to the other chair. He handed her a small but heavy package tied with a red ribbon.

With quivering fingers she untied it and removed the wrapping paper. "Ohhh." Brandelene gasped at the sight of the beautiful agate box, embellished with four ornate gold feet. The translucent quartz was variegated with bands of deep violet shading to lavender hues. "It's lovely, Kord. I . . . I don't quite know what to say."

"When I spied the box it reminded me of you."

His voice, soothing yet sensual, sent a shiver down her spine.

"It was beautiful and delicate-looking, yet beyond the fragile appearance is a substance of endurance that belies its beauty. It will stand the test of time."

Moved by his compliment, she dared not reply. She lifted the heavy agate lid and the haunting sounds of "Greensleeves" tinkled from the chest. "Ohhh," she cried again, surprised by the concealed music box and the beautiful tune she loved. In a daze, Brandelene noticed the Old English initials engraved inside the lid. B.B.B. Perplexed, she glanced up.

"Brandelene Barnett Bouclair," Kordell explained.

For a time, her gaze locked with his and she felt as helpless as if she were drowning, engulfed in a swirling whirlpool, being pulled down against her will, powerless to help herself. In her haze she could hear the hauntingly lovely melody and her mind was occupied with dreamy fantasies. Then she realized where her thoughts were leading and her eyes widened in alarm. *I'm falling in love with him. Oh, dear God, help me!* she pleaded silently as she tried to push the unbearable possibility to the back of her mind.

Somehow, she was in his arms and the world slipped away. There were only Kordell's strong arms holding her, Kordell's face buried in her hair, the pounding of Kordell's heart, the wonder of the emotions that tore through her body, leaving her weak and wanting more. And then, relaxing, she submitted completely to the ecstasy of his embrace.

Chapter 20

PEARL GLANCED THROUGH THE OPEN DOOR TO SEE Brandelene and Kordell locked in each other's arms, and frowned as she recalled her friend's vow to Dagert that Kordell would not again tempt her.

Kordell made no attempt to kiss Brandelene, but silently held her in an endless embrace that said far more than words. Her arms encircled his waist and her hands clasped his back, holding him tightly to her. For the longest time they remained thus, each unwilling to draw away from an embrace so ardent and giving.

Presently Kordell released her and looked down at her upturned face, his gaze lingering on her parted lips before dropping to the softly rounded flesh revealed by her slightly separated dressing gown. He knew her breasts would feel as soft as they looked. He could almost feel them and he cursed his desperate need to hold her in his arms, to lie next to her soft and willing body, to make love to her. As though she read his mind, Brandelene's glazed eyes captured his. With all the control he could manage, he resisted the sensuous, inviting lips she offered. He could not take advantage of her vulnerability. Not tonight.

"I'll see you in the morning, Brandy," he murmured. Then he was gone.

Brandelene stared after him, bemused. Why had she been willing? And why had he turned away?

Pearl entered the bedroom and at the reflection of misery on Brandelene's face could think of nothing to say.

"Oh, Pearl, what am I to do?"

Pearl started brushing Brandelene's long hair. "You're going to forget about everything and get in that bed, you hear? If you're determined to start working with Dagert in the morning, you're going to get little enough sleep as it is. I'm going to have to put cold cucumbers on your eyes to take away those dark circles you're going to have." But the chiding that usually pulled Brandelene from morose moods did not work this time and Pearl crooned. "Don't fret, Brandelene. Everything will be all right. I know it will. I can feel it in my bones. It's been a terrible night what with the night riders coming. When you get up in the morning and see that Virginia sunshine, you'll feel better."

Brandelene drifted into an uneasy sleep filled with nightmares. In her vision, masked riders torched Southern Oaks. She screamed for the torch-bearing men to stop, but the fire burned brighter and brighter, the orange-red blaze devouring, insatiable. Then she screamed again. As she battled her way out of the nightmare, she was being comforted by strong arms. A deep, soothing voice murmured to her; a large hand gently stroked her head and she no longer screamed.

"It's all right, Brandy," Kordell whispered. "Everything is all right. I'm here."

Brandelene opened her eyes, quickly aware of Kordell's strong arms around her, his masculine scent, disturbing yet also comforting. Sighing, she snuggled her head against his powerful chest and heard the wild pounding of his heart.

Assuming Brandelene had fallen into a dreamless sleep, Kordell pressed gentle lips to her brow, then slowly lowered her back to her pillows.

After he tucked the covers around her, he rose and slipped silently back to his room.

At dawn Pearl gently shook a protesting Brandelene awake.

Dazed from little sleep, Brandelene forced her tired body out of bed. Today she would start teaching Dagert the tedious art of growing tobacco. Hopefully he was everything Kordell had said. But she had few reservations, for she'd worked with the man over Kordell's sickbed. Fortunately the thousands of acres of wheat and the hundreds of acres of plantation food crops were already planted. She dressed hurriedly and glanced at Pearl. "Would you mind bringing a lunch out to the north field for Dagert and me today?" She sat on the edge of her bed to pull on her riding boots. "You look especially pretty in your yellow dress and Dagert hasn't seen it."

"Oh, Brandelene, I love you."

Brandelene moved to the door to leave, then turned back. "Pearl, please tell Joshua not to wake Kordell this morning. He didn't look well last night and needs his rest."

Later that morning Dagert, surrounded by the fifteen foremen who would carry out his instructions, stood in the tilled fields that last year had been planted with wheat, alfalfa, oats, and corn. With disbelief, he stared as Brandelene rode her spirited stallion toward him across the north field. She wore a primrose lawn riding habit and matching hat, embellished with a gossamer scarf that whipped behind her. As always, she rode sidesaddle. With the expertise of an experienced equestrian she reined her mount to a halt beside Dagert, removed her riding gloves, and slipped gracefully to the ground. She pulled a primrose parasol from a specially designed sheath attached to her saddle and opened it to shade her face. Smiling brightly, she ignored Dagert's astonished look. "Good morning, Dagert, gentlemen," she chirped and nodded to all the men. "You're all looking well this morning."

"You intend to show me how to prepare the soil for tobacco dressed like that?" Dagert asked.

"Of course." Brandelene smiled agreeably, amused. "This outfit is cool." At Dagert's disparaging glance at her parasol, she added, "I certainly don't intend to sacrifice my complexion for the earth of Southern Oaks. My back, yes, but not my complexion."

Dagert sighed.

"Dagert," Brandelene began patiently, "if I had dressed in men's breeches it would not change what is in my head." She bent to lift a handful of rich fertile soil and examined it. "Thank heaven Cyrus hasn't ruined the soil. The crops have been rotated as I insisted. Tobacco wears out the land in four years, Dagert, which is why most tobacco plantations are so large." Pausing, she glanced across the tilled fields, then sighed. "There's much work to be done, Dagert. Give me your hand."

He did as directed and Brandelene placed the small scoop of dirt in his large hand. "Close your eyes, carefully feel this earth, and then smell it."

Dagert did as requested.

"Contrary to what you might believe, Dagert, tobacco is extremely fragile and requires tender and constant care if it is to be of prime quality. James Barnett's Southern Oaks grows naught but prime tobacco. The world-famous Virginia Bright."

Shifting her parasol, she explained, "Men are quite selective about the aroma and flavor of the tobacco they use, in addition to being particular about how it burns. What we do now will determine if we have thin, light tobacco leaves or the large, heavy, dark green choice leaves that are worth ten times the price of the other. That fertile earth you hold in your hand will produce nothing but low-quality leaves, lugs, and cutters, which bring the lowest prices at market and would only be used for chewing, or as cigar wrapper. We are going to grow the finest smoking tobacco in the world. Southern Oaks's salvation depends on it."

Dagert examined the soil in his hand again. "This is good rich soil. What's wrong with it?"

"Feel it. It packs. Smell it. It's too damp. We'll have to till these

ields once, possibly twice more, and then rake them clean. After
hat the earth will be loose enough, dry enough." She wondered
f the task ahead of them was too vast? There was so much to do
nd so little time. Earlier, she'd gone to the seeding beds to
xamine the tobacco plants and the fragile seedlings were already
our inches high, almost ready to start transplanting, yet the fields
vere not properly prepared to receive them. Abruptly she felt so
ired. Overwhelmed. So much was at stake—the future of every
erson at Southern Oaks. The future of the plantation.

Brandelene straightened with determination. "Tobacco is re-
narkably sensitive and requires more knowledge, expertise, and
edious care than any other crop in the world. If we transplanted
ur tiny seedlings into this earth we'd risk black shank disease. If
ve planted between these shallow furrows we'd chance black root
ot. We'll have that concern anyway if we get rains that are too
eavy or last too long."

She looked around her and visualized the thousands of acres
hat must be prepared by fewer than six hundred people. "Dagert,
he seedling tobacco plants could be transplanted now, if only the
ields were ready. The longer we wait, the more their growth will
e stunted."

"We did the impossible with Kordell's illness. For a team who
an do the impossible, planting a few tobacco plants is only a
eisurely stroll. You tell me what to do, and how to do it, and I'll
ee that it gets done."

Brandelene laughed. "You're right. I had momentarily forgotten
hat this task is only next to impossible. A casual promenade in
he park for you and me. Shall we get started?"

A few hours later Brandelene straightened and rubbed her ach-
ng back. In the distance she saw Kordell riding toward them and
Pearl hanging on behind. She frowned and wished he were resting.
She wasn't quite ready to face him after their brief interlude last
night. She wiped her hands on the piece of cloth she'd brought
or that purpose, removed her lace-edged kerchief, dabbed at her
row, then brushed a smudge of dirt from the skirts of her riding
abit.

As Kordell guided his mount to her side, he doffed his low-crowned, wide-brimmed planter's hat before he leaned down and handed her a vivid red rose. He dismounted, then reached up for the checkered cloth bundle that Pearl clutched in her hand and handed it to Dagert before he lifted the young woman to the ground. "I came upon Pearl on the way out here. Apparently Brandelene instructed her to bring lunch for the two of you."

Pearl smiled shyly at Dagert.

Kordell turned back to Brandelene, a light twinkle in the depths of his golden eyes. "I must say, Madame Bouclair, you are the loveliest overseer I've ever seen." Kordell flirted openly, then turned to Dagert. "Where is your parasol, Dagert?"

A field hand nearby guffawed.

"Mock all you wish, Kordell," Dagert scoffed. "These last five hours I've learned more about tobacco from this delicate flower than any man could teach me."

"Excellent," Kordell said, "for I have come to take this 'delicate flower' home."

"You'll do no such thing," Brandelene retorted. "We're weeks behind in the planting. Every minute counts—if the rains come before we've finished, Southern Oaks will not survive." Gently Kordell brushed back a curling tendril that had escaped from beneath her riding hat, and she quivered at his touch.

"Brandy, I had no doubt that you would be the expert in tobacco you claimed to be, for you are a unique woman." Removing his hat, he ran his fingers through his softly waving tawny hair and golden lights glinted through it in the bright sun. Then he replaced his hat. "Had I expected otherwise I wouldn't be here. However, as an expert in growing coffee and cacao I also know that what you've taught Dagert today will take him and all these bondsmen a week to put into practice. Dagert won't need you for the rest of today, and I do."

Brandelene's eyes widened in alarm. "Are you ill?"

Hesitating, he looked down at her concerned face. "I'm still recuperating and I realize I'll be of no use to you or Southern Oaks if I have a relapse. Therefore, I'm going to rest for the next two weeks as Dr. Malloy advised. This morning, someone"—he gave her a pointed look—"instructed Joshua not to wake me and

I haven't been up long. Thus I am well rested, unable to work, and bored." Now he grinned, not unlike a mischievous boy, and kicked at the dirt with his booted foot. "I thought perhaps I might teach you to play chess. With Cyrus gone, I've lost a chess partner."

"You came out here to ask me to play chess with you?" Brandelene sputtered.

"I realize women can't play chess. But you're not the ordinary woman. You might give it a try."

She sniffed at the rose in her hand, pondered Kordell's request, then glanced up at the blazing sun. "Well, it is rather warm out here," she said, then narrowed her mocking eyes, "and I couldn't figure out how I was to juggle a fan, along with my parasol, and teach Dagert anything at all . . ."

As her voice trailed off Kordell realized she was openly making sport of him and scooped her up to set her on her stallion.

Dagert's mouth pursed slightly with annoyance.

Half an hour later Brandelene and Kordell sat in the library bent over a chess set. Patiently, he'd explained how each piece moved, then offered her the white pieces, which gave her the first move and an advantage. After she advanced her queen pawn two squares, Kordell was explaining why hers was not the best move for a novice to make when Ruby bustled into the room.

"Honey lamb, it seems like old times seeing you playing chess again," Ruby said happily.

Brandelene rolled her eyes heavenward and sighed.

Not noticing Kordell's expression, Ruby chattered on, "Miss Brandelene played chess with her daddy most every night from the time she was knee-high." She chuckled. "After Miss Brandelene turned thirteen, I don't think Mister James ever won a game when she played the white pieces. Mmmm-um, Mister James sure would get mad." With that, Ruby turned back to Brandelene. "Have you seen my baby? I can't find that child anywhere."

"I haven't seen her since we returned," Brandelene replied, her cheeks flaming under Kordell's scrutiny.

"I just don't know what's the matter with that child lately." Ruby shook her head and turned to leave the room.

Kordell leaned back in his leather chair, stroking his chin as he studied Brandelene. At last he broke the awkward silence. "I presume you wish the Queen's Gambit to be your first move after all."

"Yes," Brandelene replied and grinned sheepishly although her eyes twinkled merrily.

During the next three weeks the routine at Southern Oaks varied only on Sunday, which was now a half day's work instead of the usual day off. For the bondsmen raced the calendar and the rains to have the tobacco transplanted from the seedbeds in time. The seedling plants were already six inches high and time was of the essence. Southern Oaks's salvation was the stake that drove everyone, and after Shadrach's sermon in the common house on Sunday almost everyone headed for the tobacco fields.

Each morning Kordell presented Brandelene with a single rose from the bountiful gardens, then escorted her to the dining room where she sat next to him and sipped her juice and tea while he ate a hearty breakfast. Gradually, they slipped into a warm friendship and chatted easily during the meal.

After breakfast she rode to the fields, dressed in her usual cool lawn riding habit with matching hat and parasol, an ensemble she had in several different colors. There she instructed Dagert with an intensity that left no one doubting her ability or the gravity of their situation.

At midday Pearl brought lunch and Dagert smiled his welcome. Brandelene, Dagert, and Pearl shared the meal, then Dagert's flashing dark eyes watched Pearl out of sight when she left.

Each afternoon, after Kordell's nap, he rode out to meet Brandelene to escort her back to the plantation house. Upon returning to the mansion they played chess until time to dress for dinner, each a formidable opponent, making their games exciting and challenging. Then they dined. She enjoyed the stimulating conversation and flattering attention from Kordell, for now instead of treating her as a much-lusted-after wife, he courted her. He made no attempt to force his attentions on her, and she accepted this with considerable relief, for such was her attraction to him that her resistance had been sorely tested by his earlier persistence.

Still, she wondered why there was not the slightest embrace or even a single kiss. Had Kordell's previous behavior really been a charade for Cyrus's benefit? If so, why, each time she looked up, was Kordell's gaze on her? For a moment he would smile, then glance away only to return to watching her, and she wondered about his continual regard. Nevertheless, Brandelene relaxed and appreciated the companionship of the man she still suspected of being a charming rogue and penniless fortune seeker.

With each passing day Kordell felt his health and strength return while the bond between Brandelene and him deepened. Finally the day arrived when Dr. Malloy informed Kordell he could perform light work. With that happy announcement Kordell instructed Cook to prepare a picnic for him and Brandelene. As had been his routine for the previous three weeks, he rode to the fields at midafternoon. But this time, he leaped from his stallion, dropped the basket casually to the ground, and ran to Brandelene. Taking her parasol from her, he handed it to a field hand. Then he swept her up in his arms and twirled her round and round, laughing all the while.

Her arms slipped around his neck and clung to him, caught up in his joy. "Kord, what's happened? I'm getting dizzy!"

He stopped circling, but continued to hold her in strong arms. "Dr. Malloy doesn't need to see me again and I may leave my prison and resume normal activities."

"Oh, Kordell," Brandelene cried out, "I'm so happy for you." Then she hugged him in delight.

Slowly Kordell slid his hand from beneath her legs until she once again stood, though still clasped in his arms. For a moment she gazed up into his smoldering eyes before his tawny head lowered and he captured her lips in a flaming kiss that scorched her with its intensity. He crushed her to him with a power that took her breath away and a subtle magic, a riptide of emotions, rushed through her as his warm, moist lips moved sensually over hers and stole the last of her breath from her lungs. Emotions that simmered barely below the surface, feelings she'd held so tightly in control the last three weeks now rose to consume her and she cared naught for anything else. There was only this place, in the splendor of Kordell's arms, and this time, this moment of ecstasy when his intoxicating kiss told her everything she wanted to know—be it truth or lie.

Kordell, shaken by the depth of the emotions he experienced, lifted his mouth from Brandelene's. His gaze devoured her upturned face and he fought the battle that raged inside, to sweep her up in his arms and carry her to some secret place of their own where he could make passionate love to her until the day turned to dark. Instead, he reached out a hand and his fingers tenderly traced the line of her delicate cheekbone.

Brandelene closed her eyes, savoring his gentle touch and the wonder of the moment.

"I didn't intend for that to happen, Brandy."

His softly spoken words broke into her fantasies and she opened her eyes to look up at him. "I know."

Dagert, standing next to them, was completely ignored, for Brandelene and Kordell were aware of no one but each other. Dagert's only thought as he glanced at Brandelene's rapturous face was that Kordell sought to satisfy his lust, but Brandelene was falling in love.

When Kordell spoke his voice was seductively low. "I brought us a picnic basket. To celebrate."

At Brandelene's hesitation, he leaned down and murmured close to her ear, "You have my word, Brandy, I will not give in to the temptation you unknowingly place in my path."

His handsome face melted into a boyish, heart-twisting smile and she could deny him nothing.

"Marvelous!" With a lightheartedness she could not explain, Brandelene retrieved her parasol and walked toward her stallion, calling back over her shoulder, "When you're much better, I'll race you." She laughed, happily carefree. "Though I doubt your ego can bear it when I beat you."

With Brandelene out of hearing range, Dagert snapped to Kordell, "It's too bad Cyrus didn't see that display. I assure you he would've been thoroughly convinced."

"I'll speak with you later, Dagert," Kordell returned. He grabbed the basket and mounted his horse to ride to Brandelene's side.

They rode wordlessly, side by side. Under a vivid blue sky filled with billowing, puffy clouds, they went into the shadowy forest. There peace and serenity reigned supreme and chirping, twittering birds greeted their arrival and followed them as dry twigs snapped beneath the weight of the horses' hooves. Here and there a medley of flowers burst forth bringing a splash of beautiful color to the subdued hues of the forest. The sun's rays streaked through the dense woods, struggling to penetrate the leafy bowers of towering trees, or the thick needles of the pines, cypress, and junipers. Those warming shafts gloriously spread mystical diffused light, bathing the sheltered wooded area with a magical aura, and gentle, warming breezes beckoned any intruder to stay and enjoy fully the wonders of nature.

Brandelene reined in her stallion and heard the babbling creek before she saw it. Beyond the embankment a crystal-clear stream, one of many that crisscrossed Southern Oaks, cascaded over giant boulders and rushed to some unknown destiny.

Surrounded by such beauty, words were unnecessary. Dismounting, Kordell moved to her side and, clasping strong hands around her waist, gently lifted her to the ground. After he tethered their mounts he opened the woven basket and removed the red-checked cloth that contained their picnic. Moving back to his horse he untied a blanket and spread it beside their lunch; then with an exaggerated sweep of his arm and a low bow, he announced, "Lunch is ready, Madame Bouclair."

He graced her with the smile that never failed to send her heart into an erratic pounding.

After they had eaten, Kordell tapped her hand, a finger placed to his lips. Glancing in the direction he pointed, she watched a doe and fawn cautiously drink from the stream, then sprint back into the brush. Brandelene smiled at him and lay back on the blanket, resting her head on one arm. A sigh of contentment escaped her lips. A feeling of serenity she'd seldom known enveloped her in this enchanted forest.

Kordell eased himself down beside her and his hand gently covered hers, a silent action that said what he did not. She turned her palm up and laced his fingers with her own, hating the tenderness of her feelings for this man who had the power to hurt her far more deeply than Cyrus Varner ever had. Birds sang and twittered, squirrels scolded, and twigs snapped as one forest creature or another scampered on its way. Brandelene and Kordell silently savored the gifts of nature and each other's company.

Chapter 21

"I THOUGHT YOU LOVED NICOLLE!" DAGERT THUNdered.

"I do love Nicolle, and you well know it! I'll love Nicolle 'til the day I die."

Dagert paced back and forth in front of his open door. "Well, you sure fooled me with that little scene you played for all the field hands this afternoon. I can imagine what happened on your cozy little picnic. How can you do that to Brandelene?"

"Nothing happened during that picnic," Kordell bellowed. "Not a damn thing!"

"Maybe that's why you're in such a foul mood." When Kordell didn't reply, Dagert's powerful shoulders slumped and his muscular arms hung limply at his side. "Kordell, I love Nicolle like my own sister. I can't bear to think of her suffering as she did when Robert died. But I've also grown to have a high regard and respect for Brandelene. In fact, I'm extremely fond of her. And I know your reputation with women." He hesitated, noticeably distressed, for he'd not had a disagreement with Kordell since they were boys. "Kordell, if things continue as they have one of those women is going to end up with a broken heart. Which one do you care so little for?"

Kordell stared at the glowing oil lamp, silently studying in fascination the insects fatally drawn to the flame of the wick.

Dagert continued, "Loving Nicolle, as you claim, and knowing that if you consummate your marriage to Brandelene it might make her your legal wife, why do you court her? She sure didn't come riding after you today."

Kordell turned to face his friend. "If you can answer why those insects are so drawn to that flame, then perhaps I could answer your question, Dagert, for I am just as fatally drawn to Brandelene."

"But you said you loved Nicolle."

After a time Kordell sighed. "Dagert, you said you loved Nicolle as your own sister. I love Nicolle in the same way."

"But you were going to marry her," Dagert protested.

"I had never met a woman I loved as you did your wife—as Robert did Nicolle—and I reached an age where I wanted to settle down and have children of my own. Besides, I adored Nicolle's son, and the boy needed a father. Nicolle would be a perfect wife and mother." Kordell hesitated and stared at the lamp once more. "They all seemed to be the right reasons at that time. . . ."

"But not at this time?"

"I don't know, Dagert. I honestly don't know. I'm experiencing emotions I've never felt before. How can I name them? I only know I'm questioning, for the first time, whether a man should expect to marry a woman for reasons more than that she will be a good wife and mother. Brandelene's been liquid fire surging through my veins from the first day I saw her in that damn auction house, and now it's a torture devised in hell to be so near her and not possess her." Kordell laughed. "It's probably simply that I've been too long without a woman."

"Why don't you go to Petersburg and find out?"

"When I was there three weeks ago, it crossed my mind, quite strongly."

"Well?"

"Every time I looked at a woman with that thought in mind all I could see were mesmerizing violet eyes that sparkled more beautifully than the most precious of gems. Eyes that passionately beckoned me, magnetically drawing me into their depths, promising me everything I desired. So I bought the hounds and came back."

"And you've courted Brandelene from that time."

"And I've courted Brandy ever since. I'm probably caught up in her childish, fanciful dreams of wanting to marry someone she loves with all her heart and soul. For some reason I find the concept spellbinding." He moved to the oil lamp, his back to his friend, and glanced down at the dead insects that had sacrificed their lives in their quest to fly closer to the flame. "Did you love your wife with all your heart and soul, Dagert?"

"Yes."

"When you made love to her, was it any different than making love to other women?"

"Yes," Dagert replied instantly.

"How?"

"Making love to any woman is pleasurable. Exciting. But then the moment's over and later you can't remember her name, or even her face." His dark countenance grew sober and his eyes glazed in reminiscence. "Making love to my wife was an experience I'd never known before—or since. It was an incredible magic that defies description, or explanation."

"Incredible magic," Kordell repeated softly, as though to himself. He turned and walked out the door.

"But what about Nicolle and Brandelene?" Dagert asked the empty room.

Following breakfast the next morning, Kordell pulled a rolled map of Southern Oaks from under his chair. "I found the map in the library where you suggested it might be."

"That map was sketched by George Washington," Brandelene announced proudly. "He did the surveying of Southern Oaks. Those are Washington's initials down in the corner."

"Then I shall take care that it not be lost or damaged. Brandy, the life of a sedentary country gentlemen isn't my nature, and now that I'm reasonably recovered from my illness I intend to be active again. I want to start by exploring Southern Oaks—every inch of it—so I'll be camping out. I plan to leave today, as soon as I can be ready."

Caught by surprise, Brandelene protested, "Kordell, your health! There are more than two hundred fifty thousand acres of Southern Oaks. It's too soon." Then she asked suspiciously, "Why do you want to explore Southern Oaks?"

"At our reception I learned that most of the plantation owners expect a hot, dry summer. Inasmuch as Cyrus has gambled away the cash reserves, that would be disastrous for Southern Oaks. Apparently it's predicted in the *Planter's Almanac*, a source in which the plantation owners I met seem to have the utmost faith. Therefore, I want to investigate the possibility of building an irrigation system from the numerous streams to the fields."

Kordell did not mention he also wanted to be by himself, or, in reality, away from her, so he could more clearly consider the feelings that bothered him.

That morning Kordell left, and that afternoon and evening Brandelene and Pearl labored at the immense task of updating the journals of nearly six hundred bond servants, for no records had been kept during the preceding two years that Cyrus controlled the estate. This entailed tediously estimating the time worked and expenses incurred based on the previous years of the bond servants' work and expenditures. Then those estimates needed adjusting for changes such as increases in family size, work responsibility, or type of labor performed, and bonuses.

The time Kordell was gone was joyless and empty for Brandelene. She became aware of how much, during the last three weeks, she'd come to enjoy and look forward to his companionship. On each occasion they'd been together, he had treated her as a different woman, as though he knew every facet of her personality.

At breakfast his behavior had been that of reverence for a treasured wife; and during their rides from the tobacco fields, she'd been a friend and confidante; then during their games of chess he'd considered her a challenging opponent; while dining formally, she became the desirable woman subtly courted by a charming suitor; and then after dinner he'd engaged her in the intelligent and invigorating conversation he accorded a respected peer.

With each passing day, it became more difficult to leave him when he escorted her to her bedroom each night.

The second day he was away, Kordell had located the main stream of Southern Oaks's water, and started upstream in the direction of the water supply to locate its source. It would benefit nothing to perform the enormous amount of work an irrigation system would require, only to have the plantation's stream dry up in a drought. Patiently, he followed the water, stopping periodically to measure the width and depth and make notes, relieved to find the water making only gradual changes, an indication of a strong and constant source.

On the fourth day he came to the major source of the streams and creeks that ran through Southern Oaks's fertile land—a roaring waterfall from a small lake—and he wished Brandelene were here to share the beauty with him. Long ago, he'd left the boundaries of Southern Oaks behind him and now rode an unsettled area. He explored the lake, the product of a spillover from the Nottoway River. He drew a detailed sketch and made notes.

In the event of a disastrous drought that would drop the level of the lake, or even the river, he could use gunpowder to blast an area precisely big enough to create a spillover that would keep the water flowing. He'd had to do the same on the Ivory Coast for the coffee and cacao crops. Considering his experience with gunpowder, there was no question in his mind that, in the event it became necessary, he could control the amount of spillover and keep it to a minimum so there should be no flooding problem when the river or lake returned to its normal level. But if there were, he was also well experienced in building earthen dams. Satisfied, he turned back.

As the days and nights slipped by, Brandelene intruded into all his thoughts and dreams, and her face, smiling, serious, or thoughtful, haunted him. He missed her to a degree he'd not felt possible. Was he falling in love with her?

But what about Nicolle? Their two families had been the best of friends and were always together. He could not remember a time in his youth without Nicolle, and both families had expected they would wed. They had been bitterly disappointed when Kordell showed no signs of surrendering his bachelorhood.

He sighed and reflected on the effect a twist of fate was now having on so many lives. For now he was no longer willing to marry a woman solely because she would be a good wife and mother. Still, he had suggested marriage to Nicolle. Was he committed to her? He thought not, but he would write her as soon as he returned to Southern Oaks to ascertain her feelings. Despite his own sentiments, he would never hurt Nicolle. If she would not release him, then he would marry her.

Late on the seventh day of his expedition, Kordell saw the lamps of Southern Oaks, and he knew exactly what Brandelene would say when she saw him.

"You certainly took enough time to ride over Southern Oaks!" Brandelene snapped when Kordell casually strode into the library, his sun-bronzed face starkly handsome, a fact that irritated her all the more. "I could've explored the whole state of Virginia in the time you've been gone."

Kordell laughed, his tone mischievous as he teased, "Madame Bouclair, I'm touched you were so concerned. Could it be you missed me?"

At the suggestion she sighed, thankful Kordell did not know just how terribly she had missed him. She rose from her chair to leave. "There's hardly enough room in here for me and your considerable ego."

Kordell's face sobered. He spoke softly. "You're still denying what's between us?"

"There is nothing between us!"

"Isn't there, Brandy?"

Kordell's deep husky voice beckoned. The sensuality in his words captivated her, and she fought her unwanted feelings before she lifted her chin proudly. With a rustle of her skirts she swept from the room and silently cursed her weakness that was obvious even to Kordell.

The following morning Kordell heard the tinkle of "Greensleeves" from Brandelene's music box and smiled. Perhaps she was becoming more attached to him than she would admit? Or did she simply open the box to replace or remove her hairpins?

Presenting Brandelene with the ritualistic rose before he accompanied her to breakfast, he chatted comfortably all the way to the dining room, with the same ease they'd slipped into before he'd left. He informed her of what he'd learned, and said, "I'll need thirty of your strongest men to help me build a network of irrigation canals from the streams to the fields. Can you spare them?"

"Kordell, I told you at the time we reached our agreement that you wouldn't be expected to work."

The smile he bestowed on her sent shivers down her spine.

"Brandy, this is something Southern Oaks should've had long ago. But now, because there're no cash reserves, the fate of the plantation this year rests on a good crop. And that's dependent on not having the drought the other plantation owners predict." Kordell paused to pull the dining chair out for her, then asked, "Are you willing to take that risk if you don't have to?"

She tried to think, although it was difficult to concentrate, for what she really wanted to do was submit to her magnetic attraction to him—or have him thrown off of Southern Oaks so she never had to see him again. Glancing up, she found his golden gaze fastened on her expectantly. "You'd need that many? Thirty? The first harvesting of the vegetable crops was completed while you were gone, and we're planting the second now, so none of those people can be spared. Some of the field hands are involved with the wheat, alfalfa, corn, and oats. The tobacco seedlings are being transplanted from the seedbeds to the fields. So none of the tobacco field hands can be borrowed, for when that's finished they'll be worming and hoeing."

She mentally calculated. "If you really feel it's necessary, we can pull the thirty hands you need from the wheat we'd sell, but once we start topping and suckering the tobacco I won't have a man to spare."

Kordell appraised her in amazement. It was strange to discuss matters restricted to men not only with a woman, but with a woman of rare beauty. He found the experience exhilarating.

"I hate to deprive myself of your delightful company, my beauty, but first things first. I'll be working from dawn to dusk on this project, so I won't be here for breakfast, our chess games, or dinner until the canals are completed."

"Kord, your health," Brandelene objected softly, hiding her disappointment.

"I'll pace myself." He smiled at her and placed his hand over hers ever so briefly. "You'll not have to nurse me again—unless you want to."

With Dagert as chief overseer, and the foremen working under him selected from the experts who'd held that position when her father lived, the next few weeks required less of Brandelene's presence in the fields. Dagert was everything Kordell had claimed and he removed a tremendous burden from her.

The warm air of spring melted into the damp, breathless, and suffocating heat of summer. Brandelene now spent part of her day working with Pearl. They continued to update the bond servants' records and posted the ledgers with the mounting debts Southern Oaks had accumulated.

Long days dragged by and Brandelene became restless, and rode out to where Kordell and his crew were fervidly digging the canals for the irrigation system. When she rode into view, she reined in her mount. Her reaction, a heart-pounding, heated rush, left her face warm and her pulse racing. Kordell worked shirtless in the hot, enervating summer sun and from her stallion she sat admiring him.

Muscles rippled in his massive shoulders with every movement, biceps bulged when he assisted one of the men, and his powerful back shone from the sweat of his labor. Kordell's sun-bronzed body was magnificent and Brandelene was mesmerized, recognizing the strange stirrings in her body for what they were. But not only was she powerless to stop them, she was inexorably drawn in search of more. After a time she nudged her mount and trotted toward him. When he saw her coming he slipped on his shirt.

With strong arms, Kordell lifted her from her stallion, and, to her disappointment, kissed her only briefly for the benefit of the field hands. Afterward they shared a quick lunch and then he returned to work, for too many days had passed without rain. She'd barely arrived before he assisted her back into the saddle.

"Will you come again tomorrow?"

Brandelene nodded.

Thereafter she rode every day to the area where Kordell worked, took a lunch for them to share, and then returned to the plantation house feeling lonely and empty. Why did she have this compelling need to be near him?

Soon came the day she remained nearby after he went back to work, and while she sat under a tree, fanning herself, she watched him plan, calculate, instruct, and supervise the construction of the elaborate network of shallow canals.

That afternoon, Kordell took several short breaks and joined her for a few minutes each time. Thereafter, she spent time each afternoon where he worked, and gradually they drifted back into the easy camaraderie they'd shared before he'd left to explore the source of the streams. With each passing day the air between them became more charged with an unexplainable atmosphere that neither could ignore. Yet neither was willing to say, or do, anything different.

Each day that passed, Brandelene realized, was one day closer to the day when Kordell would walk out of her life forever. The thought was unbearable—so much so she refused to consider it.

By this time, Kordell and his bondsmen worked on the laterals, the smaller ditches that would carry the water from the canals to the deep furrows that flanked each side of the tobacco plants. Brandelene watched him supervise the bond servants with the confidence and air of authority of a man who not only knew what he was doing, but had done it for most of his life, and once again she wondered what he had been, how he'd acquired the skill and knowledge to engineer an irrigation system, and how he came to be on a slave ship.

But now the truth of his background no longer mattered, for she was helplessly in love with the man, whoever he was.

Unwittingly, Kordell had destroyed the possibility of any other man gaining favor in her eyes, for no other man could ever compare to him. Yet she refused to wed a fortune hunter even though Kordell was now the only man she would ever want for her husband. He was the most fascinating man she'd ever met, and although she realized she had fallen in love with the fantasy Kordell ortrayed, she also realized that she would never be satisfied with ess.

Better she had never savored the wine than to thirst for more he rest of her life.

The day came when Brandelene rode out to where Kordell vorked and added to his heavy burden. "Kord, I've just come from he tobacco fields. The growth of the crop is being stunted by the ack of rain. What are we to do? I know you've been working day nd night, but the irrigation system seems so far away."

"How much time do I have to finish?" He lifted her from her orse, retrieved and opened her parasol, and handed it to her.

"Some of the leaf is showing the first signs of a withered look ow."

"The irrigation channels will take another week to complete, lus an additional three days to finish and set the control gates, nd yet another three days to test the system."

"Kord, we don't have thirteen days. Another week without rain ould mean the plantation will produce no choice tobacco. I have o money. I can't pay the creditors until we sell the tobacco. And vithout a quality crop I won't be able to make the mortgage ayment. The bank will foreclose on Southern Oaks." Brandelene ased herself down to sit on the ground. "What am I to do?"

Preoccupied, Kordell hunkered down beside her.

She glanced up at him. "There's more."

"There's more?"

"If it doesn't rain soon, we'll lose the hundreds of acres of egetable crops that feed the plantation. We have thousands of cres of wheat, but at least the wheat crop isn't as fragile as the obacco and is considerably nearer to harvest."

Kordell's expression was intent, concerned. "If you give me hirty more men I can give you water in four days—if we don't est the system. However, I warn you, Brandy. To start irrigating vithout several testings will risk a break that'd flood part of the obacco fields. Are you willing to take that risk?"

Laughing, Brandelene dropped her parasol and leaped up to hrow her arms around his neck, almost knocking him over. "Kordell Bouclair, I've watched you in amazement while you've meticulously engineered your irrigation system. There will be no breaks. Give us the water for our thirsty crops." Then she kissed him exuberantly and skittered out of reach while the workers watched in amusement.

Four days later, as she predicted, no breaks occurred, and the life-giving water flowed down one deep furrow after another. Brandelene smiled proudly at Kordell, as elated as if she'd achieved the monumental task herself. There was a depth to her bondsman, to the master of disguise known by the name of Armand Kordell Bouclair, that she'd not suspected, and her pride in him only deepened her love.

Days passed and still there was no rain, and Kordell knew that now he also would be forced to use flood irrigation. But it was risky, for if heavy rains came while the fields were flooded, the crops would be lost. Nevertheless, the control gates were opened and water completely flooded the area. With the furrow and flood irrigation systems operating, the crops thrived.

Brandelene continued to oversee Dagert's training through each stage of the tobacco and to actively manage Southern Oaks.

Soon the children picked several varieties of berries, which were quickly made into preserves, placed in thousands of quart jars, sealed with wax, and stored in the enormous, cool, earth-floored cellars. Casks of blackberry and elderberry juice were placed in the dark cellars to ferment.

The orchards ripened and Brandelene assigned women, older adults, and older children to pick peaches, apricots, and plums, while the younger children washed and pitted the fruits that were turned into preserves or laid out in the sun to dry. Both would be stored to be eaten throughout the year. Peach and apricot brandies were made and stored in casks, next to the berry wines.

Without rain, each hot summer month burned into the next. Time ceased in the endless, slumbrous heat and the air filled with the fragrant aroma of the other plantations flue-curing their harvested tobacco crops.

Thousands of acres of wheat bent from the weight of the grain, which would be scythed and taken to the plantation grist mill. The greater part of the flour would be hauled to the Petersburg market and sold to buyers from England. Hundreds of acres of corn grew heavy with silky tasseled heads, and would be stripped of the ears, shucked, and stored in bins for the fowl and livestock. Alfalfa and oats ripened and soon would be cut and stockpiled in the barns for the livestock. All this while they still performed the labor-intensive task of worming and suckering the tobacco, and continued to irrigate the crops. For hours on end bond servants and mules plodded the earth of Southern Oaks.

As the next two weeks passed, the work took its toll on everyone. Finally, with scythes swinging in every direction, the harvesting of the wheat, alfalfa, and oats was completed, and most of the field hands began harvesting the second planting of food crops while others moved into the acres of apple orchards to pick the only fruit that could be stored until the following summer.

During those trying days, Brandelene and Kordell worked from dawn to dusk as did everyone else, except the young children, the ill, and the elderly. However, with still no rain, the day came when the water level of the stream dropped so low that Kordell rode up to the small lake and the Nottoway River to blast a spillover.

Restless with Kordell gone, Brandelene decided to check the progress of the harvesting. She galloped off toward the knoll that overlooked the hundreds of acres of Southern Oaks's food crops, and reined in her horse to watch the beehive of people, mostly women and older men, gather the crops.

Wagons, pulled by mules slowly plodding their path, were piled high with baskets before lumbering to the sorting sheds. There each item was inspected for quality prior to being stored in the outbuildings and cellars, for an imperfect piece would rot in storage.

Brandelene sighed with satisfaction, for she could see that the food harvesting and replanting would be completed before the tobacco was ready to harvest. In that moment she realized everything was better than she'd hoped for. There was an indescribable feeling of accomplishment in knowing that six hundred people would be well provided for during an entire year. The only foods they would purchase would be rice, coffee, tea, cocoa, sugar, olive oil, and spices.

She turned her mount and nudged him toward the mighty leaf, the vast tobacco crops of Southern Oaks that stretched in every direction, as far as the eye could see. Elated to see the streams start flowing again, she knew Kordell was on his way back to Southern Oaks.

This time, Kordell, with the aid of a spare horse and driving himself from daylight to dark directly to and from his destination, made the trip to the small lake, where with gunpowder he blasted a spillover, and returned to Southern Oaks in three days.

When Kordell returned, instead of flinging her usual caustic remark at him, she flew into his arms and showered him with kisses.

"I should leave more often." Kordell's casual comment belied the depth of feelings Brandelene stirred in him. Feelings he knew his burning gaze and trembling arms could not disguise from her.

The one benefit Brandelene had received laboring from dawn to dusk was to fall asleep instantly when she crawled into bed. But the night Kordell returned she lay wide awake, the summer heat oppressive. However, it was not the heat that kept her tired and aching body from sleep, but fantasies of Kordell intruding into her night, the same as he plagued her days. A heaviness settled in her chest and she ached with an inner pain. Kordell would be gone in five weeks. Gone from her life forever, as if he'd never been, and that imagining was unbearable.

Looking up, she saw Kordell pacing the balcony in the moonlight. At least she did not suffer alone, and she found the notion comforting that he had his own worries. Obviously he wrestled with some problem and she wondered if, even hoped, she was the cause of his discomfort.

Shirtless, Kordell wore snug-fitting breeches, and Brandelene could not help but admire his magnificent physique, honed to perfection by his recent labors, and so temptingly silhouetted in the moonlight.

As though to add to Brandelene's frustration, Kordell stopped at her open doors, leaned against the portal, and stared into the darkness of her room.

Chapter 22

BRANDELENE TRIED TO CONTROL HER RAPIDLY POUNDing heart, sure that Kordell could hear it from where he stood. It seemed a long time before she sat up on the side of her bed and heard herself speak softly. "Is something wrong, Kord?"

"Yes."

She picked up her peignoir from the foot of the bed, slipped it on, and moved to his side. She gazed up at his carved features, resplendent in the shadows of the full moon, and was consumed by the odd sensations that trickled through her. "What's wrong?"

Kordell clenched his hands that hung at his sides and fought to control his overwhelming desire to pull her into his arms. The months of being so near her, yet so far, of desiring her, yet remaining celibate, had finally penetrated his self-control. Never had he wanted to possess a woman so much and his continuous craving for her gnawed not only in his loins, but, now, also in his heart.

At that moment he knew. Knew he no longer wanted only to possess her body, he wanted to possess her heart, her soul.

He did not know when he'd started thinking of her as his wife, but he had. Shaken and confused, he answered her, his voice husky with emotion. "We are what's wrong, Brandy. We should be together. You know it as well as I."

Brandelene's composure shattered and sent her senses reeling in a mindless whirl. As in a dream, she reached out and slowly seared her palms across his softly furred chest and around his muscular back. She felt his responsive shudder and was drawn into a spiraling emotional vortex from which there was no recovery. With no will of her own, she succumbed to his suffocating presence and pressed her thinly clad body to his before she turned her face upward. "Hold me, Kord." Her soft cry was breathless, pleading. "Just hold me."

Kordell clasped her in his arms and pressed her head against his wildly beating heart. "You're my wife, Brandy. You're mine!" He trailed burning kisses from her ear, across her face, and stopped short of her parted lips.

Brandelene only cared that she was in his strong arms, where she wished to be. She wanted the tingling of excitement that raced through her to go on forever and slipped her hand around his nape. Her fingers tangled in his thick waving hair and she turned her face to search for his lips with hers.

Unable to resist her open invitation, Kordell hungrily claimed her parted lips.

Tenderly, he cupped her face in the palms of his hands and his mouth devoured hers, his kiss so ardent, so demanding, it set her aflame, and the hot tides of passion seared through her veins. His lips moved on hers, his tongue lingeringly tracing their soft fullness, and Brandelene gave herself freely to the thrill of his heady kiss. Gently his tongue slipped into the soft moistness of her honeyed mouth, curling sensuously around hers. Waves of pleasure crashed through the pit of her stomach with an intense urgency and she molded her body to his, clinging passionately.

The feel of her full breasts burned through the thin silk into his bare chest, and her flesh so close to his flesh aroused a raging desire that enflamed a fiery path through his loins. Slowly, lightly, his hands moved down the silky fabric covering her back to caress her hips.

Then he pulled her tightly against him and Brandelene could feel his bold manliness. Trembling, she could not catch her breath, and the room spun as she went limp in his arms. Then, with a low moan, he swept her into his arms and carried her to his bed and gently laid her there, smothering her with kisses that sent lingering shivers down her spine. There was only Kordell. Kordell kissing her. Kordell caressing her. Kordell embracing her. Kordell causing the wondrous sensations that splintered through her body and catapulted her into another world. A world where only the two of them existed.

His moist lips burned kisses into her neck, and Brandelene threw her head back in ecstasy to offer the slender column up to him, exalting in the feel of his lips that moved to the rapid pulsing at the hollow of her throat. When his hand cupped the fullness of her breast, she moaned and pulled him to her. The heart that pounded uncontrollably within her breast at the same time hammered in her head, so she could not think, she could only feel.

Once more his mouth captured hers and his tongue claimed hers to tease and taunt. Skillfully his hand caressed her body at will, roaming where it would, causing a tide of emotions to whirl up and engulf her, and she knew she was helpless to stop him. And she cared naught.

This time Kordell's hand returned to her throat to slowly slip downward, inside her nightgown, to caress the full roundness of her breasts, and before Brandelene realized what happened, he slipped her peignoir and gown from her shoulders.

His mouth moved from hers, and he lifted his tawny head to stare at the perfection of her creamy breasts that had tortured him night and day for so many months. They filled the cup of his hands, their rosy tips stiffening excitedly into taut peaks.

Then his searching lips caressed where his hands had stroked and Brandelene arched to meet his ravenous mouth that gently, sensuously, tortured her, and a warm flutter deep within her belly filled her with anticipation and desire. She tossed her head from side to side and Kordell lay down beside her, pulling her into his embrace, and she felt the arousal of his powerful manhood press into her thigh. She sighed.

At her sigh, Kordell buried his face in the softness of her fragrant hair while his fingers moved slowly under her gown and up her thigh, relishing, savoring that for which he had waited. "I've wanted you for so long, Brandy. You're all I think about. You're an unquenchable fire burning in my loins." He brushed gentle kisses across her brow, her lids, her nose, and Brandelene tilted her face upward for more.

Now his fingers massaged her naked stomach and that same fire flashed through her inner being and she ached with longing, for what she knew not.

Swiftly his breeches were off and then, impatient, he rent her gown from her willing body, his breathing heavy with restrained passion as his mouth burned down her throat to capture her breast. There his wet tongue caressed, nipped, nibbled, suckled, and her breasts surged to his scorching lips.

Expert fingers silkily caressed her thigh, then moved to her throbbing womanhood, and Brandelene gasped at the splintering pleasure of his touch.

"This night you will be my wife."

Brandelene stiffened at his words, suddenly aware of his hands on her body, his hot, naked flesh pressed to hers. Kordell had not mentioned love. He wanted her in his bed. The fortune hunter wanted her for his wife. But he didn't love her, he only wanted what was hers—her body and her plantation. With that excruciating thought, she pulled her fingers from his hair and grabbed his hands, staying them. "Stop! Kordell, stop!"

"It's all right, Brandy," Kordell said, his voice husky, his breathing rapid, his bulging manhood boldly pushed against her thigh. "You're my wife."

"I am not your wife!" Brandelene returned coldly and felt Kordell's naked body pressed intimately to hers, sensed the tremble in his warm hands that stroked her body. "Stop!"

"Dammit, Brandy . . . you can't ask me to stop now." Kordell's rasping voice broke.

"Would you take me by force?"

"Of course not!" Kordell took several deep breaths, then stilled his hands on her body. Sitting up, he gazed down at the beauty of her nudity that gleamed in the moonlight.

"I felt sure you wouldn't. Your pride would never permit you to take by force what you're sure you can win by charm."

Kordell sighed. "Brandy, need I remind you, I didn't bring you here by force." Then he groaned aloud. "I can't even think clearly anymore—you're all I think of. Dammit, Brandelene, you're like some vicious disease eating at my insides. I need you. I want you."

Flushing at his words, she turned her face away, but made no attempt to cover her nakedness, knowingly torturing him as he now tortured her. She would have given herself to him if only he loved her. But he did not. And still she'd almost consummated their marriage knowing he would then, as her husband, own Southern Oaks. Well, Kordell Bouclair would not beguile what was hers from her. With that firmly resolved Brandelene turned and looked up at him. "Please leave, so I may dress."

"You can't be serious!"

"Leave, Kord."

Wordlessly, he gazed down at her and cursed her beauty. He wondered if he had the self-control to do as she asked, his insatiable lust a physical pain tearing though him, her naked beauty a temptation rightfully his by law. His breathing was rasping, jagged. He trembled. He could not think, he could only feel.

"Please leave, Kord."

He lay back on the bed and took several deep breaths while he fought to regain some semblance of control. At this precise moment, could he deny himself the one thing he wanted above all else in order to keep his word? Rising up on one elbow, once again his gaze swept the ethereal beauty that transcended any he'd ever seen. It was a sight the image of which he had formed in his mind many times.

"I should be canonized as a saint."

Without moving, Brandelene lay staring up at him.

"Brandy! You will be my wife—in every way." His words, whispered hoarsely, breathlessly, were a proclamation. Then he rose and walked naked onto the balcony.

Though Brandelene reasoned she should feel triumphant, she felt only an agonizing emptiness. Even to own Southern Oaks, he could not force "I love you" from his lips. Silently, she grabbed the shreds of her gown and slipped back into her room.

During the night, the heat built up and lightning flashed from the sky followed by shattering claps of thunder. The storm had a frightening violence that tried to equal Brandelene's turbulent emotions.

The next three days it rained, giving the hard-working bond servants a much deserved rest and bestowing on the mighty leaf the nourishment that could only come from rain.

Housebound with Kordell, Brandelene watched the storm, her mood as dark as the Virginia sky. To her bewilderment, he treated her with warmth and affection, as though the events of that night had never happened. Even so, each time she glanced up his golden gaze rested on her, and her breath quickened, her cheeks flushed with the memory of the intimacy they had shared—and the intimacy they had not.

They played chess and talked for long hours. She educated him about the colonies of the United States, which, over the slavery issue, were slowly being divided by an invisible line into the North and the South. Kordell told her about the Ivory Coast and the horror of the ever-increasing slave traders invading all of West Africa.

On the surface, everything was the same, yet nothing was the same. Gazes met, the air between them as charged as the bolts of lightning that flashed through the air.

Except now Brandelene had tasted of the nectar of the gods and she could think of nothing else. The wonder of Kordell's intoxicating kisses, his sensuous tongue passionately claiming hers, his expert hands that had intimately seared her body and filled her with emotions she'd never experienced, constantly lingered in her memory.

When he caught her staring off into space, he would grin rakishly and she knew he was aware of where her imaginings dwelled. She wanted to hate him for it, but she could not. She loved him to distraction and knew if she followed the path she trod, it would lead directly to his bed, exactly as he had proclaimed. That notion was intolerable, for although she would then be married to the husband she loved with all her heart and soul, that husband did not love her in return. He would consummate their marriage not merely out of lust for her body but also out of lust for her inheritance. Rather she would be a spinster, or marry a man she didn't love, but who loved her the way she needed to be loved.

A solution seemed beyond her capacity. Then the answer came of its own accord. Tomorrow she would have the doctor's examination, obtain her required certificate, and have Charles Thompson file the petition for annulment. Once she informed Kordell they were no longer married, she would insist they avoid each other until he left. She could not trust herself to resist him, but with Southern Oaks forever removed from his grasp she felt sure he would not try to tempt her again.

"It's your move, Brandy."

Kordell's words interrupted her reverie and she stared blankly down at the chess board. Rising, she queried with a sudden buoyancy, "Would you mind if we finished this game another time? I remembered some things I must do." His agreeable smile tore through her heart.

Much later in her cozy bed she fought sleeplessness and listened to the rain pound on the roof and splatter on the balcony. Then the connecting door from Kordell's room flew open with a loud bang and he stormed into her room.

"Brandelene! Wake up!" Kordell boomed, looming over her. "Brandy!"

"Is something wrong, Kordell?"

"Yes. *Something* is very wrong. Joshua informed me he wouldn't be here to bring my bath in the morning because he's driving you to Petersburg in the middle of the night."

"Certainly you could arrange for one of the other servants to bring your bath without waking me."

"Damn the bath! Why didn't you tell me tonight that you planned to go? You know I'm not going to permit you to go into Petersburg unescorted."

"Not permit me? You don't tell me what I can or cannot do, Kordell Bouclair."

"When it comes to your safety, I do. As long as you're my wife, even if it is in name only, I will see to your protection.

Therefore, my beauty, I'll be going with you."

"I am not your wife . . . in the true sense of the word."

"You could be, Brandy."

At his huskily murmured words, Brandelene's heart raced frantically. "Kord . . . ."

"No!" Kordell turned to leave.

"Your escort isn't necessary, Kord. I'm leaving in the middle of the night so none of the neighboring plantation owners will see me."

"The subject is not open for discussion, madame. If I don't go, you don't go! Do we go, or do we stay?"

Sighing in defeat, Brandelene murmured softly, "We are going."

"Exactly why do you so suddenly need to go to Petersburg?"

Now her heart pounded so loudly she was sure he could hear it from where he stood by her bed. "I—I need to get away from the plantation for a while. And there are some matters personal to women I'd like to take care of."

Kordell's voice softened. "I understand, Brandy. You've been working longer and harder than many of the bond servants, and you were gently reared." His tone was understanding. "I will be happy to escort you anywhere you wish. All you need do is ask. I want to check for mail anyway. I certainly have some word by now."

"Kord, I'm taking a pistol and two flintlocks with me, and I really do need some time to myself. . . ."

"Sorry, Brandy. I'll be ready when you are. I've already given Dagert his instructions." Then he bent and briefly brushed her lips with his before he returned to his room and quietly closed the door.

Brandelene spent the hours until time to dress contemplating how to absent herself from him in order to see a doctor and her lawyer, for surely if Kordell knew, he would try to prevent her from filing for the annulment.

Shortly after four in the morning, Kordell assisted Brandelene into the brougham. The lanterns had not been lit inside the closed coach. Rain pelted on the metal roof, and when he climbed in beside her she felt intimately secure inside the cozy interior of the plushly upholstered coach. She started to object when he seated himself beside her, then changed her mind. It would not be wise to provoke him now, for she would need all her southern charm to escape him in Petersburg.

Joshua, bundled beneath a canvas poncho, pulled his wide-brimmed hat low, snapped the reins smartly, and the brougham started with a lurch.

Feeling slightly sick about her task, Brandelene leaned back against the thick squabs of the gray velvet seat, only to find Kordell's arm there. His large hand pulled her to his broad chest.

"You can sleep until we get to Petersburg."

Kordell's deep voice, his warm breath, was so close to her ear that it sent a shiver tingling down her spine. At his offer she snuggled in his embrace with her face pressed to his steely chest and soon fell asleep.

As the coach rocked over the bumpy, rain-filled ruts of the winding planters' road, the silkiness of Brandelene's hair brushed against Kordell's neck to torment him. Her delicate fragrance played havoc with his senses. The feel of her full, firm breast burned through the fabric into his chest, to torture his sanity and tear through his loins and set him afire. Staring down at her, he wondered at the wisdom of his earlier decision to truly make her his wife. His love for her had brought him nothing but misery.

When they arrived in Petersburg all Brandelene could think of was to get the distasteful business of her annulment behind her. Having slept in Kordell's arms all the way from Southern Oaks, she once again agonized at the notion of casting him out of her life. In a scant five months he'd become the whole world to her. Her being revolved around him, with him. He occupied her thoughts every waking minute. If only he wanted her for herself! It no longer mattered that he was penniless. Willingly, she would sacrifice her pride if he loved her instead of loving her inheritance.

Still it rained, and Brandelene leaned across the empty seat and tapped on the portal behind the coachman's seat. Joshua opened the small door.

"Joshua, take me to Dr. Carson's," Brandelene instructed and gave him directions.

Kordell's brow furrowed with concern. "Brandy, are you ill? You should have told me."

"I'm not ill, Kordell. I have a matter of a personal nature to be checked. This is why I didn't want you to accompany me."

"But why aren't you going to Dr. Malloy? You've said many times he's the best physician in Petersburg."

"Sweet mercy! Isn't it bad enough I have to suffer this embarrassment with you here? Must you interrogate me too?"

"I didn't mean to intrude into your privacy," Kordell apologized, frustrated.

Brandelene gave him a dazzling smile, then slipped her hand through his arm before she said disarmingly, "Forgive me, Kord. I'm afraid I'm rather irritable today." She brushed an affectionate kiss across his cheek.

The coach stopped in front of the doctor's office, and Kordell alighted, opened an umbrella, assisted Brandelene down, and escorted her to the door. From beneath the umbrella they shared while the rains pelted them, he paused to gaze down at her. "Don't worry, Brandy, everything will be fine."

At his words, she found herself feeling guilty that she'd not told him of her actual mission, inadvertently causing his concern for her health. She pledged to tell him on the ride back to Southern Oaks. Perhaps he would be as pleased as she that this charade neared an end.

A short time later, Brandelene left the physician's office with the all-important certificate, which confirmed her marriage had not been consummated, burning through her reticule.

The rain had stopped, the sun shone brightly through the dark clouds, and the air was fragrant with the freshness that comes only after a hard rain.

Kordell leaped from the coach and scooped her up into his arms to set her carefully in the brougham, then climbed in beside her. "While you were inside I arranged for the sun to shine. I felt it might brighten your day," he teased.

She loved his consideration, the gentle camaraderie they shared. Turning away, she stared out the small window and hoped he would not see the wretchedness on her face.

"Where to now, madame?"

"There's a ladies' shop near Charles Thompson's office that I've been wanting to visit."

When the coach pulled up in front of the building, Brandelene turned to Kordell. "I'd prefer to shop alone. There are some personal items I need."

"Of course."

"Kordell," Brandelene hesitated, apprehensive, "I wish to browse and take my time. If there's something you wish to do?"

"You take as long as you wish, Brandy," Kordell answered as he assisted her from the coach. "I'll check for mail and post some letters. It's been so long since I've been to Petersburg, I must certainly have mail by now. Then I'll return and wait for you."

Brandelene walked into the small shop, turned to watch the coach move down the street, then heaved a sigh of relief. Originally, she'd planned to go out the rear of the store, but now that would not be necessary and she hastily informed the shop girl, "I've remembered another errand I wish to do first. I'll be back shortly." She hurriedly left by the door she had just entered and almost collided with Dean Paul Mason.

"Brandelene!" Dean Paul tipped his hat and inclined his head. "This is an unexpected pleasure. How wonderful to see you."

"Dean Paul. How very nice." As she made trite conversation with young Mason, she swallowed the screams of frustration at her poor luck. Precious minutes were ticking by and Kordell could return at any time.

Chapter 23

DEAN PAUL'S WORDS BROKE INTO BRANDELENE'S mounting tension. "I'm sorry, Dean Paul. You were saying?"

"Will you and Kordell come to my betrothal ball to Ruth Anne?"

"Your betrothal ball?"

"Yes, Brandelene. Haven't you heard a word I've said?" Dean Paul stared at her. "Are you feeling all right?"

"I'm fine. Your betrothal ball?" Brandelene glanced up the street, but the carriage was not in sight. She looked up at him, pleased that her friend had found another. "I'm so happy for you, Dean Paul. Ruth Anne is a lovely girl." There was still no sign of the carriage. "I must go. I'm late for an appointment. You do understand?"

"Of course."

"Please send your invitation and I'll discuss it with Kordell. I'm sorry, but I must leave." She glanced up the empty street and all but ran a few doors down. Minutes later she stood in the lawyer's private office.

"Ah, Brandelene, you're looking well," the fair-haired, bespectacled man greeted her. "Please be seated."

Brandelene sat in the leather chair in front of his desk.

"I heard your reception went well. The gossip all over Petersburg was how favorably impressed everyone was with Kordell."

Brandelene smiled, her insides churning.

"Then the next thing I knew, Cyrus was pounding on my door, wanting to see James's will. He was irate at your restoring indentured servitude at Southern Oaks. After he read your father's stipulation that you did not need his permission to marry, he was rather disgusted, to say the least." Charles grinned. "Judge Jenkins said that Cyrus had been there too, and quizzed him about your marriage. Said the scoundrel even demanded to see the registry."

The lawyer leaned back in his chair. Brandelene could hear his large clock in the corner. Was Kordell waiting in front of the empty ladies' shop?

"Cyrus said he was going back to New York. Said the life of a country gentleman was too boring and not to his liking. Did he go?"

"I don't know. I haven't seen him since he left, so hopefully he did."

Thompson laughed. "It did my heart good to see Cyrus so disgruntled. The scoundrel's almost bankrupted Southern Oaks. Are you going to be able to save it?"

"I'm racing the calendar, Mr. Thompson, for the tobacco was planted late. Kordell installed an irrigation system so we have a quality crop. If I can get the leaf to market before the foreign tobacco buyers leave, I'll save Southern Oaks." She smiled broadly.

"You're a remarkable woman, Brandelene. Irrigation system, eh? Your husband is a man of many talents."

Brandelene paled. "Yes. Kordell's been a blessing." At those words a sharp pang tore through her.

"There're rumors that some of the plantation owners called on you in the middle of the night and Kordell ran them off. Is it true?"

"Yes, it's true." The ticking clock pounded in her ears.

"Exceptional man, your husband."

Instantly Brandelene felt sick, nauseated, weak. "Yes, Kordell's an exceptional man."

"Well, I'm happy it all worked out so well for you. But when I watched you two at your wedding, I was sure it would."

Recalling her disgraceful behavior at that time, Brandelene flushed, fumbled in her reticule, removed the doctor's certificate, and laid it on the lawyer's desk with trembling fingers. "I'm here to file the petition for annulment."

Charles Thompson stared at her. "Certainly you don't want to do that, Brandelene? From everything I've heard, Kordell's a marvelous husband. And you seemed to get along so well on your wedding day."

She turned crimson at his last statement, then lifted sad eyes, imploringly. "Please, Mr. Thompson, please file the petition." Nodding toward the document on his desk, she quietly added, "That is the doctor's certificate, dated today."

"Are you sure you really want to do this, Brandelene?"

"I'm sure."

He sighed. "Very well. I'll have it filed in Richmond, not here in the county. It'll be less likely to be bandied all over town, and if Cyrus returns he'll also be less likely to learn of it."

Brandelene nodded. "Thank you. Will you please take care of it today?"

"Today?"

"Yes. I want the matter behind me, so I can concentrate on the harvest. You do understand?"

"Yes, of course. I'll have my legal assistant leave for Richmond today. It will be filed first thing Monday morning. Since you have the doctor's certificate, the annulment cannot be denied. I'll send you a letter confirming the filing and approval."

Back on the street, Brandelene was surprised, since she'd been considerably longer than anticipated, that the coach was not in front of the ladies' shop. She stepped from the lawyer's doorway and hurried to the store.

Browsing through undergarments of lace-trimmed silk, lawn, cambric, and satin a few minutes later, Brandelene looked up to see the coach outside. After quickly selecting a chemise and petticoat, she left the shop with her packages and walked toward the waiting brougham.

Joshua assisted her into the empty coach. "I've been driving all around looking for you, Miss Brandelene. When you wasn't here I went to the general store and to the house of that lady who makes hats. I was sure getting worried about you. I was just about to go get Mister Kordell. He's with a gent he knows. He said to tell you that he'll be with the gentleman until you gets there."

As the brougham lumbered down the rain-rutted street, where

only a short time ago Brandelene had been relieved, she now felt distraught. Although the weather had turned into a beautiful late summer day and her sham of a marriage was as good as annulled, an inner torment began to gnaw at her. But why? Cyrus was no longer a serious threat, and the tobacco harvest should bring exceedingly high prices, thanks to Kordell's irrigation system. With the tobacco crops of most of Virginia's plantations suffering devastating losses due to the long dry season, Southern Oaks's choice tobacco should be at a premium. For a scheme that had started so disastrously the conclusion looked quite promising. But still, an unexplained sorrow weighed on her and she felt an overwhelming urge to burst into tears.

The coach stopped beside Kordell, who stood deeply engrossed in conversation with a well-dressed stranger. A foreigner, she guessed from the cut of the man's clothes. Kordell pulled his timepiece from his pocket, spoke again to the man, shook his hand enthusiastically, then turned and climbed into the coach.

He gave Brandelene a heart-tugging smile.

"I'm famished," he said. "Shall we have lunch?"

"That'll be fine." Her words were lifeless. Suddenly needing the sanctuary of Southern Oaks, she said, "I'm anxious to return home. There's nothing more I wish to do, unless there's something you need to take care of?"

"As a matter of fact, there is." Kordell grinned impishly before he instructed Joshua to drive to the Wolf's Lair Inn. A short time later they stood in the tavern common room. "Please wipe dry an outside table so my wife and I can eat outdoors," Kordell asked the tavern maid. "Bring a bottle of your best wine too." They followed the girl outside and waited while she dried the trestle table and benches. The rains had cooled the muggy heat, and the fresh scent of earth filled the air. Billowing, puffy white clouds floated in the vivid blue sky.

Brandelene's curiosity could no longer be contained. As soon as they were seated she asked, "Kord, what is happening?" Then she smiled. "You've received a letter."

"Better than that, my beauty." Kordell laughed, elated, and pulled several letters from his coat pocket.

Instantly Brandelene recognized the dainty writing of a woman's hand on the top letter and her heart lurched. Her gaze lifted to his, questioningly.

"Pierre, the gentleman you saw me speaking with, is a courier sent by my brother, Jacques." With that, he pulled a large number of bank notes from his coat pocket and handed them to her. "This should reimburse you the cost of Dagert and me, plus what you spent for our clothes, inn bills, expenses, and the music box I gave you." As Brandelene's stunned reaction turned into a questioning gaze, he reassured her, "Don't be concerned. Jacques sent enough to pay our ship fare home, expense money, and some extra."

"Kord . . ."

He raised his hand to still her protest. "I told you I'd repay you, Brandy, and I'll hear no protests."

"I didn't agree to any such arrangement, and I know it's a sum you can't afford," she argued and pushed the money back at him.

Once again he handed her the money across the table. "Put the money in your bag, Brandy. We can discuss it later. For now we are celebrating."

Rather than create a public scene, Brandelene picked up the stack of bills and placed them in her reticule. She would return the money later, for he had not denied it was a sum he could not afford. Undoubtedly it was from his wealthy Nicolle. Brandelene fought to constrain her emotions. She swallowed hard and bit back the tears that threatened to surface, then lifted her chin haughtily. "It appears, Kord, that everything has worked out well for both of us." With that, she lifted her glass of wine and toasted, "To both of us getting what we desire."

Kordell grinned and touched his glass to hers.

Their gazes met and held over the rim of their goblets.

"Are you planning to leave immediately?" Brandelene's trembling fingers on her wineglass belied the air of indifference in her casual inquiry.

She was visibly pale and Kordell did not miss any of what she tried so hard to disguise. "Do you want me to leave now?"

With her aching heart thudding in her ears, she could think of nothing to say.

It rushed through Kordell's mind that Brandelene did not want him to leave. Her refusal to submit to him the other night made it abundantly clear she did not love him. By posing as her husband nd building the irrigation system, he had served his usefulness o her, so she no longer needed him. Brandelene tried to disguise her feelings, but Kordell could see she was overwrought. With ime he'd come to know her, had discovered that her proudly lifted chin, her rigid back, and her cutting words tossed haughtily were all a facade to mask her real emotions. He had also learned to look beneath the surface to examine her true feelings. And that he did now, and could arrive at only one conclusion—perhaps he did not love him, but she had grown to care. It was not what he hoped for, but it was a beginning.

"Brandy, will you marry me?"

"What did you say?"

Gently, he placed his hand over hers on the table and repeated, "Will you marry me?"

Speechless, Brandelene swallowed her gasp and tried to think over the din that roared through her mind.

Kordell's hand tightened over hers. "Even you will admit we make a perfect team."

Stiffening at his last words, Brandelene wrenched her hand from beneath his. Make a perfect team, indeed. He sounded as though he were talking about her carriage horses. Men who could not see the color of her eyes for the color of her father's gold had proposed to her more romantically. Then, as the idea occurred to her, she owered her thickly lashed lids, looking at his hands covering hers.

"What color are my eyes, Kord?"

"Your eyes?"

Certain he did not know, she refused to glance up. "Yes, what color are my eyes?"

"Most of the time they are more beautiful than any delicate wood violet I could ever hope to gaze upon. Yet there are times, when you're laughing in the sun, that they are a crystalline amethyst, more exquisite than the most expensive of jewels. At other times when you're angry, as now, they become an unfathomabl black magenta."

Brandelene glanced up at him, cursing his smooth tongue, hi charm, his adeptness to rip her heart from her chest. Even so not a word of love did he speak. Did he still seek Southern Oaks "In answer to your question, Kordell, I'm quite surprised you'v forgotten. We are married." She picked up her reticule, silentl signaling that she wished to leave and that this conversation wa ended.

As they left the tavern, Kordell broke the uncomfortable silence "I've a few additional matters to discuss with Pierre. We'll nee to stay over."

"Take as long as you need. Joshua can drive me to Souther Oaks and return for you tomorrow."

"Brandelene! You're not leaving Petersburg without me." Kor dell's hand tightened on her elbow and he wondered what angere her now. "I'll take two rooms at the Wolf's Lair." With that, h led Brandelene, who protested all the way, back into the taver to acquire adjoining rooms.

Much later that night, Brandelene slipped from her bed to stan in her chemise at the open window. She stared out into the moonlit rain-rutted street. Her mind would give her no peace. Long ago she'd lost count of how many sleepless nights Kordell had cause her, and this night was no exception. Only her dilemma differed

On the one side, she hoped Kordell would immediately retur to the Ivory Coast where he would be out of her life forever. The she would be spared her obsession to have a man who could neve be hers on any terms with which she could live. Yet on the othe side, she had experienced what life was without him—empty meaningless, joyless, and she once again wished with all her hear that Kordell Bouclair loved her.

Through the partially opened window a breeze, scented wit the freshness of recent rains, toyed with her tousled hair an pressed her chemise against her youthfully curving body. He thoughts turned to Kordell's golden catlike eyes. Leonine eyes tha drew her magnetically, irresistibly, and she recalled when a child her parents had taken her to New York. There had been a fai with many exotic African animals. Yet it had been the lion that had captured her heart as he paced his cage with an indomitable spirit that spoke volumes. His incarceration would never break his proud spirit, for he'd been, and in his heart still was, lord of the jungle. The magnificent animal had paused to aloofly return her stare from haunting golden eyes that mesmerized her. Then, after a time, he'd shaken his mighty mane and proudly sauntered away, his majestic head held arrogantly high.

Now another magnificent animal with mesmerizing golden eyes had captured her heart, and he too was about to saunter out of her life.

Where would she find a husband who would greet her with a rose and a devastating smile each morning; would permit her to run Southern Oaks without interference; would work tirelessly beside her; would defend her and the plantation at the risk of his own life; would comfort her like a child when she had a nightmare; had an incomparable sense of humor; was impressively intelligent and educated; had more charm and charisma in his heartwarming smile than most men had in their entire being?

Where would she find a husband whose embrace thrilled her senseless, whose masterful kisses melted her and spun her into another existence? Where would she ever, ever, find another Kordell?

Now it was too late to stop the annulment. At this moment Charles Thompson's legal assistant rode to Richmond, and her aching heart kept cadence with the horse's hooves. There was no way to stop the filing of the documents, so essentially she was no longer married to Armand Kordell Bouclair.

Anguish overwhelmed her. Bereft, she stumbled blindly from the window, bumping over the small tea table, and the lamp crashed to the floor.

Seconds later the connecting door from Kordell's room banged open. "My God, Brandy!" He saw the overturned table, the broken lamp, and quickly surveyed the moonlit room for an intruder. "Are you ill? What happened? You are ill!" In swift strides he stood at her side and saw the raw agony that shimmered in her eyes. Then he pulled her into strong arms to comfort her and the more he whispered soothing words the more she trembled. Finally, unable to bear not knowing what ailed her, he set her from him and held her shaking hands in his tender grasp. He glanced down at her disheveled appearance. "What did the doctor tell you today? Tell me, Brandy."

"I'm fine, Kord." Her eyes filled with unshed tears. "That's not what's wrong. Really it isn't."

Relieved, Kordell exhaled sharply and pulled her into his arms. "Did you have a nightmare?" Soothingly he stroked her head. With all the adversity Brandelene had endured in the last five months the only time he'd seen her distraught was when she had finally submitted to her grief for her father. At a loss, if indeed she were not ill, to explain what could possibly cause her such distress, he urged softly, "You know, my darling, there's nothing we can't overcome together. We've proven that already."

At his endearment, Brandelene relaxed in his arms. "We? There is no we, Kord. You're leaving."

Once again, Kordell set her from him and tilted her chin up to gaze into her glistening, tormented eyes. "Our agreement's for one more month."

"But you gave me the money for your contract, which I'm not accepting. That wasn't the agreement."

"How could I leave you now, with the tobacco ready to harvest?" Abruptly aware, intensely aware, that she wore only her chemise, he swallowed hard and fought to control his automatic response.

"Earlier, I asked if you were leaving now and you didn't answer."

"Is that what this is about, Brandy?"

"No."

"The truth, Brandy."

"Well . . ."

She loves me! Kordell's heart sang. Whether she knows it or not, Brandelene loves me. Then he pulled her back into his warm embrace. High, firm breasts burned into his chest and he fought his desire for her. But he would put his hand in burning fire before he would press her feelings for him now, and he forced his mind from the hunger that raged through his loins as he clung to her. "Brandy," he whispered into the soft fragrance of her hair. "I gave you that money today because I know you're desperately in need of cash. I have no intention of leaving now."

"Oh, Kord, why are you so good to me?" Brandelene cried out and rose on tiptoe to brush a soft kiss against his carved lips. Then, somehow, her arms slipped around his broad shoulders and she kissed him with all the love in her yearning heart, all the pent-up passion within her scorching body.

Reluctantly he lifted his lips from hers and removed her arms from around his neck. "I'd better leave, Brandy, or I won't be able to."

Everything faded to nothingness and there was only Kordell. Brandelene could not think, she could only feel, and all she felt was her desperate need to be in his arms. She molded her body to his and gazed up at him with glazed eyes. "Don't leave, Kord."

Chapter 24

IF SHE COULD NOT HAVE HIS LOVE, BRANDELENE DECIDED she could have this night in his arms, this one night of ecstasy, where nothing else existed but her love for Kordell.

When she'd filed the documents of annulment, supported by the doctor's certificate, she had forever removed Southern Oaks from his grasp, but in its stead she now offered him herself. She whispered, "I want you."

They were not the words Kordell had hoped to hear. With her body molded against his, he shuddered. Never had he craved a woman so much. At this moment he could not even remember another woman. Overcoming the passion that raged through his body, he spoke softly, "Brandy, there will be no repeat of the other night. That's asking too much of me."

"Love me, Kord."

Her words were soft. Sensuous. Submitting.

She offered what he'd craved, yearned for, what had haunted his dreams, night and day, for five months, and yet he hesitated, made no move to entice her with tantalizing kisses, to seduce her with tormenting caresses, to persuade her with tender words, as he would have a temporary conquest, for she was the woman he loved and there must be no regrets by her come the dawn. He raised his hands to cup her face between his palms. "You realize this will mean you are my wife, for I will not file the annulment. There will be no turning back."

Startled, Brandelene stiffened at his words. Then she placed her hands over his. Capturing his gaze in the moonlight, she softly murmured, "I request two things from you, Kord. Ask me no questions. And for this night only, pretend you love me as you have loved no other woman."

Smiling, Kordell instantly understood why the other night Brandelene had turned from fire to ice in his arms. Why she had treated his proposal today with cool indifference. She needed him to tell her that he loved her, and he cursed his ignorance, even though he had never uttered those most precious of words to any woman. Tenderly he lifted her into his arms and carried her to the bed, laying her there ever so gently. Then he lay beside her and hoped he had the strength to hold himself in check long enough to do as she asked. He had waited so long—so very long.

Moonlight filled the room and Brandelene's raven hair fanned over the pillow, as he'd envisioned it during so many sleepless nights. He bent over her and his long, slender fingers traced the high cheekbones of her delicate face, then slowly moved to caress the perfection of her sensuous mouth. "After all we've been to each other could you possibly doubt how much I love you?" He lowered his head to brush the tip of her nose with warm lips. Then slowly, his caressing mouth moved upward while his hand moved with whisper lightness down her body. "I love you, my Brandy," he huskily murmured, pressing a tiny kiss to one closed lid. Then his mouth moved across her brow. "I love you," he repeated softly, seductively kissing the other lid ever so lightly.

At Kordell's gentle touch, his tender words, Brandelene spiraled into another world, a world where she could forget his words were false and his motives less than pure, and she marveled at the feelings that engulfed her. Her arms slid around his nape and her fingers entwined themselves in his thick mane of tawny hair. For this night Kordell was her lion.

And she, the lion tamer.

His moist lips trailed down her cheek while his fingers tiptoed sensuously over her body. She shuddered and his mouth hovered over hers, so close she could feel the warmth of his breath mingle with hers.

"I will love you forever, Brandy. Forever!"

At those heart-stirring words, his lingering lips claimed hers in a silken kiss of such gentleness, such tenderness, that it stole her breath away, and took her soul with it. A sigh escaped her satiny lips. Brandelene did not know what she had expected from Kordell when she asked him to play one more charade of love, but it was not this heart-wrenching display of affection that asked everything of her and left her nothing. Yet she cared naught, for this was the man she loved with all her heart and soul, and she lay in his arms hearing all the things she'd so often dreamed he would say. There was only this moment, this timeless eternity.

And she was just being born.

Then his drugging kiss deepened sensually and her willing lips parted beneath his. Their tongues entwined, but unlike the first time, when he'd explored the sweetness of her mouth with passion, this time it was a slow, deliberate caressing, and his tongue stroked the honeyed caverns ever so gently, so infinitely tender while his fingers resumed their light, slow torment of her body. Every touch, every exploration, was with reverence, as if he cherished each part of her, until she felt she could not bear the intoxicating pleasure for another moment.

Again, Kordell's breath felt warm on her ear and his moist lips nibbled at her ear to send shivers of delight splintering through her. He whispered, "A poet said, far more eloquently than I ever could, 'If I could choose from every woman on this earth, the heart, the soul, the face I would most love—they would all be yours.'" Then he cupped her face between his palms and gazed into her eyes. "I would add one thing, Brandy. If I could choose from every woman on this earth, the one whom I would spend the rest of my life with, it would be you."

At his words, Brandelene surrendered wholly, completely, and irrevocably to the seduction of her heart.

Her pulse leaped in her throat and she was suffocating, drowning in a tumultuous whirlpool of emotions. Then her gaze locked with his while everything whirled around her and she was cold, then hot, then cold again. So this was what it felt like to *explore the heavens*? This splendorous, indescribable feeling of floating, drifting on waves of pleasure as the world slipped away.

Once more, Kordell's hungry mouth covered hers, moved sensuously, eagerly to devour her lips with an urgency that had not been there before. His fingers tangled in her hair, and she yielded to the flickering flames that sprang alive within her. Moaning, her hands clasped his head and pulled him closer as the feelings that enveloped her increased. Then slowly her fingers moved down his bare back to feel the muscles she'd so often admired quiver beneath her delicate touch. After a time his ravaging mouth raised from hers and she whimpered in protest, but was soon soothed as his teasing lips dusted down the column of her slender neck to her pulsing throat, while his fingers worked at the laces of her chemise. Slowly and ever so gently, his hand slipped beneath the lacy fabric to cup the fullness of her heaving breast. He fondled, teased the pink bud into rosy hardness, and she gasped at the wild shiver that trickled down her spine.

"Kord," she moaned, arching into the palm of his hand, and she squirmed beneath the teasing of his tongue doing wondrous things to her flesh as it blazed from her throat, downward to sear a burning path to her breast. Then he pressed moist, featherlight kisses on the mounds of her breasts. Kisses that scorched into the tender flesh as his tongue delicately caressed the sensitive swollen nipples. This time, his searching mouth engulfed the softness of her breast while his fingers weightlessly trailed up the inside of her thigh. Glazed eyes flew open as she was jolted by an indescribable heat that started in the pit of her stomach and splintered through her body in a fiery path that intensified as his hand roamed her thighs, then wandered to her abdomen and hovered ever so near the fur that shielded her womanhood.

Kordell fought a battle of self-control that he slowly lost, and he groaned aloud. Seeking to remove himself from the agony of wanting to fling himself upon her and take what his tortured body desperately craved, he sat up, and with deliberate slowness gently removed her chemise. But then the action he had taken to temporarily cool his heated ardor now fired his aching loins all the more as his hungry gaze feasted on the vision of perfection who lay before him.

The moonlight cast her breathtaking beauty in soft, alluring shadows. Her figure was curving and graceful and his gaze roamed her body, mesmerized. The fullness of her lush, firm breasts beckoned him, and he reached out to trace the rosy peaks that begged him to taste fully of the pleasure there. His gaze moved slowly downward to the tiny waist his hands had easily spanned, then wandered slowly to the flared swell of her curving hips and her taut, slightly rounded abdomen, following her hips as they tapered into shapely thighs and slender legs. Then he started the long, slow journey back up her temptingly curvaceous form and searched for some tiny flaw, but found none. His slow and deliberate study of her ended only when his gaze met hers. Silently she'd watched his lengthy appraisal of her, and her soft lips now parted invitingly. She was a ravishing, raven-haired temptress of extraordinary beauty, and soon she would be his wife, in every way. He smiled at her, his eyes glazed with desire, and her innocence irresistibly beckoned. He lowered his head to hers once more.

Soon Kordell's consuming kisses were passionate, drugging, and his possessive mouth moved over hers with an intensity, a hunger that left her weak and craving more as she returned kiss for kiss. His tongue sensuously captured hers and Brandelene gasped, unable to catch her breath.

His hands skillfully massaged and caressed every curve of her yearning body to send ever new sensations streaking through her, kindling a fire that threatened to consume them both with the intensity of the heat. Then, where his hands had burned their way across her body, his hot, moist lips scorched her flesh and his tongue seared his brand into her as she writhed in ecstasy. Aflame with desire, she called his name, reveling in the exquisite pleasure she discovered in his arms.

He rolled from the side of the bed and doffed his breeches. His hungry eyes devoured her porcelain beauty in the moonlight, and momentarily, it was as though he had discovered an unattainable goddess whom no mere mortal dared to love, and if he moved to possess her she would disappear, a mystical figment of his imagination. Even so, Brandelene beckoned, irresistibly, and he slowly lowered his body over hers and her enormous violet eyes implored him to be gentle.

Kordell had never made love to a virgin. Yet many of the tavern wenches, wives, and widows whom he'd bedded throughout the years had expounded on the horror of their first night with a man and the man's insensitivity. And he determined that such would not be the memories with Brandelene. He did not want her to wake tomorrow with any regrets, and he would make any sacrifice to achieve that end—if his body would cooperate. Yet he had discovered with Brandelene exactly how weak was his flesh. With that firmly in mind, he groaned inwardly and moved his naked frame from over hers and lay beside her.

At her inquiring look, he smiled, then moved to whisper words of love, over and over. Gently he ran his fingers through her silken hair to examine the luxuriously thick raven strands that he'd so often admired, allowing his ardor to cool as much as possible, which seemed to be none at all.

Then, once again he bent over her, and his lips covered hers in a gentle kiss that quickly turned to the same fire that raged through his aching loins. For the first time in his life, he thought only of pleasuring the woman who lay in his embrace, and he began with a slow, torturous assault of her naked flesh with his ravenous mouth, his exploring lips, his pillaging tongue.

He left no part of her body untouched by his mouth, or his magically gentle hands, and Brandelene gasped and moaned in sweet agony as Kordell turned her body into a flaming inferno, where she writhed in ecstasy to be ever nearer the flame. Just when she knew she would surely die from the fiery sensations that seared through her like molten lava, his expertise sent her to even higher levels of ecstasy and the fire spread to her heart, consuming her. A passionate moan of desire escaped her soft lips and she pleaded for release from her joyous torment. It flashed through her mind that, certainly, this time she would die from the delicious pleasure that washed over her in wave after wave. Yet she cared not.

"Kord! Kord!" she cried out passionately, unaware she'd uttered a word.

With a tortured groan, Kordell moved his muscular body over hers and her hands embraced him, welcoming the weight, the strength of his body as his hungry lips recaptured hers. Weak with desire, she stiffened slightly as the power of his burgeoning manhood pressed against her thigh. Then began the slow but exquisite manipulation of her womanhood and she opened her thighs to welcome the man she loved more than anything in life. A willing vassal to his intoxicating touch, she relaxed beneath the expert explorations of his ravaging lips, his pillaging hands, before he lowered his slender hips to hers and gently entered her.

He stopped at the delicate shield that assured him no man had ever been where he ventured forth and he reveled in the knowledge.

Gasping in pain, Brandelene tried to twist free of the intrusion of her body and pushed ineffectually against the wide expanse of his furry chest.

"Trust me, my love, and I will take you to the stars." Then he devoured her lips with a fevered, savage urgency. Parted them, twisted, burned, slanted across them as though he could not get enough of the honey sweetness, sparking her passionate return, and they kissed with a wild abandon borne of unsated desperation. Their tongues mated in quivering desire, their breath merged and became one.

Their hearts thudded wildly, echoing inside their cavity where his burning chest pressed against her fevered breasts. Then he thrust and a searing pain shot through her loins and his mouth stilled her cry. Unmoving, he smothered her face with a trail of never-ending, burning kisses and murmured words of love, soothing her until the pain subsided, all the while fighting his own overwhelming passion that sought to overpower all else.

Presently, slowly, ever so slowly, he began to move deep inside her while his hands, lips, and tongue once again began their subtle magic and aroused her to a fever pitch to fill her with such exquisite pleasure that she floated in another world, suspended in timeless ecstasy, wanting this moment of unendurable, rapturous exhilaration never to end.

Breathless and yearning for what, she knew not, Brandelene instinctively arched her hips in hungry impatience to meet Kordell's searing, surging thrusts in a primitive gesture as old as the beginning of time. To race toward some unknown culmination that would release her from her exquisite torment. And then her body exploded into millions of brilliant shards that defied description and shattered her being into a black sky filled with sparkling stars where she floated above the earth as wave after wave of scorching, fiery sensations splintered through the center of her being.

A magical, mystical place where nothing existed but Kordell and she as they whirled through the heavens for a fleeting eternity, engulfed in euphoria.

And from that lofty position she could hear herself cry out his name over and over.

At the sound of Brandelene's passionate cries the fire in Kordell's loins raged out of control and with his next thrust of ardor a wild, soaring ecstasy burst forth and fused them together in a glorious, rapturous, all-consuming culmination that sent him spinning through the heavens with her on a fiery journey that melded their souls into one.

It was the most beautiful, the most awesome experience of his life.

Sometime later Kordell raised his tawny head from where it nestled in the curve of her neck to glance down at her and his look gently caressed her as she gazed up at him with wide, searching eyes, amazement etched there.

His lips gently met hers in a moving kiss of such tenderness that her heart surged at the gesture that meant far more than words.

Brandelene smiled up at him.

Kordell's returning smile dazzled her.

Then he rolled beside her, pulling her close, and placed her head on his shoulder. A contented sigh escaped his sculpted lips as he gazed down into the crystalline amethyst eyes that still glowed with passion's flame, and he marveled. Their union had been so much more than he could have ever imagined.

A sigh escaped Brandelene's lips, and she expected to feel a rush of gnawing guilt to torment her for giving herself to the man who was no longer her husband, but no such emotions came. There was only the beauty of the intimacy she'd experienced with the man she loved. She vaguely wondered why she felt such a bond of tenderness for the man who had made her a woman. It was that feeling, and the feeling of rightness she felt at being in his arms, as though here was where she was meant to be, like the sun in the sky, that frightened her. And that wholeness, that awareness of consummate, all-consuming contentment, disturbed her far more than guilt ever could.

For now her happiness was dependent upon Kordell Bouclair.

She traced a fingertip delicately across his marvelous, sensuous mouth and wistfully queried, "Is it always this way between a man and a woman?"

"Never, my love," Kordell replied huskily, lifting her chin with gentle fingers to capture her gaze. "Never!" Gentle fingers moved to caress the contours of her face with a whisper-soft touch. "What you and I shared this night can never be recaptured."

Brandelene believed him, for she could not conceive of ever equaling the experiences she'd reveled in within Kordell's arms, and to surpass such ecstasy would be surely to die.

"Ahh, Brandy," he sighed contentedly. "You have no idea how sorely you've plagued me these many months." With that his warm lips brushed hers with feathery kisses. "Now you are truly my wife. My beloved wife."

Kordell's words were uttered with a tenderness, a depth of feeling Brandelene did not expect, and regardless of his reasons for wanting to be married to her, she could not deceive him by allowing him to think they were still married. She had to tell him what she'd done. "Kord . . ."

His mouth gently, tenderly slanted across hers, interrupted her confession, and Brandelene returned his warm, fleeting kisses. "I love you, my Brandy." His lips hovered inches from hers and his eyes were suddenly pensive. "The thought of spending the rest of my life with you, growing old with you, is a heady, heady wine." Then his lips savored hers once more.

Reluctantly she pulled her mouth from his and breathed, "Kord, I must tell you . . ."

But then he once again smothered her with loving kisses. When he raised his lips from hers, he tenderly smoothed her rumpled hair and gazed at her with golden cat-eyes and what she had been about to say vanished with the quickening of her pulse. Promptly she realized that she lay naked in his tight embrace. Her arms still circled his neck, and their legs entwined intimately. Her breasts crushed against the power of his furred chest while her stomach pressed to the hardness of his abdomen, and she felt the heat of every place his flesh touched her flesh. It was deliciously warm.

Now Kordell traced his mouth searchingly along the graceful column of her throat. The fragrance that seemed so much a part of her filled his nostrils, that haunting scent that had plagued him every waking hour, every moment of his dreams.

To appease her twinge of conscience, Brandelene quickly dismissed the fact that she'd arranged for an annulment. The documents were not yet filled in Richmond. Legally, for this night, she was still Kordell's wife and he her husband.

Tomorrow morning she would tell him what she had done.

Chapter 25

BRANDELENE'S FINGERS PLAYED GENTLY DOWN THE muscular tendons of Kordell's back to his slender hips and hesitated there before she trailed her fingernails teasingly up his back, pleased by his responsive shudder. Moments later her eyes widened as she became aware of his growing desire, and her own body responded with a heated rush. Eagerly, she reached up and trailed her fingers through his hair, gasping as his lips found her breast and his warm tongue teased the pink tip to an arousing tautness. "You're a lusty lion." She laughed softly.

"Complaining, my sweet?" Kordell continued with his ardent, mind-whirling assault of her body, her low moan the only answer he received.

The feel of her body molded so intimately to his ignited a wildfire that began to burn out of control and his lips ravenously recaptured hers with a scalding intensity that torched them both. He nibbled sensuously, passionately at her kiss-swollen lips, and she mimicked his gesture. His tongue seared inside her mouth and she captured it with her own, curling her tongue around his to send their unleashed desires flaming higher. Hot, trembling hands roamed every inch of her body and she writhed with wild abandon under his skillful touch.

Kordell's hungry lips explored her body while her world careened crazily beneath the exhilarating torment, and her consciousness seemed to ebb and then flame brighter than before. A moan of surrender escaped her lips and he raised himself above her as he hungrily devoured her, then lifted her hips to accept him. Then they moved wildly together, striving for the depths of intimacy as the fire of their passion raged out of control. Swept along in the violent storm of mutual craving, she abandoned herself to the whirl of rapturous sensations that consumed her as he took her ever higher and higher.

She cried out his name and feverishly met his throbbing surges, his passionate thrusts, writhing in sweet agony for release from the fiery torture that radiated uncontrollably through the core of her being. A tremor inside her seared her thighs and groin while her body began to vibrate with a liquid fire that exploded in fiery sensations and soared her to an awesome, shattering ecstasy. Kordell joined her in a shuddering release and their souls took flight to soar above the raging fires that seared their bodies. Her body melded to his and her world was filled only with him as they drifted languorously through the heavens together.

Her fingernails still dug into his back when he gently lowered his body to hers and tenderly claimed her lips in an endless kiss. After a time, he rolled over, pulling her with him, and for a long time neither spoke. Neither knew the words to express what they felt.

"Brandy."

The husky murmur of her name interrupted her pondering and she glanced up at Kordell's handsome face.

He pressed warm lips to her brow and one hand clasped her close while the other absently roamed her body, as though, now that he'd possessed her, he could not keep himself from her. She reveled in the warm feeling it gave her.

"I didn't know it at the time," he said in a low, deep voice while his hand gently caressed her breast, "but I started to fall in love with you when you brandished your pistol and a whip to get laudanum for me."

Smiling at the remembrance Brandelene snuggled closer in his arms.

Feathering light kisses over her face, he continued, "I could no longer deny there was something incredible, magnificent, monumental, between us when we married."

His fingers massaged her taut abdomen and she once again felt the magical stirrings deep inside.

He picked up raven strands of her silky hair, carefully examining each curling tendril before he let it fall to her naked shoulder. "After you nursed me through the fever, I had foggy recollections of the hell you put me through, but I realized that was probably what had saved my life, and I could not imagine another woman doing what you'd done, and I agonized over my growing feelings for you, even then."

At his words, Brandelene stiffened with confusion. Why was he saying these things to her? She had only asked that he pretend he loved her, which he'd done with an expertise that almost allowed her to believe it. She had satisfied his lust. Now he believed himself to be her husband, and as such controlled Southern Oaks. Why did he still torment her with words she wanted more than anything to believe?

Kordell laughed softly. "When I saw you in Dean Paul's arms at our reception, I wanted to kill him." He paused. "Brandy, I've never felt that way before."

At the words she wanted so much to believe, her heart lurched, his lips found hers, and she fervently kissed him with all the ardor, all the love, that filled her heart to overflowing. Releasing her lips, he leaned back into his pillow and pulled her against the wide expanse of his muscular chest, and she could hear his pounding heart.

"When you aimed your rifle at Harold Mason that night at Southern Oaks, I think I knew I would never give you up. And the weeks we spent together after that, while I recuperated, I knew what was happening to me, but still I couldn't admit it." His hands resumed their sensuous roaming.

"I was falling in love with my wife."

Brandelene placed gentle fingertips over his carved lips to still his words, then guiltily pulled free of Kordell's embrace. Sitting up, she devoured the splendor of the masculine body lying naked next to her. She drew in her breath sharply, for her proud lion was a majestic animal. Hungrily, she appraised the length of him, admiring his massive broad shoulders and muscular biceps, to his powerful chest that tapered to a narrow waist and slender hips.

Then her eyes widened as she stared at the burgeoning masculinity that had taken her to such rapturous heights.

"Wifely curiosity?" Kordell grinned devilishly.

Brandelene flushed crimson. "You're a lusty rogue, Armand Kordell Bouclair."

"Is that a complaint, madame?"

"Yes," she answered dreamily before she bent over him to press a sensuous kiss to his lips. She lifted her mouth only enough to seductively breathe her next words, "You've a reputation to maintain and you've neglected me far too long." Then her lips captured his in a fiery, intimate kiss.

Twice more she was his, before they collapsed in blissful exhaustion, temporarily sated, and their naked bodies glistened from the moisture of their scorchingly passionate lovemaking. They slept in each other's arms with legs entwined, clinging to one another, lovers, each fearing what the dawn might bring.

Kordell's lips awoke Brandelene in the morning, and when his twisting, tormenting mouth finally lifted from hers, she smiled happily, contentedly, and slipped her arms around his neck to gaze into his leonine eyes. "Good morning, Kord," she whispered sleepily and nibbled at his chin as he bent over her, her voice more seductive than she'd intended.

"Good morning, Brandy." He grinned at her. "I feared I'd wake to find last night only a magnificent dream."

Drowsily, she flushed at the recollection of her behavior, marveling that only a few hours ago she'd been an innocent girl. What was it about this one man that could inspire her to behave in a manner she would have considered disgraceful yesterday? "You must think me shameless."

Kordell's eyes sparkled. "My sweet, if your conduct last night was shameless, I beg you—be shameless the rest of our lives." With that he crushed her to him, kissing her senseless while she happily disgraced herself again.

Sometime later Brandelene lay contentedly in Kordell's arms, marveling at the ecstasy she'd shared with him during the previous few hours. Each time he'd made love to her she'd felt it impossible to experience a more rapturous journey without expiring from the pleasure of it all, and each time he had taken her to new heights. "Kord," she protested halfheartedly while she lay in his warm embrace, "we really must start back to Southern Oaks. We were expected home last night."

Kordell chuckled and kissed her briefly. "Brandy, last night was our wedding night. Considerably belated, granted, but our wedding night, nonetheless. We've endured much these last months, not to mention how hard we've worked. Don't you think we deserve this day for ourselves?" For a moment he was disturbed because instead of finding himself completely sated after spending the night making love to her, he whirled helplessly in a vortex, his appetite for her as insatiable as a man consumed by a powerful drug.

Brandelene sighed and stretched her arm around Kordell's slim waist. What difference would one more day make? Legally she was still his wife until Monday, and this was only Saturday. What more harm could be done if she spent this day in the charade they both acted out?

One whole glorious day to live a fantasy with Kordell.

Tomorrow she would tell him what she had done.

Besides, what harm to let Kordell have his dream for one day, that as her husband he now owned Southern Oaks? After all, he had not taken anything she had not willingly, too willingly, given. What wrong to pretend, for one more day, that Kordell loved her with all his heart and soul, as he had pretended last night, as she loved him? Sighing again, she nodded her assent, then was soon asleep in his arms.

But while Brandelene slept, Kordell was wide awake. With his obsessive craving temporarily assuaged, he was thinking clearly and he sensed something was wrong. It now occurred to him that for all his declarations of love, not once through the long and glorious night had the word "love" crossed Brandelene's lovely lips. Unquestionably, she did not consummate their marriage unintentionally. But why had she said, "Ask me no questions"? His arm unconsciously tightened around her sleeping form and he wondered if her trip to Petersburg had some purpose other than what she said. He drifted into an uneasy sleep pondering why

Brandelene had tried to sneak into Petersburg without him.

It was midday when Brandelene awoke in Kordell's arms and sighed contentedly. Wishing she could stop time, she refused to think of anything unpleasant on this day. She had asked for one night of fantasy and she was being given two nights and a day. She would permit nothing to spoil her only remaining day and night.

Brandelene rose up on her elbow and gazed into his golden eyes. Smiling, she brushed her lips across the sensuously carved mouth that sent her heart racing every time she glanced at it. "My lusty rogue, would you please pull the bell cord and order us a hot bath and change of linen. I find something has given me a ravenous appetite and after a night and morning in bed with you, I hardly dare leave the room until I have my bath." Then she gave Kordell a mischievous grin and lightly kissed him again.

Kordell grabbed her and pulled her down onto the bed. "The only thing I hunger for is you, my lovely wife."

Sometime later he ordered two baths, a change of linen, and dinner with wine brought to their room. At his suggestion, they used one tub to bathe in and the other to rinse. Together they squeezed into the small tub, laughing and splashing like children, the water overflowing.

Wrapped in bath sheets, they dined, laughed, and drank wine.

"What," Kordell queried with glinting eyes and one rakishly raised brow, "shall we have for dessert, my sweet?"

She laughed gaily. "Kord, you're insatiable."

"Pleading a headache already, wife?"

"Never!" Giggling delightfully, she jerked the bath sheet from his lean hips.

He scooped her up in his arms and carried her to their freshly made bed, and the lovers once again journeyed to that magical place that contains no walls or time, only ecstasy and space.

Later, as he lay in bed with Brandelene clasped in his arms, Kordell's thoughts again roiled with all the unanswered questions that plagued him. "What pretty things did you buy yesterday, love?"

"A petticoat and a chemise."

"That's all you could find to buy during all that time I talked with Pierre? My darling, most women I know would've bought out half the store. Where else did you go?"

Brandelene's heart raced crazily. Could Kordell or Joshua have seen her slip down the street to Thompson's office? Or perhaps Joshua had mentioned to Kordell that he'd come for her only to find the ladies' shop empty, and had searched everywhere before he returned. Gathering her wits, her sweeping lashes that shadowed her cheeks flew up.

She gazed up at him from the violet eyes that turned him weak. "Where else could I go, Kord? You had the coach."

As a young man, Kordell had learned that when a woman asked him a question he did not want to answer, he avoided answering by posing a question of his own. Brandelene had just done the same thing. He bent to kiss her, putting her at ease. "I thought perhaps, seeing as you haven't been to Petersburg since our reception over four months ago, that you might've seen someone you knew, or heard some news of Cyrus." He stroked her hair, aware of her deep inhalation of breath, the slight stiffening of her body, her damning silence.

"It might be a good idea to check with Thompson before we leave, Brandy, to see if Cyrus is up to anything."

Shattered by Kordell's suggestion, Brandelene fought to maintain her fragile control, then forged ahead, hoping to divert him. "Yes. Perhaps we should check with the lawyer. However I'm sure if there was any problem, Charles Thompson would've sent a message to us. Besides, it's so cozy in this bed. . . ." Her pulse raced frantically as she hoped her ploy would work. She snuggled closer. Striving to distract his thinking from the lawyer, she said, "Oh, I did run into Dean Paul Mason. He's getting married and invited us to attend his betrothal ball." She hesitated when she felt Kordell's body tense. "Although I refuse to go, I told Dean Paul I'd discuss it with you and send a reply after his invitation arrived."

With a controlled voice that betrayed none of the tumultuous feelings tearing through him, Kordell casually asked, "Where did you see Dean Paul?" Then he condemned himself for his jealousy, wondering if he was so besotted he would never have another rational thought regarding Brandelene.

"I almost collided with him when I left the ladies' shop. Dean Paul seems quite taken with this girl he's to marry." Brandelene sighed happily, grateful her friend had found someone else. "So much for Dean Paul's vow of eternal love for me."

"Why do you think Dean Paul doesn't still love you?"

"I know."

Kordell knew too. All the pieces of the puzzle started to fall into place. Months ago Brandelene had deceived him when she denied being in love with young Mason. All this time she had loved Dean Paul. That was why she'd been so distraught last night. Dean Paul was marrying another. With the man she truly loved forever lost to her, she cared naught whom she married. Last night she had turned to him for consolation and that thought, a knife that ripped though him, shredded his insides. He was married to a woman whom he loved to distraction but she loved another man.

Inwardly sick, Kordell hated her for having duped him, and bitterly cursed his stupidity. All he cared about was hurting her as she had him and took her as he would a harlot, with neither love, nor tenderness, nor gentleness, or any of the loving consideration that had been in all their previous unions.

But when he rolled from her, the satisfaction he expected by treating her so was not there. He felt only pain and guilt. He had turned the most beautiful experience of his life into merely a sordid encounter that satisfied his physical needs, but neither his emotional needs nor the needs of his bleeding heart.

Love! He grimaced silently, then cursed himself for surrendering his heart to such sweet hell.

Brandelene wondered why Kordell had treated her so. Why had he seemed so angry? What had she done, or said? Indeed, she'd simply told him about Dean Paul in hopes to distract him from the lawyer. Dean Paul! Her shock and pain turned to understanding, and then exhilaration, as the words Kordell had whispered to her last night rushed back: "When I saw you in Dean Paul's arms at our reception, I wanted to kill him." She smiled inwardly, for whether Kordell realized it or not, he was falling in love with her. He must be, he had to be, and she was hopefully ecstatic. But it was too late to stop the annulment, and to tell him now would ruin everything.

She had resolved her problem with Cyrus, certainly she could find the solution that would give her Kordell's heart. The answer came unprompted. For the next month she would play the part of his wife and not tell him she'd filed the annulment. What more harm could be done? She had already surrendered her virtue. During the month, with Kordell believing her to be his wife, she would find out his true character. There would be no more need for pretense on his part, and his disguise would be stripped away. Perhaps, when she discovered the real Kordell Bouclair, she would even get over her obsession for him. Or perhaps he was the man that with all her heart she wished he were, and she could win his love. If so, she would confess all at that time and they could remarry. Satisfied with her plans she turned to Kordell.

"Brandy, I. . . ."

Delicate fingers pressed against his lips to interrupt him. "No apologies, no explanations. I know it won't happen again."

Overwhelmed by guilt, regret, and love, Kordell cradled her in his arms. Never would he have imagined that a woman could weave such a web of enchantment around him. Never had he believed it possible to love someone as he did her, and now he vowed to win her love from Dean Paul.

Dean Paul might have her heart—for now—but the fair-haired Mason had never known the pleasure of hearing her call out his name in ecstasy. Of that he was positive and he reveled in that knowledge. In his arms was the one place Brandelene did not think of her wonderful Dean Paul. So if he had to keep her in his bed for the next year to make her forget her love, he would.

He groaned inwardly, recalling how coldly he'd possessed her in his hurt and anger, and smothered her face with delicate kisses, determined to erase that memory from her mind.

The next morning Brandelene slept contentedly in Kordell's arms during the ride to Southern Oaks. While she napped, Kordell read the letters he'd received from Nicolle. Sweet, loving, encouraging letters that contained no mention of marriage. His guilt engulfed him, for he now considered himself married to Brandelene. There would be no annulment. He could tell from the tone of Nicolle's missives that she hadn't yet received his letter asking her to find another.

Kordell glanced out the window, then down at his sleeping wife. He smiled, for he'd seen to it that Brandelene received little rest last night.

Neither the jogging of the coach through the myriad rain-filled ruts nor the rattle of the passing mule-drawn tobacco wagons disturbed her sleep. For this he was grateful. He did not want her to see the miles of rolling tobacco on its way to market. Tobacco already cured and ready to sell, and Southern Oaks had not yet started harvesting. They were three to four weeks behind the other plantations, due to Cyrus's negligence. They were still at the mercy of the weather. An early frost or heavy rains and all would be lost.

The coach and four turned into the wide lane, shaded by the leafy bowers of towering trees that lined the long driveway to Southern Oaks. Ahead rose the white, three-storied mansion with its series of massive columns. The manor had been designed to impress, and it achieved that admirably.

Ruby, Matthew, and Pearl stood on the veranda as Joshua halted the rumbling brougham and the horses pranced in place.

Kordell swept a drowsy Brandelene into his arms and carried her up the veranda steps. Her arms were wrapped firmly around his neck, her face sleepily buried in the soft fabric of his coat.

"Matthew, have two hot baths and lunch brought to our room. It's been an exhausting two days and we want to rest. The harvesting of the tobacco begins tomorrow. Madame and I won't be leaving our room today."

"Yes, sir," Matthew responded respectfully, seeing the raised eyebrows and questioning glance Ruby exchanged with their daughter.

Pearl followed to assist Brandelene.

Pausing at the bottom stair, Kordell turned to the young girl. "Thank you, Pearl. I'll attend to my wife's needs."

"It's all right, Pearl," Brandelene said softly.

Pearl nodded, then glanced at her mother, and both women hustled off together while Kordell carried Brandelene up the wide, curving staircase to his room.

The next morning Brandelene awoke to the sound of singing birds, and she sat up and stretched, her own heart singing too. Kordell's arm hugged her waist and one long leg was flung across hers. Today began the harvesting of the tobacco and she wondered how she would ever get through a hard day's work. She was exhausted. Happy, she bent and kissed him, then trailed her fingertips through his softly waving locks. Her gesture was met with his amorous gaze as he pulled her into his arms. Briefly, she wondered how a man who'd been so devastatingly ill five months ago could have so much stamina, be so virile. Then her thoughts vanished in the intensity of his arousing kiss.

Before they went down to breakfast Brandelene handed Kordell his contract of indenture, torn into several pieces, and the money he'd given her in Petersburg. "Some time ago, I tore up your contract, and then it occurred to me that you might not believe I had destroyed it, or that perhaps you might wish to keep the contract—as a memento." She chuckled. "The money is yours, Kord. It wasn't our agreement that you buy your freedom—you've earned it. This isn't a subject open for discussion. However, I do appreciate your offer. It's quite generous of you."

A short time later, at Brandelene's request, Dagert joined them for breakfast. She flushed under the big man's scrutiny, for there was little doubt that Pearl had told him of Kordell's and her behavior after they returned from Petersburg yesterday.

"Dagert," Brandelene said, "I want to thank you for looking after Southern Oaks while Kord and I were detained. I'm sure Kordell will give you all the details later. His brother sent a courier to take you both home. He's waiting in Petersburg until the tobacco is harvested. I know you must be relieved to hear that."

Dagert's smile was endearing.

Then he sobered. "But. . . ."

"I'll go over everything with you later," Kordell quickly interjected and flashed Dagert a warning look for his silence.

Brandelene said, "Kordell is staying for the harvest. Can I also depend on you to see me through the harvest, Dagert?"

"Yes, madame. Of course," Dagert replied.

"Dagert, I should've talked to you about these things yesterday but . . ." Brandelene's voice trailed off and when Kordell cleared his throat, she deliberately avoided looking at him. "We must begin harvesting the leaf today. We planted late in the season and we're the only plantation in the area that hasn't finished the harvest. An early frost would defeat everything we've all worked so hard to accomplish."

"What can I do, Brandy?" Kordell asked. "I certainly won't be needed at the irrigation system."

"I don't expect you to work again, Kord." She smiled tenderly. "I never did. That wasn't the agreement."

"Damn the agreement! I'm not a gentleman farmer." He grinned at her. "Besides, the agreement has been slightly altered."

Brandelene flushed a deep scarlet while Dagert stared first at her, then at Kordell. She gathered her composure and spoke avoiding Kordell's gaze. Under the table, his hand moved to rest on her knee. Ignoring it as best she could, she said, "I'll go with you to the north fields, Dagert, the first fields we planted, and show you how to prime."

At their questioning look Brandelene smiled. "That's tobacco language for slicing the leaves off the stalk and doing a basic grading in the fields to select the choicest leaves. We'll do the final grading in the sorting sheds." Slowly, Kordell's hand started to move up her thigh and Brandelene turned to her husband. "Kord, why don't you stay with me today? I'll see to it that some of that excess energy you seem to have is worked off."

Kordell threw back his head and laughed heartily, then Brandelene laughed with him, and their gazes met and held.

At that, Dagert realized the truth of his suspicions. Heartsick for Nicolle, concerned for Brandelene, and angry at his friend for the first time in his life, he jumped up. "I'll meet you in the fields."

After Dagert left, Brandelene asked, "Is he upset because of Nicolle?"

"Probably. But don't be concerned, my beauty. He doesn't understand Nicolle's and my feelings for each other. Besides, Nicolle will have no problem finding another husband, for men are standing in line at this moment. I'm sure the man she marries will be more suitable than I."

Shortly thereafter, Brandelene sat on her stallion, beside Kordell and Dagert, among the dark green tobacco plants that stood almost as high as her mount. She smiled with satisfaction as she glanced across the fields, a sea of green in every direction as far as the eye could see. It was not Southern Oaks's best crop, for the drought, even with Kordell's irrigation system, had taken its toll. But she knew it was the choicest tobacco Virginia would produce this year, and she was elated.

"My father would have been proud of me."

Kordell had never heard her refer to James Barnett as anything other than "Daddy."

"My father would be proud of us all, for I couldn't have done it without the two of you." She smiled at Kordell and Dagert. "Ordinarily, we would prime the leaf, cutter, and lug at the same time, sorting as we go, but I'm afraid to risk it. We are harvesting late, so we're going to prime all of the leaf tobacco first. Those choice larger, heavier, dark green leaves on the top part of the plants are the valuable leaves, worth ten times the remaining. Then we'll come back and prime the cutters and lugs. Now, gentlemen, I'll teach you the rest of what separates the experts from the amateurs in tobacco. It begins with the priming and sorting."

When Brandelene had finished her instructions, Kordell swung easily into his saddle and said, "If I remember correctly, some months back you challenged me to a race when I felt better. You may not have not noticed, but I'm feeling much better. . . ."

Violet eyes glinted in amusement and a gentle laugh rippled through the air. "I really hadn't noticed, but now that you mention it . . . Well, Monsieur Bouclair, every race worth running must have a wager—to make it interesting, wouldn't you agree?"

"Absolutely. What do you suggest?"

She nudged her stallion forward, out of hearing range of Dagert. Kordell moved his mount beside hers and she leaned toward him, intimately resting her hand on his knee. "If I win you will play my maid for a week." She smiled seductively. "You will brush my hair, give me a massage before dinner and before bed, and serve me breakfast in bed on Sunday."

"Is that if you win, or if I win?"

"And if, by a considerable stretching of my imagination, you should be lucky and win, what would be the price I would pay?"

Kordell sobered, and his gaze locked with hers. "I would ask of you what you asked of me." Then his hand covered hers where it still rested on his knee, his voice especially serious.

"That, this night only, you pretend you love me as you have loved no other man in your life."

Chapter 26

BRANDELENE PALED, AND HER HAND TREMBLED BEneath Kordell's. Searching for a reason he would ask her to feign that she loved him, her eyes probed the depths of his, but found no answer, and her face revealed her pain. "No. I refuse. I will not." Her tremulous words were barely audible and she turned away.

"It's only one more charade to you, Brandy. Or are you afraid?"

Brandelene whipped her head around to face him. "Me afraid? Sweet mercy, what would I be afraid of?"

"That you might discover"—Kordell brushed his knuckles softly across her rosy cheek—"that you have feelings you don't wish to admit to."

"My arrogant Bouclair. You still believe every woman who meets you is dying of love for you, don't you?"

"No. I've never thought that, Brandy, but I had hopes that one woman might." His hand squeezed hers where it still rested on his knee. "Is it a wager, or are you afraid? I'll understand if you're afraid."

Biting back the insults she wanted to hurl at him, Brandelene stared at Kordell's chiseled face, devastatingly handsome, then lifted to his golden eyes before moving to his mane of dark tawny hair, glinting with streaks of gold. Rising to his challenge, she exclaimed confidently, "Agreed!" Then she nudged her booted heel into her mount and the stallion bolted forward.

They raced, head and head, down the lane between the fields of tall tobacco. Brandelene's hat flew off and her raven hair whipped in the wind, shimmering blue-black in the bright sun. The sorting sheds came into view and Kordell's stallion spurted forward to leave her behind. Aware that he'd restrained his powerful horse, so he would not win by too great a distance, she smiled inwardly, for she'd won also. At least in this race.

Kordell leaped from his horse, and stood tall and triumphant as Brandelene halted her panting mount beside him.

Kordell lifted her from the saddle. Reverently, his hand moved to her glossy wealth of raven hair, tumbling in wild disarray down her back. Wisps of curling tendrils framed her face, and he gazed down at her, overwhelmed by the range of emotions that raced through him. He was a besotted fool, he told himself, and he hated the power she held over him. Thanking a merciful God that she did not know of his feelings, he solemnly vowed she never would unless she came to love him too. He had not uttered a word of love to her after the night he first possessed her, when he had poured his heart out like a lovesick schoolboy. But those most important words had never slipped from her lips even during their most frenzied of passionate lovemaking.

Now he regretted the damn wager, for he knew her words tonight would be hollow, meaningless, and he resolved she would never hear the word "love" from his lips again until the cursed Dean Paul was exorcised from her heart. Kordell Bouclair danced to no woman's tune.

Suddenly he needed to be away from her. "I'll get your hat."

He mounted his stallion and reined the animal in the direction from which they'd just come.

"Kordell."

"Yes."

"What time have you?"

Kordell questioningly studied her as he pulled his watch fob from his pocket. "Ten minutes after eight."

"Thank you." Brandelene watched him ride away, the earth spinning around her, and she grabbed her stallion's mane for support. Kordell was no longer her husband. The annulment surely had been filed. What had she done?

In Kordell's arms, in the afterglow of passion, she believed she could play out this charade for another month, but now realized she could not. He was no longer her husband and her protesting conscience would not permit her to share his bed. This evening, she would tell him. With that much resolved she forced her thoughts to other matters. Urgent, pressing matters. The salvation of Southern Oaks.

Brandelene spent a long and exhausting day. She alternated between riding the aisles of the covered, open-air sheds, where the tobacco was sorted into grades, and directing that work advanced as expected in the curing barns. Kordell coordinated the unloading and reloading of leaf to be sorted and sent to the curing barns.

At dusk Brandelene turned her stallion toward the plantation manor. Although elated with both the quality and quantity of work accomplished today, she was assailed by doubts. For the first time, she, and she alone, was in charge of the most critical, the most crucial, phase of tobacco—the sorting and curing of the leaf. Many tobacco plantations were ruined by a lack of expertise in these two vital areas.

Brandelene knew that for the next weeks she would work fourteen- and sixteen-hour days in the sorting sheds and curing barns. However, she also realized that her willingness to work hard would be useless if she'd not retained everything her father had taught her. What she did now determined whether they produced a prime quality Virginia Bright, or tobacco that brought one-tenth the price at market. And following that excruciating notion came another; what if the sale of the tobacco did not bring enough money to pay the mortgage?

Exhausted, with every bone in her body aching, she wondered how she would survive tomorrow, for they would start the kilns to begin curing, a procedure that at first would require her constant supervision. It was the process of curing that fixed the color of the tobacco, the beautiful lemon yellow from which it got its name, Virginia Bright. The color as well as the quality of the tobacco leaf determined the price, for the beautiful and unique color of a choice Virginia Bright leaf always impressed tobacco buyers.

With no cash reserves Brandelene could not make one error in judgment, and her mounting trepidation bordered on panic. Was she really the expert James Barnett taught her to be?

She straightened in the saddle and lifted her chin high with a sense of conviction. She could not afford self-doubts now.

With that resolved, she determined to do whatever necessary to increase the income, starting with a hand-delivered letter to the warehouse proprietor in Richmond, accompanied by the first cured Southern Oaks's Virginia Bright leaf. With luck, that, since it was so late in the year, would keep the foreign tobacco buyers from leaving before she could get the leaf to market.

Wordlessly, Brandelene and Kordell rode side by side to the mansion, each lost in troubled thoughts. Inside the house she turned to Kordell. "I'm so tired," she flatly declared. "I'm going to soak in a hot bath and go to bed. I hope you don't mind dining without me."

"I'll have dinner brought to our room," Kordell offered. "The day will come when you won't be working like this, Brandy. I promise you."

"I don't mind the hard work, Kord. Actually, it's a truly rewarding experience, and when times are better I'll appreciate, in a way I never could have before, what is done at Southern Oaks." Turning away so he could not see the anguish on her face, she added, "Please don't bother with dinner for me. I'm much too tired to eat." With that, she instructed Matthew to have a maidservant other than Pearl attend her, for Pearl had worked long and tirelessly with the timekeepers to make certain each bondsman was credited with the proper work assignment and bonuses.

As Brandelene started up the stairs, Matthew handed her a silver tray with a letter resting on it.

"This arrived for you today, Miss Brandelene."

The letter was addressed to Monsieur and Madame Kordell Bouclair. Glancing at the beautifully addressed envelope, she knew it was the invitation to Dean Paul's betrothal ball.

Sighing, for she had more important concerns, Brandelene briefly told Kordell, "It's for Dean Paul's ball." She turned to Matthew, "Place it by my plate. I'll open it in the morning."

Kordell swept her up in his arms and started up the stairs. "The least I can do for the chief overseer is see her to her bath." Brandelene, too tired and heartsick over the annulment, did not protest.

Although Brandelene and Kordell had bathed together the previous two nights, she had no intention of continuing with the masquerade of being his wife. So, with that resolved, when he stood her on her feet in his room, she drawled, "Kordell, I need to relax in a hot tub. I'll bathe in my room." With those hastily murmured words, she walked into her bedroom and quietly closed the door.

Physically and emotionally exhausted, Brandelene used this excuse to absent herself from him, for she could not tell him tonight that they were no longer married. She was not prepared for his reaction.

Kordell cursed himself for pressing her too soon with the ridiculous wager on their horse race. Then he damned the timing of Dean Paul's announcement. Briefly, he reexamined his original plan to win her heart through their mutual desire, their passionate fervor for each other, and again he arrived at the same conclusion. It was the only way.

Sometime later Brandelene sank lower in the fragrantly scented bath. Although her aching body felt considerably better, instead of being relaxed she felt as taut as a bowstring. She sighed and asked Ivy to rinse the soap from her hair before she stepped from her bath.

Slipping into a gossamer nightgown and wrapper, Brandelene sat at the dressing table while Ivy towel-dried her thick hair and she despondently mused that the timid young girl did not have the gentle touch Kordell had used when he dried her hair last night. When she slipped between the covers of her bed, she felt unexplainably lost and alone.

Before long a soft knock sounded from Kordell's connecting door. Though wide awake, she turned her back and feigned sleep. The door opened and Kordell called her name. Although her room was dark, the lamplight from the other room shone across her form.

Kordell swiftly crossed the room. "Brandy!"

She stared at his large shadow cast on the wall she faced. Closing her eyes, she did not answer.

Kordell lit her lamp and sat on the edge of her bed. "I know you're not asleep, Brandy, so shall we dispense with the pretense?"

"I'm tired, Kordell." She rolled onto her back to gaze up at him. The lamp cast shadows across the face she loved, accentuating his carved features, and her heart raced. She turned away. "I ache all over, and I need to get some sleep."

"I understand, Brandy. However, you're my wife. And tired, sick, or passionate, my wife sleeps in my bed." With that, he pulled back the covers and swept her up in his arms and carried her to his room where he gently laid her on the large tester bed.

"Kordell," she stammered, realizing she had no choice but to tell him about the annulment now. "I . . ."

"Hush and turn over."

"What?"

"Brandy, I'm not going to ravish you. If sleep's what you want tonight, then you shall sleep."

Suspicious, she rolled onto her stomach. Then before she knew what happened Kordell had slipped her nightgown up to her neck and was gently kneading her back. Silently she marveled again at the tenderness his large hands could display. Slowly she felt herself relaxing beneath his touch, relieved that his hands never slipped lower than her waist, and the last thing she remembered was his gentle fingers massaging the muscles of her shoulders.

Later that night Brandelene awoke unable to move. Her naked back pressed against Kordell's muscular chest, her head rested on his one arm while the other cinched her waist, holding her close, and his long leg covered hers, pinning her to the bed. From his even breathing, she knew he slept soundly and she lay there, contented, fighting the thought that this was where she belonged. The clock chimed midnight.

Surprised it was no later, she vaguely remembered that Kordell had removed her gown and then massaged her back, shoulders, and arms and she'd fallen into a deep, peaceful sleep. Now, with much of the ache and tiredness gone from her body, she lay in his arms, vividly aware of the rise and fall of his chest against her back. Serene, she could feel the steady beating of his heart and the soft furring against her skin. Then she became acutely conscious of his naked thigh that intimately warmed the flesh of her slender leg, cognizant of his fingers, which could perform magic with their gentleness, possessively holding her to him, and she felt a heated quivering begin deep inside her abdomen. She had to get away from him before she submitted to the craving that already stirred in her body. Slowly and tediously, she maneuvered herself onto her back and waited. Sure that he still slept, she maneuvered her legs from beneath his, lifted his hand from her waist, and rose up on one elbow to glance down at his motionless form, barely discernible in the moonless, starlit night.

"You'll never know how much I love you, my magnificent lion," she whispered, her voice barely audible.

"Don't, Brandy. I should never have asked it of you."

Brandelene gasped.

Kordell was awake!

Her heart thudded in her ears and her pulse raced erratically. Then her face was clasped between the palms of Kordell's hands. He kissed her tenderly, breathlessly, and she kissed him back with all the love in her aching heart.

With the resolve of earlier this morning forgotten, for she had a wager to pay, Brandelene bent over Kordell and whispered words of love, passionately kissing him while her hand hesitantly roamed his body.

Her touch, delicate and painfully teasing, drove him into a frenzy of passionate rapture, and Kordell inhaled in ecstasy, rolling her over to possess her with an urgency that took them to the pinnacle of new horizons.

Morning came too soon and now Brandelene defended herself to her conscience. "I love him," she said and allowed that to justify the night.

Back at work Brandelene once again supervised the most crucial task of all, the curing of the tobacco. It was that which fixed the lemon color of the choicest leaves. Her tension mounted, for too much or too little heat would ruin in a matter of minutes the twenty-five acres of crop that cured in each barn. During her lengthening absences to oversee the curing procedures, the task of riding the aisles behind the sorters was added to Kordell's heavy work load.

She assigned more men to assist the fire tenders at each curing barn, for careful guard was required lest the red-hot flues start a fire. A continuous check needed to be maintained inside the barn during the four-day process for each curing. A broken rack of tinder-dry leaf that fell on a hot pipe could cause a disaster.

The twenty-five flue-curing barns, located a considerable distance from the plantation house, had been built well apart from each other in anticipation of a fire. Even so, it would still be impossible to stop the blazing fire of a barn full of dry tobacco from spreading from one barn to another. So the plantation operated on the hopes of snuffing a fire at the beginning. Barrels of water surrounded each barn, but they would only be useful at the start of a fire. Although a large bell hung at each barn to sound an alarm for help, Brandelene knew that no amount of help would stop the devouring flames if they reached the curing leaf, and she shuddered at the thought of ever hearing that bell.

Her memories flew back in time to when she was a child. There was a tobacco fire at one of the neighboring plantations, and her grandfather and father and all their slaves had scrambled to help, but it had been useless.

From their veranda, she and her mother watched the eerie orange-red glow that lit the sky from one horizon to the other.

The entire tobacco crop, slave quarters, and most outbuildings were lost, and only good fortune saved the manor, for the storage barns had been built too close to the house, with no consideration to high or shifting winds. Shivering, Brandelene forced the unthinkable from her mind.

That evening established a routine for the following weeks. Kordell carried her up the curving staircase to the large master bedroom, where they bathed together, then dined in their room. They spent the next eight hours in their large tester bed where they talked at length, exploring each other's minds and feelings, and gradually their lovemaking became less frenzied and more fulfilling. Although neither mentioned the word, their love deepened into something ever more beautiful and wondrous.

The way they slept remained the same. Kordell's shoulder pillowed Brandelene's head while his arm cinched her waist, intimately clasping their naked bodies together, his leg casually covering hers. At first, she'd felt pinned, almost trapped, but quickly came to treasure the security of his arms and wanted it no other way. Contented, she ignored her nagging conscience.

The day came when the choice, bright yellow, flue-cured tobacco leaf almost overflowed the storage barns. The thousands of acres of plantation leaf had been cured, and the tobacco needed to be transported immediately to market. The risk of fire, or mold in the event of too much rain, or of the foreign tobacco buyers leaving was too great to wait.

The tedious process of the final sorting of the leaf had been completed. The tobacco had been intricately graded, for a prospective buyer quickly examined each wooden cask, called a hogshead, in only a few seconds, and based his offer on the poorest quality leaf contained in that particular barrel. Thus the more uniform the quality of a hogshead, the higher the return. A small fortune could be, and often was, lost to the seller simply because he did not uniformly grade the quality of each cask.

After grading, the leaves had been tied, by twisting one leaf around the stem of approximately twenty leaves, into small bundles called "hands" and stacked in the storage barns. Soon the hands would be transferred into the hogsheads, loaded onto the mule-drawn wagons, and transported to market in Richmond where they would be sold.

Brandelene stood with Kordell in one of the barns, breathing deeply of the aromatic, cured tobacco as she studied the ceiling-high, bulked leaf. With satisfaction, she reached out and carefully examined a bright yellow leaf. "Perfect," she said, glancing up at Kordell. "Do you remember how dry and brittle the leaf was when we removed it from the curing barns, and how carefully it had to be handled so it wouldn't break?" At his nod, she said, "Feel the leaf now. It's absorbed natural moisture in the storing and is supple. It almost feels like leather." A shiver of pride wriggled down her spine, and her arms prickled with gooseflesh as her eyes scanned the Southern Oaks's choice Virginia Bright leaf. "My father taught me well."

"Have I ever told you that you are an incredible woman?"

"No."

Laughing, he murmured, huskily "Brandelene Barnett Bouclair, you are an incredible woman."

Brandelene would have preferred that he tell her that he loved her, but she was content—for now—for his eyes revealed what his lips refused to say. She gave him a dazzling smile, then pressed a dainty finger to his carved lips, gently tracing them. "Have I," she whispered so softly it was almost inaudible, "ever told you that you have an incredible mouth?"

Desire flashed through Kordell's loins, and he kissed her passionately.

At that moment Dagert walked into the storage barn. How Brandelene and Kordell felt about each other was secret to no one on the plantation, for during the fourteen hours a day they worked the sorting sheds and curing barns, they could not keep their hands, or gazes, from one another. And the house servants told everyone how the master and mistress disappeared into their room for hours every evening, even taking their meals there.

"You sent for me?" Dagert asked.

At the untimely interruption, Kordell reluctantly released Brandelene. "Yes, Dagert. You've done the impossible, getting the leaf primed so quickly. Now we need your help here." Striding up to his friend, Kordell extended his hand. The two men shook hands. "I've missed you, Dagert."

Glancing at Brandelene, then back to Kordell, Dagert grinned. "Not from what I've heard."

Laughing, Kordell bantered lazily, "Well, somewhat." Then he sobered. "Brandy and I need to take the leaf to market in Richmond. I want you to assign your second-best foreman the task of chief overseer to finish priming the cutters and lugs. We need you and Noah to take over the responsibility of the sorting sheds and the curing barns until we return. The two of you can work with Brandy and me for the next two days to learn what needs to be done." At Dagert's concerned look, Kordell calmly reassured him. "Don't worry about your inexperience. The men sorting and curing are experts at their jobs. Under Brandelene's guidance it's now a smoothly run operation that requires your skill to supervise and maintain the flow that is already in operation. You will be in charge. The fire tenders and sorters are all excellent, experienced men. It's a matter of coordination, supervision, and making certain all the precautions against a fire are continuously observed. Nothing you can't handle."

"Fine. When do you want the change?"

"Tomorrow morning."

"We'll be here." Dagert glanced around the barn at the bright yellow leaf. Then he turned to Brandelene. "My compliments, madame. You're an amazing woman."

"Why, thank you, Dagert." She smiled proudly. "Coming from you, I consider that the highest of compliments."

"I meant it to be," Dagert said.

Chapter 27

TWO DAYS PLUS SOME HOURS LATER, IN THE MIDDLE OF night, Kordell assisted Brandelene into the carriage, then swung into the saddle on his prancing stallion. She glanced down the cavalcade of lantern-bearing, mule-drawn wagons escorted by mounted armed guards. A smile crossed her face at the strange-looking convoy she and Kordell would lead to Petersburg. The first of Southern Oaks's choice Virginia Bright leaf was being taken to the large tobacco market in Richmond, and since Petersburg was situated on the Appomattox River, the hogsheads would be transferred to a river barge and transported by water up the James River to Richmond.

Earlier, after Brandelene had agreed for Kordell to accompany her and the entourage, Kordell had sent Joshua to Petersburg with two letters.

One message went to the lawyer, Charles Thompson, requesting that Thompson hire two trustworthy white stewards to stay at the plantation during the two or three weeks that Kordell and Brandelene expected to be gone. In the event of trouble from the plantation owners surrounding Southern Oaks, only a white person would be permitted to act on their behalf. Also state law made it mandatory that at least one white person reside on each plantation, so there was dual reason for the white retainers. Two days later a middle-aged couple and their nineteen-year-old son had arrived and, to Kordell's relief, had met with his and Brandelene's approval.

The other missive had been to Pierre, briefly explaining their situation and requesting that Pierre work with Thompson to hire twenty white men to act as armed guards. It was illegal for a black person to carry a gun, so they could not draw from the plantation help.

Three guards remained at the plantation, under instructions from Dagert, while the retainers acted as the legal white authority. The other seventeen armed men escorted the train of tobacco wagons to Petersburg. Brandelene and Kordell agreed they could ill afford the risk of having their precious cargo of prime-quality tobacco leaf raided and burned by a group of marauders hired by the local gentry.

Four mules pulled each lantern-equipped wagon, loaded high with the hogsheads of tobacco. Two bondsmen, with food and water for their personal needs, alternated driving. A thick cornshuck and straw tick pallet lay under the high, wide seat, for the drivers to alternate sleeping during the several twenty-four-hour days the drays would travel back and forth from Southern Oaks to Petersburg. In addition, there were wagons of relief mules and horses; of hay, grain, and barrels of water for the animals; of wheels, sideboards, tongues, and all manner of wagon parts, tools, and equipment. Also a wagon filled with food, water, and thick cornshuck and straw tick pallets, for the guards who would keep the same nonstop schedules as the drivers, accompanied the train.

The heavily burdened tobacco wagons crawled over the rutted dirt roads. Except to switch mule teams and horses, or to unload the hogsheads on the docks in Petersburg and reload at the plantation, the men and wagons would not stop traveling until the entire crop of Southern Oaks's tobacco had been transported to Petersburg. The mules and horses were relieved at each return to Southern Oaks.

The continuous stream of rolling tobacco eventually stretched from Southern Oaks to Petersburg, and was guarded by fourteen patrolling armed men, while three rotating guards slept. The empty wagons returning to the plantation to be reloaded continuously passed loaded wagons of Southern Oaks's tobacco on their journey.

Many hours later Brandelene and Kordell boarded a small riverboat in Petersburg for Richmond, leaving two of their most dependable bondsmen on the docks to keep a third tally and oversee the unloading of the continuously arriving wagons of hogsheads onto the river barges.

Kordell was disappointed they passed through Petersburg too late to get his mail, for the long awaited letter from Nicolle had surely arrived by this time.

Two mornings later, Brandelene dressed in the gown she had worn the day she purchased Kordell's contract of indenture—a white-silk charmeuse trimmed with burgundy.

At the sight of her wearing the gown that was indelibly imprinted in his mind, Kordell's vivid recollections slipped backward in time to the first moment his gaze had fallen upon her in the hell of the auction house. At first, Brandelene had seemed not unlike an angel appearing before him in a vision, a gift not of this earth come to comfort him in his misery. But then, after she'd spoken with him and he misinterpreted her words, he imagined her to be all that he detested, disguised as the most exquisite woman his tortured gaze had ever fallen upon. Later, she'd brandished a whip to secure laudanum for him and he realized that she was neither of his previous conceptions. In that moment she had stolen his heart.

Twirling for his approval, Brandelene explained, "I realize it's inappropriately late in the season to be wearing white, yet . . ."

Kordell's reverie faded, for Brandelene had paused in what she'd been saying. He lifted his gaze from the gown that rekindled so many memories to the face that stirred so many feelings and repeated, "Yet?"

Uncertain, she bit her lip, then glanced away before she continued, "Yet . . . the last time I wore this gown I had such good fortune. I found you . . . and Dagert, of course."

Kordell wanted to read so much into what she said, but realized the folly of doing so. Proffering his arm, he smiled tenderly down at her. "Shall we go, my lovely wife? We have considerable tobacco to sell."

A short time later, as they neared the tobacco warehouse, Brandelene gasped. An enormous canvas sign hung outside the warehouse, flapping in the breeze, and for a moment her heart stopped. The sign read: JAMES BARNETT'S SOUTHERN OAKS TOBACCO.

Pride swelled in her breast at the gentle tribute to all her father had achieved—with freed slaves and bond servants. As the carriage drew nearer, her tear-glazed eyes fell on the gathering of men. Although it was late in the season, the warehouse Brandelene had selected, the same her father had always used, was abuzz with buyers, as it had been during the tobacco-buying season. The proprietor, Walter Harrell, to whom she'd sent the sample hogshead and a brief letter—a request rather than instructions—had not only done what she had asked, but had far exceeded her suggestions.

Brandelene realized the owner's incentive was the hefty sum he would collect as his fee to weigh, warehouse, and sell what she was sure would be the only choice leaf to come out of Virginia this year. She knew naught of any other plantation with an irrigation system such as Kordell had built. The warehouse owner would well deserve his percentage, inasmuch as the gigantic canvas sign he'd had painted was nearly three times the size she expected. The sign, printed exactly as Brandelene had requested, obviously had been responsible for drawing the representatives of the major foreign tobacco processors, the tobacco brokers, and the speculators. For there was not a buyer of importance unfamiliar with the prime quality of James Barnett's leaf, or with the fact that James was deceased.

Walter Harrell had broken open the sample hogshead and spread the large, leathery, lemon-yellow leaves on a large table set up for that purpose. Over the table a sign read: Southern Oaks's Mighty Leaf.

"Mighty leaf," Brandelene whispered with misty eyes. For some time she stared at the sign, her breath caught in her lungs, for the term "mighty leaf" was the highest compliment their crop could be paid.

They had done it. Kordell, Dagert, she, and nearly six hundred bond servants. Bond servants—not slaves.

It had been this remarkably high quality sample, offered in a year of partial drought, which had kept those same tobacco buyers long after they ordinarily would have departed for their foreign shores.

From her lofty position in the carriage Brandelene glanced around the enormous warehouse that could hold two million pounds of tobacco at one time. She smiled with satisfaction, for the Southern Oaks's hogsheads had been arriving throughout the night. She could see from the disarray of the top hands of leaf that every hogshead had already been broken open and examined, probably in disbelief, and then examined more closely.

At that moment Walter Harrell, a large, muscular man, hurried to the carriage to greet Brandelene and Kordell.

"Please join us, Mr. Harrell," Brandelene invited, "I'd like to have a word with you."

Climbing into the carriage, the warehouse owner lowered his large frame into the opposite seat.

"Mr. Harrell," Brandelene began, "we have a unique situation here. I'm sure I've brought you the most quality leaf to come out of Virginia this year. Is that correct?" At his nod, she continued, "The buyers, quite naturally, must have been extremely upset with the poor grades they've been forced to buy, or go without. What are they going to offer the tobacco user who not only is used to, but demands, a quality smoke and aroma? In two or three years from now, after this year's tobacco has mellowed, are they going to be able to apologize and explain about the Virginia drought for not having any quality tobacco for those who can afford the best? No, they are not. But I offer them not only the prime-quality leaf they are begging for, but also a substantial quantity."

Brandelene felt Kordell's curious gaze upon her, for she'd not discussed with him what had captivated her thoughts. "It appears to me, Mr. Harrell, as they say in the gentlemen's world, 'I hold all the cards' and I would like, with your permission, to take advantage of this position. I want to do something that's never been tried before in tobacco. I would like to auction each hogshead."

"Auction them? It's unheard of."

"Yes, auction them. I had occasion last spring to attend an auction of human beings, which permitted me to see firsthand that if the circumstances are right an auction is the most profitable way to sell something of value. We have here the best possible situation for any type of auction—a large group of buyers who want the merchandise that's for sale, buyers who desperately need the merchandise, more demand than goods, and merchandise that cannot be obtained elsewhere—we have no competition."

At Harrell's astonishment, Brandelene continued, "In addition, Mr. Harrell, I recognize many of these men from when I attended the tobacco markets with my father. We have buyers whose quantity requirements are small, and buyers whose needs are large. If we auction each hogshead individually, the bidding should be brisk."

"But how would we ever have time to auction thousands of hogsheads individually?"

Brandelene leaned forward, her face alight with anticipation. "You've already marked each hogshead with the weight and grade of leaf. I realize there's no qualified auctioneer who would know the tobacco market, and that tobacco experience is essential to know what the starting bid should be. At the auction I attended the opening bid determined the selling price, for buyers will only bid up so many times. However, you have that experience, Mr. Harrell, and I'd pay you well for that service. You could walk the aisles beside the auctioneer and give him the starting bid on each hogshead. An expert auctioneer could auction off the leaf at the rate of one hogshead a minute, and the cutter and lugs at two or three a minute. That's an average of about nine hundred hogsheads a day. I'm sure the buyers will be agreeable to spend a few more days in Virginia in order to buy the choice Virginia Bright leaf their customers will demand."

Kordell leaned back in the seat of the carriage, stretched his long arm across the back of Brandelene's seat, and smiled, content in the knowledge that there was not another woman in the world who could compare with his wife.

"When I saw the sample hogshead you sent it looked like gold," Harrell admitted. "But I don't know if these gentlemen—"

"If they leave without bidding," Brandelene interrupted, "these buyers will have to explain to their employers when the word gets out—and they realize it will. Why don't you send a messenger for the best auctioneer you know, so we can discuss it with him? Then you may introduce me to your buyers."

The next three weeks were exhausting, tension-filled days of attending the tobacco auction, for Brandelene insisted on being there every minute the leaf was auctioned.

The atmosphere was charged with the chanting of the auctioneer and the excited shouts and cries of the buyers as the bidding went higher, then higher. Brandelene reveled in the chaos of the auction, and the hogsheads rolled out of the warehouse as fast as they rolled in.

Not a buyer there doubted the cunning or shrewdness of James Barnett's daughter, and her presence was a constant reminder.

Each evening after Brandelene left the warehouse, she became the loving and carefree playmate of Kordell, his passionate, insatiable wife. They made love as though it were the first time, or the last.

They browsed the historical sights of Richmond and the quaint English antique shops, dined, and were entertained at the sumptuous Bell Tavern. Brandelene glowed under Kordell's tender and loving care. Never in her life had she been happier.

At the end of three weeks, when Brandelene and Kordell left Richmond, the Southern Oaks's leaf had been auctioned off at an unprecedented high price, and the cutters and lugs had not yet been put up for auction. Indeed those hogsheads still arrived every day.

When Brandelene paid off the mortgage on Southern Oaks, she felt the weight of that tremendous burden slip away. Then, with an exuberance she'd not felt since she was a child, instead of accepting Kordell's hand up into the carriage for the return trip to Petersburg and home, she threw her arms around his neck and smothered him with loving kisses.

She considered telling Kordell about the annulment, so they could remarry in Richmond. If only she knew he loved her, and not her once-again prosperous plantation. She loved him. But she would give him up before she would marry a man who loved naught but her wealth. Certainly now, with the strain and concern of a successful tobacco crop behind her, and the mortgage paid, she could relax and contrive a scheme to determine if Kordell actually loved her, and not simply her plantation. And she could best do that at the sanctuary of Southern Oaks. Besides, she'd always wanted a Christmas wedding. By Christmas, Kordell would be her husband . . . or be gone.

When they arrived in Petersburg, Kordell asked, "Brandy, why didn't we travel this route from Richmond when you bought Dagert and me? It seems a much shorter distance."

She grinned. "I took a roundabout course hoping to keep Cyrus from inquiring about me in Richmond. Since everyone in Petersburg knows me, Ruby, Joshua, and the carriage on sight, I couldn't allow us to disembark from the river barge from Richmond. The way I came with you, if Cyrus questioned anyone in Petersburg, he'd learn that we came by road from the direction of Norfolk, and not by river barge."

"Aha. You thought of everything, didn't you, my lovely wife?" Kordell gave her a quick kiss and alighted to pick up his mail, anxious to receive the all-important letter from Nicolle. The clerk, fumbling nervously, handed him a large stack of mail. At the man's strange behavior Kordell glanced up.

"Uh, Mr. Bouclair. A letter came for your wife sometime back. The postmaster now refuses to deliver any mail to Southern Oaks, so I put it with your mail, sir. I, uh, I hope you understand."

"Yes, of course. Thank you." With that, Kordell returned to the carriage. "To the Wolf's Lair Inn, Joshua. Then take a message to Pierre. Ask him to meet me at the inn tavern at seven this evening, for dinner."

"Yes, sir."

Kordell glanced down at the top letter, addressed in Nicolle's hand. A premonition snaked down his spine.

In their room at the Wolf's Lair, Kordell and Brandelene bathed, made love, and dressed for dinner. Brandelene was rolling her long hair into stylish curls when he picked up the stack of letters that included several from Nicolle. He stared silently, anxiously, at Nicolle's handwriting and a rush of shame stifled him. What if she, in her gentle, loyal way, had insisted on waiting for him? Guilt penetrated his soul. How could he have permitted himself to fall in love with Brandelene before he received Nicolle's letter? How could he have done that to Nicolle?

"I'm ready, Kord."

He set the pack of mail down, deciding to read the letters after dinner, and escorted Brandelene downstairs to the tavern common room. Pierre rose as they approached his table. Kordell introduced Brandelene to the well-dressed man.

Pierre nervously glanced toward the small sitting area nearby, then back at Brandelene. "*Bonjour*, madame." He bowed over her hand and his eyes glinted with admiration. Anxious, he turned to Kordell. "I, ah, indeed I did not realize Madame Bouclair would be joining us, *mon ami*. I had no idea your, ah, wife was so lovely, Kordell."

"You're very kind, sir," Brandelene drawled to the dark-haired stranger, and seated herself in the chair he held for her.

The older man turned to Kordell, then glanced again toward the empty sitting room. "May I have a private word with you, Kordell? Indeed, I only hope 'tis not too late."

"You're free to speak in front of my wife, Pierre. What is it?"

Glancing uncomfortably from Kordell to Brandelene, then to Kordell, Pierre hesitated.

"Well, out with it, Pierre. What is it?"

"Madame Montcliff is here," Pierre blurted, then stammered, "I—I had taken the liberty of asking her to join us. I, ahh, I did not realize Madame Bouclair was with you."

Astonished, Kordell said, "Nicolle is here? In the United States?"

"*Oui*. This very day, and in the Wolf's Lair Inn. She arrived yesterday. 'Tis most distressing." Pierre once more glanced toward the sitting area. "Indeed, at this exact moment Madame Montcliff should be here."

Chapter 28

NICOLLE! HERE AT THE WOLF'S LAIR? THE LAST SIX months of Brandelene's life flashed before her. She was drowning, helpless, about to draw her last breath, and her dreams were drowning with her.

"I—I—I had no idea Madame Bouclair was such an exquisite woman. I only hope . . . 'Twould be best, Kordell . . ." Pierre paused to compose himself. "No doubt, Kordell, you might wish to meet Nicolle in the anteroom, to, ahh, to prepare her, indeed so she is less surprised than I, under the circumstances. . . ."

"Yes. Yes, of course." Kordell rose and turned to Brandelene. "Excuse me, Brandy. I know you understand."

Sick and confused, she watched Kordell walk to the small sitting area, then Pierre's voice broke into her thoughts.

"I realize, madame, you and Kordell are living not as man and wife. However, for a man's intended to find him married to a woman of your extraordinary beauty . . . Regardless of the circumstances, 'twill no doubt be quite a shock. Madame Montcliff is an exceptional woman. She doesn't deserve to be hurt. You do agree, *oui*?"

Brandelene nodded, her nightmarish agony almost overcoming her control. The smile that crossed her lips did not reach her eyes. What could there be about a woman that every man adored her, sought to shelter and protect her? At that moment she saw a willowy, fair-haired woman, angelic in primrose silk, cross the anteroom toward Kordell. The woman drifted into Kordell's arms, and he hugged her tightly.

"Dear God!" Brandelene gasped and all color drained from her face. He loves her. He loves her.

Hearing Brandelene's cry, Pierre glanced at her, then at Nicolle in Kordell's arms, abruptly realizing, from Brandelene's expression, that she also loved Kordell.

"*Mon Dieu!*" Pierre muttered.

Brandelene did not hear, for she floated in the world of her tormented thoughts, her aching heart, and the sight of the fair-haired Nicolle still in Kordell's arms.

Presently they separated and Kordell motioned Nicolle to sit on the settee, where he joined her. Nicolle's companion, a middle-aged maidservant, hovered discreetly nearby.

Unable to tear her gaze away, Brandelene wordlessly watched the two as they sat talking and laughing. She shuddered when Kordell's tawny head bent close to Nicolle's elaborate coiffure. He looked so happy to see her, and that knowledge seared inside Brandelene. Then Nicolle rested her gloved hand on his, and his fingers enclosed hers. Her bare shoulder pressed lightly, familiarly, comfortably against his arm.

Brandelene had never been jealous in her life, but now the emotion consumed her, engulfing her.

"Would you care for some wine, Madame Bouclair?" Pierre queried anxiously as he nodded toward the tavern maid waiting at her elbow with a bottle.

"Yes, please," Brandelene replied, forcing her regard from Kordell and Nicolle, to fasten on the rough-hewn beams behind Pierre. She took a sip of wine and glanced at him. "Perhaps, monsieur, considering the rather awkward circumstances, you should call me Brandelene."

"*Oui! Oui,* indeed that would be best. Madame, ah, Brandelene, please accept my apologies. I should have realized you would be with Monsieur Bouclair. This unfortunate situation 'tis my fault. I—I knew Madame Montcliff was anxious to see Kordell, and I fear I did not think."

"Please don't concern yourself, Pierre. It was understandable." Brandelene felt devoured by Pierre's admiring glance. Nevertheless, she was delighted she'd decided, at Kordell's urging, to wear the low-cut gown that matched her violet eyes to perfection. At least she was as elegantly gowned as Nicolle. Avoiding looking at Kordell and Nicolle, she asked Pierre, "Did Madame Montcliff's son accompany her?"

"*Non.* Nicolle believed the trip too taxing for a young boy. Two menservants and a ladies' companion accompanied her."

Glancing back at the couple, Brandelene saw Nicolle rise and slip her arm through Kordell's, as though she had done it all her life. Then Nicolle glided toward them. Her grace, proud bearing, elegant gown, and dazzling diamonds were evidence of a gently reared woman possessing considerable confidence and wealth. Hidden behind a composed facade, Brandelene, stunned by Nicolle's angelic perfection, shuddered at the wretched look on Kordell's face. Although her heart was shattered, she forced a smile. All thought was impossible.

"Nicolle, I'd like you to meet Brandelene Barnett Bouclair," she heard Kordell say, the misery in his voice apparent.

"Brandelene, may I present Madame Nicolle Montcliff."

"Brandelene . . . such a lovely name," Nicolle said softly. "Kordell has written me so many letters about you that I feel as though I know you. It is indeed a pleasure to meet you."

"The pleasure is mine, Nicolle," Brandelene responded, heartsick. "Please, be seated." Unbidden, Dagert's words flashed through her mind. "She has hair the color of cornsilk and eyes as blue as the sky." Dagert had not exaggerated, for Nicolle was a flawlessly delicate beauty, conjuring up visions of a genteel woman who spent her days on needlework, painting watercolors, and having men vie to protect her.

Somehow Brandelene forced cordial words from her lips. "It's unfortunate we didn't realize you were coming, madame, or we could have arranged to meet your ship. I do so hope you weren't inconvenienced."

"It's considerate of you to be concerned, Brandelene, but my servants took care of everything. I wrote Kordy when I would arrive, but apparently he's been involved with the harvest and didn't receive my letter until today," Nicolle said sweetly, her soft French accent lilting. She patted Kordell's arm affectionately and smiled up at him with adoring blue eyes. "In fact, Kordy tells me he still hasn't had the opportunity to read my letter."

Kordell returned Nicolle's smile with love and pride in his eyes.

Brandelene was devastated. "I trust your trip was comfortable. Hopefully you didn't run into a storm. I understand severe storms at sea are a dreadful experience," she rambled, unaware of what she said, wishing she could leap up and run from the room instead of making inane conversation with the woman Kordell unquestionably loved. How could he have so convincingly played the charade of loving husband? "Were your accommodations satisfactory?"

A soft, tinkling laughter escaped Nicolle's petal pink lips. "I'm sure my accommodations were much better than poor Kordy's on his trip here." Her wide blue eyes glittered at Kordell and then her lovely face sobered. "Oh, Kordy, we were so worried about you before your letters came. We had given you up for dead. However, I've never seen you look better. Brandelene has certainly taken good care of you." Before Kordell could reply, Nicolle turned back to Brandelene. "Kordy wrote me that you brandished a pistol and whip to get laudanum for him? Is it really so?"

Humiliated that Kordell would have revealed her unconventional behavior to a genteel lady, Brandelene flushed. "Yes, it's true."

"Astonishing! How I envy your spirit, Brandelene. I would've fainted at the idea of doing such a thing. The most daring thing I've ever done is to make this voyage with two well-armed menservants and a ladies' maid."

"Kordell had been terribly abused," Brandelene replied. "He was in considerable pain and needed help. I—I could think of naught else to do. . . ."

Nodding, Nicolle smiled. "Nevertheless, it was a brave thing for you to do. Kordy also wrote that you saved his life when he had the fever."

Brandelene shivered in vivid recollection, her gaze turning to Kordell, and the agony of those terrible days shimmered in her eyes for a moment before she said, "Dagert, the doctor, and I managed to pull him through. I—I was sure we were going to lose him."

"You're too modest, Brandelene," Nicolle protested. "Kordy has written me pages and pages of what you've done for him. You've been marvelous. However," she scolded pleasantly, "Kordy forgot to mention in his letters how young you are, or how beautiful."

"I also didn't write you what a hard taskmaster she is, working me from dawn to dusk."

"Kordell! How ungrateful of you," Nicolle chastised affectionately. "After all this lovely girl has done for you."

Amusement flickered in Kordell's eyes, then he laughed with sudden good humor, glancing at Pierre. "I think I had best keep my mouth closed, Pierre. How can I win against two women?"

Pierre laughed. "*Oui*, Kordell. *Oui*."

Suddenly Brandelene was suffocating. For not one minute longer could she sit at this table and behave as though everything was wonderful when her world was falling apart. It would have been easier if she could hate the woman Kordell loved, but she could not, for Nicolle seemed a genuinely kind and gracious woman—and so trusting; she had not the slightest suspicion that Brandelene shared Kordell's bed.

Brandelene felt nauseated and deceitful, and so terribly guilty. She could not even fault Kordell, for she'd bargained him into her bed. Turning to Nicolle, a forced smile touched the corners of her lips. "Nicolle, we have just come from the tobacco market in Richmond. It's been an exhausting trip and I'm very tired. Please excuse me. I'm going to my room now. It has been a pleasure meeting you, enjoyable talking with you. You're as lovely as everyone has said." Brandelene's voice broke and she paused. "I know how happy Kordell is to have you here. I'm sure you two have considerable to talk about."

"I'll walk you to the room," Kordell offered somberly, rising to assist Brandelene from her chair.

Brandelene stared at him, for he had said *the* room, not *our* room. Obviously he did not want Nicolle to know where he slept. "Thank you, Kordell, but that's not necessary."

"I insist." Then he turned to Nicolle, who gazed at him with doting eyes. "I'll be back shortly, then the three of us can catch up on everything that's happened while I've been gone."

Judging by Kordell's look of agony, Brandelene mused, apparently he also waged his battle with guilt. Her gaze fastened on the beautiful, fair-haired woman who looked like a fairy princess in her primrose silk gown with yards of matching sheer. Kordell believed himself married to her while Nicolle, the woman he surely loved, was now within his reach.

Wordlessly, she walked beside him to their room and wondered if Nicolle also had detected Kordell's distress. She hoped not, for the woman was but an innocent victim of fate. Brandelene sighed. It was best that Kordell had escorted her to their room, for now she could tell him what she should have told him weeks ago—that they were no longer married. Then he could happily return to Nicolle, who seemed to be everything Brandelene had admired in her mother—sweet, caring, considerate, and giving.

Glancing up at Kordell's solemn expression, a flash of wild grief ripped through her, leaving her empty, bereft. How could she live without him? How could she go to sleep knowing Nicolle would be in his arms, sharing everything with him she had once shared, being everything to him they had been to each other? The thought tore through her like a jagged blade, cutting the heart from her body, leaving her lifeless.

When Kordell unlocked the door to their room, Brandelene did not remember how they came to be there. Then they were inside and he closed the door and turned up the oil lamp.

"Brandy, I'm extremely sorry," Kordell said from behind her. "I had no idea . . ."

His voice trailed off and Brandelene lifted her head high. She did not want his pity. Anything but his pity. Knowing what she had to do, she whirled to face him. "No apologies, Kordell," she said softly and her heart lurched as she gazed up into his devastatingly handsome face. Her gaze captured his, and she stepped back from his overpowering nearness.

"Kordell, there's something I've tried to tell you during these last weeks . . . but somehow it never seemed the right time. Somebody interrupted, or something happened, or . . ." Sighing, with the searing pain in her heart shimmering in her eyes, she blurted, "Kord, we are not married, and haven't been for some weeks."

Kordell stared at her in disbelief. "What did you say?"

Swallowing the choking lump in her throat, she repeated, "We are not married, Kordell."

In two long strides, he clasped her arms in strong hands and his face darkened. "Would you care to explain that?" he challenged, bridled anger in his voice.

"I've had our marriage annulled."

"Exactly how could you do that, considering you've shared my bed? I want an explanation, Brandelene. Right now. Do you hear? Now!"

Startled by his wrath, Brandelene glanced away. For a moment her mind raced in confusion. Why was he so irate? She'd felt sure he would be ecstatic, for now he was free to wed his perfect Nicolle.

"Answer me, Brandelene!" Kordell boomed, shaking her. "Answer me!"

"I filed for the annulment before we . . . before we . . ."

At the meaning of her words, Kordell's astonishment melted into shock. "Look at me, Brandelene."

Reluctantly she glanced up into his fiery golden eyes.

"Do I understand correctly that you had our marriage annulled before I made love to you?"

Faltering, Brandelene nodded, and Kordell's fingers tightened on her arms until she flinched.

Enraged, he ignored her grimace of pain. "When?"

"The last time we were in Petersburg," Brandelene replied and turned away from his glare.

Kordell's eyes widened. "The day you met your wonderful Dean Paul? The day he told you of his betrothal? Was that the day?"

Confused, Brandelene was uncertain what Dean Paul had to do with any of this.

"Answer me, dammit!" Kordell shook her again.

"Let me go, you bully!" Brandelene snapped and struggled free of his iron grip.

"Was that the day, Brandelene?"

Refusing to cower beneath the blazing glower that pierced her soul, she said, "Yes, Kordell, that is the day. Although I don't see what—"

"Tell me, my *beloved* wife, did you acquire this annulment before or after you met the illustrious Mr. Mason?"

"After. I went to see Thompson after I saw Dean Paul. What difference could that possibly make?"

"Why, Brandelene? Why?"

"Why? I don't understand what you're asking, Kordell." Edgy, Brandelene shifted from foot to foot. Why was he so angry? His pride?

Kordell stepped forward. "Why did you file for the annulment?"

Brandelene stepped back. "That was our agreement, was it not?"

Kordell's eyes narrowed. She'd avoided answering him. "I will damn well have some answers, Brandelene. Why did you file for the annulment at that time?"

"I . . . I wanted to make certain the annulment would be final before you left, so there'd be no problems," she lied and, with her heart aching, turned away to walk to the window and blindly stare out into the dark night.

Trembling with barely controlled rage, Kordell followed her. "Is that why you went to the doctor that morning? To get your damnable certification?"

"Yes!"

"You look at me when I'm speaking to you, Brandelene. Now!"

Brandelene reeled to face his accusing glare.

"Where did you meet your Dean Paul?"

"Outside the ladies' shop."

"I see. And exactly when did you see the lawyer?"

"Kordell, I've already told you. After the coach left, I talked to Dean Paul, then I walked the few doors from the ladies' shop to Thompson's office."

"So our marriage was as good as annulled when we dined and I asked you to marry me?"

Wordlessly, Brandelene looked away.

"All these weeks, after all we've been to each other, after all we've shared, you still allowed me to play the fool, thinking I was your husband. Why didn't you tell me?"

Her silence was his only answer.

Reaching out he turned her to face him, his expression clouded with rage. Then he tilted her chin up until her gaze met his.

"And when I made love to you . . ." Halting, Kordell hesitated to ask what he really did not want to know. "When I made love to you, you knew that Dean Paul was betrothed to another and you were no longer my wife?"

Stiffening at his question, Brandelene turned again to stare sightlessly out the window.

"Answer me!" Kordell roared.

"Yes." Her single word was soft, hushed, barely audible.

Kordell knew the answer to his next question, but he had to hear it from her own lips. "Why?"

Vowing she would not bare her soul to a man who did not love her, she again turned away, then replied, "It simply happened."

Her answer destroyed him, cut him to the heart. In their bed he had made love, but Brandelene had merely sought solace. Now he wanted to hurt her, as she'd devastated him. "Do you know what that makes you, Brandelene?"

Brandelene whirled and slapped him across the face. "That makes me no worse than you, who sought to get me into your bed while your lovely fiancée waited trustingly for you!"

"I was right. You are a black widow spider. A deadly one!"

With that he crushed her to him and kissed her savagely, setting her aflame, leaving her mouth to burn with the fire of his kiss after he released her.

"Have you forgotten, Kordell? Your betrothed awaits you downstairs." Brandelene sneered, hiding her wildly beating heart behind an icy facade.

He spun around to leave.

"Kordell, get another room, for you'll not be sleeping here tonight." Then she added softly, "If not for me, do it for Nicolle. She's a lovely woman. There is no need to hurt her."

Kordell jerked open the door.

"I'll have your trunks sent here tomorrow. You'll not be returning to Southern Oaks."

Kordell slammed the door behind him, so hard that it shook the wall.

Brandelene threw herself on the bed, refusing to submit to the sobs that tore through her tortured heart.

Downstairs, Kordell, outraged, stunned, and hurt, rejoined Nicolle.

She stared at him. "Kordy, what is wrong?"

"Pierre, would you excuse us? I would like to talk with Nicolle privately."

"Please stay, Pierre," Nicolle bade gently, then turned back to Kordell. "Kordy, we would compromise Brandelene's, yours, and my reputations if we were to dine alone." She smiled, understanding in her eyes. "I'm sure you don't want that. Pierre is a trusted friend. Why don't we have him take us for a carriage ride and we can talk? I'm not really hungry."

Kordell nodded.

Nicolle tapped Kordell's arm with her fan. "I'll go and freshen up. My maid and I will meet you in fifteen minutes."

After they left Kordell's thoughts turned to Nicolle. Had she not received the letter he'd written her, asking her to forget him, suggesting she find a more suitable husband? Certainly she had, for he'd written it months ago, after he returned from his search for the source of the water on Southern Oaks. After he realized he was falling helplessly in love with his wife.

But now Brandelene had filed the annulment, proving she would never love him, they were no longer married, and nothing was the same.

How different the two women were. He wondered if he'd ever heard Nicolle raise her voice, and he couldn't think of a time. He tried to recall if he'd ever seen her upset, other than at Robert's death, but he could not remember once. She was a lady, in every sense of the word. Could he possibly tell her that he could not marry her? Could he be so cruel when she'd crossed an ocean to be with him? No, he could not do that to Nicolle. Not now.

There was no longer a reason to.

So Kordell threw a few coins on the table and left the tavern common room to meet Nicolle. While married to Brandelene these last weeks, he had known the ultimate joy, experienced the pinnacle of pleasure, attained a wholeness he would never find with another woman. If it were not Brandelene to whom he was married, it didn't really matter whom he wed. For no woman, not even Nicolle, could ever replace in his heart what he felt for the black widow spider who had entangled him in her silky web.

If only Nicolle had not come . . . but she had.

Kordell opened the carriage door and forced a happy smile to his face.

"Welcome to the United States, Nicolle," Kordell said, climbing into the carriage. "I've missed you!"

Chapter 29

"OH, KORDY, WE HAVE SO MUCH TO TALK ABOUT, I don't know where to begin." The glowing lamps inside the coach revealed the plain features of the maid who sat opposite them, next to Pierre. Nicolle continued to gaze at Kordell. "I do believe, Kordy, you're more handsome than ever." Laughing softly, she said, "It's disgraceful that one man should be so handsome."

"Ahh, Nicolle." Kordell lifted her gloved hand to squeeze it affectionately. "You're a balm to my anguished soul. I don't need to tell you how beautiful you are, for you've every other man in the world to tell you that. But you have a radiance about you that I haven't seen since Robert died. Tell me everything that's happened while I've been gone."

"It was terrible when you and Dagert didn't return. Jacques organized search parties and led the searches himself. He didn't sleep for days, but you know what it's like in the bush country.

He located the village in Mali where you and Dagert had acquired sixty laborers, but he couldn't find any clue after that. It was as though you'd disappeared from the face of the earth. Jacques has been marvelous, Kordy, the way he came in and took charge." Her blue eyes gleamed and her face glowed.

Kordell glanced curiously down at her, but said nothing.

"Kordy, you'd be so proud of Jacques. You wouldn't know your brother today. He looks after little Bobby and me as well as you did. And he's running both plantations with an expertise that is astounding. I suppose it's the Bouclair blood."

Kordell laughed heartily, fascinated. "Are we talking about the same Jacques? My younger brother, the irresponsible, devil-may-care Jacques Bouclair?"

"Yes. Isn't it incredible?" Nicolle squeezed the hand that still held hers, and her face sobered. "Jacques has lived all these years in your shadow, Kordy. He never had a chance to show anyone what he was really made of. You were always more handsome, more charming, more confident, and, yes, more capable. You invested your father's remaining wealth and tripled it in only a few years. I think Jacques simply concluded there was no use trying. He could never compete with you."

Nicolle paused, and her eyes searched Kordell's for understanding. "But Jacques has other qualities. He's such a caring man, Kordy. He's so sensitive and has a compassion and insight one would never expect to find in the man he seemed to be. Now he's assumed all the responsibilities of West Winds that you always carried by yourself, as well as overseeing my plantation too. He's even muddling through your many investments trying to manage them. After I return, he plans to go to France and England to check on your estates and investments there. The combination of his new maturity with the naturally loving, affectionate person he really is . . . is irresistible."

"And you love him." Kordell smiled tenderly, his heart taking wings.

"You know I love you, Kordy," Nicolle said hastily. "And I always will. But somehow it's different with Jacques . . . I don't know how to explain it."

"You love me, but you're in love with Jacques." Kordell's eyes softened.

"Yes, that's it. Exactly! Is it so obvious?"

"No more so than your vivid blue eyes, my sweet Nicolle." Kordell was suddenly ecstatic.

"Oh, Kordy, I knew you'd understand. Jacques or I had to come to America to make certain that . . ."

When Nicolle's words trailed off, Kordell glanced down at her. "Make certain of what?"

"That you had truly fallen in love with your Brandelene. Each letter from you reflected all the more how you felt about her. But then, when I received your letter suggesting that it would be best if I found someone else, and you didn't mention Brandelene, and your letter implied that you might not be returning for a while—of course all doubt was removed today in the Wolf's Lair anteroom. You glowed every time you mentioned Brandelene's name. But if that weren't enough, a person would have to be blind not to realize how you feel when you look at her." She paused, then added, "Well, I had to come and make certain that I wasn't merely hoping."

"And to make certain I was all right?"

"And to make certain you were all right," she agreed. "Although I knew Pierre would have that well in hand. Jacques couldn't leave himself, what with the tremendous responsibilities he'd taken on, but we both felt one of us needed to explain to you . . ."

At her last words, Kordell grew preoccupied, his mind on Brandelene, but Nicolle did not notice.

"I suppose the next thing to do is to ask for your blessing."

"I'm sorry, Nicolle. What did you say?"

"As soon as I return to the Ivory Coast, Jacques and I want to announce our betrothal. I hope we have your blessing."

"Of course you do," Kordell answered absently. "Most certainly, Nicolle. How could you question it? I couldn't be happier for both of you."

"I think you know, Kordy, that no one will ever take Robert's place in my heart," Nicolle said. "I thought I could never feel this way about another man, and I've been too long without a husband. Your last letter said you weren't sure how soon you'd return. Will you come back for the wedding?"

Kordell smiled down at the beautiful face that radiated happiness. "I don't know, Nicolle. I don't really know."

"What's wrong, Kordy? Please, don't tell me I'm wrong about you and Brandelene."

He glanced from Nicolle's companion to Pierre, then looked out the window. "We're outside of town. Why don't we walk awhile?"

"That would be nice. However it'll seem strange walking without the sounds of the jungle."

Kordell called out for the coachman to stop, then assisted Nicolle from the carriage. Glancing from the dirt road to Nicolle's silk and sheer gown, he said, "Perhaps rather than walk we can pretend we're kids again, and sit on the ground as we used to. I need to talk to you, Nicky."

"Of course."

Kordell removed his cutaway and placed it on the grassy roadside, assisted Nicolle, then sat on the ground beside her. "Brandelene told me when I escorted her to her room tonight that she's had our marriage annulled."

"Annulled! How can it be? You didn't . . . you haven't consummated the marriage?"

Hesitating, Kordell replied. "No. No we didn't."

"Oh, dear! Ohhh, dear."

"Don't worry, Nicolle. You were right. I'm in love with Brandelene. Hopelessly in love with her. But she loves another man."

"Oh, Kordy, no! I can't believe it. How could any woman you wanted not be in love with you?"

"How could you not, Nicolle?"

"It's different between us, Kordy. You've always been like my big brother. That's why, when you brought up the subject of marriage, I suggested we talk after you return. You and I were so close. Our families were so close. Whenever I imagined sharing a bed with you, as I had with Robert, it felt wrong. I needed time to consider if I could overcome those feelings, and while you were gone I decided I couldn't. Besides, I knew you weren't in love with me. Not the way Robert was, the way Jacques is. And your halfhearted proposal was hardly that of a besotted man."

"Why? What did I say?"

"If I remember correctly, you said, 'I suppose we ought to get married. What do you think?' "

"I said that?"

"That's exactly what you said. But I was as uncertain as you, so please don't feel bad. That's another reason I said we'd talk about it after you returned from Mali. I decided to decline, if indeed that was a proposal, after you returned."

Kordell smiled down at her, loving her sweetness, and asked, "You don't feel it's wrong with Jacques?"

"No. Jacques was always with my younger sister or one of his friends. You, Dagert, and I were always together. There was never that closeness with Jacques when we were children. It only started to grow after you disappeared."

"I truly am happy for you, Nicolle. You deserve more than I could have given you, and I see you've found it with Jacques."

They talked for quite a while. Kordell was hesitant to put into words that which he'd known for many months. "Now, to complicate matters, Brandelene will soon realize Southern Oaks is doomed."

"Southern Oaks is doomed? How can that be?"

"Southern Oaks cannot be saved."

"Kordell, are you saying that Brandelene will lose Southern Oaks?"

"Yes. Unless she converts back to slavery. Which she will not. Without the enormous cash reserves her stepuncle gambled away, her plantation is lost. With more bondsmen gaining their freedom each year there won't be enough money to replace them, or pay them wages, even with the most bountiful of crops."

"Brandelene doesn't realize this? Certainly she must know. How can she not?"

"After your father died, did you know if your plantation was rosperous, or perhaps in jeopardy?"

"No. Not until you went over the ledgers and told me."

"Exactly. The records at Southern Oaks haven't been kept for ver two years. The journals and ledgers are being brought current ow, so there's no way to determine how bad the situation is until hey're completed. Besides Brandy's had no one to advise her. he's only nineteen years old, Nicolle. She was barely seventeen hen her father was murdered, and her stepuncle immediately ent her north for two years to school. They don't teach women o manage a plantation or to analyze required future cash reserves nd depletions in such schools."

"But why haven't you told her of the grim future of her plan- ation?"

"It was never the right time. When is the right time to tell a oung girl whose father has been murdered and her heritage windled from her; when is the right time to tell a young girl who till has the heart to come back fighting, working from dawn to lusk, that she fights for a lost cause? That she's won the battle his year, but she can't possibly win the war?"

"You could salvage Southern Oaks with the money you throw way every year on your loose women. Tell her how wealthy you re, Kordy."

"Brandy will marry me for love, and love only, or I will walk ut of her life forever."

"Kordy!"

"Nicky, Brandy is like no other woman I've ever known. If she narried me for my fortune, she'd feel she'd been bought and her ride, her damnable pride, would never allow her to grow to love ne. Besides, I could never live with the knowledge that I had ought her. We would both be miserable. That was why I asked ou, in the sitting area of the inn, not to reveal anything of my vealth or heritage. Brandy believes me to be a pauper, and Dagert's worn to secrecy too."

His voice softened. "I had felt, this last month, that she was tarting to love me, until I realized the truth of it tonight when he told me about the annulment."

"What happened?"

"Why don't I start at the beginning. It's the only way I know of being fair to Brandy."

Nicolle laughed. "Kordy, I know you too well for you to need to worry about defending your Brandelene. But I would love to hear the whole story. I have the feeling it will be fascinating."

Kordell told Nicolle everything. He left out nothing and also admitted to his instantaneous attraction to Brandelene, something overpoweringly compelling that he had never felt for any other woman.

Later they returned to the inn, and when Kordell stepped from the carriage, he turned to Nicolle before he hurried inside. "It's time I tamed a hellcat!"

He hesitated in the anteroom, contemplating whether to acquire another room as Brandelene had requested. But now there was no need to protect Nicolle from the truth, for she knew everything. With a grin, he decided he would sleep in their room. Brandelene might have started their love affair, but she was not going to end it so easily. Thus decided, Kordell started for the stairs when the innkeeper's voice stopped him.

"Mr. Bouclair," the man called out, "your wife left a message for you."

Frowning, Kordell crossed the room to take the letter from the man's hand. Moving toward the stairs as he broke the seal, he paused and leaned against the balustrade to read.

Dear Kordell,

Deep regret forces me to write this letter. You have done so much for me, gone so far beyond the confines of our agreement to help me, that mere words could never express my gratitude. It is because of you that I still have Southern Oaks.

Never will I regret what we have shared these last weeks and that brief period in time will always be a beautiful memory to me.

It is for these reasons that I feel such pain at our parting in anger, and if I have hurt you please know that I never intended to.

I will forever cherish the thought that, together, we accomplished the impossible. I pray that someday you too will be able to look back, without bitterness, on what we endured, and smile.

I wish the best for you, Kord, in everything you do. May you find the love and happiness with Nicolle that you deserve.

Brandelene

Turning to the innkeeper, Kordell boomed, "When did my wife ive this to you? When?"

"Right before she left, sir."

"My wife left the inn?"

"Yes, sir. She seemed in a hurry, and your coachman escorted er."

"How long ago did she leave?"

"I reckon about a half hour."

"Where is the livery?"

"They'd be closed now, sir."

"Send someone to open it—immediately!" Kordell bellowed nd threw some coins on the counter. "Get me the fastest horse ıey have."

"Yes, sir."

"Well, move!" Kordell barked, and the innkeeper scurried off. Curse that independent woman! Dammit to hell. Damn!"

At this moment Pierre was escorting Nicolle and her maid into ıe Wolf's Lair. Taking one look at Kordell, Nicolle hurried to is side. "Kordy, what's wrong?"

"Brandelene left for Southern Oaks." His face darkened with oncern.

"Oh, is that all." Nicolle laughed, relieved. "For a moment I hought . . ."

"Nicolle, Brandy's riding unprotected, in the dark of night, in he same carriage and on the same road on which her father was nurdered. Every plantation owner between here and Southern Oaks knows that carriage on sight."

"Oh, merciful God!" Nicolle gasped. "What can I do?"

"Pray! Please pray, Nicky. If anything happens to Brandy . . ."

"Oh, Kordy. Kordy, you must go after her."

"I am. On the fastest horse I can find. I only hope I can overtak her." Then he turned and ran for the stairs, calling back over hi shoulder, "I'm going to see if she took any guns with her."

Minutes later Nicolle was pacing the sitting area when Kordel returned with a pistol shoved into his waistband and a flintloc in his hand.

"At least Brandelene has a pistol and a musket," he said grimly "Nicolle, I'll send a coach for you and your servants tomorrow. want you at Southern Oaks. Will you bring my things? They'r still in our room."

"Certainly," Nicolle assured. "Kordy, everything will be all right I know it will. It has to be. Hurry!"

Kordell raced out the door, jerked the reins from the startle groom, and galloped off into the night.

He urged his horse faster. At long last, in the moonlight h spied the carriage traveling at a moderate speed. He heaved a sig of relief, for he knew, since the barouche moved at a relaxed pace that all was well. At least Brandelene had had the good sense t raise the folding top and not light the exterior lamps. He pulle his stallion beside a frightened Joshua and called out for him t stop the carriage.

Inside the barouche, terrified, Brandelene cocked her pistol, he heart pounding in her ears. Was it the same man who'd kille her father? Trembling, she vowed that if she were to be murdere this night, she would not die alone.

Chapter 30

CAUTIOUSLY, KORDELL RODE TO THE REAR OF THE topped barouche, knowing Brandelene would not panic and shoot t simply anything that moved. He tied his winded horse to the ear and carefully approached the carriage. "Brandelene, it's Kordell. Don't shoot."

There was no response.

"Did you hear me, Brandy?"

At that, the carriage door swung open and Brandelene demanded coolly, "What are you doing here, Kordell?"

"The question is, madame, what the hell are you doing here?" With that, he swung up into the barouche, wanting to pull her nto his arms and never let her go. Instead he roared, "This was ridiculous stunt."

"Apparently you forget your place, sir. You aren't my husband. You no longer have a place in my life, Kordell, nor are you esponsible for my welfare." Pausing, she added haughtily, "And ou don't tell me what to do."

Kordell tiredly eased his large frame onto the seat beside her nd replied, "Can you order me not to care what happens to you, Brandy?"

Brandelene commanded her racing heart to be stilled and did not reply.

"I've ridden hard to catch you," he said, unable to tell her of he tremendous relief he felt at finding her unharmed. "I should ub my horse down. I'll be back shortly. The animal will need to est, then I'll escort you to Southern Oaks." With that, he jumped out of the carriage and disappeared into the darkness.

A short time later, when he opened the door, Brandelene's words rushed at him from the darkness within. "Please take the opposite seat."

Pausing partway in the door, Kordell challenged, "Why?"

"We are unescorted. You're betrothed to . . . another. You shouldn't be here at all."

"This is absurd! You are . . . you were my wife—in every sense of the word."

"Does it give you pleasure to keep reminding me?" At Kordell's silence she softly added, "Besides, that is precisely the reason I'm asking you to sit opposite me."

Swinging into the carriage, Kordell sat facing her. "Brandy, we need to talk."

"Does Nicolle know you're here?"

"Yes. Of course she knows I'm here."

"Then you should consider yourself fortunate to have such an agreeable fiancée. Happily, I'm not your betrothed, for I wouldn't be so understanding."

"Why?" When he received no answer Kordell, in a hushed tone pressed, "Is that why you were never possessive of me, Brandy? Because you don't love me?"

Stunned by his question, Brandelene stammered, "Did I . . . did I ever claim to love you?"

Kordell smiled to himself. She had avoided his question. It was not much, but still it was a place to start. "There was one night you did." The instant the words left his mouth, he regretted saying them.

Brandelene inhaled sharply, battling to maintain her composure. She recalled, in heartbreaking detail, every memory of that night. She felt her arms embrace Kordell, felt her lips hungrily kiss his magnificent, carved mouth, felt her hands intimately caress his powerful body; she saw his passion-glazed leonine eyes; smelled his masculine, musky scent; heard the words of love she'd whispered, meaning every one with all her heart.

"Brandy, forgive me. I didn't mean it the way it sounded. Please forgive me."

"Please leave, Kordell," Brandelene whispered weakly. "Please."

"I won't leave you on this road unprotected."

"You've had your revenge, or whatever it is that you seek, for my not telling you when I filed the annulment." Her words were barely audible. "I would've thought your joy at learning that you're free to marry the woman you love would permit you to forgive me for bruising your ego. Regardless, you've avenged your injured pride. Now, please leave me in peace. Go back to Nicolle. She needs you. I don't."

"I'll follow the coach on horseback," Kordell replied and opened the carriage door.

"You can't do that! You'll be an open target. Please . . . go back to Nicolle. I don't ever want to see you again, Kordell. Not ever!"

Wordlessly, Kordell stepped down from the barouche and shut the door. After he untied his horse he mounted and rode up to Joshua. "I'll be following at a short distance, Joshua, so it's home to Southern Oaks."

"Yes, sir." Joshua beamed.

Alone inside the carriage, Brandelene wrapped herself in a cocoon of anguish and despair. Once again she was unable to cry to relieve her grief, as when her father had died, and her feelings of wretchedness broiled inside of her with no way to find relief.

Much later, in the middle of the night, the carriage arrived at Southern Oaks. The door swung open, and instead of Joshua, Kordell stood there to assist Brandelene. She hadn't realized Kordell had followed her, and she quickly sought to maintain her composure. Never would she let him see what he had done to her. Unable to trust herself to speak, she extended her hand for assistance, but instead of taking her hand Kordell reached up to encircle her tiny waist and lift her down, as he always did.

The moment her feet touched the ground she brushed his hands from her.

Kordell grabbed her arm, staying her. "Brandy, is there any chance you carry my child?"

Crying out, Brandelene slumped against him.

Instantly Kordell swept her up in his arms and carried her into the mansion, up the stairs, and into their bedroom. Gently, he laid her on the bed and bent over her.

"Don't you touch me. Don't you ever touch me again! Save tha for your mistress, or fiancée, or whatever Nicolle is."

"Nicolle is not now and never has been my mistress. That i your distinguished position—by choice. Don't ever let me hea you assassinate Nicolle's character again." His words were grounc out, his barely controlled rage obvious. "Have I made myself clear?'

"Perfectly. And let me make something quite clear to you. I you ever put one finger on me again you'll live to regret it . . . i you live at all."

His expression wretched, Kordell replied, "I'll ring for Ruby t assist you." He rose and left.

Ruby hustled into the master bedroom to find Brandelene desolate, sitting on the edge of the bed. "What's the matter wit my little lamb?"

"Oh, Ruby! I'm so miserable, I could die."

"Is that handsome rascal plaguing you again, honey?" Rub wrapped Brandelene in plump arms and rocked her as she hac when Brandelene was a child. "Now, don't you let that man ge you down. Sometimes, men are more bother'n they're worth."

At that, Brandelene stiffened, then straightened. "Will yo please help me out of this confounded gown?" She stood anc moved toward the bedroom she'd not used in weeks. "I refuse t stay in this room another minute."

"Mmmm-um." Ruby followed Brandelene to unfasten her gown "He sure got you in a huff this time. And you two been close than two peas in a pod, just like my baby and that charming buck Dagert. Lordy, you two are putting every gray hair in my poo head, and that's a fact."

Stepping out of her gown, Brandelene glanced up. "Pearl anc Dagert?"

"That man is gonna leave and break my poor baby's heart, o he's gonna leave and take her with him, and break my poor heart.'

"Dagert's leaving?"

Nodding, Ruby helped Brandelene out of her petticoats. "H told Pearl he won't live where he can't feel free. Where he can' even go hunting 'cause it's against the law for black people to have a gun."

"When is Dagert leaving?"

"He said he wouldn't know for sure until you and Mister Kordell returned from Richmond."

"And he and Pearl are still together?"

"Every minute possible." Ruby sighed. "Thank the Lord, Pearl's been real good about not being alone with him. I told her if she keeps swishing her backside at that man, she's gonna get what she's asking for. But she just walks around with her head in the clouds and he gives her one of his dazzling smiles and struts his beautiful body in front of her, like some proud peacock, and Pearl starts acting like she hasn't got a lick of sense."

"Oh, Ruby, darlin', you don't need to worry about Pearl. She has good sense—which is more than I can say for myself."

"What you talking about?"

Brandelene told Ruby everything.

"Honey lamb, if you want Mister Kordell I know you can have him. He doesn't love Nicolle. I've seen how that man looks at you. Besides, it was you he followed home, wasn't it?"

"I don't want him. I hate him! The only thing Kordell sees when he looks at me is my inheritance."

"What about her inheritance?"

Ignoring Ruby's question, Brandelene turned her eyes to the woman who'd helped raise her and blurted out, "What if I'm carrying Kordell's child?"

"Oh, Lordy! When did you last have your monthly flow?"

"I can't remember exactly. Sometime before Kordell and I left for the auction."

"Oh, Lordy!"

"I've certainly made a mess of things, haven't I?" Brandelene sighed unhappily and lay back on her bed. "How could everything that was going so well suddenly go so wrong?"

"Now don't you be fretting, lamb. Ruby's gonna fix you some hot chocolate. You get some rest, child. We can talk tomorrow. Maybe it's just that you've been working too hard." Ruby tucked Brandelene under the covers and bustled downstairs.

Pacing the veranda, Kordell heard Ruby come down the staircase and hurried into the foyer. "Is Brandelene all right?"

"That child's got her daddy's strength. You don't need to be worrying about her." Ruby glanced up at Kordell's tormented expression reflected in the flicker of the candle and shook her head. "I knew when I saw you walk out of that bathhouse that there was gonna be trouble. I knew it."

Kordell stared down at her and nodded. "I think I knew it too, Ruby."

"Mister Kordell, I want to ask you something. Are you after Miss Brandelene's inheritance?" Ruby's dark eyes bored into him.

"I think you know better than that, Ruby."

"Do you love Miss Brandelene?"

"You know the answer to that too."

"I just wanted to hear you say it."

"Yes, Ruby, I do love her. I love her with all my heart."

"I knew it! I knew it all the time." Ruby grinned. "But what about this Nicolle woman?"

"I love Nicolle as a sister. And she's going to marry my brother after she returns to the Ivory Coast."

Ruby's eyes widened. "Miss Brandelene never told me that."

"She doesn't know it. Brandy didn't give me a chance to tell her."

"Mmmm-um. That child sure is mule-headed." Ruby grinned widely. "I'm gonna fix Miss Brandelene some hot chocolate so she can sleep. She's loved it since she was knee-high. You look like you can use some sleep yourself, Mister Kordell, so you can let Miss Brandelene know about Miss Nicolle tomorrow." Then she moved off toward the kitchen.

"Good night, Ruby," Kordell called after her.

Pausing, Ruby turned back. "Miss Brandelene's in the other bedroom. If you want to sleep in your bed it's empty. I'll bring you some hot chocolate too."

"Thank you, Ruby." Kordell smiled affectionately.

At noon the next day Brandelene rode out to the sorting sheds and curing barns. The rich aroma of the last of the curing lugs and cutters filled the air. The autumn day was cool and nature's beauty surrounded her, abounding wherever she looked, in the radiance of fall, in the brilliant orange, gold, and red of the leaves.

The largest, and last, harvesting of food crops was completed and the older children now picked walnuts, hickory nuts, and chestnuts. The plantation swarmed with activity as barrels of some vegetables were stored fresh in the dark of the enormous earth-floored cellars, while those that would not keep were pickled or dried.

It was Brandelene's favorite time of year, but today she could find no joy in the beauty.

She saw Dagert, on horseback, lean down to give Pearl a brief kiss. She reined in her stallion to watch them, her heart aching with longing.

At that moment Kordell rode up behind her. "How are you feeling, Brandy?"

"Why are you still here?"

"We have considerable to talk about."

"*We,*" Brandelene retorted, "have nothing to talk about. Perhaps you confuse me with your betrothed."

"Now that you mention it, I didn't have the opportunity to finish my conversation with Nicolle. You may recall I had to leave rather hurriedly. However, for the convenience of us all, I've sent the coach and an armed guard for Nicolle. She should be here for dinner."

Brandelene's eyes blazed. "How dare you humiliate me in my own home by bringing your fiancée here!"

"And how dare you file for an annulment and allow me to believe you're my wife these past weeks," Kordell parried, his face darkening in anger. "Besides, Nicolle is not my betrothed."

"I don't believe you."

"I didn't think you would," Kordell replied sharply, a chill hanging on the edge of his words. "You can hear it from Nicolle when she arrives. She's going to marry my brother."

"Your brother! Are you telling me you've been jilted? By Nicolle?"

"You could express it that way," Kordell ground out, humiliated not in the least. "As for myself, I feel only tremendous relief and happiness for Nicolle and Jacques."

"My, what a shock it must have been to discover, all in the same day, that you'd lost the two opportunities you had to marry a woman of means."

Kordell's eyes narrowed and he leaned forward to rest his arm on the pommel of his saddle, his golden gaze capturing hers. "Tell me, Brandelene, if you can. What have I done to you that you would turn so vicious? Have I ever, even once, intentionally harmed you?" His voice was hoarse, yet strangely gentle. "These last weeks with you have been the happiest of my life. And I know you were not unhappy. What's changed all that?"

"Nicolle."

"Nicolle is no longer involved."

Brandelene squirmed in her saddle and avoided Kordell's intent regard. "Now that everything is in the open I will not go back to . . . to being your mistress, if that's what this is all about."

"Why did you become so to begin with?" Kordell's gaze never left her face. "Was it because you love Dean Paul and realized you can never have him?"

"Dean Paul? You're a fool, Kordell Bouclair!"

Kordell reached out to grasp her arm in an iron grip. "You listen to me, woman, and you listen carefully, for I don't intend to repeat it. I'm not going to tolerate any more abuse from you! I have not earned it."

Jerking free of his hand, she spat, "Don't play the dominating husband with me. It doesn't suit you. Besides, you're no longer my husband. I want you off Southern Oaks. Now!"

"Not as long as there's a possibility you carry my child."

"And if I do?"

"Then you will marry me. Again."

"Water will burn first!" With that she kneed her mount and sprinted off.

Sometime later Brandelene, at Kordell's insistence, walked with him onto the veranda to welcome Nicolle. The three retired to the drawing room while Nicolle's maid and two men servants were shown to their rooms.

Shortly, Kordell excused himself and privately instructed Matthew to assemble every house servant, including Ruby and Pearl, in the foyer, cautioning the butler that he did not want one person missing. Then he returned to the drawing room, closed the double doors behind him, and casually suggested Nicolle tell Brandelene her wonderful news.

Nicolle related to Brandelene how she and Jacques, Kordell's younger brother, had fallen in love, and why she'd come to the United States. When Nicolle finished Brandelene was convinced that Nicolle told the truth, for she radiated happiness.

Matthew interrupted, "The servants are all assembled, sir."

"Thank you, Matthew," Kordell said.

"Yes, sir."

Rising from his chair Kordell smiled at Nicolle and Brandelene. "Ladies, will you please come with me and I'll introduce Nicolle to the servants."

After the three stood in the foyer, Kordell addressed the gathered servants, "I would like to present Madame Montcliff, my brother's fiancée, and a special house guest. Madame Montcliff will be staying with us for a few days before she leaves to marry my brother, and I ask all of you to extend her every courtesy, the same as you do Madame Bouclair and me. She is to have anything she wishes."

With that Kordell turned to Matthew. "Matthew, do you have Madame Montcliff's rooms in the *east wing* prepared for her and her maid?"

"Yes, sir."

"Good. Please show Madame to her quarters. I'm sure she'll wish to rest before dinner."

"Yes, sir, Mister Kordell."

Kordell smiled. "You may dismiss the staff now, Matthew."

As the roomful of servants dispersed, Brandelene wordlessly crossed the foyer and ascended the wide, winding staircase.

Quickly Kordell followed. "Brandelene, I hope this has eliminated any discomfort you may have felt due to Nicolle's presence here."

Surprise crossed her face before she could mask her feelings, and without answering, she continued up the stairs.

When they reached her bedroom, Kordell opened the door, then stepped aside for her to enter and said, "I'll escort you to dinner." It was an order, not a request. Then he softly closed the door.

After Brandelene's bath, Ivy towel-dried the thick hair, then brushed the tresses to a high sheen. Sighing aloud, Brandelene wished Pearl were with her. Ivy tried hard to please her mistress, but Brandelene needed the comfort of her friend, needed to talk to Pearl. Still she could not take Pearl away from her remaining time with Dagert. Everything had changed, and none for the better.

It seemed to take forever for the inexperienced Ivy to dress Brandelene's hair in the intricate style she wanted, piled high on her head in numerous large curls with a garland of tiny flowers surrounding the crownlike curls. Her hair in the back, drawn to the side, was curled into one thick ringlet and pulled forward over her shoulder to hang down her breast. Nothing would do but to look her best. Nicolle was an exceptionally beautiful woman and Brandelene was convinced that Kordell was devastated over losing her, and only accepted the loss because the man involved was his brother.

She'd decided, when she saw the misery on Kordell's face in the Wolf's Lair common room, that he was part of her past. Even so, her pride would not permit her to look anything but her best tonight. Carefully she selected a rust silk moiré gown, trimmed with matching velvet, wriggled into her petticoats and gown, then examined her image in the cheval glass. When she was ready, she lifted her skirts, crossed the room, and tapped lightly on Kordell's door. She entered at his response.

Inhaling deeply, Brandelene gave no visible sign of how marvelous Kordell looked. Never had she seen a more handsome man, but she'd die before she let him know it.

"I am here, as commanded." Her eyes narrowed in warning as he reached to take her elbow. Wordlessly they left his room and walked, side by side, untouching, downstairs to dinner.

As expected, Nicolle looked stunning in a canary gown the exact color of her hair. She was exceedingly gracious throughout dinner, though Kordell had little to say. Since Brandelene completely ignored Kordell, the atmosphere was strained, with Nicolle and Dagert doing most of the talking. Brandelene could barely wait for the meal to be finished.

"My compliments on dinner, Brandelene. It was delicious. I hope all of you will understand if I retire to my room. I'm unusually tired." A footman pulled back Nicolle's chair and she rose. "Oh, Kordy, when my manservant packed your belongings at the Wolf's Lair, there was a stack of your mail. I put it in my valise for safekeeping. I'll have my maid bring it down." Then Nicolle smiled fondly at him. "You wouldn't want to miss my letter telling you that I'm coming." With that, Nicolle turned to Brandelene. "Thank you, Brandelene, for extending me your hospitality. You're a lovely hostess and Southern Oaks is a beautiful home. Perhaps we can visit tomorrow. I would enjoy getting to know you better before I leave."

"I would like that too," Brandelene replied. Perhaps, she thought, she could learn of Kordell's past from Nicolle.

Brandelene retired early in order to avoid Kordell, and had prepared for bed when a knock sounded from Kordell's connecting door. She ignored it, but it came again louder.

"Yes?"

"Brandelene," Kordell's deep voice queried, "may I come in?"

"No."

"I have a letter for you." Kordell sighed patiently. "I'm sure you'll want it."

"Who is it from?"

"Brandelene, I'm not going to stand here and bellow through the door."

"Come in." Brandelene pulled the covers up to her chin, covering her silk and lace nightgown.

"You needn't bother. I've seen you in considerably less."

"Give me the letter and get out."

"It's from Charles Thompson and more than likely confirms that your treasured annulment is granted. That should help you sleep better."

Trembling, Brandelene broke the seal. She glanced up at Kordell and frowned. "I thought I told you to get out."

"You, my beauty, do not order me what to do. However, under normal circumstances I would comply with whatever you ask. But in this instance, I will stay to hear the confirmation."

Chapter 31

BRANDELENE BENT TO READ THE LETTER FROM Charles Thompson, surprised that it was dated weeks earlier.

Dear Brandelene,

En route to Richmond, my legal assistant was held up by highwaymen. He was transporting a substantial sum of money for a client to a bank in Richmond. Unfortunately, your petition for annulment and doctor's certification were in the same satchel as the money, and were also stolen.

Consequently, your documents have not been filed. If you wish me to file the remaining signed document in my possession, I will need a new certification from your doctor.

If you do not wish to acquire another doctor's certification, you do have the option of having Kordell sign a new petition and I can file that.

I caution you that if you choose not to obtain a new doctor's certification, the annulment could, at some later date, be contested by Monsieur Bouclair. Additionally, the court would have the right to refuse to grant the annulment. Taking into consideration your present standing with the state, since you have freed your slaves, it might be the wisest and safest decision for you to simply acquire a new certification.

In either case, I advise you and Monsieur Bouclair to come into my office to sign another petition for annulment. I prefer not to surrender the only signed petition if we can still acquire another.

I realize you are anxious to have this matter behind you and apologize for this inconvenience at your busiest time.

With best regards,
Charles Thompson
Attorney-at-law

"Brandy, what is it?" Kordell asked, staring at her ashen face.

She glanced up, only now aware that Kordell still stood there. She wadded up the letter and threw it at him. "I hate you, Kordell Bouclair! I hate you!"

Kordell bent and picked up the letter.

"Get out of here. I'd rather be married to the devil himself than a cad like you who preys on vulnerable women," she ranted, her eyes sparking fire, her face clouded with wrath. Glaring at him, she vowed to divorce him at the earliest possibility. "At least the devil doesn't disguise himself to be . . ."

Glancing up from the letter he'd begun to read, Kordell asked, "To be what, Brandelene?"

"Get out of here! I'd rather be wed to a wharf rat than the likes of you." With nothing else close at hand, she grabbed her pillow and threw it at him.

Kordell returned to his room to read the letter that had put Brandelene into such a rage. As he read and reread, his smile of satisfaction turned to a grin. This would give him time to tame the fiery wildcat he'd married—the rest of his life.

His door crashed open.

"Why am I just now getting that letter? It was written over a month ago."

His hungry eyes feasted on the temptation standing before him, her beauty thinly veiled beneath the silk and lace. Knowing that Brandelene once again legally belonged to him was a heady brew, and it sent a familiar fire flashing through his loins. He dragged his gaze from her and quietly questioned, "You were asking?"

"Why am I just now getting a letter written over a month ago?"

"The postmaster now refuses to deliver mail to Southern Oaks, or so I was informed."

Brandelene whirled around and slammed the door behind her. Instantly it flew open again and she glared at him. "Do not think you've bested me, Kordell. I am a Barnett, and I will prevail." She shut the door with a bang.

"Wrong, Brandy," Kordell murmured to the barrier. "You are a Bouclair now. Legally, in body, and someday in mind, spirit, and heart, I promise you."

Later that night Kordell showed Dagert and Nicolle the letter from the attorney. "Brandelene can't annul our marriage for she cannot obtain a new doctor's certificate, and I certainly won't sign another petition for annulment." Then he paused. "Brandy might be expecting our child."

"What're you going to do?" Dagert asked.

"Tame the shrew," Kordell replied. He was not smiling.

The next four days Kordell worked with Dagert until dark while Brandelene and Nicolle became acquainted. After dinner each night, Brandelene avoided Kordell by retiring to her room while Nicolle, Kordell, and Dagert visited until early in the morning.

At those times Nicolle insisted that her maid remain in the room with them, and requested that a Southern Oaks servant be close by.

Brandelene realized Nicolle took such precautions to protect her, Brandelene, from servants' gossip and she appreciated her thoughtfulness.

During those four days Brandelene found herself drawing close to the genuinely loving and considerate Nicolle. She readily acknowledged that it was impossible not to care for someone as warmhearted and compassionate as Nicolle, finally understanding why Kordell, Dagert, and even Pierre loved and admired her. Nicolle saw only good in everyone and everything.

From time to time, Brandelene subtly tried to discover the truth of Kordell's position in life, and confirm his wealth—or lack of it. Yet with every attempt, Nicolle seemingly misunderstood what Brandelene wanted to know, or managed to answer without reealing what she sought, or changed the subject altogether. On he third day, after one more not quite so subtle attempt that Jicolle once again avoided answering, Brandelene knew the voman was deliberately evading giving her the answer she sought. Her only alternative was to ask Nicolle directly. "Nicolle"—she esitated hopefully, then rushed on—"is Kordell penniless?"

With no hint of surprise at Brandelene's improper question, Niolle smiled sweetly. "Perhaps you should ask Kordell, Brandelene."

"Of course, you are right, Nicolle. Please forgive me for placing ou in an uncomfortable position." But Brandelene had her answer. No woman who loved a man as Nicolle did Kordell would decline o praise his high station in life—if he held such.

The following morning Brandelene's discovery that her monthly low had started was met with mixed emotions—disappointment, or she had started to find pleasure in thinking she might carry Kordell's child—and relief, for now, hopefully, Kordell would not ontest a divorce, if she made it rewarding enough for him. Then he remembered Nicolle was leaving this morning and her mood larkened, for she now thought of the caring woman as her friend. She crossed the room to knock on Kordell's connecting door.

"Come in," Kordell called out, surprised to hear a knock from Brandelene's side. He slipped on his cutaway coat as she opened he door. Silently, he drew in his breath as she entered his room n a flowing jade velvet dressing gown, her raven hair tumbling reely over her shoulders.

"You'll be relieved to know I'm not expecting your child. If you urry you can have your belongings packed and leave with Nicolle." With that Brandelene whirled to return to her room.

"Brandy!"

Kordell's voice halted her steps, but she stubbornly refused to urn around.

He spoke to her back. "I am not relieved."

His voice, oddly tender now, sent a shiver down her spine.

"Nicolle is well escorted and doesn't need my assistance. Besides, ou are my wife. Why should I wish to leave with another man's etrothed?"

Brandelene continued on into her room. She should have known the fortune-seeking cad would not easily give up Southern Oaks, and especially now that they had received such a high price for the tobacco leaf.

A short time later Brandelene walked the veranda with Nicolle while her servants loaded the coach. Dagert had decided to stay awhile longer, so he and Kordell waited to tell her good-bye. Somber, for other than Ruby and Pearl, Nicolle was the only woman she called friend, and now she would never again see her.

Nicolle, upset because she'd been unable to help Brandelene and Kordell resolve their differences, glanced at Brandelene, seeing her distress. "Brandelene, Kordell is a wonderful man," she murmured for Brandelene's ears only and placed her arm around the smaller woman's shoulders while they walked. "Perhaps, like you, he permits his pride to stand in the way of what he wants. I know you love him—" She held up her hand when Brandelene started to protest. "Please, allow me to finish. I know you love him, but he needs to know it too."

Brandelene hesitated, but decided against confiding in Nicolle. After all, Nicolle was first Kordell's friend. Distressed, she asked, "Will you write to me?"

Nicolle hugged Brandelene to her and smiled brightly. "Of course I'll write to you. Pages and pages. And you must write me too."

Brandelene nodded her assent, unable to say all she wanted. "Address it to the postal station in Petersburg." Then she lifted her chin and laughed. "The postmaster won't deliver mail to Southern Oaks."

"I will miss you, Brandelene," Nicolle said and tears filled her eyes. "I wish we could live close to each other." Then she moved to hug Kordell and Dagert good-bye.

Brandelene watched Kordell pull Nicolle into his arms, and she turned away when he bent his tawny head to whisper in Nicolle's ear.

Then Nicolle sat in the coach while everyone waved as the brougham started down the oak-lined driveway, followed by an armed guard on horseback.

Presently Brandelene walked toward the small pillars guarding the portals of Southern Oaks. Kordell stepped aside to permit her to enter the foyer. Pausing, she glanced up at him. "I would have a word with you in the library, Kordell." With a swish of her skirts, she swept into the mansion.

Kordell followed her into the library and closed the door.

Instead of facing him, Brandelene presented her back. "So that there won't be hard feelings because I didn't inform you in advance, as before, I wish to advise you now." She hesitated. When she spoke, her softly murmured words were almost inaudible.

"Kordell, I'm going to Petersburg to file for a divorce."

Stunned by her words, Kordell paused for a moment to regain his composure. "Divorce? On what grounds, Brandelene?" he queried huskily, glancing at the blue-black glint of her hair in the ray of sunlight that streamed through the French doors. "Let's see, what grounds could you possibly have? Do I beat you? There's not a man who'd fault me if I did, for the Lord knows you could use a good lashing."

Brandelene whirled to face him and gripped the edge of her father's large carved oak desk. Her violet eyes darkened to black magenta.

"What other grounds could you have for divorce? Do I drink?" His golden gaze captured hers briefly before his eyes narrowed and his voice took on an angry tone. "No? I sure as hell don't know why I haven't started, for your vicious tongue could drive the best of men to drink."

"If you're finished—"

"I'm not."

He stepped forward, until he stood so close she could feel the heat of his body.

"There must be some other reason that you could obtain a divorce, madame. Could you accuse me of being unfaithful? Not hardly! After all, I was celibate for a damnable five months after we married, and now find myself in the same miserable position again. However, perhaps that is a situation I should give consideration to changing. Any normal man would have run into the arms of the first woman he met, if only to receive a kind word." Then he glanced down at the perfection of her flawless face and cursed her beauty that disguised the deadly black widow spider within, and then he cursed his own weakness for permitting her to weave her web around him.

As Brandelene moved to leave, Kordell blocked her path.

"I don't intend to stay here and listen to your idiotic ramblings. I've better things to do, even if you don't," she said heatedly, brushing against her father's large globe of the world, held in a carved wooden floor stand, almost knocking it over in her anxiety.

"You are staying until I'm finished."

Wordlessly, Brandelene glared up at his face, now darkening. An outrageously handsome face that exuded a magnetic masculinity and set her pulse racing. She moaned inwardly. Why was she unable to resist this one man?

"Have I mismanaged your estate, Brandelene? I don't think even you would accuse me of that. Perhaps you might say I have been lazy, inattentive, inconsiderate, uncaring, or have a total disregard for your happiness. No? Have I failed to protect you? No? I don't believe you can say I'm not well educated for I graduated from Oxford with honors, or even that I lack the comportment of a gentleman, when it's required. And other women don't seem to find me unattractive."

"Let me pass, you bully. I don't intend to listen to you spout any more accolades to yourself. You are naught but a conceited boor."

Now Kordell's hand flashed out to grab her arm, staying her. "Conceited? Because I admit women have found me attractive? Grateful, yes. Conceited, no. I can't take any credit for my appearance, for that is my parents' doing. And if I take pride in something I've personally achieved, then I say I've earned feeling good about a job well done. If that makes me conceited, then I am guilty."

After a moment he released her, but his piercing glare pinned her to the spot.

"What have I overlooked, Brandelene? Ahh, yes. Could it be that you find me an unsatisfactory lover?"

Instantly his golden leonine eyes glimmered with the unmistakable look she had seen many times, and had learned to recognize.

"I will be the first to acknowledge you are a passionate woman, my *beloved* wife. Was I unable to satisfy your appetites? I think not."

"You are crude and disgusting! I hate, loathe, and despise you, Kordell Bouclair."

"I don't believe that's grounds for divorce, madame."

"You are a fraud! A fortune hunter who preys on helpless women."

At that Kordell roared with laughter. "Helpless women? You—helpless? You're about as helpless as a black panther. In fact, I wouldn't be the least bit surprised to find you'd been suckled in a lair by a she-cat." With that he picked up a curling lock of her tresses. "You even have the same shining black hair. Tell me, my beauty, does a black panther have violet eyes?"

Slapping his hand free of her hair, Brandelene retorted, "Your humor at such a time is sorely lacking."

"So is yours when you call me a fortune hunter. Besides, you don't really believe that, Brandelene. If that was true, I would have wed Nicolle years ago." With that, he grinned. "And need I remind you, it was not I who seduced you into my bed to consummate our marriage."

Turning a vivid scarlet, Brandelene snapped, "Do you refuse to give me a divorce?"

"Why do you want a divorce?"

"To find the man I could love."

"Such as your wonderful Dean Paul?"

"Dean Paul?" Brandelene laughed. "He's a boy."

"So you've finally realized that, have you? And now that you've tasted of the wine of passion you're going to add 'virile lover' to the long list of attributes your husband-to-be must possess?"

"You're detestable! Will you give me a divorce?"

"I will consider it. But until I decide, you are still my wife. And as such you *will* share my bed."

Violet eyes sparked as they challenged golden ones. "When I refuse, what will you do?" Brandelene asked haughtily. "Divorce me?"

"A woman of your passion won't sleep alone the rest of her life."

"I want a divorce!" Brandelene stormed persistently and stamped her foot as her voice rose to a piercing level.

"And if I refuse?"

Brandelene wanted him to feel the pain, the anger, the humiliation she felt, and would say almost anything to achieve that end. "I'll take a lover before I'll share your bed again." The minute the words left her lips she regretted them. How could she have uttered such words? Surely he must think her no better than a trollop. Now she'd probably lost the one feeling that Kordell did have for her—respect, and she could not bear the thought.

A fiery look of rage covered Kordell's face. Then one iron hand loosely clasped her throat. "As long as you are my wife, you will know no other man."

"And if I do?" Brandelene said coldly, showing no fear.

"I'll kill any man who touches you!"

Instantly she knew he meant it. "Take your hands off of me, Bouclair."

Kordell removed his hand. "Heed my words well, Brandelene. They are not spoken in jest."

Chapter 32

BRANDELENE THOUGHT ABOUT THE KIND OF WOMAN who had surfaced in her behavior toward Kord, and she did not like what she saw. Kordell was right, she did have a vicious tongue. Perhaps, with considerable effort, she could become a woman she could admire—a woman somewhere in between Nicolle and the sharp-tongued Brandelene. Possibly she could become the lady her mother had wanted her to be.

The following morning Brandelene dressed in a rust wool riding habit, for the days of late autumn had grown chilly. Following

Nicolle's arrival, she'd allowed her responsibilities to be borne by Dagert and Kordell, and now she wanted to check on the progress of the never-ending work to be done this time of year. But first she wanted to make Kordell the offer she had decided on last night. She did not want the dread of it to hover over her the entire day. She crossed the room, determined to contain her temper, her insults, her biting tongue, to become a woman to be admired. She tapped lightly on Kordell's connecting door.

"Come in, Brandy." After Kordell's temper had cooled he'd admitted to himself that he had been too hard on Brandelene and was anxious to apologize.

"Kordell, I'd like to speak with you a few moments, please, if you have the time. It's of a personal nature, so it can't be discussed over breakfast with servants present."

"Of course, Brandy. But first I would like to apologize for my behavior—"

"No apology is necessary," she interrupted softly, then returned his puzzled smile. "Perhaps we could talk on the balcony."

Nodding his assent, Kordell gestured for her to precede him and he followed.

Once outside, Brandelene walked to the balustrade and looked out over the beauty of the oak-clustered, manicured lawns of Southern Oaks. The air was crisp and cool, but the sun shone brightly. Autumn neared its end and the trees shed their leafy bowers of scarlet, orange, and gold. It was the kind of day that, normally, she felt like racing across the lawns with the sheer joy of living, but today she felt joyless and empty, as though something inside of her had died and would never live again. Inhaling deeply, she turned to face the curious golden eyes of Kordell. "I realize we both lost our tempers yesterday, and possibly said things we didn't mean. . . ."

"I said nothing I didn't mean, Brandy. Only things that might best have been left unsaid."

Furious at his affront, she bit back the retort she wanted to fling at him. She would become a lady to be admired if it killed her—and it just might. After a moment she looked up at him, her face innocently regretful. "As I wrote in my letter to you, in

Petersburg, I never intended to hurt you, to cause you any pain, and I don't want us to part in anger. You've been too many things to me to ever want that, Kord. Now, I want to get on with my life, and I'm sure you'd appreciate being able to do the same." She paused and looked down at her trembling hands and hoped she could say that which needed to be said. After a time she glanced back up at him, then sighed. "I'm prepared to make you an extremely generous offer in exchange for a divorce, or an annulment if I can still get one."

Kordell's eyes narrowed. "What exactly do you mean by extremely generous?"

"I'll give you a cash settlement so you will be comfortable until . . ."

Instantly, Kordell's strong fingers bit into the soft flesh of her shoulders. "If you were a man I'd . . ." His breath came raggedly, in barely controlled rage, as he fought to maintain his composure. Presently, his grip loosened, but his expression remained thunderous. "I know you to be an intelligent woman, Brandelene, so therefore you couldn't have misunderstood the many times I've made it clear I don't want your cursed money, or your plantation. So that leaves only one explanation. You still don't believe me. Well, Miss High and Mighty, Miss Don't Trust Kordell, you are throwing happiness away." He released her with a jerk and glowered down at her. "You bought me once, Brandelene, but you'll never buy me again. If I decide to give you your damnable divorce it won't cost you one penny."

"Then you'll give me a divorce?"

"I'll consider it."

"When will you let me know?"

"After I've made my decision."

"How long . . ."

"Don't press your luck, Brandelene," Kordell warned, then turned, stalked through his bedroom, and slammed the door behind him.

Brandelene calmly walked from the balcony, through the house, and downstairs to her waiting stallion, fighting to control her temper. She would become the lady her mother had wished her o be if she choked trying, and the lump in her throat threatened o do that exact thing.

During the next two weeks Kordell did not mention the divorce, or little else, and their relationship drifted into one of polite strangers. Brandelene decided to wait until after the harvest celebration to approach him on the subject again. Still, living under he same roof with the man she wanted more than she'd ever wanted anything, and knowing she couldn't have him under any conditions she could tolerate, wore her nerves raw. With each passing day her desire for Kordell mounted.

The barns, outbuildings, their basements, and the immense cellars beneath the common house overflowed with the stored foods that would help feed the near six hundred at Southern Oaks until the next harvest. Barns that housed the animals were filled o the rafters with hay, and the granary and corn bins bulged. Nothing would need to be purchased to feed the plantation animals and fowl. The last of the tobacco cutters and lugs were being sorted, cured, and shipped to Richmond. Fall neared its end.

Wholeheartedly, Brandelene now strove to control her impatience, her temper, and her sharp tongue, smiling at those times when Kordell expected an explosion from her, but received none.

Brandelene's presence was no longer needed at the sorting sheds or curing barns and she turned her attention to working in the library with Pearl on the records. At the end of the day she closed her ledger, leaned back in her chair, and sighed. The closer she came to completing the financial journals and ledgers, the more she realized that Southern Oaks was in jeopardy.

The morning of the harvest celebration dawned bright and beautiful with not a cloud in sight, and the treasured pianoforte was carried from the common house to the common grounds. Brandelene asked Dagert to assemble everyone on the lawns, where, mounted on horseback, she thanked the near six hundred people for their hard work and dedication.

Then the banjo players, fiddlers, and the tinkling keys of the pianoforte began, accompanied by the quick-stepping feet of dancers. Hands gnarled by hard work enthusiastically clapped in time with the music, and everywhere she looked eager, happy faces smiled. Sides of beef and pork roasted on the outdoor spits and already filled the air with delicious aromas, and the happy sounds of music, children, and laughter rang across the grounds of Southern Oaks. Casks of brandies, wines, and cider were broken open for the celebration.

Unable to force herself to join in the festivities, a gloomy Brandelene slowly led her stallion through the throng of people and trotted toward the forest. She could think of naught but her looming financial problems.

Kordell watched her disappearing figure, contemplated going after her, then decided against it. He knew what bothered her—the damnable divorce, and he had not as yet resolved how to give them both what they wanted. Brandelene wanted a divorce and he was not ready to consider it, for he needed the confines of their marriage to try to win her love without revealing his own position of immense wealth.

Late on the third and last night of the harvest celebration, Brandelene was asleep when Pearl banged on her door.

"Brandelene! Brandelene!" Pearl cried out, but received no answer. Slowly, she opened the door and seeing the sleeping form rushed to Brandelene's bedside to shake her awake.

At the same time Kordell, lying sleepless, leaped out of bed and hurriedly slipped on his breeches. Never in the seven months he'd been at Southern Oaks had either of them been awakened after retiring unless there had been a serious problem. Donning a shirt, he pulled on his boots and rushed into the hall to stand outside Brandelene's door.

"Dulcie needs you right away," Pearl panted excitedly. "Hurry! Hurry!"

"Quick, Pearl. Get me a dress." Brandelene threw back her covers, now wide awake. "What's the matter? What's wrong?"

"Dulcie has big trouble with Magdalene!" Pearl shrieked, snatching a muslin gown from Brandelene's dressing room. "She doesn't know what to do. She said to get you to help her, quick. There's no time to send for a doctor."

Slipping on her gown, Brandelene turned for Pearl to fasten it.

Then she raced out her door and ran into Kordell.

"Kordell, grab the laudanum, and hurry," Brandelene said. "It's Noah's wife. There's a problem with the delivery."

Kordell threw his cloak around her shoulders, ran into his room for a bottle of the medicine, then raced after Brandelene and Pearl as they fled down the stairs through the house and across the grounds toward the birthing cabin.

Rounding the corner of a row of bond servants' cabins Brandelene heard Magdalene's screams, and saw the crowd gathered in front of the cabin door. The three of them burst into the cottage.

Dulcie glanced up, then heaved a sigh of relief. Then the tall, stern-looking midwife saw Kordell. "Ain't no men allowed in here!"

Brandelene turned to Kordell. "Please wait outside, Kordell. It's an unwritten law."

Nodding, Kordell stepped outside with the others.

Magdalene's cries pierced the air again, and Brandelene glanced at the woman thrashing in heavy labor. Brandelene rushed to the foot of the bed where Dulcie sat, with head in hands. "Oh, dear God," Brandelene whispered half aloud. The shoulder of Magdalene's unborn infant protruded from the birth canal. Feeling faint, she drew in her breath, and calmly commanded herself to maintain her control. "What have you tried, Dulcie?"

"I've tried everything, Miss Brandelene," the midwife groaned. "Everything."

Magdalene's shriek rent the cabin as she again strained to force the baby from her body.

"If we don't do something immediately they'll both die," Brandelene whispered to Dulcie, and the thin gray-haired woman nodded. Calm now, Brandelene glanced up at Pearl. "Get Kordell!"

Pearl's eyes widened, then she turned to Dulcie.

"You can't shame this poor woman like that," Dulcie protested. "You can't!"

"Better shamed than dead," Brandelene retorted, her words almost drowned out by Magdalene's next spine-shivering scream. "Pearl, I said get Kordell."

Pearl ran to the cabin door to summon Kordell.

"Two of you women grab a blanket and get on each side of

the bed. Hold the blanket up in the air so the gentleman cannot see below Magdalene's shoulders," Brandelene instructed and poured alcohol over her hands.

Now Kordell stood inside the cabin door, and Brandelene could hear the mumbled protests from outside. "Kordell, please go to the head of the bed. I need your help. If I cut Magdalene open, she would not live. I don't know if I can do what I'm about to try, but I know naught else."

Another shrill wail filled the cabin and Brandelene inhaled deeply, then breathed a silent prayer. She could not see Kordell for the blanket. "Kordell, give Magdalene a large dose of laudanum. Do whatever you have to do in order to make her swallow it."

"Right, Brandy," Kordell replied.

While Kordell forced the opiate-based laudanum down Magdalene's protesting throat, Brandelene apprised him of the situation. "The baby is turned in the birth canal, Kord, and is coming shoulder first. Magdalene's had two other children and knows she must push the infant out and that's what she's trying to do now. That's the worst thing she can do—for the both of them." Brandelene waited for the latest scream to die away before continuing, "I need you to hold Magdalene's shoulders down so she can move as little as possible. Then talk to her, tell her anything to make her stop pushing. She's in so much pain she doesn't understand much. When she quits pushing, I'm going to try to force the baby back up the birth canal far enough to get it turned headfirst. At least we might have a chance to save Magdalene." Another holler echoed through the room. "Do you understand, Kord?"

"I understand, Brandy."

For a never-ending fifteen minutes, Brandelene listened to Kordell's deep, resonant voice murmuring instructions to Magdalene, over and over, in comforting, patient tones, and it soothed her too while she worked over the woman. Finally she pulled the infant free of its mother's body.

"I know it's useless," Dulcie whispered, picking up the baby and whacking its tiny behind.

A weak wail of protest came from the infant boy who had endured so much to survive.

One of the women took the crying baby to bathe before placing him in his mother's arms, while another woman hurriedly moved to where Kordell stood, to wash Magdalene.

Brandelene stood up. "If I'm not needed, I think I'll leave," she murmured weakly, but no one on the team of efficiently working women seemed to hear. Glancing up, she caught Kordell's gaze above the blanket and smiled. She scrubbed at the basin and they walked out the cabin door together.

Kordell placed his cloak around Brandelene and she smiled up at him. He walked up to Magdalene's pacing husband and extended his hand. "Congratulations, Noah. You have a son."

"How is my wife, sir? How is my Magdalene?" Noah, Southern Oaks's best foreman, asked.

Kordell waited for Brandelene to reply.

"She had a difficult delivery, Noah," Brandelene reported, "but with plenty of bed rest and loving care she should be fine."

"I thank you, Miss Brandelene." Noah wept softly, then said, "God bless you, ma'am. You're a mighty fine lady."

"Thank you, Noah," she replied, smiling, "and congratulations. Your son is a real fighter. You can be proud of him."

Turning away, Brandelene and Kordell walked wordlessly to the plantation house.

In the foyer, Kordell moved to light a candle to show the way up the staircase.

"Thank you, Kord."

Turning at her words, Kordell stared down at her in the candlelight. "Brandy, that was a marvelous thing you did tonight. You saved two lives. Where did you learn so much about doctoring?"

"It takes six hours to get a doctor out here, and that's if we can find the doctor, and if he can come right away. So when anything serious happened with any of the people, Mother always assisted until the doctor arrived. She always had me go with her, to learn. I've assisted Dulcie many times. I've watched animals birth. I've watched Dr. Malloy cut open a woman, but I don't know enough to do that. Still, I never get used to a birthing complication like tonight." She swallowed, the room spinning around her.

Kordell caught her swaying form, then set the candle down. He lifted her in his arms and carried her up the stairs.

Her head rested against the hard wall of his chest and she could hear his racing heart. Her own kept cadence.

Outside her bedroom, Brandelene reached out a hand and pushed open her door. Kordell carried her inside and to her bed. He eased her onto the edge. "Are you feeling better? I'll unfasten your gown. Can you get into bed yourself?" At her nod, he bent and with shaking fingers unhooked her gown, then turned and left her room, closing the door behind him.

After Kordell left, Brandelene undressed, freshened herself, and slipped into her lace-trimmed, pink satin nightgown. She turned and stared at Kordell's connecting door, fighting her longing to go to him, to feel the strength of his arms around her again, to feel his marvelous mouth on hers. Her lips tingled in remembrance of his sensuous, heart-stopping kisses, her body ached for his touch. Turning away, she walked to her canopied bed and slipped beneath the covers, hungering for their shared passion.

A knock from the hall interrupted Brandelene's reverie and she called out, "Yes?"

Her door swung open and Kordell stood there with a steaming cup in one hand and a candle in the other. "I've brought you some hot chocolate to help you sleep. May I come in?"

"What woman could refuse such a considerate gesture? Please come in, Kord."

Setting the candle down, Kordell handed her the cup of hot chocolate.

"How did you know I like hot chocolate when I can't sleep?"

"A man learns a few things about his wife in seven months. I know you like hot chocolate, but sometimes I feel I've learned little else about you." Pointing to the edge of her bed, he asked, "May I sit down? I'd like to talk with you for a moment."

With her heart racing out of control, she hesitated, then replied, "Yes."

Kordell lowered himself to the side of her bed. Capturing her gaze, he searched for some sign of encouragement, but found none there and turned away.

He had never been in love before and now he felt possessed, bewitched, beguiled. His whole world, his every thought, every deed, revolved around Brandelene, and he once again wished he'd never found her. Countless times he'd told himself, the pleasure was not worth the pain.

But like the moth that is helplessly drawn to the flame, he was powerless to stay away from her. Everything about her intoxicated him—her blue-black hair that glinted like a raven's wing in the sun; her wood violet eyes, jeweled violets, where a man could lose his soul gazing into their depth; her full pink lips that softly parted inviting a man to taste of the pleasure he could find there; her voluptuous body that took him to heights of passion he'd never felt before, a rapture he had not imagined possible. These were the things that attracted him, but what captured his heart, what held him enthralled, what caused him to ever seek out her company, was her indomitable spirit, her depth of character, her enchanting sense of humor, and her magnetic personality, and he knew he would love her still if she were plain. Even so, he could not let her control his life. She was his wife. If he remained a man, something had to change. Brandelene would not emasculate him.

Finishing her hot chocolate in silence, Brandelene set the cup and saucer on the night commode. Kordell had sat wordlessly at her bedside and his nearness spiraled unwanted emotions through her. Unable to bear it any longer, she broke the silence. "You wanted to talk to me?"

"Brandy, I'm leaving for the Ivory Coast in the spring. My own affairs have been neglected far too long. I've given the matter considerable thought, and if you still want a divorce when I'm ready to leave, I'll sign whatever papers are required. If the state will accept them, I'll sign new annulment papers. It would be better for you than a divorce."

Instead of being overjoyed Brandelene was devastated. Thoughts of what it would be like without Kordell at Southern Oaks overwhelmed all else. It seemed as though he'd always been there, and always would be, and deep inside she knew that when he left he would take a part of her with him, a part that would never again live. But all her wishing would not change what was.

Never would she let him know how badly she wanted him to stay. She lifted her head high and asked aloofly, "Do I have your word?"

"You have my word," Kordell vowed solemnly. His hand covered hers where it rested on the bed. "There is one thing I would ask of you. It's not a condition, Brandy. I want to make that clear. When I leave, you may have your divorce, or an annulment if you can get one." He paused, hesitant to voice it. "I realize you don't love me, but since there doesn't seem to be an available man whom you do love, I would ask that we both try, until it's time for me to leave, to make our marriage work."

Gasping aloud, Brandelene stared wide-eyed at him. His hand burned into hers.

"Whether you agree or not, I will still give you the divorce you want."

"Try how?" she whispered.

"By calling a truce." Kordell lightly traced his fingers over her hand and wrist. "By resuming the relationship we had when I first believed we were married . . . and by your returning to my bed, our bed. Why should we deny ourselves the pleasure we can give each other? You are my wife."

A heated rush raced through Brandelene. Why was it only Kordell who filled her heart? Why did he have such power over her that she could deny him nothing? Why could one rakish gaze from his golden cateyes melt all her resistance? If she agreed, could he possibly tear any more of her heart from her than if she said no? Unable to concentrate any longer, she asked, "Why should I?"

"Why shouldn't you?" Kordell leaned forward to make his point. "Would you prefer to live the way we have for the last three weeks, or as we did the weeks I believed you were my wife? You're a passionate woman, Brandy. I can give you the pleasure you have come to enjoy. You were willing to play my mistress for those weeks. Why wouldn't you play my wife for a few months? We are married."

Brandelene was aware of nothing but Kordell's magnificent carved lips, so temptingly close she could lean forward and touch them with her own. The vision of being in his strong arms again eft no room for thinking, and the remembrance of the close, ender camaraderie they'd come to share flooded over her. But nce more her pride reared. "Charades again?"

"Even you cannot call what we shared in our bed charades."

Raising her hand, Brandelene stroked the cheek, the jawbone, he chin of Kordell's handsome, chiseled face. "No. Even I cannot ay that."

"Is it agreed?"

Chapter 33

"IT IS AGREED," BRANDELENE MURMURED. UNABLE TO esist Kordell one moment longer, she moved her hand upward o twine her fingers in his softly waving hair before slowly pulling is head down to hers. Their lips met in a gentle kiss of such enderness she felt she would surely die from the joy of it.

Kordell's loving kiss caught fire and his mouth voraciously lundered hers to seal the victory he already knew was his. Brandelene responded passionately. He raised his lips from hers and, nable to wait, ripped her gown down the center. His gaze feasted n the perfection of her body in the soft golden glow of the lickering candle.

Lifting thickly lashed lids, her glazed eyes adored him and she miled. He returned her smile, then she watched his hungry gaze lrop and slowly roam her body. "Why should you be permitted what I am not?" Brandelene breathed and reached out to unbutton is shirt with trembling fingers before she lightly trailed her fingertips through the soft furring of his muscular chest.

Kordell groaned, tossed the shirt aside, and eased her back or
the soft pillows.

Passions flared and their hunger grew.

His mouth captured hers in a fiery kiss, their lips ravaging, a
a white heat consumed them.

Her lips parted and the flames of his tongue flickered aroun
hers and a surging hotness flooded her abdomen.

Kordell's kiss relentlessly demanded, and his hands burned a
searing path across her quivering flesh to memorize each temptin
curve.

Uncontrollably, her heart pounded, and heat splintered dow
her stomach to the core of her being. Soft breasts pressed int
the wide expanse of his powerful chest and she moaned. The
his lips moved from hers to her lids, her ear, and traced a pat
of searing kisses down her pulsing throat to the fullness of he
heaving breasts. Another frail moan escaped her lips as he gentl
kissed the rosy nipples, before his mouth captured the swolle
mounds, one after the other. The fire flamed, low, deep in he
stomach. Her fingers threaded through his waving hair and hi
hands boldly roamed her body to caress and torment her int
mindless pleasure.

Brandelene's soft lips brushed his bronzed throat, and partin
her lips, her tongue sensuously teased his flesh.

His hands and tongue erotically assaulted her body and sen
her spinning deliriously, writhing in agony and ecstasy for fulfill
ment. She whimpered when he paused to swiftly doff his boot
and breeches, and with him now naked, her hand boldly roame
his body. He groaned, then her caressing lips followed where he
hand had been, exactly as he made love to her. Her gentle finger
moved up the inside of his thigh, to explore the manhood tha
pleasured her so.

Shuddering, he groaned again, his hunger urgent, wild. Layin
her down, he hovered over her and murmured sensual word
before his open mouth once again closed over hers. Urgently, h
parted her thighs with his knee and his turgid manhood entere
the throbbing, honeyed smooth flesh of her. Groaning, his cravin
for only her insatiable, he thrust into her.

The power of his driving passion filled her with a glorious, wantonly unrestrained intensity that crashed through her body.

His victory of Brandelene's submission was a heady wine, surpassed only by the unfathomable euphoria of possessing the woman he loved with an obsession beyond imagination. Then his mouth feverishly devoured hers and his surging need for her was in every possessive plunge, in every protesting withdrawal. Brandelene wrapped her legs around him, arching to meet every frenzied thrust, every ravenous drive, her hands on his buttocks urging him on. Unable to get close enough, he crushed her to him, then lifted his head to watch her passion-shrouded face. Her glazed eyes met his and while gazing into each other's eyes, a blaze flashed wildly through their joined bodies, spiraling them into the stratosphere, their essence locked in the delirium of love.

Brandelene was living and dying, unable to catch her breath, unable to surrender it.

The first and second time they made love they were the passionate, insatiable lovers whose craving for each other could only be temporarily assuaged. But the third time there was a gentleness, a reverence for each other and for what they had almost surrendered that made their culmination a gloriously awesome experience of wonderment they had never before shared—the mystical joining of the other half of their soul.

Brandelene lay contentedly sated in Kordell's arms and her thoughts touched on everything but next spring as she drifted into a peaceful sleep.

In the morning, when Brandelene opened her eyes, Kordell gazed down at her and she smiled up at him. He grinned disarmingly, then brushed the tousled hair from her face.

"Again?"

"Again!"

Sometime later she stretched and wrapped her arms around Kordell's neck.

Kordell hugged her to him. "Do you realize this is the first time you've awakened with a man you knew to be your husband? Which way do you prefer me, Brandy? As lover or husband?"

"I really wish you wouldn't keep reminding me of that," Brandelene said softly and removed her arms from his neck. "I never really intended for it to go on after the first night."

Instantly one brow shot up. "I thought you never intended for it to happen at all."

"I—I didn't," she stammered the lie and avoided his gaze.

Now Kordell stared thoughtfully at her, and unbidden, her words flashed through his mind, "Dean Paul?" she had laughed. "He is a boy." She might feel that way now that she was a woman, but could she possibly have felt that way before? Could he possibly be mistaken about her being in love with Dean Paul? That the only obstacle he had to overcome was her opinion that he was a fortune hunter? Let it be so, he prayed silently.

With her face averted from his, Brandelene started to have second thoughts about her latest agreement with him. Kordell knew her too well. Alas, at times he could almost read her mind. Also, it disturbed her that not a word of love had crossed his lips during the night when their passion carried her to such heights that she had to fight her will not to cry out her love for him.

With gentle fingers, he cupped her chin and forced her face toward his. When his gaze locked with hers, he sighed aloud, "Ah, Brandy, Brandy. How will I ever leave you in the spring?"

"Don't tease me, Kord. You'll most likely have trouble remembering my name by the time you reach Norfolk."

His eyes twinkled. "I have work to do. Do you think I can dally all day in this bed with you? Kiss me, wench, whatever your name is."

She did. Enthusiastically. Much later, they dressed and went downstairs for a late breakfast, and there was not a servant who did not know everything was back to normal with the master and mistress of the plantation.

After breakfast Kordell rode off to consult with Dagert. The tilling of the thousands of acres of harvested wheat was starting today in preparation for next year's crop, and men and mules plowed the earth.

Brandelene instructed Noah, the foreman of the work crews that were going into the plantation forests. New land would be cleared for the voracious tobacco crop, trees would be felled, and the winter supply of firewood would be cut. The other timber would be hauled by mules to the plantation sawmill to make hogsheads, barrels, kegs, and casks, plus the planks and clapboards that would be sold to England.

A short time later Charles Thompson's law clerk delivered nearly six hundred documents of manumission and a like number of contracts of indenture for the Southern Oaks's bond servants. They were placed in the library until the records were summarized. Once again Brandelene pored over the bond servants' journals and posted the ledgers while Pearl performed the task of updating the time records. The adjustments for the more than two years when there was no time-keeping were almost finished. After that was done, Brandelene, Pearl, and Shadrach could fill in the blanks on the contracts and give out the documents of manumission. Then slavery at Southern Oaks, legally as well as spiritually, would be a thing of the past.

With each set of figures that Brandelene added, the bleaker Southern Oaks's future became. When she'd verified the same numbers for the third time, she closed the bond servants' journal and pushed back her chair. "Oh, Pearl, Ruby was right!"

"How's that?"

Wretched, Brandelene cried, "After mother died, Ruby always said I was growing up wild. She kept telling me I was getting too big for my britches. That something would bring me down to size. She was right, Pearl. Southern Oaks has serious problems."

"That does it, Brandelene," Pearl said. "It's far too beautiful a day to look at figures. Let's check on Magdalene and the baby, and then we'll fix Kordell and Dagert a hot lunch and ride out to see what they're doing."

A short time later Brandelene and Pearl set the baskets of delicacies from yesterday's feasting on the table next to Magdalene.

Magdalene, although weak and exhausted, beamed with pride, for this was her first son. The baby's face, head, and shoulder were badly bruised, not only from trying to be forced from the birth canal in the wrong position, but also from Brandelene's fingers when she'd maneuvered the infant into the right angle. Otherwise he was beautifully shaped, healthy, and nursed enthusiastically. Everyone knew the bruises would disappear in time and an air of joy filled the cabin.

"I can't thank you enough, Miss Brandelene," Magdalene said. "Everyone told me what you done. I don't remember too much."

Smiling broadly, Brandelene replied, "I'm happy I could help, Magdalene. Have you named your son yet?"

"Oh, yes, ma'am. We named him Noah Kordell."

Blinking back the tears, Brandelene assured softly, "Kordell will be so pleased."

"I still remember Mister Kordell talking to me when I just knew my son and me was dead. He kept telling me not to give up, that we was gonna be fine. And him, a fine gentleman, he pressed his cheek next to mine. He told me I didn't have to think, that he'd tell me everything to do. His voice was so soft, and crooning, like my daddy's when I was a little girl." Tears streamed down Magdalene's cheeks.

"You and Noah Kordell rest now, Magdalene." Brandelene smiled. "I'm going out to the fields to see Kordell now. I'll tell him what you named the baby."

"Oh, you don't need to, ma'am." Magdalene smiled broadly. "I told him when he stopped by earlier. He was right pleased. He sure is a fine man."

Brandelene smiled, surprised to learn Kordell had checked on them. "Yes, I know he is, Magdalene. You rest now. God bless you both."

Then the woman attending Magdalene and the baby opened the door for them to leave, and Brandelene wondered how she could ever give Kordell up.

That night she slipped into her gossamer and lace nightgown and smiled, for she knew it would be removed as soon as she walked into the master bedroom.

Kordell's gaze devoured her. "You are a vision, my lovely wife." The diaphanous fabric did little to conceal her body and his gaze followed her as she crossed the room to the bed. "However, I don't know why you trouble yourself with putting on such lovely gowns, unless you enjoy having me remove them."

"And if I do?"

"It's my pleasure to accommodate you, madame."

He held out his arms to her. By the firelight, he looked like an Adonis.

He swept her up to carry her to the rug in front of the hearth and stretched out beside her. "Why is it you are the one woman in the world I can't get enough of?"

Sometime later they lay entwined in each other's arms, the fire blazing as hot as had their now-sated passion. Drowsy and contented, she glanced up at Kordell, who lowered his head to claim her lips in an endless kiss that took her breath away.

Filled with emotion, he stroked her silky tresses. "This night, and every night hereafter, Brandy, you are going to pretend you love me. Pretend that I am the man you would have chosen, above all others, to be your husband."

Brandelene stiffened. "I will not!"

"I'm not asking you, Brandy, I'm telling you. Remember, love, you agreed to try to make this marriage work."

His gentle hands performed their magic on her body leaving her weak, powerless.

His gaze had never left hers and now he lowered his face so close to hers she could feel his warm breath. His fingers slowly massaged her abdomen, then traced down to her inner thighs to send the liquid fire searing through her veins.

"Why?" she whispered, eyes glazed with passion.

"You once requested of me not to ask any questions."

His warm lips nibbled at her ear while his hand roamed at will and heated flashes splintered through her. She could not speak, she could only feel.

"I respected that request, Brandy. Now I'm asking the same of you."

"And you?" she asked blissfully, her voice barely audible as she succumbed to the fire that raged through her.

Kordell moved over her, his strong thighs imprisoning her hips between them. "I'll do the same."

"So now we are to carry our charades into our bed?"

Her passion-clouded face tormented him. "If you wish to think of it that way, yes."

"How else could I think of it?" She squirmed to set herself free.

"Have you already forgotten? No questions."

With that, he again lowered his body over hers and, with masterful domination, kissed her senseless while his masculinity sent spirals of ecstasy splintering through her, and she writhed beneath him, crying out his name for fulfillment.

His hands moved beneath her buttocks, and lifted her hips to receive him. "I love you," Kordell whispered tenderly. "Say it, Brandy. Say it!"

"Kord, please," she pleaded, her head tossing back and forth in that whirlpool of time between scorching torment and the bursting sensations of rapturous, uncontrollable pleasure.

"Say it, Brandy," he commanded and stilled all movement.

Opening passion-glazed eyes, Brandelene looked up into the face she adored. "I love you, Kord," she whispered, "I love you, I love you, I love you!"

Kordell vowed that someday she would mean those precious words, then plunged frantically, again and again, and with a burst of shuddering, ecstatic sensations, he took her to the lofty pinnacles of that other world they shared, where, together, they dipped and soared through timeless space with the wings of an eagle and floated on the quintessence of clouds of rapture.

The next morning the aroma of the smokehouse where hams, pork ribs, chops, and slabs of bacon slowly cured over burning hickory filled the chill air. At the same time, pork roasts and assorted parts of the butchered hogs were salted and placed in barrels for storage in the meathouse.

Now men and women worked at new duties, the multitude of seasonal chores of a large plantation. Women mixed hot tallow with wood-ash lye and water, to cool and cut into brown soap, while others made short, stout candles and the thousands of tapers needed for the next year; still others made mattress ticks to be stuffed with cornshucks, straw, and moss, and yet others dyed into different colors the white cotton bought to make clothes with. Drying bright fabric draped nearby clotheslines and bushes. Some women spun the carded bats of wool, from Southern Oaks sheep shorn last spring, into thread, while others wove the woolen thread into cloth, and the seamstresses cut and sewed winter clothes.

The majority of the men tilled the fields for spring planting, felled trees, or worked in the sawmill, while the artisans tanned hides that would be fashioned by the cobblers and leather workers into shoes, clothes, belts, saddles, mule and horse collars, and harnesses. But a few of the older men and younger boys happily fished the abundant streams.

The week sped by for Brandelene, the days joyous as they'd been the first weeks she'd played Kordell's wife. Now she lived for night, when their amorous, passion-filled hours merged with whispers and gestures of everlasting love.

Every night each sought to exceed the previous night in expressing *their* love, and with each passing night it became easier to believe the charades each believed the other played.

Brandelene pensively speculated that surely her heart would burst from the joy of it, except next spring ever lurked around the edges of her mind.

One night, after Kordell made love to her, she lay in his arms as usual, but this night she would get no rest until she knew the answer to something Nicolle had said. "Why did you write Nicolle last summer and suggest she find another?"

Silence greeted her question, for he was not sure he wanted to answer. After a time he pressed warm lips to her brow, then quietly said, "So Nicolle told you that?"

"Yes." Brandelene traced her fingers across his softly matted chest. "Why did you?"

"Because I realized I had fallen in love with you."

Gasping, Brandelene whispered, "I don't believe you."

"Believe it, Brandy. It's true."

"Believe your charades? Believe the words you whisper in the dark or in the heat of passion?"

Kordell's mouth covered hers and kissed her into silence.

The next day Brandelene and Pearl once more sat at the library table working on the financial journals and ledgers. Pearl had finished posting the time and work performed on each bond servant's journal. Everything was current on those long-neglected records. Now Brandelene was completing the multiplication and addition to determine which and how many bond servants had earned their freedom. Suddenly she stiffened and closed the last journal, unable to force herself to post the disastrous figures in the ledger. Her stomach churned with anxiety, frustration, and dread.

"Oh, Pearl! Southern Oaks cannot be saved. Pearl, Southern Oaks is lost!"

Pearl jumped at Brandelene's cry. "What are you talking about? What do you mean Southern Oaks can't be saved? You sold the tobacco for a record-high amount."

"I can't see any way I can ever salvage Southern Oaks. One hundred sixty-eight bondsmen have earned their freedom. One hundred sixty-eight! Southern Oaks operates shorthanded now. How can I replace these people if they choose to leave? With no cash reserves to replace the bond servants, each year the plantation will go deeper into debt, for we'll produce that much less tobacco. I'm not sure there's even enough money left from the tobacco to pay their wages for a year if they stay. I had no idea there would be that many who'd worked their way to freedom. And what about next year?"

"How can there possibly be that many?" Pearl blurted, almost knocking over her ink pot. "Perhaps you've made an error."

Brandelene gave a choked, desperate laugh. "There's no error, Pearl. There are that many because it's been two and a half years. And I owe some of these people considerable wages, in addition to their freedom. I had hoped to purchase another fifty bondsmen, so we wouldn't be so shorthanded. Yet even with the high price I received for the tobacco, less the mortgage repayment, I can't possibly do that and pay additional wages to one hundred sixty-eight people. And I certainly could never replace them."

Staring off into space, Pearl twirled her quill pen. "Brandelene, it can't be that bad. It can't be. You got so much money for the crop. I can't believe it. You must've made a mistake."

"Pearl, every figure's been checked twice. Some three times. And there's more."

"Oh, Lord, woman, there's more?"

Brandelene groaned. How could she force the words from her lips? How could she pronounce Southern Oaks's death knell? Her head bowed and her body slumped in despair. But she had to face the realities. She knew that the first step in overcoming an insurmountable problem was to face it. And she did that now by voicing the rest of her fears. "You know how fragile the tobacco crop is. What am I to do if we get a late spring hailstorm and it destroys the crop? Or if we get heavy rains that last too long? Or an early frost? And God forbid that we ever suffer a fire during curing, or a blight. There won't be enough money to see us through six months if we lose a crop. How could I not have realized this before? Pearl, I don't know what to do!"

Pearl's trembling hands reached across the library table and covered Brandelene's. "You're going to ask Dagert and Kordell. That's what you're going to do. They know everything. They'll know what to do. It just can't be that bad, Brandelene. They'll have some answers. Now don't you fret, honey. Let's go find Kordell right now."

"Kordell!" Brandelene exclaimed, wide-eyed. "Pearl, Kordell will leave when he finds out I'm not a woman of wealth. No, I can't talk to him yet. I have to think, Pearl. Surely I'll think of something." With that she leaped up and ran from the room.

The following morning at breakfast Kordell studied Brandelene with concern. All evening she'd been quiet, withdrawn. She'd heard little he'd had to say, her mind elsewhere. Yet she would not share with him what bothered her. He had tried several times, but she dismissed his attempts, saying she was just tired.

Kordell knew better. So during the night he'd decided it was time to quit playing charades. Spring was not that far away. If Brandelene would not believe his declaration of love, whispered in the dark of night, then perhaps she would believe it in the light of day. After that, possibly she would trust him and he could discover what troubled her and help her to resolve it.

"It's a marvelous day, love. Will you go riding with me?"

Chapter 34

"GO RIDING?" BRANDELENE SHOOK HER HEAD. "NOT today, Kord."

"Yes, Brandy, today," Kordell insisted. "You've been gloomy long enough. This is the perfect time to try your new riding habit."

She started to refuse, but Kordell interrupted her.

"Change, Brandy. Now. Or I'll take you back to our room and you'll have to make up for your lack of enthusiasm last night." He grinned and raised one brow rakishly.

She smiled.

Minutes later Brandelene stepped into the library. "Pearl, I'm going riding with Kordell. Will you take the bond servants' journals to the common house and ask Shadrach to help you fill in the blanks on the contracts of indenture? I'm anxious to have them done."

Pearl smiled cheerfully. "I'll be happy to. Are you feeling better?"

"Somewhat."

"Did you ask Kordell?"

"Not yet, but I will."

"Don't worry, Brandelene," Pearl said. "I'll have Isaac help me carry the records over now, and we'll get started on them right away. Enjoy your ride."

Brandelene changed into her forest-green velvet riding habit with matching hat and sheer trailing scarf. Then she twirled in their bedroom, for Kordell's approval.

Laughing, Kordell teased her, "If you're looking for a compliment, I suppose I had better tell you how ravishing you look in green velvet. But I still prefer you with nothing."

"Kord, you're impossible." She blushed happily, suddenly deciding she would put Southern Oaks out of her mind for today. This was to be a happy day. She would worry about Southern Oaks later. "Are all men as lusty as you?"

"I will see to it that you never know, my beauty." He laughed again and escorted her downstairs.

They raced their mounts, side by side, across the meadows to the edge of the forest. Kordell signaled Brandelene to rein her stallion in, then lifted her to the ground.

Brandelene wandered to a large tree, now barren of leaves, and leaned against the gnarled trunk, glancing up at the vivid blue, cloud-filled sky. Even though it was November the sun shone brightly, but the air was crisp and chilly. "It's such a beautiful day, Kord." She sighed, glancing around, the musky smell of fallen leaves filling her nostrils.

"Yes it is." He watched her as he walked to her side.

"It's so beautiful in Virginia, every season of the year."

Kordell braced his hands against the trunk of the tree, on either side of her head, pinning her between his arms. "You can feel the nip of winter in the air, even though the sun's shining brightly." His husky voice was seductive, though his words were not. Bending, he brushed a warm kiss across her upraised lips.

"Kord, why do you court me? I'm your wife. You control Southern Oaks. I share your bed, under your terms." Her gaze locked with his, and his lips hovered inches from hers. "What more could you possibly want from me?"

"Something I value much more than anything else."

"Which is?"

"Your love."

Caught off guard by the proclamation of this unpredictable man, her heart thudded uncontrollably in her chest. Too surprised to speak, she searched his earnest face. Could he possibly be telling the truth? Yet she was unable to think of any reason for him to lie. Through her confusion, she fought to control her swirling emotions, her glimmer of hope. Under his intense scrutiny it was impossible to concentrate, and finally she managed to ask, "Why?"

"Why?" Kordell repeated bemusedly. "Because I'm in love with you, Brandy. I knew it long before you first invited me to your bed."

Then he kissed her tenderly, an intoxicating kiss that captured her heart and sang through her veins.

Lifting his mouth from hers, he gazed into her eyes. "I'm telling you this in the light of day, love, not the dark of night. It is not our charades. They are not words murmured in passion. I love you, Brandy."

At those treasured words, Brandelene circled her arms around his neck and ardently kissed him with all the pent-up love her heart had harbored for so long. But still she could not tell him what he also wanted to hear in the light of day. When they finally separated, she refused to meet his gaze. Could Kordell really love her? Would he stay if he knew Southern Oaks's disastrous financial condition? Suddenly she needed to be away from him so she could think more clearly, and she moved toward her stallion. "The horses should be rested. I'll race you to Southern Oaks."

Grinning, Kordell said, "Well, Madame Bouclair, every race worth running must have a wager, simply to make it interesting. Wouldn't you agree?"

Glancing at him suspiciously, she hesitated, then ventured, "What do you suggest?"

"Ladies first."

"Well," Brandelene said playfully, "since I still haven't won what I first wagered, I'll bet that again. If I win you'll play my maid for a week. You'll brush my hair, give me a massage before dinner and before bed, and serve me breakfast in bed on Sunday."

Kordell's eyes gleamed. "I'll do that, madame, even if you lose—which you will."

"If you win," she taunted, "what devious scheme do you have for me to pay?"

At her question, Kordell stepped forward and rested his hands against the flank of her horse, once again pinning her between his arms. "If I win, you will play my infatuated love during our days as well as the nights, until spring."

At that, Brandelene vainly scrambled to free herself from his entrapping arms, from his heart-stopping nearness. "Why?"

"Why not? The arrangement is working out exceedingly well at night. Or need I remind you?"

Crimsoning at his taunt, she retorted, "It's but a charade."

"An extremely pleasurable charade."

Her heart shattered at his admission. His heartrending words of love, only minutes earlier, were false, but another ploy to keep her inheritance, to seduce her from the divorce.

"It's only until spring, Brandy."

She could feel the shards of her heart pierce her breast.

"Then I'll be out of your life forever . . . if that's what you want."

Lifting enormous violet eyes to his gaze, doing her best to ignore his body that pressed into hers, she replied, "I cannot."

"You did agree to try to make our marriage work." Then his eyes narrowed at her look of agony, and he was ripped apart, but his pride would never permit her to know it. Softly, he baited, "I never knew you to walk away from a challenge. However. . . ."

Brandelene haughtily exclaimed, "It's a bet!"

Lifting her onto her sidesaddle, Kordell leaped on his stallion and spurted forward, urging his mount far ahead and staying there.

When he arrived at the plantation house, Kordell dismounted and waited for Brandelene to gallop to his side. He reached to lift her from the saddle and her arms encircled his neck. Slowly he slid her body intimately down his. "What did you say, Brandy?" he asked, refusing to set her on her feet.

"I said I love you, Kord." Her barely whispered words were stiff, forced.

"Certainly, Madame Bouclair, you can show a little more enthusiasm."

Unable to look at him, Brandelene brushed her lips against his neck. "I love you, Kord." She sighed softly.

Kordell nuzzled her neck while he held her in his arms. "I can't hear you, love."

Now Brandelene buried her face in his neck, loving the masculine scent of him. "I love you. I love you. I love you!" Then she clasped his face between her hands and gazed at him. "Kord, I love you with all my heart."

Kordell's eyes widened at the words for which he had so long yearned to hear, then he hugged her until she gasped for air, and he twirled her around and around until they both became dizzy. Finally he set her down. "If this is a charade, Brandy, don't ever tell me the truth!"

Then his mouth possessively devoured hers in a flaming kiss that torched her soul, and she returned fire with fire.

When his lips lifted from hers, her arms still clung around his neck and she smiled wickedly up at him. "Now, you'll never really know for sure."

"Never know what for sure?" Kordell's arms tightly clasped her to him.

"If I intentionally let you win."

His eyes widened at her meaning.

Then his hungry lips claimed hers with a scorching kiss of searing intensity, the soldering heat that joins metal, and sent fiery shock waves through her entire body. When he dragged his mouth from hers, Brandelene was breathless.

"I love you, Brandy. God help me, but I do." After that he swept her up into his arms and carried her into the mansion and up the curving staircase, two stairs at a time.

"Mmmm-um," Ruby mumbled to Matthew. "Those two are gonna burn this house down yet."

"If," Matthew grumbled, "Pearl and Dagert don't beat them to it. Every time I look at those two they're cuddling."

Sometime later Brandelene and Kordell came down the stairs, hand in hand.

"As long as we've already missed half a day's work, why don't we take the rest of the day off?" Brandelene suggested happily, for this day she'd made a decision; if she had the choice she would never give Kordell up, even if he did want to remain for all the wrong reasons. He was her husband and somehow she would win his love. It mattered naught that he was not a man of means. Besides, it was simply a matter of time until her own inheritance would dwindle away. She also decided to tell him the fate of Southern Oaks tomorrow. Perhaps Pearl was right. He might know something she had not considered, or perhaps the situation was ιot as bad as she suspected. Nevertheless, today was to be a happy lay. "It's too beautiful a day to waste when we could walk the ;rounds."

"I'll get our cloaks." Kordell chuckled and briefly kissed her ›efore bounding up the stairs to return quickly with their wraps. Ie placed her cloak around her shoulders and pressed lips to her ιeck before donning his own.

Once outside, she slipped her hand into his and Kordell smiled lown at her. "Do you remember the day I bought your contract ›f indenture?"

"Remember! When I glanced up in that auction house and saw ʼou, I knew I had died and gone to heaven."

"And when you walked out of that bathhouse you took my ›reath away," she admitted, laughing. "I was speechless." Now he leaned her head against his shoulder, and his arm encircled ιer waist to pull her close to him while they strolled among the ;iant trees of Southern Oaks's leaf-covered, rolling lawns. "I knew was falling in love with you when you further risked your life o marry me while you were so ill. But I fought my feelings with ıll the strength I could muster. I didn't want to love you then, ınd I don't want to love you now, but I cannot help myself."

Kordell stopped and pulled her into his arms, gazing down at ιer. "Why don't you want to love me, Brandy?"

Trembling a little, feeling vulnerable, she glanced up at him, or now she had another fear that plagued her. That Kordell would ιot want her when he realized she was not a woman of wealth, ınd she could not live with that threat hanging over her head. I'm afraid," she answered softly.

Brushing the wind-whipped tresses from her face, Kordell quesioned, "Afraid of what?"

She bit her lower lip and glanced away. No more procrastination, he must tell him about Southern Oaks now. Today, not tomorrow. 'You haven't married a woman of wealth as you think, Kord," he said apprehensively. "Even though we received an incredibly ιigh price for the tobacco, each year . . ."

When her voice trailed off, Kordell finished for her. "Each year vhen there'll be an average of fifty or sixty indentured servants who acquire their freedom, Southern Oaks cannot possibly replace them on the profits from the tobacco. A substantial cash reserve is needed to do that."

Brandelene stared up at him in amazement.

"Therefore," Kordell went on, "each year you'll be forced to work with less help, which will mean less production and a smaller profit. Then will come the year when a late spring hailstorm continuous rains, early fall frost, or possibly a disease will destroy part or all of your crop, and without significant cash reserves Southern Oaks cannot survive."

"How did you know?" she gasped, astonished.

"You forget, my love, or possibly you didn't believe me, I am an expert at managing plantations."

"How long have you known?"

"From the time you first told me you intended to reinstate bonded servitude at Southern Oaks," Kordell answered gently, still holding her firmly in his arms. "Long before I ever set eyes on your estate."

Brandelene drew in her breath sharply. "Then you really haven't been after my inheritance all this time? You knew eventually there'd be nothing left."

Kordell smiled down at her. "Ah, my love, I thought you'd never figure that out."

"Oh, Kordell, I've been such a fool."

Kordell pulled her against the hard length of his body to comfort her, wanting to protect this woman who had more inner strength than most men, overwhelmed by his feelings of tenderness and love for her, and her alone.

Leaning back in his arms, Brandelene asked, "Why did you never tell me I couldn't save Southern Oaks?"

"It was something you needed to discover for yourself. If I had told you, either you wouldn't have believed me, or you'd have hated me for telling you." He pulled her to him and rested his cheek on her head. "I started to tell you several times after . . . after I thought we'd consummated our marriage, but I couldn't bring myself to do so."

"What are we to do, Kord?" she whispered into his chest.

Fighting his desire to tell her she had naught to worry about, for he could buy her twenty Southern Oaks, he remained silent. During his life, he'd always kept his emotions under tight control, but with Brandelene, he was as vulnerable as a boy. He had to be sure of her love before he would reveal his wealth, had to know that everything Brandelene had said today was not mere charades, payment of her lost wager. In a week, if he were convinced of her love for him, he would tell her the truth.

"What are we to do?" she repeated.

"I'll think of something, love, but not today. Today there is only us." With that, he feather-kissed the tip of her nose, then her lids, and finally his mouth tenderly possessed hers in a lingering kiss as gentle as the early winter breeze.

They strolled the grounds, and in a playful moment Brandelene bent down and grabbed two handfuls of leaves and threw them at him, then ran away, laughing. Kordell gave chase, and when she glanced over her shoulder, she tripped and fell to the ground. He pounced on her, and they rolled together among the fallen leaves, frolicking like children.

"Your hair is full of leaves, Monsieur Bouclair," she gaily taunted, laughing as he bent over her where she lay on the cold ground. "How undignified! What if one of our aristocratic neighbors should decide to come calling? Whatever would they say?"

Laughing with her, for she also had leaves in her hair, he pulled each leaf from her long tresses, spread fanlike in wild disarray upon the ground. "I love you, Brandy. God, but I love you!"

Violet eyes examined his sober countenance, then she wrapped her arms around his neck. "And I love you, Kord. More than you'll ever know. More than I ever dreamed possible." Then she pulled his tawny head down and nibbled on his carved lips before he kissed her passionately.

Much later, they both squeezed into the tub in the master suite, still laughing as lovers are wont to do. They soaped each other's bodies while Kordell good-naturedly grumbled that he would come out of his bath smelling like a dandy or a fop. Then he washed Brandelene's long hair, dried her lovely body, and carried her to the rug in front of the blazing fire. After they made love he ever so gently brushed her raven hair to a high sheen, then led her to their bed where he massaged her entire body with scented lotion, as he'd promised before their horse race.

Dinner was extremely late.

"Hmmph!" Ruby grumbled to Matthew. "Doesn't that man ever get tired?"

Matthew's brow shot up. "Woman, either you're getting old, or your memory's getting short."

"Don't you tell me I'm getting old, Matthew. I don't see you keeping me locked in my room all day and night." Then she giggled, not unlike a young girl, and her dark eyes sparkled. "But I sure remember when you did."

The following day Brandelene and Kordell traveled to Petersburg. Kordell wanted to inform Pierre that he could return to the Ivory Coast now, before winter set in, while ships still sailed. They planned to stay overnight and return late the next day. After that, he promised, they would discuss Southern Oaks. It was now too cold to permit Joshua to drive the brougham. Kordell had the young coachman stop, and Kordell picked up their mail before he sent a message to Pierre.

Kordell climbed into the coach and handed two letters to Brandelene and shoved the others into his pocket. "Yours are from the lawyer." He grinned, his eyes sparkling, ever the mischievous little boy. "He's probably wondering why we haven't been in to refile for the annulment."

"I suppose I should tell him why." Brandelene placed the unopened letters in her reticule, then chuckled. "Charles Thompson was so astonished that we hadn't . . . that I still had my virtue intact after five months of marriage to a lusty rake like you, and now I'll have to astonish him all over again."

"Madame!" Kordell feigned shocked disappointment, dramatically clasping his hand to his heart. "I'm crushed that you would malign my character so freely." Then he gave her a wink and they laughed.

Later, Brandelene sat in the tiny anteroom of the Wolf's Lair and waited for Kordell to return from talking with Pierre. She pulled the lawyer's letters from her reticule and opened one, noticing it had been written on the day Nicolle arrived, almost five weeks earlier. She sighed and silently chastised the postmaster for refusing to deliver mail to Southern Oaks, then read the letter.

Dear Brandelene,

I am relieved to inform you the highwaymen who robbed the coach were apprehended.

Of more importance to you, the pouch containing your petition for annulment and the doctor's certificate was recouped.

Realizing your anxiety to have this annulment finalized, I have dispatched my law clerk to Richmond and in all probability your annulment has been filed as you read this letter.

With best regards,
Charles Thompson
Attorney-at-law

"Oh, dear God!" Brandelene gasped aloud. "Kordell and I are no longer married."

She glanced around to see if anyone had heard her outburst, but there was no one in sight. With trembling fingers she shoved the abominable letter into her reticule and opened the second one, written a week later.

Dear Brandelene,

This letter is to inform you that your annulment has been granted and is recorded in Richmond.

You may resume your maiden name of Barnett.

Congratulations on the successful completion of your plans.

With best regards,
Charles Thompson
Attorney-at-law

What was she to do? What was she to tell Kordell? Closing her eyes, Brandelene attempted to gather her scattered thoughts. If she told him now, he might leave with Pierre. How could she bear to let him go? Better to wait until spring. That was it, wait until spring. With that resolved, she heaved a deep sigh and leaned her head back against the plush, high-backed chair to wait for Kordell. But her conscience gave her no peace. If Kordell sought a wealthy wife, and were free to choose, he would have no reason to stay, as he did being her husband. She no longer had a claim on him for their six-month agreement was satisfied. After all he'd done for her she could not repay him with deceit; she must tell him they were no longer married and that he was free to leave.

The pain and anguish of Kordell being forever gone from her life was overwhelming and she closed her eyes, beyond tears.

Forcing her thoughts from Kordell, her mind would permit her to think of naught but losing Southern Oaks. Kordell's confirmation, yesterday, of Southern Oaks's ultimate demise rushed to further plague her: "Without substantial cash reserves Southern Oaks cannot survive."

Today she considered those words from an entirely different perspective, for she no longer had a husband.

Charles Thompson's letter nearly placed her in the position she had originally planned. In that scheme of so long ago, she intended to be in Boston now, in the middle of the winter social season, seeking a husband of means whom she could love. Brandelene sighed. If she continued with her original plans, she would no longer be hindered by wanting to find a husband she could love, for never would she love any but Kordell. Now, any wealthy man who would treat her with consideration and be a good father to their children would do. Involuntarily, she shuddered at the idea of sharing her life, of sharing a bed, with anyone but Kordell. Could she do it?

Could she not?

James Barnett had made the supreme sacrifice for Southern Oaks—his life's blood. Could she do less than make any sacrifice herself?

"Brandy," Kordell's deep voice queried, "are you all right?"

Opening her eyes, Brandelene glanced up at Kordell's beloved face, the pain in her heart a sick and fierce gnawing. She could do naught but nod.

"Shall we have dinner, my lovely wife?"

Brandelene indicated the chair opposite her and softly urged, "Please sit down, Kord."

Concerned by her pallor and the solemnity of her countenance, Kordell seated himself and leaned forward. "What is wrong, Brandy?"

With fingers that refused to stop shaking, she withdrew the first letter from Charles Thompson and tried to hide her inner misery from Kordell's probing stare before she handed him the letter.

Kordell read the letter and glanced at her. Before he had an opportunity to say anything she handed him the second letter. Quickly, he read that too. He smiled and his eyes reflected understanding for her concern. Rising, he extended his hand to assist her from her chair and said softly, "Don't worry, my beauty. Everything will be fine. Trust me."

But his words of comfort could not pacify the tumultuous feelings that ripped through her and tore her apart. For now she knew she would be forced to choose between Southern Oaks and Kordell, and either choice would leave her devastated. She accepted his hand and looked up at him from eyes that could not disguise her anguish.

"Would you like to go for a ride, and we can talk?"

Brandelene nodded and turned for him to place her pelisse around her shoulders, then slipped her hand through his arm and walked to their waiting coach. Kordell assisted her into the brougham, instructed the coachman to drive about Petersburg, then climbed in beside her.

He slipped his arm across the seat behind her, picked up her gloved hand, and leaned toward her to press gentle lips to her lips, her nose, her closed lids. Tilting her chin up, he waited until she opened her eyes, and gazed into their depths.

"There can be little doubt in your mind that I love you, Brandy, for I love you with all my heart. I always shall. Forever. Will you marry me?"

Chapter 35

KORDELL'S GOLDEN CAT-EYED GAZE CARESSED HER. Swallowing a sob, Brandelene pleaded for understanding.

"I cannot, Kord," she whispered painfully. "I cannot. . . ."

Astonished, Kordell stared at her and waited for some explanation. Receiving none, he asked, "Why?"

Biting her lower lip, Brandelene turned away and refused to answer. After a time she asked, "Kord, will you give me every suggestion you can think of so that I might save Southern Oaks?"

Her question told him everything he did not want to know; her heart, as well as her first concern, was with Southern Oaks, and not him as he'd wished. Disheartened, he leaned back in the rocking coach, knowing this was not the time to press his suit. "Do you want the objectionable solutions as well as the preferable?"

"Yes," Brandelene replied as she stared sightlessly out the small window.

A bond servant's labor was only for the length of the contract, usually between five and seven years. But a slave was owned for a lifetime. If a slave was treated well he or she could work hard for thirty years and be sold or used for less laborious work for another ten to fifteen years. In addition, and the most profitable, the children of a slave became the owner's property, which meant the owner, with every child that was born, ultimately obtained a slave at no cost to himself.

Kordell began to explain, "With the exception of this year, when you received an unusually high price for your leaf because of the drought, you'll never have a high profit margin because a plantation that operates with bonded servants or free people cannot possibly return the yield of a slave operation. You're aware of that, Brandy."

"I had barely turned seventeen when my father died," she replied, absently smoothing the ruby wool folds of her fur-lined cloak. "Daddy hadn't time to teach me the finances or management of a plantation. I realize slavery has to be more profitable, but I have no idea how much more. I assume Southern Oaks cannot hope to compete against the slavery plantations."

"You have to compete," Kordell corrected. "Therefore you won't have the profits. James Barnett knew this, but he had the cash reserves to make the transition. He knew he would never be a man of great wealth again, but he was a man of conscience and willing to sacrifice his wealth for his values. He was a man of considerable honor."

"What are my choices now that I've paid off the mortgage and creditors, and I have limited reserves left from the auction?"

"Financially, you'd only have a small problem if you converted the plantation into a slavery operation, but I know you wouldn't consider that—"

"Never!"

"You could terminate all freed persons, sell the remaining servitude of the other bondspeople, and sell all or part of Southern Oaks."

Brandelene gasped. "Southern Oaks is my heritage! My mother and father are buried there. My grandparents are buried there."

"Another alternative is that you could immediately terminate all freed persons, so that you're not paying wages, but then you wouldn't have sufficient labor, so you'd have to plant less tobacco and allow the plantation to slowly dwindle away. Or you could sell half of the land, terminate all freed persons, and sell the remaining servitude of another two hundred bond servants. That would give you the minimal cash reserves you need and permit you to live modestly. No expensive gowns or jewels such as you now have."

"All of my jewels were Mother's, and I have no need for costly gowns, for I'm never invited anywhere, nor would I extend invitations." Lost in contemplation, Brandelene asked, "If I sold half of Southern Oaks and the remaining servitude of two hundred bondsmen, who would protect them from unscrupulous agents or slave traders turning them into slaves again? A sizable fortune could be made by a slave trader in the South who might buy the remainder of a black indentured servant's contract and then transport him to the new Louisiana Territory and resell him as a slave. Who would prevent that from happening? That black indentured servant would have no one to turn to for help, for Virginia is pro-slavery and there are no laws established in the new territory. In the South bond servants have no rights, and besides, most wouldn't know how to protect themselves. For the most part, only the younger people have learned to read, write, and cipher adequately enough to look after themselves. But even with them, I'd have concerns that slavers would whisk them off to the new territories of the Louisiana Purchase, and turn them into slaves. You've read the *Virginia Gazette*. You know the demand for slaves is unprecedented. The color of their skin hinders them in that regard, for no one in the South questions a black person being a slave. I imagine it would be the same in the new territory."

"Then you'd definitely have to sell their servitude in the North to protect them."

"I know there's employment for free blacks in the North, but you aren't familiar with the United States, Kord. I don't believe anyone in the North would buy the servitude of a person who's been a field hand all his life."

Brandelene sighed in exasperation. "From my understanding northern farms are too small and too poor, because of the short growing season, to buy an indentured servant. In the North most indentured servants are artisans, tradesmen, house servants, or can read and write sufficiently to perform other types of work. According to the newspapers I read while I was in school in Boston factories won't buy indentured servants. I doubt if there'd be a market for unskilled and uneducated indentured servants in the North. If that's the situation, it means I cannot sell the contracts of indenture."

"If you love me, Brandy, marry me and we'll work it out."

Gazing up into Kordell's penetrating golden eyes, Brandelene's heart lurched. "Show me how we'll work it out, Kord. Tell me how to save Southern Oaks. Prove to me it can be done."

"Brandy, please trust me."

"I cannot! The risk to the people of Southern Oaks is too high. You ask too much of me."

"Brandy . . ."

"Kord, I need to go home. I need to think. Please take me back to Southern Oaks."

He nodded. "All right, Brandy. We'll leave today."

Torn between responsibility and her heart's desire, she wrestled with her conscience. James Barnett had given up much of his considerable wealth plus the friendship of his peers for a slave-free Southern Oaks. He had died for Southern Oaks. Now she, in turn, would have to forfeit the only man she would ever love. How could she live with herself if she refused to do otherwise? It would be the same as turning her back on her father's sacrifice. With an aching heart, she knew she had to go to Boston.

Kordell questioned softly, "Have you thought of something I haven't, Brandy?"

"Yes . . ." She paused, unable to force the words from her lips. After an interminable minute, in a hushed voice, she said, "I'm not unattractive. I could marry a wealthy man." At his swift intake of breath, Brandelene paused again, then continued in sinking tones, "I can run Southern Oaks myself, so my husband would not have to involve himself. I can learn to manage . . ."

"You would throw away what we have?" Kordell accused angrily.

Wanting to scream at the new coachman who seemed to hit every rut and pothole in Petersburg, Brandelene turned to gaze into Kordell's eyes and forced her words to chilling coldness. "What do we have, Kordell?"

"You can ask that after yesterday?"

"Yesterday?" Brandelene said with feigned bewilderment. "Yesterday was naught but a charade to pay my wager on the race. Surely you didn't consider it otherwise?"

Kordell stared down at her. "You are lying, Brandelene." He scowled heavily. "Perhaps you don't love me as much as I would like to believe, but I know you love me."

"It's true I am fond of you, but given a choice, you're not the man I would choose as my husband," she lied, hurting with an inner pain that threatened to destroy her. Then she lowered her sweeping black lashes before she murmured the deceit she would give anything not to utter—anything but Southern Oaks, "Now that I have a choice I will marry a man I prefer."

"I don't believe you!"

Kordell crushed her to him, his hungry kisses melting her defenses. His hand cupped the roundness of her breast and, helplessly, her arms slipped up to encircle his neck, to let the world slip away. Submitting completely, she eagerly responded to his skillful kisses with a passion that left them both breathless, and she wanted to yield to the burning sweetness that seared through her. But at the same time, she cursed her weakness for this one man who could melt all her resolve with one sweet word, one gentle touch, one intoxicating kiss, leaving her with no will of her own.

Kordell dragged his lips from hers and recklessly baited, "Now tell me you don't love me."

Afraid to reply, Brandelene battled to regain her composure. After a time, she uttered the fabrication, "I cannot deny you've conquered my body, Kord, but you'll never capture my heart." Avoiding his eyes, she added, "I intend to find and marry the man who can save Southern Oaks for me. You and Dagert are free to leave." Then she twisted free of his arms and sat rigidly straight, staring out the side window of the coach. "I'll appoint Noah chief overseer of the cultivating, and I'll confer with Dagert if there's anyone on the plantation even remotely qualified to replace him. Naturally, I'd prefer one of our own bondsmen to acquiring an outside man. Of course, I realize it will be impossible to find another Dagert." Sighing, she turned toward Kordell. "However, I'll be there at the crucial time to instruct the new overseer, exactly as I did Dagert."

"Precisely where do you expect to find this husband of means?" Kordell quizzed, then continued on before Brandelene could answer, "The husband who will permit you to operate Southern Oaks under a system with little or no profit when he could easily restore the plantation to an exceedingly profitable slavery system? The husband whom you will love with all your heart and soul? Tell me, my beauty, are you going to search the auction houses again?"

"There are times, Kordell, that your sense of humor is extremely lacking."

Kordell laughed at the irony of it all. "You will never find with another man what we share, Brandy," he said scornfully, and cupped her chin with gentle fingertips before he turned her face to his gaze. "Never! You'll spend the rest of your life yearning for a love like ours—for what you are throwing away."

Brandelene said what she felt she had to, so he would willingly release her. "Your considerable ego simply won't allow you to believe every woman isn't dying of love for you, will it?" She laughed cruelly. "Consider, Kordell. Have I ever voluntarily said I love you, unless it was part of some ridiculous agreement or charade?" As the deceitful words escaped her lips, she felt something inside die.

In that moment Kordell realized that if Brandelene did harbor any love for him, it was not sufficient. And although he would never love another woman, he refused to buy the one he did love. If Brandelene would not come to him willingly, with her heart full of love, he would give her up.

Tapping on the small driver's portal, Kordell instructed the coachman to return to Southern Oaks. Then he said quietly, "So as not to interfere with your plans, Brandy, I'll leave immediately for the Ivory Coast."

The trip to Southern Oaks was made without conversation. Brandelene was extremely hurt that Kordell had not sought to change her mind and then she said a silent prayer that he had not, for she did not know if she had the strength to resist anything he might say.

As soon as they arrived, Brandelene hurried to Dagert's cabin and asked if she could speak to him. Nodding, he stepped onto his porch.

"Dagert, when Kordell and I were in Petersburg, we picked up the mail. The cursed postmaster refuses to deliver mail to Southern

Oaks now. Of course, it was never his obligation to deliver the mail, but it's a service he's always performed for the plantation owners, for a fee, of course. But now . . ."

"Is something wrong?" Dagert interrupted, realizing Brandelene had not come to his cabin at this time of evening to ramble about the postmaster.

"Yes."

"Would you like to step inside out of the cold?"

"Yes, please."

He stepped aside and Brandelene walked into the small sitting room. The oil lamp burned brightly.

Glancing at her pallid face, Dagert asked, "What's wrong, Brandelene?"

Her lower lip trembled, and her hand dove into her reticule to retrieve the two letters from the attorney. Wordlessly, she handed them to Dagert.

After he read the letters, Dagert looked up questioningly.

"Kordell's leaving for the Ivory Coast right away. I want you to know that if you wish to leave with him, I'll have your wages, bonus, and passage fare ready first thing in the morning." She paused, choked up. "Dagert, I can never thank you enough for all you've done for me, for Southern Oaks."

"It was my pleasure, madame. My pleasure indeed. It's very satisfying to know that something good came out of being captured by slavers." Dagert inhaled deeply. "Have you and Kordell discussed his leaving?"

"Yes." All her pain and agony was in that one word.

Thoughtful, Dagert stared down at his work-roughened hands. After a time, he glanced at Brandelene. "If it's all right with you, I'd like to marry Pearl as soon as we can arrange it. We had planned to wed at Christmas, but I want Kordell to stand up at my wedding."

At the pronouncement, Brandelene smiled. "If Ruby and Matthew are agreeable, I certainly am, Dagert."

"They've given us their blessings." He grinned, his dark eyes danced, and his face cast that special appealing glow.

Brandelene hugged him fondly. "Then you know you have my

blessing too. I couldn't have found another good enough for Pearl." She paused. "Well, I had better leave. I'll have much to do to help Pearl get ready for a wedding before Kordell . . ." Her words trailed off, for she could not utter them.

"If you have no objection," Dagert said hesitantly, "we'd like to wait until spring to leave."

"Then you're still going to leave?" Brandelene frowned.

"Yes."

Quietly, Brandelene turned away. Her whole world was falling apart. Kordell would be gone. Now Pearl and Dagert also would be leaving. What if Ruby and Matthew left with them? Then she would have naught but Joshua and a new husband she did not love. Distraught and unable to speak, she wrapped her cloak around herself and ran from Dagert's cabin to race blindly toward the plantation house, the chilly wind whipping her.

Abruptly Brandelene changed her direction and went directly to the common house. If the contracts of indenture were completed, she wanted to have them signed tomorrow and then the documents of manumission could be given out the day after. Then she could leave for Boston after Dagert and Pearl's wedding.

Shortly after Brandelene left Dagert's cabin, Kordell knocked on his door and hurried inside out of the cold wind.

"I figured you wouldn't be too far behind." Dagert chuckled. "Brandelene left only minutes ago."

"Ah, then she's told you everything?" Kordell's voice broke miserably.

"She showed me the letters from the lawyer and said you were leaving for the Ivory Coast right away. She said I could leave with you if I chose."

"Did she also tell you why I'm leaving?"

"No."

"Brandy won't remarry me, Dagert. She's going north to find a wealthy husband who'll subsidize Southern Oaks."

"You didn't tell her you're wealthy?"

"No."

Dagert nodded. "What would you do if the situation were reversed, Kordell? What if it were West Winds?"

"For Brandy, I would give up West Winds and everything else I own. In a minute!"

"You expect an awful lot from a young girl," Dagert chided, noticing the strain in Kordell's voice, the grim look on his face. "I can't believe you're going to let her go. That woman's in your blood. Why do you have to be so stubborn? Tell her you're wealthy."

Shaking his head, Kordell replied, "It wouldn't work, Dagert. Brandy would never let herself love me if she believed I had bought her, any more than she would if she felt she'd bought me. Her pride would never let her forget. We'd take something that could be paradise on earth and turn it into a living hell and I couldn't bear that. I'll give her up first."

"Brandelene loves you, Kordell."

"Apparently not enough, friend."

"And you're leaving for the Ivory Coast right away?"

"Tomorrow morning I'll start for Norfolk and stay there until I can make arrangements." Kordell sighed. "I'll talk with Brandy once more before I go, but I doubt anything will change. Even a fool knows when to cut his losses. I may be in love, but I'm not worse than a fool."

"Would you delay your trip a couple of days and stand up with me when I marry Pearl?"

Kordell's face broke into a wide grin. "It's about time you realized you'd better not let that woman get away. Of course I'll wait. You couldn't force me to leave knowing this." Then his countenance sobered. "At least for one of us something has turned out right in this fiasco." At those bitter words, Kordell clasped Dagert's hand and threw a strong arm around his shoulders. "I'm happy for you, Dagert. Pearl will make you a very contented man." With that, he released his friend and quietly left.

The following day was a day of no work as over four hundred bond servants signed their names or made their marks, and all was witnessed by Shadrach. The plantation preacher read the contracts to the bond servants, explained what each item meant, and answered all questions. The large room of the common house abounded with happy chatter and laughter. When Shadrach announced that everyone had finished the signing of the contracts, those one hundred sixty-eight protested that they had not signed. With a most sober face, for those who had earned their freedom had not been told, Shadrach assured them that they need not fear, for they would still receive their documents of manumission tomorrow, during the celebration, along with everyone else. Happy rejoicing and the decorating of the common house for the celebration, and upcoming wedding, continued throughout the day.

The next day the celebration began. The sun shone brightly in the chill air and Kordell stood beside Brandelene on the common house grounds. The nearly six hundred bond servants gathered around. Except for those who had earned their freedom, Brandelene called out each bond servant's name and handed him, or her, a paper.

The treasured document of manumission.

The document that stated he, or she, was free, no longer a slave. And that document guaranteed his or her children could never be sold, for under their newly signed contracts of indenture, children of a bond servant did not become the property of the contract holder, as under slavery.

"I have an announcement to make," Brandelene called out, smiling broadly. "We have completed the records for the period that Cyrus Varner lived here. To date there are one hundred sixty-eight of you who have worked your way to freedom. Complete freedom. They are those of you who weren't asked to sign a contract of indenture. Congratulations!" she shouted. "You are free!"

Cries of surprise drifted through the air, then prayers of thanks, and finally the dreams of a future carved out by one's own achievements.

Living in freedom.

Unfettered.

Free!

And on that small grassy knoll, deep in the heart of slavery, those glorious rays of freedom radiated a brilliance awesome to behold.

Shadrach brought Brandelene a box of rolled documents, and she announced each name of those one hundred sixty-eight, again congratulated each, then handed him or her a document of manumission and a silver dollar—his or her first dollar earned as a free person. Every name called was greeted with piercing cheers, shouts, and applause. That was followed by a handshake and congratulations from Kordell and Shadrach. All too soon it was over, and Brandelene and Kordell were surrounded by the joyful, teary-eyed faces that were Southern Oaks.

The next evening was Pearl and Dagert's wedding. A ravishing Pearl, on the arm of Matthew, glided into the music room in a beautiful white wedding gown, her lovely face veiled by a crown of yards of illusion. Dagert's face radiated its own sunshine as he beamed at Pearl and proffered his hand. Ruby smiled proudly, for she'd spent almost a year making her daughter's gown.

There Pearl and Dagert married in the sight of God, in a ceremony performed by Shadrach. The licensing and service required by the state would be performed a few days later in Petersburg.

Assailed by memories of her marriage to Kordell, Brandelene turned away to meet his penetrating gaze.

After the ceremony, a toast and the beginning of the celebrations started in the ballroom, then moved to the common house for a bountiful buffet, and the populace of the plantation celebrated the wedding of two of the most popular people there.

It was late when Brandelene saw Dagert sneak off with Pearl, and Brandelene smiled wistfully, happy that her faithful friend had followed her heart.

Seeing her look of longing, Kordell crossed the crowded room to her side. "We could be next, Brandy."

Startled, Brandelene glanced up into his golden eyes, her heart aching. "I cannot," she whispered and gathered her skirts to run to her bedroom.

With a choked cry, Brandelene moved to her writing desk, hoping now she could write the brief note she had attempted so many times during the past three days. She picked up the quill and dipped it into the ink pot. This time, the words flowed.

Dear Kordell,

I cannot bear to gaze upon your dear face when you leave Southern Oaks. Please forgive my inconsiderate behavior—and my sentimentality.

Words are inadequate to express my gratitude for all that you have done for me, for Southern Oaks, so I shan't try.

May you find the love, the wealth, and the happiness you deserve. God be with you.

Brandelene

Inside the letter she folded the expense money and passage fare to the Ivory Coast. With her anguish threatening to surface, she placed her sealing wax over the fold and wrote Kordell's name on the front. She placed it on her desk where the maid could not miss it.

In the dark of night she left for Boston.

Chapter 36

A FEW DAYS LATER, BRANDELENE AND IVY ARRIVED IN the frigid wintry city. High-masted ships filled the harbor, and the ever-present sea gulls circled overhead. The landscape was encased in white and the falling snow swirled wildly on brisk, freezing winds. In the numbness of her grief, it was a scene that matched her icy heart.

For the most part, Boston was steeped in religious convictions and propriety. Not even a theater was permitted in the city, and social life, much as on plantations, centered around the home. Therefore, the society of the aristocracy was exclusive, the only opportunities into the inner circles by invitation. Thus Brandelene's success was dependent upon Madame Duval's introductions.

The following day, Brandelene called on Madame Duval at her school and explained her predicament.

"My dear, I thought you realized I present only unmarried young women." Madame Duval smiled regretfully. "Surely though, I can be of assistance. I'm familiar with a widowed lady of quality whose lineage traces back to the titled nobility of England. Rumor has it that she's fallen upon hard times. Mrs. Vandersall has a magnificent estate and is accepted by society's elite. Indeed, when her husband lived, she was the grand dame of Boston's society. I shall make discreet inquiries. Perhaps, for the right sum, this woman could be persuaded to present you. Although she hasn't acted as hostess since the time of her husband's passing, I know she attends all the social functions. She lives with her servants in an enormous mansion, so, considering your background, she might even permit you to live at her estate—for a price, of course."

The next morning, Brandelene sat in the salon of the elderly Celia Vandersall. Apparently Madame Duval had not made Brandelene's marital status clear and Mrs. Vandersall assumed Brandelene was a widow. Now she did not know how to rectify the unfortunate misunderstanding without losing the woman's possible patronage.

"Madame," Celia inquired, "why do you want me to present you?"

Brandelene, taken unaware, met the penetrating stare of Celia's questioning sapphire-blue eyes. "I'd prefer not to marry, but because of my plantation, I need a husband."

"I see. So that we don't waste each other's time it might be advisable if you were more specific about what qualities you look for in a husband."

The snow continued to fall outside the windows and a fire blazed in the hearth. Momentarily unable to voice it, Brandelene did not answer.

"Madame Bouclair?"

"Please, Mrs. Vandersall. Call me Brandelene."

"Certainly," she responded. "Brandelene, do I understand correctly that you look for an arranged marriage, that you do not require a love match?"

Staring at the roaring flames of the fire, Brandelene set forth her requirements. "I'd prefer an arrangement at the earliest possible date. I do not expect, or want, a love match. I would hope, however, to marry someone I don't dislike." She paused and inhaled deeply before continuing, her gaze still fastened on the licking flames of the fire, "The gentleman must be a man of considerable means. He must be anti-slavery and allow me to run my plantation as I see fit. I'll insist on an agreement to that effect before we marry. I realize the law states that when I marry my property legally belongs to my husband, but my lawyer assures me a premarital agreement will give my husband pause to consider, in regard to the operation of my plantation, before he tries to usurp my will."

At Mrs. Vandersall's continued silence, Brandelene glanced at her and spoke again, "I don't require that my husband live exclusively at Southern Oaks. He'll be free to live where and how he chooses. I do not entertain at my plantation and do not intend to start. However, if my husband requires a social life of which I am to be a part, I'll travel to his home as often as my responsibilities at the plantation permit."

"Then you really don't want a husband to operate your plantation?"

Brandelene's gaze locked with the woman's, pleading for understanding. "No."

"Yes, I understand that now," Mrs. Vandersall said. "Exactly what are you looking for, Brandelene? His wealth?" Her sapphire-blue eyes pierced the distance. When she received no answer, the elderly woman took Brandelene's silence to be affirmation. "The Barnett name is not unknown in Boston. Nevertheless, let us examine what you offer, then we can better determine what kind of man to seek. Do you intend to take a lover?"

"Of course not!" Brandelene shot back, appalled at the suggestion.

"Good," Mrs. Vandersall said approvingly. "Then we should have no problem filling your needs. I know several young men of considerable means who not only would be anxious, but would pay any price to marry a woman of your gentle birth. A woman who possesses your beauty and savoir-faire . . . as long as they could continue their frivolous bachelor life."

A silence more familiar to bereavement than a marriage arrangement filled the room, and after a moment Mrs. Vandersall spoke again, her tone gentle and compassionate. "Brandelene. The arrangement we have spoken of will mean a joyless life for you. Why would you settle for that? I had understood you to be a woman of means. Was I incorrect?"

At that, Brandelene explained the circumstances of her plantation.

"I see," Celia replied thoughtfully. Then she brightened. "It appears, my dear, we both have our burden to bear. Do not worry. We'll find you the husband you seek, and who knows, perhaps you'll grow to love him as I did my Fairfax. Please call me Celia. We have too much to accomplish to be bothered with formalities." She smiled encouragingly.

The financial arrangements were made, and that afternoon Brandelene and Ivy moved into Vandersall Hall, which was the ultimate in luxury and graciousness.

That same night Brandelene, accompanied by Ivy, was reintroduced into the elite society of Boston by Celia Vandersall, at a ball given by the Farnsworths.

For her presentation to Boston society, Brandelene wore an opal silk gown, fashioned with a glittering cape of opal beading, the same as trimmed the modest décolletage. Wispy, curling tendrils escaped the shining raven hair that swept into an intricately woven chignon on the crown of her head, and a delicate diamond butterfly nestled in the elaborate coiffure of clustered curls piled on top. She received a nod of approval from the elderly Celia Vandersall, and admiring eyes caught her entrance.

The dowager knew everyone on a first-name basis and was held in the highest esteem. Two taps from her cane would silence the most pompous of Boston's elite. An introduction by Mrs. Fairfax Vandersall was to be automatically and unquestionably accepted by these Boston aristocrats who socialized together.

All introductions were performed with the same casual grace, and without one word of variance. "Allow me to introduce Madame Brandelene Barnett Bouclair, of the Barnetts of Virginia. Madame Bouclair will be staying with me at Vandersall Hall until spring."

The combination of the benevolence of the aristocratic Celia Vandersall and Brandelene's beauty made her the belle, and the gossip, of the ball. Periodically, when she needed to catch her breath between dances, she would join the elegant, bejeweled Celia, whereupon she was informed of whom to avoid in the future, due to the gentleman's lack of sufficient wealth, improper breeding, objectionable reputation, or the fact that he was a poor relation and a fortune seeker.

As Brandelene danced through the night she compared each man she met to Kordell, and found them all considerably lacking. Propriety dictated she not dance with the same man twice, and she felt relieved, for as the evening dragged on interminably all she could think of was to end it. So, as the tall, blond, handsome Terrence Farnsworth whirled her around the floor, Brandelene closed her eyes, wondering if she would ever recover from the pain of losing Kordell.

"Are you ill, Madame Bouclair?" her escort queried.

"I believe I've danced a little too much." Brandelene smiled charmingly. "Would you mind if we sit this dance out, Mr. Farnsworth?"

"I have a better idea, madame," he genially offered, his deep voice gentle as he devoured her upturned face. "Why don't I show you through the estate. I'm sure you'll feel better once you're not being whirled around the dance floor."

"I would enjoy that," Brandelene responded dryly. "If you'll advise my maid and one of your footmen to accompany us."

Disappointment briefly crossed the man's perfect features, then he said, "I shall return shortly." He flashed Brandelene a disarming smile and left, soon returning with Ivy and a footman. When he offered his arm, she placed her gloved hand on it and followed his lead while the two servants trailed at a short distance.

Celia Vandersall's sapphire-blue eyes hopefully brightened ever so slightly. Terrence Farnsworth was the catch of Boston. Exceedingly handsome, but he was a bit too arrogant; notably stylish, though a little too foppish for her taste; and wealthy in his own right, for he had inherited his maternal grandmother's immense fortune. Also, he would inherit the Farnsworth wealth. However, Terrence did have the reputation of being a bit of a rakehell with the ladies. Moreover, she could not imagine the handsome young man as a country gentleman on a plantation.

Terrence Farnsworth, a sybarite, had never worked a day in his life and spent his time in the idle pursuit of pleasure—horse racing and polo in the summer, fox hunting and games of chance at his private club in the winter, plus being with the right woman at the right events year around. It was well known that Terrence never stayed with one woman long enough to be pressured into marriage, and Celia had heard that he even frequently changed the mistresses he kept in nearby Cambridge. He was not a man she would have chosen for herself. True, Terrence was considered Boston's prize; nevertheless, after reconsidering, she decided to warn Brandelene about him.

Meanwhile, Terrence escorted Brandelene throughout the showy Farnsworth mansion, using all of the tremendous charm at his disposal, to no avail. Brandelene was captivating, but coolly aloof. By the time the four returned to the ballroom she had not warmed toward the man women always found irresistible.

An intrigued Terrence escorted Brandelene to the chair beside Celia Vandersall and decided he would possess this magnificent, fascinating woman, at least until he tired of her. For him the thrill was in the chase and then he quickly grew bored. Nevertheless, Madame Brandelene Bouclair definitely promised to be an exciting chase.

Bowing slightly, Terrence, with an air of self-assuredness, said, "I shall call on you tomorrow. Say about one."

Bestowing her most devastating smile, Brandelene replied softly, "I'm sorry, Mr. Farnsworth. I'm not as yet receiving callers." With that, she briefly lowered her sweeping black lashes, then lifted her violet eyes to return his gaze. "However, you may send your card to Vandersall Hall and perhaps we'll see each other at one of the holiday soirees."

Celia Vandersall's reserved demeanor showed no sign of Brandelene's snub to Boston's most eligible bachelor.

Astonished by Brandelene's dismissal, Terrence Farnsworth swallowed and his face darkened. No woman had ever treated him with such indifference. "You may be assured, madame, we shall meet again."

Brandelene was relieved when the evening finally ended and could not wait to leave, for she'd thought of no one but Kordell.

At last, they huddled in the brougham, bundled with fur lap robes against the icy cold of Boston, the warming pans on the floor doing little to comfort them.

Celia Vandersall broke the silence, "I've never seen Terrence Farnsworth so discomposed as when you declined his offer to call on you. It did my heart good to see someone set that pompous young man in his place. I truly don't believe it's ever happened before. The rake couldn't keep his eyes from you the rest of the evening." Celia reached up and released the tieback from the velvet curtain, then pulled the heavy fabric across the small, frosted window. "Remind me later, when I'm rested, and I'll tell you more about that much-sought-after charmer."

The next day was Thanksgiving. The servants had the day off and Celia Vandersall was away visiting friends.

Left to her own devices, Brandelene could not prevent her fantasies from lingering on Kordell. Where was he today? Was he already on the high seas? Was he thinking of her? She had started up the stairs hoping she could succumb to sleep when the door knocker sounded. Hopeful, and with a wildly beating heart, she stopped and called out, "Please answer the door, Ivy."

Ivy opened the door and stared at a liveried coachman.

"I have a message for Madame Bouclair," the coachman announced.

"Invite the man in, Ivy." Brandelene sighed.

The swirling snow accompanied the man as he stepped into the marble-floored foyer and handed Ivy a written message. The young girl hurriedly took the note to Brandelene.

Brandelene quickly read Terrence Farnsworth's invitation to escort her to the pageant that evening. Glancing at the coachman she said, "Please give Mr. Farnsworth my regrets." She gave no apology or explanation, but turned and continued up the stairs.

The surprised coachman turned and trod into the lightly falling snow.

That evening Brandelene accompanied Celia to the first night of a pageant at the Presbyterian Church. Everyone of importance was there. Brandelene's concentration was broken by Terrence Farnsworth's continuous stare. She could feel his scrutiny from where she watched the religious pageant in Celia Vandersall's box. Without glancing up, she knew the unusually attractive man's eyes gleamed cold and arrogantly proud.

During intermission, Terrence slipped into the Vandersall box to cordially exchange pleasantries with Celia. Then he turned his devouring regard on Brandelene. "I would have thought you'd have an escort, Madame Bouclair."

Though annoyed, Brandelene still smiled. "I fear I am too selective, Mr. Farnsworth. I've not yet met the man with whom I choose to spend an evening." With that, she turned away to slowly scan the congregation.

Terrence, provoked but undaunted by Brandelene's affront, turned his most dazzling smile on her. Never in thirty-four years had a woman treated him with scorn as Brandelene had last night. Now, that same woman had just told him that he, the Terrence Farnsworth whom women fawned and fought over, did not meet her standards. That Boston's most eligible bachelor was not charming enough to spend one evening with. Instead of being enraged, Terrence was fascinated, and the challenge of conquering the compelling woman of incomparable beauty only served to whet his appetite. And conquer her he would, he silently vowed. Again, Terrence's flashing, cobalt-blue eyes roamed Brandelene at will. Modestly but elegantly gowned in black velvet trimmed with blue satin, she was breathtaking. Terrence swallowed and his survey came to rest on her high, full breasts so temptingly covered by the tautness of her black velvet gown. Whatever it took, he determined, he would possess this woman of ethereal beauty.

Aware of Terrence's continuing appraisal, Brandelene turned and glared up at him. "Shouldn't you return to your box, Mr.

Farnsworth? Surely you don't wish to miss any of the pageant."

"Madame Bouclair is right, Terrence," Celia interjected and tapped his arm with her cane. "However, you hardly have time to return to your box now, and this is most entertaining. Why don't you join us?"

"How gracious of you, Mrs. Vandersall," Terrence replied and brashly seated himself next to Brandelene.

Seething inwardly, Brandelene ignored him each time he leaned toward her to make trite comments throughout the remainder of the church play.

Not discouraged, Terrence once again asked permission to call on Brandelene, and she icily declined.

Afterward, Celia and Brandelene mingled with the congregation in the palatial church. Eligible men, young and old, assembled around them, vying for an introduction to, or an acknowledgment from, Brandelene, and with each new introduction she became more miserable.

While Brandelene conversed with an anxious would-be suitor, Terrence Farnsworth maneuvered Celia aside. "Mrs. Vandersall, I believe your guest, for some unknown reason, has taken a dislike to me." He took her gloved hands in his. "I assure you my conduct has been above reproach. Perhaps if you extended me an invitation to your magnificent home, there I would have the opportunity to correct any misconceptions the young lady might have about me."

Celia weighed the possibilities. If Terrence were this taken with Brandelene, perhaps he would consider a wife with a southern plantation. "It would be my pleasure, Terrence, if you'd come to lunch. Shall we say the day after tomorrow, at one o'clock?"

"You are a most gracious lady, Mrs. Vandersall," Terrence replied and bowed over her hand. "I look forward to your company. One o'clock on Saturday." Then he moved off into the crowd, a smug expression on his handsome face.

The following morning, as Brandelene breakfasted with Mrs. Vandersall, her thoughts, as usual, were on Kordell.

"Brandelene, tonight is the annual charity ball for the orphanage. An elegant affair that starts the beginning of the yule season, and usually lasts far into the morning. I'm too old to stay up so late, and will leave long before the ball's over. Therefore, you'll need your maidservant as well as a footman to accompany us, so you'll be properly accompanied during the drive home."

"Of course," Brandelene replied absently.

The charity ball that evening was a festive occasion, and under different circumstances Brandelene would have had a marvelous time, but tonight her frozen smile reflected her icy heart. For charity, with each dance the gentlemen in attendance bid to dance with the lady of their choice, with all proceeds going to the orphanage. The starting bids were high, as would be expected among the affluent.

Brandelene danced only with Terrence, for he outbid all others. Some of the exorbitant sums he paid, so another man's arms would not surround the beautiful widow this night, caused murmurs among the guests. Terrence had never behaved so scandalously before, giving the gossips much to chatter about.

Although Terrence's comportment was above reproach and his self-assured charm disarming, Brandelene still could not warm to the man. So he paid a considerable sum to spend the evening being disregarded or spurned by the most desirable woman he had ever met. However, instead of being discouraged he became more determined, confident the enchantress in his arms would be in his bed before the new year. In fact, before the evening ended he'd made a sizable wager with one of his friends to that effect.

At Vandersall Hall, after the ball, Brandelene flung herself onto her pillow. Life had become an empty bed, an empty heart, an empty reality, and loomed endlessly ahead.

The following afternoon, in Celia's drawing room, Terrence Farnsworth did his charming best to thaw a frigid Brandelene, with little success. Then, unwittingly, he made a humorous remark to Celia and Brandelene chuckled. Encouraged by a reaction from the aloof woman who had heretofore expended only the minimal courtesy expected, Terrence changed his tack. Instantly, his approach went from the charming suitor to the humorous casual friend with no other apparent motive than to entertain the two lovely women with whom he spent the afternoon.

Hours later, with considerable satisfaction, Terrence pulled his watch from his waistcoat. Rising, he exclaimed, "An afternoon with two such delightful women has permitted the time to escape me. I must take my leave." He crossed the room to where Brandelene sat and casually lifted her extended hand to bow low over it. He murmured softly, "I cannot remember when I've enjoyed myself more, madame. Perhaps you'd permit me to escort you to the Barrington reception this evening?"

"Thank you, but no, Terrence," Brandelene replied warmly.

"Then I insist you join my family and me tomorrow for a midday Sunday supper. It's a ritual that I dine with my family on Sunday afternoon, and besides, I've not yet told you of the unforgivable faux pas I committed with the Prince of Wales."

"That should be lovely, Brandelene," Celia encouraged. "I'll be gone for most of the afternoon. I'm sure Terrence will see to it that you're home early enough to dress for the Cornwalls' soiree."

"Of course I will," Terrence anxiously assured. "And your maid and footman, if you wish, will dine splendidly with our servants."

Unconsciously Brandelene pressed delicate fingers to her waist, for her stomach ached from laughing most of the afternoon at the entertaining Terrence Farnsworth. Now she tried to remember if, before today, she'd laughed once since leaving Southern Oaks and could not think of a time. Glancing up at his expectant face, Brandelene smiled, then replied, "Yes, I would enjoy that."

Chapter 37

THAT EVENING AT THE BARRINGTONS', WHILE BRANdelene dined she conversed with the two eligible bachelors seated on each side of her. Although she remembered having danced with both gentlemen the night Celia Vandersall introduced her, she remembered little about either man. She wondered if dark-haired, dark-eyed Edward, the reserved, devoutly religious man seated on her right, would make few husbandly demands on his wife. At the thought, she shuddered and turned toward Edward to smile charmingly.

During the evening, Terrence danced with Brandelene several times. However, he did not pursue her with the fervor he'd displayed at the charity ball. With the respite from Terrence, she took the opportunity to assess each suitable man there, in an attempt to determine the least objectionable. Mentally she dismissed one man after another. Which left Edward Sanderson. Sweet, gentle Edward. On such short acquaintance she could find no reason not to consider him for a husband, save one. With Edward Sanderson's devotion to his faith, he would never maintain a mistress, or be unfaithful to his wife. Consequently, he would expect to live continually with Brandelene, and share her bed full-time as well. Her refusal to submit to him would be grounds for divorce, and in that event he would become the legal owner of Southern Oaks. Would not a wealthy, philandering Terrence be preferable?

Unwilling to ponder such a disturbing notion this soon, she decided to become better acquainted with the not unattractive

Edward. She graciously declined all invitations to dance, and instead chatted with Edward, a pleasant but uninteresting man.

The evening passed tediously.

The following afternoon, at Sunday supper with the Farnsworths, Brandelene was pleasantly surprised to find Terrence a considerate and loving family man, for he had a close and warm relationship with his parents and two sisters. Also, the affection he shared for his nieces and nephews was obvious as they all clamored for his attention. At that, Brandelene decided perhaps she should not so quickly dismiss his suitability. If what Celia had told her about his excellent prospects was true, there would be definite advantages in marrying him. Additionally, there was also the probability of his extended absences while he pursued his idle life of pleasure.

Another day ticked tiresomely by.

During the following week, Brandelene spent more time with Terrence. With her candidates narrowed down to two men, the next five days were emotionally trying as she tried to determine the least undesirable man for a husband, Terrence or Edward.

One or the other man was in constant attendance, either in the afternoon or at one of the numerous holiday balls or soirees during the evening.

The days stretched on endlessly. Was there no end?

Brandelene floundered helplessly, detesting every minute she shared the company of Terrence or Edward. Her reasoning was clouded with thoughts of Kordell, her vision colored with precious memories of him. Living had lost all meaning. There was no joy. No sunshine. No Kordell.

By the time the evening of the holly ball arrived, Brandelene had finally accepted that, somehow, she must exorcise Kordell from her mind, if not her heart, and seriously consider the selection of her husband. She favored Terrence, but now wondered if the confirmed bachelor could be motivated to marry. So as not to waste precious time on a useless pursuit, she needed to find out immediately. A one-month betrothal period would be the shortest time acceptable by social standards and that gave her only three weeks to extract a proposal from her choice. She could not afford to miscalculate.

Brandelene was attending the holly ball with Terrence. The invitations requested ladies to wear red or green ball gowns. Wretched, Brandelene walked to her dressing room to select a gown, moving in a befuddling fog. It would be more appropriate to wear black, she commiserated and reached for the first gown that caught her eye, a forest-green silk taffeta, trimmed with matching velvet.

At the ball, Brandelene had to force every word from her lips and coerce every smile to her mouth. This evening as never before, the reality of living without Kordell engulfed her. With senses drugged, she whirled in the arms of the tall, handsome Terrence through a bizarre dream filled with elegant red and green ball gowns, hundreds of flickering candles, and her grieving heart.

Brandelene's aloofness, her apparent boredom, encouraged Terrence all the more. Never had a woman been so unreceptive to his charm, and never had he desired a woman more than the cool beauty he held in his arms. He vowed he would conquer the irresistible enigma.

Brandelene made her decision. Thereafter she spent her time exclusively with Terrence, accompanied by Ivy and Celia's footman, Arnold. She did not have the time to play a game of cat and mouse with the reluctant bachelor by encouraging Edward Sanderson's suit. Somehow she needed to extricate the proposal of marriage from Terrence as soon as possible.

During a long and sleepless night Brandelene decided upon a scheme, an arrangement between Terrence and herself that would not make her life completely unbearable—if Terrence were agreeable. And that depended on how much he wanted an heir, and to what degree he desired her. She determined to find out the next day. If Terrence were unreceptive, she would not waste any more time with him. With Kordell gone and Dagert leaving in the spring, she would not again be able to leave Southern Oaks long enough to search in the North for a husband of means.

Late Sunday afternoon Brandelene and Terrence returned to Vandersall Hall after Sunday supper with his family. She told him she wanted to speak with him privately and invited him into her drawing room. Skittish now, Brandelene traversed the large room, pondering how to broach the subject.

Terrence moved to the black-veined marble fireplace, leisurely leaned an elbow on the mantel and allowed his gaze to follow Brandelene while she paraded back and forth. A footman arrived with wine. Lifting his glass to Brandelene, Terrence toasted, "To us."

Controlling a shudder, Brandelene raised her goblet, accepting the toast, then sipped the warming drink. She drifted to Terrence's side, her heart pounding wildly in her ears. Contemplating the classically handsome features of the man, she could find nothing in him that attracted her. For a fleeting moment golden leonine eyes in an outrageously handsome, masculine face flashed before her eyes. She blinked and the unwanted apparition disappeared, but it was immediately followed by the vision of Kordell on the high seas, sailing ever nearer the Ivory Coast, ever farther from her. Why had he not come after her before he sailed for the Ivory Coast? She had told Ruby and Pearl where she was going. Why had he let her walk out of his life so easily? Could she have been wrong in believing that he loved her? Apparently so, for he, like Dean Paul, had been able to quickly forget her. However, realizing Kordell had so easily walked out of her life made her next task slightly easier to perform, for never again would she suffer the pain and agony of desperately loving a man who did not love her the same.

Reaching out, Terrence took the glass from Brandelene's hand and set it on the mantel beside his, then pulled her into his arms and kissed her demandingly. She commanded herself to succumb to the forceful domination of his lips, then pulled away before he could turn the kiss into an intimacy she could not tolerate.

"I want you, Brandelene," Terrence whispered huskily. "I want you."

His words gave her the opening she sought. "How much," she boldly asked, "do you want me, Terrence?"

"You're the most desirable woman I've ever known. I will do anything to possess you. Anything!"

Leaning back in Terrence's arms, she said, "I am yours, Terrence. But there is a price."

"Name it, Brandelene," Terrence murmured. "I'll pay any price. A luxurious townhouse. Jewels. All the elegant gowns you desire. No price is too high."

"No price?"

"No price!"

"I would require an arrangement with you . . . an agreement, actually." Brandelene's hand moved up Terrence's arm to rest with her palm against his chest, holding him at bay.

Trembling at her touch, Terrence replied, "I've thought of no one else since first I laid eyes on you. I'm a wealthy man. Any arrangement. Any agreement. Anything you want."

Brandelene turned her face up to receive his devouring kiss. But when he attempted to part her soft lips she once again pulled free.

"Do not tempt me so, Terrence, before you've heard my demands," she scolded gently, promptly disgusted with herself for the ruse she played. She could not enter a marriage based on deceit. If she were open and honest about her feelings, then it would be Terrence's decision if he entered into a loveless, arranged marriage. She moved to the sofa to sit and compose herself to do what she must.

At her sudden aloofness, Terrence rushed to sit beside her and his arm moved to the back of the sofa behind her. "Brandelene, I've committed myself. What more do you want? What kind of arrangement? What agreement? Name your price."

She turned to Terrence and said, "I have three conditions. The first being marriage."

Terrence stared at her in speechless astonishment.

"I love my former husband with all my heart, Terrence. I will never—never love anyone but him. Not you—not any man. But I have need of a wealthy husband, and what I have to offer in return might be of interest to a worldly man such as yourself."

Terrence's cobalt-blue eyes slowly examined the ravishingly beautiful woman who was slowly becoming an obsession with him.

At his continued silence, Brandelene said, "I am suggesting an agreement, Terrence. An arrangement rather than a conventional marriage. Since I'm not in love with you, I'd make no demands on you as would most wives. You'd be free to go where you wish, when you wish, and with whom you wish, exactly as you are now. I wouldn't even require your discretion, except in Petersburg. You would not have to deny yourself the pleasure of children, and an heir, simply because you don't wish to be tied to a woman, for with me there would be no strings attached. I would bear your children and be a loving mother. I've considerable to recommend my qualifying to be the mother of your children, for my heritage is not unworthy. Also, aside from those times I'm needed at my plantation, I'd oversee your households and hostess any affairs you choose, except at my estate."

Overwhelmed by Brandelene's proposal, Terrence could do nothing other than stare at her in disbelief.

Brandelene pressed her suit. "There also would be numerous other advantages, Terrence. If you were married to me, you'd still have the carefree bachelor life you apparently prefer, yet you wouldn't have the concern, or the scandal, of an unplanned or unwanted marriage. Additionally, the comfort and stability of a home life would be there for you—when and if you wanted it. Southern Oaks, my two-hundred-fifty-thousand-acre plantation run by almost six hundred bond servants and free persons, is one of the finest in the South. A country home you could take pride in and enjoy when you were there. You've indicated you find me attractive, so that wouldn't be a problem. As well, if it's of any importance, I would never take a lover even though our separations might be numerous, or lengthy."

At her last words, Terrence frowned. "I would have your word that you would never take a lover even though . . ."

As his words trailed off Brandelene was consumed with wretchedness. Terrence was actually considering her proposal. She felt faint, felt the finality of it.

"Yes. You have my word."

"Why?" Terrence demanded, his tone suspicious.

"I have known the once-in-a-lifetime love. I've no delusions of ever finding that again. Why would I shame my children, my husband, and myself for a few moments of pleasure?"

Turning away from her Terrence stared sightlessly at the orange flames licking at the hearth.

"What is your second condition?"

"My plantation must be operated without slavery."

"I abhor slavery. What is the third condition?"

"I'll explain in detail later, but briefly, my inheritance was squandered away by my guardian. I don't have the cash reserves needed to operate my plantation. My inheritance will slowly dwindle away to nothing and I'll lose Southern Oaks. I would ask you to give me that substantial sum that I need."

"Brandelene, I want you more than any woman I've ever known. Money is no object. I'll give you whatever you need for your plantation. I'll buy you a townhouse. You'll have jewels and furs fit for a queen. We'll travel the world. I offer you my protection. . . ."

At that, Brandelene rose. "It has been enjoyable knowing you, Terrence. Your company has been charming. Please excuse me. I'll have one of the servants show you out." With that, she turned with a swish of her skirts and swept across the room toward the arched opening.

"Brandelene, wait!" Terrence cried out and jumped from the sofa to rush to her side.

She glanced up expectantly at him.

"Are you telling me the only way I will ever possess you is if I agree to . . . to this arrangement that includes marriage?"

"Yes, Terrence. That's exactly what I'm telling you."

Terrence scanned her upturned face. She was so exquisite. A woman befitting his status. He capitulated. "My immediate reaction is to say yes, but I suppose I should consider your proposal." Then he reached out and touched a strand of her hair, as though to examine it more closely. "The money would be no problem. You could consider it a wedding present. And I'd never be a slave master." He turned to stare out the window at the snow-burdened branches of the trees. Presently, he pulled a gold watch from his waistcoat and glanced at it. "I'll give you my decision this evening when I call for you."

A few hours later when Terrence arrived to escort Brandelene to the Hollisters' soiree he was in exceptionally high spirits. "Aren't you going to ask for my decision?"

"No. If you've arrived at a decision you'll tell me."

Grinning confidently, Terrence announced, "The arrangement you've suggested is most appealing to me. Actually, the more I considered it the better I thought of it. A man could not hope for more, and I've decided to accept. You, my dear, have the honor of being the woman who has captured Terrence Farnsworth." With that, he eagerly pulled Brandelene into his arms where she endured his kiss.

Moments later, slipping free of Terrence's unwanted embrace, Brandelene smiled sweetly. With a heavy heart, she once again wondered why a man as handsome as Terrence could not stir her even the slightest. Sighing, she softly scolded, "Really, Terrence, you mustn't tempt me so. Besides, we don't want to be more than fashionably late to the Hollisters."

Later that night, after Brandelene returned to Vandersall Hall, the quiet, lonely rooms closed in on her. Life was empty. Meaningless. Would it always be so? She wished Kordell would saunter through her door and gaze at her with those golden eyes that melted her. Then she wondered why, when nothing had changed, she still yearned for him to come. But she did. If only to play a game of chess, or sit with her, or simply work beside her. Anything—only for a day, an hour, a minute. Quickly she banished the tormenting fantasy, for she had to accept—it would never be. She'd been in Boston for weeks now, and Kordell surely was on the high seas. She sighed. She would do what she must. And she must marry Terrence Farnsworth. For marrying Terrence would solve all her financial problems.

Why did she hesitate?

That same night Brandelene wrote to Charles Thompson for the agreements Terrence had willingly agreed to sign. Immensely wealthy, he did not care that her plantation would only earn a modest profit, or even sustain a loss. Thus she felt secure that if she married Terrence, Southern Oaks would remain her personal property and never be operated with slaves as long as she lived.

Now for the next step. The truth. When next Brandelene saw Terrence she told him the actuality of her marriage and annulment, ending with, "Kordell is on the high seas right now, en route to the Ivory Coast."

Terrence studied her. "I would prefer that you were widowed, Brandelene. However, it's unlikely anyone I know will learn the truth, and I certainly don't intend to spend much time stuck out in the country on some plantation. So I suppose it makes no difference that everyone there knows."

"Then I will marry you, Terrence. As soon as possible."

"I warn you though, Brandelene. If this Bouclair, whom you imagine yourself to be so in love with, ever returns after we're married you are not to see him. If I have the slightest suspicion otherwise, I'll divorce you. My wife will never have a lover."

"You have my word, Terrence. I shall be a loyal wife. I will not be unfaithful."

Kordell was now part of her past.

Three days later the Farnsworths announced the betrothal at their holiday soiree. The wedding date was set for Saturday, January 21.

There was much to be done to prepare for a wedding and reception of the magnitude expected for the only son of a Farnsworth. It would be the social occasion of the new year. Mrs. Farnsworth had insisted on handling the entire affair herself, and a relieved Brandelene agreed. Solemn, she sat in the salon with Celia, sipping hot tea and discussing the coming event. With troubled eyes, she watched the snow swirl wildly. It was a gray, gloomy day, matching her mood. A blizzard brewed and the wind howled and raged.

Even Mother Nature protested what she was doing.

In the middle of their discussion, Harrison announced, "A gentleman is calling for Madame Bouclair. He refused to give his name."

"Show the gentleman in here, Harrison," Celia instructed. "It must be important for anyone to come out in this weather."

Chapter 38

At the sound of footsteps, Brandelene glanced up, then gasped. Too stunned to speak, the blood siphoned from her face. Her heart pounded wildly, crazily.

"Kord!" she cried, then jumped from her chair and ran toward him. Midway across the room she halted, remembering Celia, remembering she was betrothed, remembering nothing had changed. She stood, staring at Kordell, shaken to the core of her being. His gaze clung to hers while her heart trip-hammered at the sight of his beloved face.

His eyes echoed her love—and it both soothed and tortured her aching heart.

Perhaps, Brandelene hurriedly reasoned, she could sell Southern Oaks, except for the family cemetery, free all the indentured servants and ask Ruby, Matthew, Joshua, and a couple of other favorite servants to stay. She and Kordell could be remarried and live modestly in the city. But then her protesting conscience asked if she could kneel at her father's grave and explain that she had sacrificed her birthright for the man she loved, the heritage for which James Barnett had died? If she followed her heart, her father would have died for naught, simply because his willful daughter wanted to wed the man she loved.

Brandelene tore her gaze from Kordell and strove to regain her composure. "Kord, how nice to see you." She crossed the room to where he stood in the arched opening and extended her hand.

For only a moment, Kordell's gaze held hers. "Brandy," he huskily acknowledged, his single word an intimate caress. Then he took her proffered hand in his and bent to briefly brush warm lips there.

Brandelene trembled. As though dazed, she said, "Celia, may I present Monsieur Kordell Bouclair. Kordell, this is Mrs. Celia Vandersall."

"My pleasure, Mrs. Vandersall," Kordell said.

"Monsieur Bouclair," Celia acknowledged.

"Please excuse us, Celia," Brandelene said with no further explanations, and departed for her private drawing room. To her relief, Celia neither objected nor asked any questions.

Once inside the elegant receiving room, Brandelene whirled to face Kordell. "What are you doing here? Is something wrong at Southern Oaks?"

"Southern Oaks is fine."

"Why are you here?"

"After you left I realized I can't leave until I know if you're carrying my child."

"No!" Brandelene cried out softly, paling visibly, glancing past him to see if anyone had heard. Relieved that no servant stared at her, she turned and walked to the settee, slumping onto the cold, unwelcoming pillow. How could she not have considered the possibility? Previously, she hadn't been overly concerned, content to let fate have her way, for at the time she'd believed she and Kordell were legally wed and she had not known about Southern Oaks's fate. But now . . . Feeling slightly sick, she glanced up to find Kordell's penetrating gaze burning into her.

After a moment he strode to her side, then lowered his large frame down next to her. Resting his arm on the sofa behind her, he leaned forward. "Do you know if you're expecting my child, Brandy?"

Brandelene stared at Kordell, her panic mounting.

At the look on her face, pain squeezed Kordell's heart, then turned into a hard rock in the pit of his stomach. How could he have believed she was falling in love with him? A tormenting sense of loss, an overwhelming emptiness, enveloped him. Yet all he could think of was the pain he was causing her. "Are you with child? Do you know, Brandy?"

"No, I don't know." Sick at heart, her voice barely above a whisper.

"Shouldn't you know by now if you're not?"

When she lifted her gaze to his, the pain of her predicament flickered there. She sighed, clasped her slender hands together, and wordlessly stared at them.

"Brandelene!" Kordell's voice was low, but firmly threatening. "Hear me well. If you carry my child, you will marry no one but me, I promise you."

"You can't do this to me, Kordell. I won't stand for it."

"If you are with child, you will be my wife," he warned again. "Even if I have to drag you before a minister. Have I made myself clear?" At her silence, her obvious misery, he gently assured her, "I don't want to hurt you, Brandy. I won't interfere with your plans in any way until I know for sure. Your cycle must be past due now. We should know definitely in a week, or two at the most."

Quietly, she stared at him, her features drawn and worried. "I cannot explain your presence," she whispered anxiously. "I shouldn't be here with you now. I don't know what to tell Mrs. Vandersall that won't cast aspersions on my respectability. It would be impossible to survive one or two weeks of your calling on me, without irreparable damage to my reputation. My situation's intolerable enough as it is, Kord."

"Well, perhaps there won't be any problem at all." Kordell grinned halfheartedly, in a feeble attempt at humor. "You might be carrying our son."

Brandelene's sudden anger at his jest disappeared when she saw the misery in his eyes, and she realized his teasing had not been malicious. Once again, she found herself hoping that she carried Kordell's child within her, leaving her no choice but to marry him. With that hope in mind, her heart instantly filled with all the love she felt for this one man alone. She smiled at him and the agony in her eyes was not because she might be carrying his child, but rather that she might not be. After the first night of their reconciliation she'd consulted with Dulcie on how to prevent such a happenstance, but such precautions were unreliable and still there was that first night . . .

"My betrothal was announced last night, Kord."

Trying to conceal the stabbing pain that wrenched through his heart, he said, "That was quick work, madame—even for you. Someone you knew previously?"

"No."

"Ahh, a true love match. And this from the woman who, on the day we met, told me she'd do anything to save Southern Oaks—but she'd *never* spend the rest of her life married to a man she doesn't love. She would first buy a bondsman or become a chambermaid and wear rags. Apparently,'never' is less than eight months."

"I have not said," Brandelene pridefully flung back, "that I don't love the man."

Kordell leaned back in the settee and studied her tormented countenance. After a time he asked softly, "Do you love him?" When he received no answer, he pressed on, "Tell me, Brandelene if you will. Why would you betroth yourself to a man you've known a scant three or four weeks rather than marry me?"

"His money can salvage Southern Oaks."

"In the event you're not expecting a child, what are you going to tell your husband?"

"Tell my husband?" Brandelene repeated, confused, shifting to face him.

"How are you going to explain the fact that your marriage was annulled, Madame Bouclair"—Kordell's gaze roamed her flawless figure, demurely gowned in creamy velvet—"yet your virtue isn't intact?"

Flushing under his intimate regard, Brandelene stammered hesitantly, "Mrs. Vandersall mistakenly assumed I—I was a widow I've never found the right opportunity to correct that assumption My presentation into the Boston society was as a widow, and since I believed you had left for the Ivory Coast . . ."

"I should have known you'd think of some clever guise. Tel me, my beauty, do you never tire of charades?"

"I have somewhat explained the truth of the matter to my

fiancé," Brandelene explained defensively. "Will you leave for the Ivory Coast as soon as I can confirm your suspicions are unfounded?"

"If you want me to."

"Kord, we have already had this discussion."

"Then yes. I'll leave as soon as I know the truth."

Nodding, she glanced at the open portal, expecting Celia to appear at any moment. "You had better leave now. I'll send word to your hotel."

Rising, fighting his urge to pull her into his arms and tell her everything, Kordell questioned, "What are you going to tell your benefactress?"

"I don't intend to explain. I won't lie to her. It's bad enough she already believes I'm a widow." She sighed. "It seems I've done nothing but live a lie since first I thought of my poorly devised scheme to purchase your contract." Without another word, Brandelene rose and Kordell followed her to the salon.

Kordell's smile was cordial. "Please forgive me, Mrs. Vandersall, for interrupting your morning unannounced. I'm expecting to sail for the Ivory Coast in a few days and wanted to speak to Brandelene before I left. It has been a pleasure meeting you."

"Monsieur Bouclair," Celia urged, "since you're a relative of Brandelene's, in a manner of speaking, and one she might never see again, I'm sure she would enjoy the pleasure of your company until you leave. That is, when she isn't with her betrothed." When Celia received no unusual response to her last words, she continued, "Please feel free to call as often as Brandelene is available. It would be most enjoyable to have your company again tomorrow morning."

"You're most gracious, Mrs. Vandersall," Kordell assured. "I appreciate your invitation." Then he turned to Brandelene. "If you have no plans, Brandy, I'll call in the morning."

"Kord!" Brandelene protested, then realized Terrence would be arriving at any moment. "That will be fine."

Brandelene's afternoon and evening were deplorable. She could remember neither what she heard nor what she said. She walked through the day in a fog, her mind on Kordell, and her insoluble problem; torn between choosing either the man she loved, or the plantation for which her father had died. How would she endure it with Kordell here in Boston?

During the ride home from the Brightons, Brandelene absently chatted with Terrence and paused to glance out the frosty coach window. She realized they were traveling the route to the Farnsworth estate. "Why," she quizzed suspiciously, "are we going this way?"

Terrence pulled Brandelene roughly to him. "My sweet, we are betrothed," he said, with no regard for Ivy and the burly footman, Arnold, seated opposite them. "I thought we could stop by my rooms for a time."

"Take me home immediately, Terrence," Brandelene snapped. "I may be a"—she glanced at Arnold—"widow, but I'm not a loose woman!"

"And we both know the truth of that, don't we?" Terrence laughed and his hand slipped under her cloak to fondle her breast.

Struggling free of his unwanted attentions, Brandelene stormed, "Take me home, or I shall ask Arnold for assistance."

"You can't be serious."

"I am very serious. Stop this coach immediately."

"You do realize, Brandelene, that you're forcing me into the bed of my mistress."

"Terrence, I am forcing you nowhere," Brandelene retorted, then her voice softened. "However, if that's your decision I'll understand, as I know you understand that I'm not the kind of woman who will share a bed with a man who isn't my husband, or whom I do not love deeply. I'd be surprised and disappointed, Terrence, if you would expect less from a woman you'd make your wife."

At her chastisement, Terrence tapped on the coach portal and bellowed to the coachman to drive to Vandersall Hall. The remainder of the trip was made in silence. After the brougham stopped in front of the mansion, Terrence assisted Brandelene from the conveyance, then said, "I'm going hunting with my friends for a week in the north country. Since you are so agreeable, my wife to be, I know you understand. I'll call on you when I return."

Earlier, Brandelene had decided that although she might never love Terrence, she did hope they could be friends, for she found unbearable the thought of being married to a man with whom she could not at least share a friendship. Smiling up at him, she squeezed his hand that still held hers. "That's fine, Terrence. I'm sure you'll have a marvelous time. I'll miss you."

Frowning, Terrence stared down at her, all anger now gone. "I'd better take care I don't fall in love with you, Brandelene. For some reason I don't think it would be wise." Then he smiled and escorted her into the mansion.

During the long and lonely night, Brandelene decided she would make the most of this week with Kordell. It might be the last she would ever have with him. But for this week she could still look up and see him. She refused to think of next week, for in her heart there was no next week, when she would be spending all her time with her betrothed, no next month when she would marry Terrence Farnsworth, no next years, stretching endlessly ahead.

In the morning, giddily happy, for she would have one joyous week with Kordell, Brandelene joined Celia and him in the game room where they played dominoes. Glancing up, Kordell gave her a heart-stopping smile when she gaily waltzed into the room. "Terrence has gone hunting for a week. It's a marvelously beautiful day and the three of us can build a snowman."

Soon Celia watched from the dining-room window as Brandelene and Kordell built a snowman behind the mansion. Their carefree play was innocent and harmless to her. Only the knowing eye would see the easy way they worked together, laughing, their bodies comfortably brushing when they rolled the snow; the longing on Kordell's face when Brandelene slipped while they shaped a roly-poly chest, and he caught her before she fell, holding her a little too long, a little too close; their gazes that clung lovingly when they worked on opposite sides of the icy white man; Kordell's hand that lingered on Brandelene's as they fashioned the face of snow; or the tenderness of Brandelene's gloved hand brushing the snow from Kordell's hair when they stood back to admire their jolly snowman.

All too soon, Kordell stood in the foyer, bundled against the winter cold in his caped greatcoat. Content, with no thoughts beyond this one precious week, Brandelene stood with him. Other than their observed romp in the snow, it was the first they'd been alone today. Aware that servants hovered nearby, they stood untouching. He gazed down at her and she shivered in response, then glanced away, for fear the love in her eyes would betray her.

"My love, what are you doing to us?" Kordell murmured low, so his intimate words could not be overheard. "Brandy, this is one charade you can't play out. You will destroy two lives if you try, for I know you love me." Gently, he pressed a long finger to her lips when she started to interrupt, then, remembering they might be overseen, quickly removed it. "Perhaps you don't love me as I do you, but you will never find with someone else what we shared together, and I am referring to everything we've been to each other outside our bedroom. You're so young, love, you don't realize the special love we share. There is a magic between us. A magic that defies explanation. Give it up, Brandy."

"I cannot," she whispered, her eyes pleading. With that, she stepped back and said aloud, "It's been nice today, Kord. We'll see you in the morning."

Kordell turned and walked out into the frosty air.

The next few days were a flurry of wonderful times shared by Brandelene, Kordell, and Celia. The three of them rode past the numerous church spires of Boston, and by the State House with its gold-leaf dome, past the gulls, gathered in midstream on the floating ice of the Charles River, and outside of Boston. There they selected a yule tree, which Kordell chopped down. They played dominoes, went Christmas shopping, rode to The Commons and watched the ice skaters at the frog pond, or simply chatted. Kordell rented a large double sleigh and they bundled up a protesting Celia until only her sapphire-blue eyes showed, and the three rode across the fields of crusty snow with bells jingling and then warmed up in front of a blazing fire, drinking hot buttered rum. A deepening affection developed between the three.

Those days, Kordell sought Brandelene's admission of love. When none came, he softly told her of his feelings and quietly left. Although they shared not even a kiss, Brandelene's barely controlled desire for him left her burning with frustration, and she tossed sleeplessly for hours each night, living only for the moment, refusing to think of when Terrence would return.

During those evenings, while Terrence hunted and after Kordell returned to his hotel, Brandelene accompanied Celia to the various holiday soirees, concerts, and festivities. Then, all too soon only one day remained.

The morning of the day before Terrence was due back from the north, Brandelene opened her eyes to the gray of morning. Outside, the snow danced wildly, fluttering on gusty winds, creating an obscure wall of white. A blizzard. Kordell would never get through this weather. Jumping from her warm bed she ran to the window, her vision unable to penetrate the briskly swirling snow, the landscape obliterated. A knot formed in her stomach, her heart ached. How could she have this precious day wrenched from her?

Brandelene went downstairs, astonished to see Kordell, ensnared by Celia into playing dominoes. When he glanced up and grinned, her heart soared.

The day was a marvelous gift, a day with no tomorrows. A day of snowball fights and romping in the snow that blanketed Boston; a day of trimming the Christmas tree, under the contented gaze of Celia, with the decorations brought down from the attic; a day of popping corn in the hearth, of intimate gazes that could not be denied, of cozily sipping hot chocolate while the storm raged outside. Evening arrived, and still the winds howled, blowing icy particles against the windowpanes.

"I can't send my coachman out in this weather, Kordell," Celia announced over tea. "If he managed to get to your hotel, he most likely wouldn't get back. It looks as though you'll be my guest tonight."

"No!" Brandelene gasped, jumping to her feet, her face ashen.

"It's—it's most improper, Celia."

"I'll have a room prepared for him in the north wing, and you're well chaperoned. Certainly, no one can criticize that. Besides, we have no choice. There's no going out in this storm. It appears we'll be playing dominoes this evening. I'll have Cook add another plate for dinner."

The evening was one of pleasure and pain for Brandelene and Kordell, of being together, but unable to share so much as an intimate word or a loving touch. When the time came to retire, Arnold helped a tired Celia to her room and Kordell went to the north wing of the mansion while Brandelene withdrew to the south wing. With tensions mounting, it was a relief for Brandelene and Kordell.

Kordell brooded alone in his room. For the first time, he'd realized that if Brandelene did carry his child he might never know the truth of her feelings. If that event forced her to marry him, her stubborn pride might become a barrier between them as surely as if she felt he had bought her with his considerable wealth. The wealth that could provide Southern Oaks's salvation. He needed Brandelene to come to him willingly, out of love, with no other coercion. Had he misread her feelings on all the days of this last week? He had to know. Somehow he must force the truth from her lovely lips. He would seek her out tonight, after he was certain the household slept.

Sometime later that night Brandelene's door opened and Kordell entered silently, bearing two steaming cups on a small silver tray. Unable to sleep, she watched him set the tray on her bedside commode, knowing she should be angry at his presence, but so happy to see him, she could not pretend otherwise.

Chapter 39

KORDELL GRINNED. "I BROUGHT YOU A CUP OF HOT chocolate."

"And how," Brandelene inquired, her eyes twinkling, "did you know I wanted a cup of hot chocolate?"

"I knew it would help you sleep, love."

"And how did you, being in the wing at the opposite end of this enormous mansion, know I was still awake?"

"Why, how could you possibly go to sleep when I haven't kissed you good night?"

"How, indeed?" Brandelene took the proffered cup and sipped the warm chocolate before returning it to the night-table. "How did you know this was my room and not Celia's?"

"I've already made that error. I just came from Celia's room. She told me which was your room."

Brandelene gasped. "You didn't!"

Chuckling in amusement, Kordell brushed the wisps of mussed hair from her face. "No, my beauty, I didn't. Celia's rooms would, quite naturally, overlook the front grounds. I saw the firelight under this door that is not at the front of the house."

She smiled.

He smiled.

Then her gaze lifted to his compelling, golden catlike eyes, brimming with tenderness and understanding, and her heart caught in her throat.

Holding her gaze, Kordell lowered himself to the side of her bed and pulled her into his arms, reverently holding her for the longest time. After he released her, he glanced down, searching her upturned face. "Brandy," he murmured softly, intimately, reaching out to gently brush her cheek with his knuckles.

At Kordell's familiar touch, Brandelene unconsciously moved toward him.

Unable to resist, he bent to kiss her brow and her arms slipped up encircling his neck. "Tell me you love me, Brandy. End this idiotic charade now. Tell me you love me. I need to hear you say it."

With Kordell's face inches from hers, Brandelene's heart pounded in her ears, her pulse raced crazily, and she fought the overwhelming urge to pull his head down to hers and satiate the desire already coursing through her body. Losing the battle, she entreated, "Kiss me, Kord."

"That's asking too much of me now, Brandy."

"How," she taunted with a lightheartedness she did not feel, turning his earlier question back on him, "will I get to sleep if you don't kiss me good night?"

"That, my love, is something you may ask yourself the rest of your life, if you continue with this." He stood up and walked to her door.

He left her to agonize over his parting remark. She slipped from her bed and paced her room. Restlessly, she stared at the blazing fire, then turned her gaze to the steamed window, watching the condensation trickle down the cold pane of glass. She picked up the agate music box Kordell had given her and absently ran her fingers over the cool stone of the lid. Unable to help herself, she lifted the heavy top and listened to the haunting strains of "Greensleeves," recalling the night Kordell had given it to her, the night he'd defended Southern Oaks from the plantation owners.

Doubts assailed her mind and now she could not bear to be in the same house with him—so close, yet beyond reach. Regardless of the weather, Kordell had to leave in the morning. He had to return to his hotel and quit calling at Vandersall Hall. He must. A week ago, spending this time with him had seemed a marvelous idea, but now it was a torture devised in hell. Besides, Terrence would be back tomorrow, and her sanity and her plans necessitated Kordell's leaving. If she turned her back on Terrence now, before she was certain she was with child, it would be the same as turning her back on Southern Oaks. With that resolved in her mind, she grabbed her peignoir and slipped from her room into the pitch-black of the hallway.

With no candle to light her way, she slowly made her way along the dark hall, down the stairs, and through the main rooms of the mansion until she came to the stairs that led to the north wing. She felt her way up the dark stairs and saw the firelight shining beneath his door. Pausing, she leaned against the cold wall, inhaling deeply, listening to the wild pounding of her heart. Was it beating uncontrollably at the fear of being discovered? Or the notion of being alone with Kordell? She clasped her hands over her face. Memories, pressed between the pages of her mind, assailed her at every turn. Her heart ached for the sight of Kordell's beloved face, and her body ached for his loving caresses. Never would she be able to resist him. How could she have been so foolish? She was turning to make her way back down the dark stairs when Kordell's door flung open and the light shone fully across her startled form.

Brandelene inhaled sharply. But then all she was aware of was Kordell silhouetted in the doorway. Kordell, frozen in surprise, his devouring gaze riveting her to the spot. Kordell's hungry eyes.

Fires danced in golden eyes, flames sparked in violet ones.

Time hung suspended. Seconds ticked into an eternity.

Without a word, she raced into his extended arms. She could neither force her gaze from his nor move from his crushing embrace. With only this brief moment in time, the world slipped away. There was only Kordell. Nothing mattered but that she was where she wanted to be, locked in his strong arms. His manly scent made her senses reel and she slipped one hand into the luxurious mane of his tawny hair to cup the back of his head while the other hand encircled his neck.

Gazing into her desire-glazed eyes, Kordell reached up and pulled the pins from her hair. Her silky tresses cascaded over his arm. Then he bent to ravish her parted lips with demanding mastery.

She returned his blazing kisses with an urgency, a desperation, that kindled them both, and when his lips moved from hers, Brandelene implored, "Love me, Kord."

Her heart beat erratically while her gaze fastened on his passion-glazed eyes. "I need you. I want you," she whispered and her lips parted, her tongue moistened them invitingly, and her body moved seductively against his.

Groaning, his mouth seared ravenously over hers in a mind-drugging kiss that sent all lingering awareness into oblivion. He swept her up into strong arms, kicked the door closed with his booted foot, and carried her to the hearth. There, with his lips still clinging to hers, he clasped her buttocks and sensuously slid her body down his to feel the boldness of his desire. Slowly he stood her on her feet.

Brandelene shuddered and arched her back, pressing closer to his swollen need. He crushed her to him. Trembling hands moved from the tangles of his hair to cup his face while his hungry mouth pillaged hers and sent splintering sensations crashing through her.

When he dragged his mouth from hers, Brandelene moaned in protest. With breath harsh, uneven, Kordell gazed into her half-closed eyes before he smothered her face with moist, burning kisses. Nibbling at her earlobe, his tongue tickled her ear while his hand slipped beneath the fabric of her gown to caress the fullness of her heaving breast.

Brandelene shivered and cried out his name.

His body ached to take her, to consume her, to love her until he dropped. Her delicate fragrance teased him, taunted him, and then, with a singeing craving that would not wait, he ripped the filmy gown from her body. Her knees buckled and together they slipped to the rug in front of the roaring fire. He kissed her savagely, his mouth devouring hers, his hands hungrily, voraciously, exploring her body.

Ragged and uncontrolled, her breath came in short surrendering moans and her body was consumed by a wild fire, burning out of restraint. Kordell groaned and kissed her senseless, and his darting tongue explored her mouth with a desperate intensity that torched them both. Ablaze, her hands clutched his broad shoulders, then moved to his back, feeling the controlled power of him. She pulled him closer. But try as she did, she could not get close enough to the flame.

One hand cupped her swollen breast, teasing the nipple to tautness, while the other fumbled with the buttons of his shirt.

Quivering with raging desire, she reached up and impatiently rent his shirt down the front, vaguely aware of the sound of popping buttons. Then her fingers trailed through the soft matting on his muscular chest and he tossed his shirt aside.

Leaving her mouth, he scorched a path down the column of her neck to her breasts. His tongue nipped and nibbled at her sensitive pink nipples while gentle fingers sensuously slipped up the inside of her thigh to fondle her to a scorching heat that begged to be extinguished.

Brandelene flung her head back, feverishly twisting up against him, arching herself ever nearer the flame that devoured her. As if of one mind, they both reached for his buckle, frantically freeing it, then the buttons of his trousers.

Now naked, his flesh burned into hers. Kordell whispered his love, and Brandelene pulled his mouth to hers, and once again he claimed her kiss swollen lips. Moist kisses trailed to her erect nipples while his fingers again moved up her thigh to her throbbing womanhood. Trembling with excitement, she pulsed beneath his expert touch. Once more, his mouth feverishly ravaged, his tongue swirlingly tormented, his fingers gently plundered, taking her to the brink of insanity before he moved over her to blur everything but the feel of his body on hers, in hers. Ardently, she thrust her body upward to receive him, crying out his name, writhing insatiably while turbulent passions blazed a fiery path through her abdomen, her heart, her head.

Consumed, overwhelmed, their lips and bodies fused in a searing white heat. They made love in a frenzy, wildly, passionately, savagely.

She writhed and moaned beneath him, clinging in a senseless

abyss. Brandelene took ravenously from him, gave passionately to him.

With fingers buried in her hair, Kordell's eyes burned with passion and hunger. His golden gaze locked on the glazed violet of hers to observe her pleasure and hunger, to witness the moment of his conquest.

"You're mine, Brandy," he whispered huskily. "Mine!" And he dared fate to take her from him.

Devoured by his ravishing kisses, possessed by his plundering drive and plunging thrusts, consumed by his engulfing passion, Brandelene was swept by a flaming agony, a rapturous ecstasy; and the same mindless wildfire raged through Kordell as his powerful lunges obliterated all reality except the sensations splintering, arcing, raging through them both. Moments later they shot from the bounds of earth writhing in fulfilled ecstasy as Brandelene yielded her being to her love. Soaring through space, they reveled in their passion, their love.

Afterward, they lay entwined in each other's arms, languorous. Wordlessly, they kissed, caressed, and nuzzled in a wondrous awe of their love, savoring each kiss, each caress, each gaze, for this endless moment that would disappear all too soon.

Sated, Kordell rose up on one elbow to examine the beauty of her nakedness. She was a golden goddess in the flickering firelight. His eyes worshiped her, his smile cherished her, his touch treasured her. And his heart revered her.

Brandelene thought her heart would burst with a euphoria she'd never before known. Her hands slipped up his muscular chest, up his corded neck to caress every plane of his beloved face.

Kordell closed his eyes, reveling in her gentle touch, luxuriating in the feel of her fingers exploring his chiseled features, his carved, sensuous lips.

Her heart thundered, she was a thirsting soul drinking in nature's sustaining nectar. Wrenching herself away from her preoccupation with his devastatingly handsome face, Brandelene sat up and smiled at him, her regard roaming at will. He was a magnificent animal, her golden-eyed lion. He held his head nobly high, majestically high, and his body was awesome in the fire's glow. When he moved, the muscles rippled in his broad shoulders and she could still feel the powerful strength of his muscular arms, his sinewy thighs. Hungrily, her gaze moved down his brawny chest, down his tapered waist, down to his slim hips, his muscular thighs and hard, firm legs. For her there was no tomorrow. There was only now, only Kordell. The agonizing weeks they'd been separated were forgotten. They were together. Nothing else mattered.

Silky raven tresses fell softly over her shoulders, her gaze melted into his and she opened her arms, beckoning to him. "Love me, my lion," she murmured before he rolled her to her back. Flaming desires of love could not remain appeased.

Their first loving had been the joining of two bodies; lovers, in a frenzied, uncontrollable passion too long denied. But their second union was the slow savoring of each other and the depth of the love they felt, yet could not share. The splendorous joining of two souls, magically fused into one through the power of love.

The second time he made love to her, Kordell told Brandelene, in every way possible, how he loved her, and it was a heart-crushing baring of his soul that she yearned to return, but she agonizingly prevented herself from letting the words he needed to hear slip past her kiss-swollen lips. Once again, however weakly, she resolved not to deny James Barnett his peaceful resting place at Southern Oaks. She would pay the highest price of all, the love of the only man she would ever love, before she would put her own desires before James Barnett.

Now, lying with Brandelene in his arms, Kordell wondered if he could give her up even if she were not carrying his child. Then his mind slipped backward to the day she'd lost the horse race, as it had so many times since that fateful day when he had been so sure his wife had fallen in love with him. Every moment of that day was burned into his memory, and once again he examined everything she had done and said. Could anyone play a charade that expertly? He thought not, but when his gaze moved to Brandelene's masked features he once again had doubts. Everything that had passed between them tonight bespoke love as well as lust; yet not one word of love had passed her lips. Once more, he questioned if her feelings were only passion as she'd claimed before leaving Southern Oaks. Why else had she come to him tonight? Somehow he must make her admit her love for him, then he could reveal his status to her and they could be remarried.

Sitting up, he gazed down at her, then lowered his head to brush feather-soft kisses on her closed eyes, her nose, her mouth. "Tomorrow, my love, we'll leave and be married en route to Southern Oaks." One hand clasped her naked form to his while the other freely roamed her body.

Attempting to hide the love reflected on her face, glowing radiantly in the flickering firelight, Brandelene replied in a weak and tremulous whisper, "I cannot." Her voice was still breathy from their passionate encounter and she quickly lowered her thick-lashed lids, so her eyes would not betray her heart.

"You will not leave this room, Brandy," Kordell threatened, "until you have told me you love me . . . or that you do not." His deep voice, raspy and sensual, was firmly insistent.

With an agony that left her bereft, Brandelene forced the cutting words from her lips. "You're a marvelous lover." With those devious words, she glanced up at Kordell with a feigned nonchalance. Swallowing the wretchedness that threatened to choke her, her heart near to bursting at the pained expression that crossed his face, she asked, "Certainly you didn't love every woman with whom you shared a bed?"

Kordell studied her expressionless face. She had avoided his request by posing a question of her own. "You may choose to tell yourself we share nothing but passion, but don't try to convince me, Brandy. I don't believe it—and neither do you!" With that, he rose, quickly dressed, and left the room, closing the door softly behind him.

Flinging her arm across her eyes, she silently pleaded for the strength to resist him. A short time later, disconsolate, she slipped into Kordell's robe, snatched the remnants of her gown and peignoir, and fled to her bedroom.

Once there, she was plagued with remorse and examined her motives in going to his room. Deep inside, had she known what would happen? Surely she had. She was consumed with guilt, for she was betrothed to Terrence Farnsworth. But then, she rationalized, Terrence did know the truth of her love for and relationship with Kordell. She and Terrence were not yet married, and if her flux did not start soon she would not be marrying the illustrious Mr. Farnsworth. That realization appeased her conscience, somewhat, until she admitted there was no justification for what she had done.

The next morning Brandelene discovered her monthly flow had started. Flinging herself onto her pillow, she fought the sobs that threatened to come, refusing to give in to tears.

Her fate was sealed.

Kordell Bouclair would never be in her future.

Glancing at her mullioned window, she saw the storm outside had stopped, but the one inside her raged on.

A short time later Ivy appeared at the salon door. "Excuse me, ma'am," she said shyly.

Celia glanced up. "Yes, Ivy?"

"Miss Brandelene said to tell you she wouldn't be down for breakfast, ma'am. She doesn't feel so good."

"What is wrong, Ivy?" Kordell asked, a concerned frown furrowing his brow. "Does she need a doctor?"

"No, sir."

"What is the matter with your mistress, Ivy?" Celia asked, her tone conveying that she would have an answer.

Hesitating, Ivy shifted from one foot to the other, her dark eyes darting to Kordell, then to Celia. "Miss Brandelene has a woman's headache."

Celia nodded her understanding. "That will be all, Ivy."

Kordell's eyes narrowed in discovery. Brandelene's cycle had arrived.

Later that morning Terrence's coachman came with a message informing Brandelene that Terrence would call for her at eight. She wanted to send his messenger with a return note stating that she was ill and would not be going out, but tomorrow was Christmas Eve, and tonight at the Carltons' was the largest ball of the holiday season, for Christmas Eve was spent with family. Thus, so as not to draw suspicion, Brandelene morosely acknowledged Terrence's engagement.

By noon, Brandelene pulled the remnants of her tattered emotions together. It was clear what she needed to do. Kordell must leave for the Ivory Coast. She could not bear to marry Terrence while Kordell was within reach. How could she force herself to submit to Terrence if Kordell were in the same city, in the same country, on the same continent?

After dressing, she went downstairs to find Kordell alone in the salon, lost in thought. Celia had taken a chill and was napping.

"Brandy," Kordell acknowledged somberly, standing up.

Then he strode toward her and she moved away, fearing his touch would destroy her resolve. "I need to talk privately with you, Kord. Would you please join me in my drawing room?"

Moving to the hearth, she stood in front of the blazing fire and stared at the flickering flames that warmed the room, but could not warm her. With her back to him she anxiously confided, "Kord, I'm not expecting . . ." Her voice broke, and when he made no reply, she continued, "There is no longer a reason for you to stay in the United States. When will you be leaving?"

"When you tell me you don't love me," Kordell replied, his low voice gentle.

"You are asking me to choose between Southern Oaks and you," Brandelene agonized, whirling to face him.

"I promise you that you won't lose Southern Oaks if you marry me."

At that declaration, Brandelene gasped. "How can you promise such a thing, Kord? Do you know something I don't? If you do, why won't you share it with me? Would you keep such knowledge from me to force me to marry you?"

"What if I did have a knowledge that would save Southern Oaks? Would you marry me?"

"Yes!"

A gentle and loving curve touched Kordell's lips. "Then I'd be in the position you refused to permit yourself to accept. I would never know if you married me out of love, or because I had the key to Southern Oaks's salvation. Can you ask me to accept less than you were willing to accept? To know that I am loved for myself?" He stood staring down at her bemused expression, wanting desperately to take her in his arms and tell her the truth. But he could not betray himself. He would accept nothing less than her love, and least of all her gratitude.

"Trust me, Brandy. If you love me, you will trust me and marry me."

Chapter 40

BRANDELENE GLANCED AWAY, FASTENING ON THE long fringe trimming the heavy, velvet drapes. Was it possible Kordell knew how to save Southern Oaks? Her heart pleaded that it was so. Dare she risk all in the name of love? Surely, if Kordell loved her, he would not keep the key to the plantation's salvation secret if she did not marry him? With that disturbing notion she felt desolate and turned back, her eyes challenging his. "I can say the same to you, Kord. Trust me enough to confide in me. If you truly love me, you will trust me."

"It seems we are at an impasse, Brandy."

Suffocating, Brandelene walked to the window. "What I'm having to do is difficult enough without you here, Kord. You had said you'd leave Boston after we knew. . . ." Her voice broke and she lowered her brow to press against the soothing, icy windowpane. Inhaling deeply, no longer caring what became of her, she continued, "When are you leaving?"

"Are you telling me you don't love me?"

Shivering, her back still to him, Brandelene steeled herself to say the lie. After a fleeting eternity she forced the words from her lips in a barely audible whisper, "I don't love you."

Kordell's hands gently clasped her shoulders from behind and

Brandelene closed her eyes, hiding her torment.

"You're lying, love," he murmured into her hair. Then his powerful chest pressed lightly against her back while his hands slipped tenderly down her arms to encompass her waist, his warm cheek resting against hers. He held her like that for an endless time before his deep voice broke the silence. "I realize you might be willing to marry another man in order to save Southern Oaks, but you love me. All I ask is for you to admit it, Brandy."

All the while, Kordell's soothing, yet confident voice was understanding and compassionate, and Brandelene fought her turbulent emotions. But at the same time she knew that if she did what he asked, she would be lost. Along with those three most precious of words would also go her restraint. At her silence, Kordell's voice, a velvet murmur, broke into her thoughts.

"You're mine, Brandy! You belong to me. Why don't you stop this torturous charade—for both our sakes? I love you," he admitted, his husky voice betraying the battle waging inside him, and setting his pride aside, he forced the words from his lips, "I need you to tell me the same."

At his confession, Brandelene's heart lurched painfully. Twisting in his arms, she looked up at his beloved face, so temptingly handsome. Did she have the strength to deny him when every fiber of her body yearned to embrace him, to tell him she loved him more than she'd ever envisioned it possible to love anyone? Could she summon the willpower to turn him away when his touch turned her body to fire? How could she deny him when he'd betrayed his vulnerability by admitting he needed her love? Then she remembered the reason she could not do as he asked, and she stiffened. "I cannot say that, Kord. I cannot."

"Why?" he pressed, pulling her closer to his muscular chest, enfolding her more tightly in strong arms. Then he buried his face in the fragrance of her silky hair while one hand lovingly stroked her head. "Why, Brandy?" At her silence, he lifted his head from hers to stare at the torment in her eyes. "Brandy," he moaned, smothering her face with tender kisses. "I love you! I know you love me. I know it. But I need to hear you say it. Say it, Brandy!"

Brandelene shook her head, unable to speak.

At that, Kordell cupped her face in his strong hands, forcing her gaze to his. "Then look me in the eyes and tell me you don't love me," he gently demanded. "Say it when your back's not to me."

"Didn't last night convince you," Brandelene lied, "my interest in you is of a more physical nature?"

"Know that I love you, Brandelene Bouclair," he murmured tenderly. "I love you with all my heart, with all my soul."

For one wild moment she considered giving in to her heart, but her protesting conscience prevailed. She would not turn her back to James Barnett's sacrifice. Tearing herself from his grasp with a choking cry, Brandelene flung the words at him, "I need you to leave, Kord! Please, please leave Vandersall Hall. Leave Boston. Leave me. I don't want you here and I don't love you!"

"Then this is good-bye, Brandy."

Destroyed, she could not reply.

After Kordell was gone, she felt so cold, so excruciatingly alone. Never to see him again. Numb, she cried, "Oh, God, I want to die."

Snow softly blanketed Boston when Kordell called on Celia that evening. Earlier, she had said that she was staying home this evening. He came to tell her good-bye, at a time he knew Brandelene would not be there, and to leave some papers for her. He sat in the salon with Celia.

She snuggled contentedly under her lap robe, sipping hot tea. "It's been a long time since I've enjoyed anything as much as this last week, Kordell."

"That pleases me greatly, Celia. I said my good-bye to Brandy earlier, so I won't be back. I wanted to thank you for your gracious hospitality and to leave some papers for Brandelene." Kordell crossed the room and handed Celia a packet of papers, then knelt down to hug and kiss her good-bye. She hugged him with thin arms.

"Good-byes are always difficult. Please remember me kindly."

Celia placed the papers on her table, picked up the silver bell, and rang. "I'll remember you most kindly, Kordell Bouclair. Godspeed."

Harrison appeared.

"Show Monsieur Bouclair out and have one of the footmen carry me upstairs. I am much too tired."

"I'll take care of it, Harrison," Kordell volunteered, moving to gently lift the frail woman in his arms. He followed the maid up the staircase and down the wide hall, past Brandelene's room, to Celia's rooms overlooking the front grounds of the estate. Patiently, he held the slight woman while the servant turned down Celia's bed, plumped the pillows, and moved the bed warming pan between the sheets. Then he carefully set Celia on the edge of her bed and quietly left her room, closing the door behind him.

Striding down the hall, Kordell paused at Brandelene's partially open door, assailed by memories, inhaling deeply at her familiar fragrance. Pushing the door wide, he stood in the hall, slowly scanning her room. The oil lamp on her bedside commode glowed softly, awaiting her return, as he did, as he always would. He had not believed it possible to miss someone as he missed her when they were separated. A deep longing filled him. Sighing, he reached to close the door as it had been when his gaze fell on the agate music chest he had given her. It rested on the tea table by the door.

Lost in reflection, he reached out and lifted the lid. The strains of "Greensleeves" tinkled hauntingly, and he envisioned Brandelene placing or removing her hairpins, just as he'd imagined so often when he heard the melody at Southern Oaks.

He had to go. It was agony to leave Brandelene behind, and he tormented himself by lingering. It was over. Finished. He moved to close the lid and his hand stopped in midair. He stared into the box in disbelief.

Inside were the faded remnants of a dried red rose.

His thoughts flew backward in time, recalling the many times he'd given her a red rose. The first time had been the day they married, but surely this was not that rose. Was it? But it mattered naught which rose he had given her that she valued. He knew she loved him. He gently closed the lid, and, laughing aloud, turned and ran down the hall, down the stairs, and into the salon for his packet of papers. He was going to the Carltons' soiree. Brandelene would marry him if he had to carry her before a minister in fetters.

Sometime later Kordell entered the Carltons' mansion, ablaze with thousands of candles. He handed the butler his cloak and top hat, explained a matter of urgency required Madame Bouclair elsewhere, and strode toward the noisy gathering. He scanned the crowded room to find Brandelene's lovely form. She stood chatting with a group of people and he scowled at the sight of the blond man's hand resting possessively on her arm.

Ivy, seated in a dim corner of the room, instantly saw Kordell and jumped up to hurry to his side.

"Summon Arnold and get your wraps," Kordell said, his glare fastened on Brandelene and Terrence. "We're leaving."

Thinking he meant to leave without Brandelene, Ivy said softly, "Mister Kordell, I don't know why you don't love Miss Brandelene no more, but you can't let her marry that Mister Terrence when she loves you."

"I don't intend to, Ivy." Kordell smiled fondly at the usually shy girl, his eyes dancing. "I suppose I never did. Now, go find Arnold. We're leaving. I'll get Brandy."

At his words, Ivy grinned, then turned and ran from the room.

What Kordell wanted to do was to knock Farnsworth's hand from Brandelene's arm, sweep her up, and carry her to the coach. But he realized he must handle the situation so as not to cause any damage to Celia's reputation. That meant no embarrassment to Farnsworth. He cursed under his breath and walked back into the foyer. "Please summon Madame Bouclair here immediately," he ordered a passing footman. "She is urgently needed elsewhere."

"Of course, sir," the footman replied and hurried off.

Brandelene appeared, accompanied by Terrence. She looked up at Kordell and her face reflected her elation at seeing him.

When she quickly masked the look of joy, Kordell wondered how he could have been so blind, for so long. "You must come with me immediately."

"Is something wrong?" Brandelene asked anxiously. At his silence, she pressed, "Is Celia all right?"

"Celia is fine," Kordell replied. He smiled down at her.

Suspicious, Brandelene persisted, "Perhaps you should tell me what's happening."

Kordell glanced at Farnsworth, resisting the urge to rearrange the man's handsome features. "It's a private matter. We must leave immediately."

"Who is this man, Brandelene?" Terrence asked.

"It's all right, Terrence," Brandelene said. "Something must be wrong at Southern Oaks. I'll speak with you later."

Kordell wrapped Brandelene in her fur-lined velvet cloak, then donned his own cloak and top hat. They hurriedly left, followed by Ivy and Arnold.

Terrence was heading back toward the soiree when his eyes narrowed with realization. "Bouclair!" he gasped.

Large white flakes drifted lazily down from a dark sky, turning the Carlton estate into a wintry wonderland.

Stopping, Brandelene demanded, "Kord, what is it? Is something wrong at Southern Oaks?"

Kordell smiled. "Everything is fine at Southern Oaks. Everything is fine, love. With everything and everybody. For the first in a long time. Too long a time. I will explain in private." He carefully pulled Brandelene's hood up and over her elegant coiffure, fighting the temptation to drag her into his arms and kiss her senseless. At the personal gesture, she glanced quizzically up at him, but said nothing. Ivy, grinning broadly, followed with Arnold.

After a silent ride, they arrived at Vandersall Hall, and Kordell assisted Brandelene from the frosty coach, continuing to clasp her hand in his firm grip. When Ivy had alighted from the brougham, he said, "Ivy, pack all Madame Bouclair's and your belongings. We'll be leaving in the morning. My things are already in the boot of the coach."

"You'll do no such thing, Ivy. What is this about, Kord? I insist you explain yourself this minute."

"Do as I told you, Ivy, while I speak with Madame." Kordell's tone brooked no argument.

"Yes, sir, Mister Kordell," Ivy chirped happily and scampered through the snow toward the mansion.

Arnold hesitated, but at Ivy's tug on his arm he followed the young maidservant.

The snow drifted to the ground, clinging possessively to everything it touched. Tree branches bowed under their heavy burden while evergreens took on ghostly white shapes. Everywhere the eye could see a world of white magically shimmered and sparkled, as though millions of sparkling diamonds had been scattered, creating a wondrously alluring fantasy land.

Kordell swallowed the lump that rose in his throat when he gazed down at Brandelene's upturned face. Her hood had fallen back and snowflakes slowly nestled among her raven tresses. Boldly he pulled her into his embrace and his eyes openly adored her.

"To explain simply, my proud beauty, we are getting married. Again. If not tomorrow, then the day after."

He crushed her to him, kissing her mindless before she could protest. Moments later her arms, exerting a will of their own, slipped around his neck and she returned his wildly passionate kisses. Breathless and weak, drawing on what little of her own will remained, she reluctantly pulled her lips from his, bending her head back to gaze up at him. "I cannot, Kord," she said bitterly, the snow clinging to her long, thick lashes. "I cannot!"

"My love, I'm not asking if you will." Kordell delicately kissed the tip of her nose before recapturing her softly parted lips in a fiery kiss that melted all her resolve. After a time, he lifted his mouth from hers to murmur huskily, "I am informing you." Then again he smothered her lips with demanding mastery.

She gasped for breath. "Kord, my father died, was murdered, for Southern Oaks. If you love me, how can you possibly ask me to turn my back on that for which my father gave his life?"

"No, Brandy. You're wrong. Your father didn't die for Southern Oaks. James Barnett died for his values, for what he believed in—that no man should be a slave. Those values live on in his daughter."

Her eyes widened with realization. Kordell was right! Her father had not died for Southern Oaks, but for his convictions that all people should live free—that no man should be a slave. With that conclusion, one monumental barrier to marrying Kordell disappeared. Suddenly it occurred to her, and this time, she asked herself the question that gave herself pause to consider; Would she ask her children to sacrifice their lifelong happiness in order to preserve their heritage, Southern Oaks? No, the answer came instantly. No. She would not. And she knew that if she would not ask it of her children, her father would not ask it of her. At that moment Kordell's lips once more claimed hers.

His kiss stole her breath away. After an eternity, he traced her swollen lips with his and his velvety whisper broke the wintry silence, "Now be a good girl and tell me you love me."

Brandelene could no more have denied him than she could have refused to breathe. "I love you, Kord," she answered tremulously, sensuously, her silky words spoken in a broken whisper. "I love you! Oh, I love you, love you, love you!"

At the words he'd waited so long to hear, Kordell cupped her face gently between the palms of his hands and his heart pounded wildly in his chest. They stood in the falling snow with locked gazes for an endless time before his tawny head lowered to tenderly, reverently touch her lips again.

How long Kordell had been kissing her before their lips caught fire, sending a searing flame leaping from her soaring heart to blaze hotly in the pit of her stomach, she did not know. She only knew that nothing in this world mattered more than being with Kordell tonight, tomorrow, and all the rest of her tomorrows.

And when he swept her up in his arms and set her in the coach, she clung to him submissively, joyously, and now with a clear conscience.

The next morning at his hotel, Brandelene and Kordell rose early. Surrendering to her heart, and with a clear head, she decided it mattered naught that Kordell was not a man of means. Pearl had been right; Brandelene was lucky she could afford to buy a man such as Kordell Bouclair. She would release all the indentured servants and sell Southern Oaks, except for the family cemetery. Ruby and Matthew would probably go to the Ivory Coast with Pearl and Dagert. She would keep Joshua with her, and she and Kordell could live modestly.

So, with joy in her heart, she happily rode with Kordell to Vandersall Hall, where they picked up Ivy and bid Celia a happy farewell.

It was a beautiful, crisp, clear winter day and the sun shone brightly on the brilliant snow, as well as in Brandelene's heart. After they left Vandersall Hall, she glanced up at Kordell and he smiled down at her, giving her a tight squeeze.

"Kord, I would like to stop by the Farnsworths'. I owe Terrence an explanation."

"But of course," he replied and assisted her, then Ivy, into the coach.

Sometime later Brandelene sat in Terrence's salon while Kordell and Ivy waited in the coach. Brandelene had explained, then apologized, and was relieved at Terrence's calm acceptance.

"You know you're making a terrible mistake in giving me up, Brandelene," Terrence chastised teasingly, then grinned. "If you had loved me as you do Bouclair, I just might have given up my wild ways." He paused, a look of feigned horror on his handsome face. "What am I saying? I must be getting senile!"

She laughed. "Oh, Terrence, thank you for being so understanding."

"Understanding, my dear? Perish the thought." He rolled his eyes. "Wait until the word gets around that you called off our engagement. You'll never dare to show your face in Boston." He laughed again and gave her an affectionate hug. "If I were Monsieur Bouclair, I would be quite worried about you being in here for so long with a dashing fellow like me."

"I'll never forget you, Terrence."

"Of course you won't," he jested, then turned serious. "Nor I you, Brandelene. Have a happy life."

Brandelene and Kordell left Boston on Christmas Eve. When their ship docked at Norfolk, they immediately boarded a riverboat and sailed up the James River to Richmond. Once there they went directly to the Richmond Inn. Kordell requested, and received, the room he'd occupied the night Brandelene purchased his contract of indenture at the Richmond auction house. While Brandelene oversaw the unpacking, Kordell left and arranged for a special license.

The following day, in a small church, with only the minister and his pleasant wife as witnesses, Brandelene and Kordell remarried.

Many hours later Brandelene lay sated in Kordell's arms, and watched him drowsily. "Why did you wait so long to come to Boston?"

"I stopped in New York for a day, but mostly I wanted to give you time to realize what you were throwing away," he said huskily, lifting a lock of her long raven hair. "Now I have a question for you. What rose that I gave you do you keep in your music chest?"

"How do you know about that?" Carved lips hovered over hers, making her feel deliciously warm.

"You didn't answer my question, my beauty."

"Actually, my beloved husband, there are two roses in there. The first one that you gave me, when first we said our vows, became dreadfully crushed in the baggage en route to Southern Oaks, so there are only pulverized remnants of that exceedingly special rose." At the look of astonishment on his face, she continued, "The other rose is the one you gave me the morning after you defended Southern Oaks from the night riders." She laughed softly, squirming delightfully in his arms. "You had no idea how long I've loved you, had you?"

At those most treasured words, Kordell kissed her lovingly, longingly.

Endlessly.

Rising from their bed, he moved to the large mahogany wardrobe and removed a packet of papers from his coat pocket. He smiled mischievously and her heart leaped. How could she have considered giving him up? She returned his magnetic smile, and with her gaze boldly roaming his powerful physique, she flushed at his rakish grin.

Seating himself on the edge of their bed, Kordell handed her the folded papers. "For my inquisitive wife." Her flush deepened to an appealing crimson.

Brandelene reached for the proffered papers. Unfolding the

documents, she read the copy of Kordell's instructions to a New York Bank transferring an enormous sum of money from his bank in London to the Southern Oaks's reserve account. Gasping, her wide-eyed gaze flew to his.

Long ago, Kordell had decided that no one but he would give Brandelene her cherished Southern Oaks. "I want you to know, Brandy, I have never lied to you about my background, about my wealth, or how I ended up on a slave ship. I've never lied to you about anything."

"But . . . ?"

A tanned finger on Brandelene's lips stilled her question. "We have a lifetime to discuss how and why. Right now there are more important things." With that, his hand moved from her inviting mouth to the fullness of her breast, expertly fondling a pink nipple to tautness. Then, with a low groan, he admitted huskily, "I have wanted to tame a certain feisty hellion, a certain 'lady of quality,' as the auction guard painfully reminded me, since the day that lady slapped me in the auction house. I have thought of little else since that day." Once again, he bent to claim her lips. Only this time, the palms of her hands flashed up to press against his muscular chest, staying him where he leaned over her naked body.

Violet eyes flashed challengingly. "You, Kordell Bouclair, will never see the day you tame me!"

"Ahh, but, love," he protested roguishly, "think of all the pleasure we can enjoy while I try."

Glancing up at the rakish grin that never failed to set her heart aflutter, she sighed, then slipped her hands up his granite chest, up his muscle-corded neck, up to play in his thick mane of waving hair. "Well, my golden-eyed lion, since you have thought of little else for such a long time, perhaps . . . perhaps you should start trying." With those throatily murmured words, the "lady of quality" pulled his tawny head down to hers.

With passions blazing high, they fed the sacred flame of love.

BRENNA BRAXTON-BARSHON attended the University of Ohio in Akron and the University of California at Santa Barbara. A former financial controller and accountant, she now writes full-time. She currently lives in Las Vegas, Nevada, with her husband and daughter.